CLARKESWORLD YEAR 3

CLARKESWORLD YEAR 3

EDITED BY NEIL CLARKE & SEAN WALLACE

WYRM PUBLISHING

CLARKESWORLD: YEAR THREE

Wyrm Publishing
www.wyrmpublishing.com

For more information, contact Wyrm Publishing:
wyrmpublishing@gmail.com

ISBN: 978-1-890464-20-2 (Trade Paperback)
ISBN: 978-1-890464-18-9 (Ebook - EPUB)
ISBN: 978-1-890464-19-6 (Ebook - MOBI / Kindle)

Visit Clarkesworld Magazine at:
clarkesworldmagazine.com

*With special thanks to the staff at Clarkesworld
and our families that let us live there.*

Contents

Introduction

NEIL CLARKE

I'm one of those people who skips the introduction to every anthology they read. I understand the point in having them, but they stand between me and the stories and the stories win every time.

I never expected to have to write one of these things. When I graduated from college, being a writer or editor wasn't even on the table. I was a Computer Science major with an interest in educational technology, a field in which I still find myself over twenty years later.

Reading science fiction was what I did for pleasure, but somewhere along the way, my technical skills and love of books morphed into a side business. Through my new connections as an online bookseller, I found the talented people with whom I would eventually launch *Clarkesworld Magazine*. The bookstore may be long gone, but the magazine marches on. I've discovered a job that I'd love to make my only one, but unfortunately, it seems to come with the price of writing introductions.

Interestingly, no one says that I have to write at length or tease you with what is to come, so I won't. *Realms 1* and *Realms 2* originally started off our series of annual anthologies. What you are currently holding in your hand is the third volume and first of the group to proudly bear the Clarkesworld name.

The origin of the magazine's name comes from the online bookstore mentioned above and that in-turn, received its name from the family domain it was hosted it on. To make a long story longer, it was pure lazyness with an unintended side-effect of making people we were paying homage to Arthur C. Clarke—who isn't even a distant relative of mine.

I have to admit, it has taken a while for me to fully embrace our name. I am however, quite proud to have my family name associated with all this magazine has become. It's the best job I've ever had and thanks to our reader's generous support over the years, I've been allowed to continue doing it. I still have the day job, but maybe someday, this will be it.

Enjoy the stories.

Neil Clarke
June 2012

Non-Zero Probabilities

N. K. JEMISIN

In the mornings, Adele girds herself for the trip to work as a warrior for battle. First she prays, both to the Christian god of her Irish ancestors and to the orishas of her African ancestors—the latter she is less familiar with, but getting to know. Then she takes a bath with herbs, including dried chickory and allspice, from a mixture given to her by the woman at the local botanica. (She doesn't know Spanish well, but she's getting to know that too. Today's word is *suerte.*) Then, smelling vaguely of coffee and pumpkin pie, she layers on armor: the Saint Christopher medal her mother sent her, for protection on journeys. The hair-clasp she was wearing when she broke up with Larry, which she regards as the best decision of her life. On especially dangerous days, she wears the panties in which she experienced her first self-induced orgasm post-Larry. They're a bit ragged after too many commercial laundromat washings, but still more or less sound. (She washes them by hand now, with Woollite, and lays them flat to dry.)

Then she starts the trip to work. She doesn't bike, though she owns one. A next-door neighbor broke an arm when her bike's front wheel came off in mid-pedal. Could've been anything. Just an accident. But still.

So Adele sets out, swinging her arms, enjoying the day if it's sunny, wrestling with her shitty umbrella if it's rainy. (She no longer opens the umbrella indoors.) Keeping a careful eye out for those who may not be as well-protected. It takes two to tango, but only one to seriously fuck up some shit, as they say in her 'hood. And lo and behold, just three blocks into her trip there is a horrible crash and the ground shakes and car alarms go off and there are screams and people start running. Smoke billows, full of acrid ozone and a taste like dirty blood. When Adele reaches the corner, tensed and ready to flee, she beholds the Franklin Avenue shuttle train, a tiny thing that runs on an elevated track for some portions of its brief run, lying sprawled over Atlantic Avenue like a beached aluminum whale. It has jumped its track, fallen thirty feet to the ground below, and probably killed everyone inside or under or near it.

Adele goes to help, of course, but even as she and other good Samaritans pull bodies and screaming wounded from the wreckage, she cannot help but feel a measure of contempt. It is a cover, her anger; easier to feel that than horror at the shattered limbs, the truncated lives. She feels a bit ashamed too, but holds onto the anger because it makes a better shield.

They should have known better. The probability of a train derailment was infinitesimal. That meant it was only a matter of time.

Her neighbor—the other one, across the hall—helped her figure it out, long before the math geeks finished crunching their numbers.

"Watch," he'd said, and laid a deck of cards facedown on her coffee table. (There was coffee in the cups, with a generous dollop of Bailey's. He was a nice-enough guy that Adele felt comfortable offering this.) He shuffled it with the blurring speed of an expert, cut the deck, shuffled again, then picked up the whole deck and spread it, still facedown. "Pick a card."

Adele picked. The Joker.

"Only two of those in the deck," he said, then shuffled and spread again. "Pick another."

She did, and got the other Joker.

"Coincidence," she said. (This had been months ago, when she was still skeptical.)

He shook his head and set the deck of cards aside. From his pocket he took a pair of dice. (He was nice enough to invite inside, but he was still *that* kind of guy.) "Check it," he said, and tossed them onto her table. Snake eyes. He scooped them up, shook them, tossed again. Two more ones. A third toss brought up double sixes; at this, Adele had pointed in triumph. But the fourth toss was snake eyes again.

"These aren't weighted, if you're wondering," he said. "Nobody filed the edges or anything. I got these from the bodega up the street, from a pile of shit the old man was tossing out to make more room for food shelves. Brand new, straight out of the package."

"Might be a bad set," Adele said.

"Might be. But the cards ain't bad, nor your fingers." He leaned forward, his eyes intent despite the pleasant haze that the Bailey's had brought on. "Snake eyes three tosses out of four? And the fourth a double six. That ain't supposed to happen even in a rigged game. Now check *this* out."

Carefully he crossed the fingers of his free hand. Then he tossed the dice again, six throws this time. The snakes still came up twice, but so did other numbers. Fours and threes and twos and fives. Only one double-six.

"That's batshit, man," said Adele.

"Yeah. But it works."

He was right. And so Adele had resolved to read up on gods of luck and to avoid breaking mirrors. And to see if she could find a four-leafed clover in the weed patch down the block. (They sell some in Chinatown, but she's heard they're knockoffs.) She's hunted through the patch several times in the past few months, once for several hours. Nothing so far, but she remains optimistic.

It's only New York, that's the really crazy thing. Yonkers? Fine. Jersey? Ditto. Long Island? Well, that's still Long Island. But past East New York everything is fine.

The news channels had been the first to figure out that particular wrinkle, but the religions really went to town with it. Some of them have been waiting for the End Times for the last thousand years; Adele can't really blame them for getting all excited. She does blame them for their spin on it, though. There have to be bigger "dens of iniquity" in the world. Delhi has poor people coming out of its ears, Moscow's mobbed up, Bangkok is pedophile heaven. She's heard there are still some sundown towns in the Pacific Northwest. Everybody hates on New York.

And it's not like the signs are all bad. The state had to suspend its lottery program; too many winners in one week bankrupted it. The Knicks made it to the Finals and the Mets won the Series. A lot of people with cancer went into spontaneous remission, and some folks with full-blown AIDS stopped showing any viral load at all. (There are new tours now. Double-decker buses full of the sick and disabled. Adele tries to tell herself they're just more tourists.)

The missionaries from out of town are the worst. On any given day they step in front of her, shoving tracts under her nose and wanting to know if she's saved yet. She's getting better at spotting them from a distance, yappy islands interrupting the sidewalk river's flow, their faces alight with an inner glow that no self-respecting local would display without three beers and a fat payday check. There's one now, standing practically underneath a scaffolding ladder. Idiot; two steps back and he'll double his chances for getting hit by a bus. (And then the bus will catch fire.)

In the same instant that she spots him, he spots her, and a grin stretches wide across his freckled face. She is reminded of blind newts that have light-sensitive spots on their skin. This one is *unsaved*-sensitive. She veers right, intending to go around the scaffold, and he takes a wide step into her path again. She veers left; he breaks that way.

She stops, sighing. "What."

"Have you accepted—"

"I'm Catholic. They do us at birth, remember?"

His smile is forgiving. "That doesn't mean we can't talk, does it?"

"I'm busy." She attempts a feint, hoping to catch him off-guard. He moves with her, nimble as a linebacker.

"Then I'll just give you this," he says, tucking something into her hand. Not a tract, bigger. A flyer. "The day to remember is August 8th."

This, finally, catches Adele's attention. August 8th. 8/8—a lucky day according to the Chinese. She has it marked on her calendar as a good day to do things like rent a Zipcar and go to Ikea.

"Yankee Stadium," he says. "Come join us. We're going to pray the city back into shape."

"Sure, whatever," she says, and finally manages to slip around him. (He lets her go, really. He knows she's hooked.)

She waits until she's out of downtown before she reads the flyer, because downtown streets are narrow and close and she has to keep an eye out. It's a hot day; everybody's using their air conditioners. Most people don't bolt the things in the way they're supposed to.

"A PRAYER FOR THE SOUL OF THE CITY," the flyer proclaims, and in spite of herself, Adele is intrigued. The flyer says that over 500,000 New Yorkers have committed to gathering on that day and concentrating their prayers. *That kind of thing has power now,* she thinks. There's some lab at Princeton—dusted off and given new funding lately—that's been able to prove it. Whether that means Someone's listening or just that human thoughtwaves are affecting events as the scientists say, she doesn't know. She doesn't care.

She thinks, *I could ride the train again.*

She could laugh at the next Friday the 13th.

She could—and here her thoughts pause, because there's something she's been trying not to think about, but it's been awhile and she's never been a very good Catholic girl anyway. But she could, maybe, just maybe, try dating again.

As she thinks this, she is walking through the park. She passes the vast lawn, which is covered in fast-darting black children and lazily sunning white adults and a few roving brown elders with Italian ice carts. Though she is usually on watch for things like this, the flyer has distracted her, so she does not notice the nearby cart-man stopping, cursing in Spanish because one of his wheels has gotten mired in the soft turf.

This puts him directly in the path of a child who is running, his eyes trained on a descending frisbee; with the innate arrogance of a city child he has assumed that the cart will have moved out of the way by the time he gets there. Instead the child hits the cart at full speed, which catches Adele's attention at last, so that too late she realizes she is at the epicenter of one of those devastating chains of events that only ever happen in comedy films and the transformed city. In a Rube Goldberg string of utter improbabilities, the cart tips over, spilling tubs of brightly-colored ices onto the grass. The boy flips over it with acrobatic precision, completely by accident, and lands with both feet on the tub of ices. The sheer force of this blow causes the tub to eject its contents with projectile force. A blast of blueberry-coconut-red hurtles toward Adele's face, so fast that she has no time to scream. It will taste delicious. It will also likely knock her into oncoming bicycle traffic.

At the last instant the frisbee hits the flying mass, altering its trajectory. Freezing fruit flavors splatter the naked backs of a row of sunbathers nearby, much to their dismay.

• • •

Adele's knees buckle at the close call. She sits down hard on the grass, her heart pounding, while the sunbathers scream and the cart-man checks to see if the boy is okay and the pigeons converge.

She happens to glance down. A four-leafed clover is growing there, at her fingertips.

Eventually she resumes the journey home. At the corner of her block, she sees a black cat lying atop a garbage can. Its head has been crushed, and someone has attempted to burn it. She hopes it was dead first, and hurries on.

Adele has a garden on the fire escape. In one pot, eggplant and herbs; she has planted the clover in this. In another pot are peppers and flowers. In the big one, tomatoes and a scraggly collard that she's going to kill if she keeps harvesting leaves so quickly. (But she likes greens.) It's luck—good luck—that she'd chosen to grow a garden this year, because since things changed it's been harder for wholesalers to bring food into the city, and prices have shot up. The farmers' market that she attends on Saturdays has become a barterers' market too, so she plucks a couple of slim, deep-purple eggplants and a handful of angry little peppers. She wants fresh fruit. Berries, maybe.

On her way out, she knocks on the neighbor's door. He looks surprised as he opens it, but pleased to see her. It occurs to her that maybe he's been hoping for a little luck of his own. She gives it a think-over, and hands him an eggplant. He looks at it in consternation. (He's not the kind of guy to eat eggplant.)

"I'll come by later and show you how to cook it," she says. He grins.

At the farmers' market she trades the angry little peppers for sassy little raspberries, and the eggplant for two stalks of late rhubarb. She also wants information, so she hangs out awhile gossiping with whoever sits nearby. Everyone talks more than they used to. It's nice.

And everyone, everyone she speaks to, is planning to attend the prayer.

"I'm on dialysis," says an old lady who sits under a flowering tree. "Every time they hook me up to that thing I'm scared. Dialysis can kill you, you know."

It always could, Adele doesn't say.

"I work on Wall Street," says another woman, who speaks briskly and clutches a bag of fresh fish as if it's gold. Might as well be; fish is expensive now. A tiny Egyptian scarab pendant dangles from a necklace the woman wears. "Quantitative analysis. All the models are fucked now. We were the only ones they didn't fire when the housing market went south, and now this." So she's going to pray too. "Even though I'm kind of an atheist. Whatever, if it works, right?"

Adele finds others, all tired of performing their own daily rituals, all worried about their likelihood of being outliered to death.

She goes back to her apartment building, picks some sweet basil and takes it and the eggplant next door. Her neighbor seems a little nervous. His apartment is cleaner than she's ever seen it, with the scent of Pine Sol still strong in the bathroom. She tries not to laugh, and demonstrates how to peel and slice eggplant, salt it to draw out the toxins ("it's related to nightshade, you know"), and sauté it with basil in olive oil. He tries to look impressed, but she can tell he's not the kind of guy to enjoy eating his vegetables.

Afterward they sit, and she tells him about the prayer thing. He shrugs. "Are you going?" she presses.

"Nope."

"Why not? It could fix things."

"Maybe. Maybe I like the way things are now."

This stuns her. "Man, the *train fell off its track* last week." Twenty people dead. She has woken up in a cold sweat on the nights since, screams ringing in her ears.

"Could've happened anytime," he says, and she blinks in surprise because it's true. The official investigation says someone—track worker, maybe—left a wrench sitting on the track near a power coupling. The chance that the wrench would hit the coupling, causing a short and explosion, was one in a million. But never zero.

"But ... but ... " She wants to point out the other horrible things that have occurred. Gas leaks. Floods. A building fell down, in Harlem. A fatal duck attack. Several of the apartments in their building are empty because a lot of people can't cope. Her neighbor—the other one, with the broken arm—is moving out at the end of the month. Seattle. Better bike paths.

"Shit happens," he says. "It happened then, it happens now. A little more shit, a little less shit ... " He shrugs. "Still shit, right?"

She considers this. She considers it for a long time.

They play cards, and have a little wine, and Adele teases him about the overdone chicken. She likes that he's trying so hard. She likes even more that she's not thinking about how lonely she's been.

So they retire to his bedroom and there's awkwardness and she's shy because it's been awhile and you do lose some skills without practice, and he's clumsy because he's probably been developing bad habits from porn, but eventually they manage. They use a condom. She crosses her fingers while he puts it on. There's a rabbit's foot keychain attached to the bed railing, which he strokes before returning his attention to her. He swears he's clean, and she's on the pill, but ... well. Shit happens.

She closes her eyes and lets herself forget for awhile.

The prayer thing is all over the news. The following week is the runup. Talking heads on the morning shows speculate that it should have some effect, if enough people go and exert "positive energy." They are careful not to use the language of any particular faith; this is still New York. Alternative events are being planned all over the city for those who don't want to come under the evangelical tent. The sukkah mobiles are rolling, though it's the wrong time of year, just getting the word out about something happening at one of the synagogues. In Flatbush, Adele can't walk a block without being hit up by Jehovah's Witnesses. There's a "constructive visualization" somewhere for the ethical humanists. Not everybody believes God, or gods, will save them. It's just that this is the way the world works now, and everybody gets that. If crossed fingers can temporarily alter a dice throw, then why not something bigger? There's nothing inherently special about crossed fingers. It's only a "lucky" gesture because people believe in it. Get them to believe in something else, and that should work too.

Except . . .

Adele walks past the Botanical Gardens, where preparations are under way for a big Shinto ritual. She stops to watch workers putting up a graceful red gate.

She's still afraid of the subway. She knows better than to get her hopes up about her neighbor, but still . . . he's kind of nice. She still plans her mornings around her ritual ablutions, and her walks to work around danger-spots—but how is that different, really, from what she did before? Back then it was makeup and hair, and fear of muggers. Now she walks more than she used to; she's lost ten pounds. Now she knows her neighbors' names.

Looking around, she notices other people standing nearby, also watching the gate go up. They glance at her, some nodding, some smiling, some ignoring her and looking away. She doesn't have to ask if *they* will be attending one of the services; she can see that they won't be. Some people react to fear by seeking security, change, control. The rest accept the change and just go on about their lives.

"Miss?" She glances back, startled, to find a young man there, holding forth a familiar flyer. He's not as pushy as the guy downtown; once she takes it, he moves on. The PRAYER FOR THE SOUL OF THE CITY is tomorrow. Shuttle buses ("Specially blessed!") will be picking up people at sites throughout the city.

WE NEED YOU TO BELIEVE, reads the bottom of the flyer.

Adele smiles. She folds the flyer carefully, her fingers remembering the skills of childhood, and presently it is perfect. They've printed the flyer on good, heavy paper.

She takes out her St. Christopher, kisses it, and tucks it into the the rear folds to weight the thing properly.

Then she launches the paper airplane, and it flies and flies and flies, dwindling as it travels an impossible distance, until it finally disappears into the bright blue sky.

The Second Gift Given

KEN SCHOLES

Go-on-all-fours-sometimes-upright tracked the three-horn spoor alone. He moved along the ridge in the red of the day when the Greater Light swallowed the sky and heat danced over stone.

Below, the big waters licked at the land. In the days when he was young, Go-on-all-fours remembered eating swimmers the People used to pierce in the shallows while the children played on the shaped rocks that the Oldest People had left behind. But the swimmers were rarer now than even the three-horns and the big waters drank those rocks long ago. Rememberer-of-forgotten-days said someday the big waters would drink all of the land and the People as well. But Rememberer-of-forgotten-days also said that the People had walked *across* the big waters before they were so big, in the days before the sky burned red. And Rememberer-of-forgotten-days had difficulty remembering where (and sometimes when) to make water.

Go-on-all-fours picked up a pebble and put it in his mouth. Hunger chewed at him; there'd been no meat for twenty days. He clutched his piercer, its sharpened tip burned hard in fire, and went on threes with his nose to the ground. His hackles rose. He crested the ridge and stopped. The scent of blood made his tight stomach rumble.

Now he went upright, stretching his neck, working his nose, darting his eyes over the place where the broken rock became gray scrub and spider trees. Blood. The three-horn lay in the shadows, sides heaving, a small piercer protruding from its neck. Go-on-all-fours-sometimes-upright growled a warning in the speech of the People, raising an octave into inquiry. No response.

He shuffled forward cautiously, piercer ready. Laying beside the dying three-horn was a bowed stick, the ends tied together with a strand of dried gut, and a pile of small piercers. He sniffed them, inhaling a strange, sweet smell like nothing he'd known before.

Turn.

The compulsion spun him around, a panic boiling in his chest. He lost his footing and fell.

Compassion. No fear.

A female upright walker stood a throw away. Her hairless skin radiated in the copper light and she stood straight and very tall. She held a similar bowed stick in her hands and her mouth curved like the stick, her teeth shining white.

Go-on-all-fours scrambled backwards, dropping his piercer. Her smell—strange, sweet—overpowered the three-horn's blood-smell.

Watch. Learn.

She pulled the string, holding a small piercer point facing out The small piercer blurred across the ground, sinking into the three-horn's throat beside the other piercer. The three-horn bleated and died. She lay the thrower down, then turned and walked away.

Frozen and whimpering, he watched her go and tried to remember what she looked like.

Go-on-all-fours-sometimes-upright pounded the dirt and howled to be heard. Rememberer-of-forgotten-days handed him the horn and he spoke. "Scared. Not harm. Golden-upright-walker *People.*"

"Harm," said Best-maker-of-fire, gesturing at the two throwers and the bundle of piercers. "*Not* People. *We* People. Upright walker eater of People."

They had argued long after the last of the three-horn had been devoured, the women and children banished to their caves. As night drew on, the mountains cooled and the Lesser Lights throbbed and sparkled overhead. Rememberer-of-forgotten days taught the People they were dead hunters guarding them while the Greater Light slept. He also taught that the Greater Lesser Light, fat and white in the night, was a mother who chased her young to bed. Perhaps the upright walker gave the gift because *she* was a mother, too, taking care of her young. Go-on-all-fours wondered about this and poked a stick into the fire, despite Best-maker's growl of protest.

Rememberer coughed. He was the oldest of the People, and blind now though he once had been their best hunter. "Upright-walkers make gift." He smiled toothlessly at Best-maker-of-fire. "Not eat Go-on-all-fours-sometimes-upright. Could."

No-child-in-stick laughed and made a spitting sound. "Go-on-all-fours-sometimes-upright too skinny."

Everyone else laughed, except for Best-maker. He scowled, picked up one of the throwers and tossed it into the fire. Go-on-all-fours leaped to his feet and burned himself pulling it out. "Not people," Best-maker said. "Eaters of people."

When the angry growls died down, they all went to bed. He had not told them about the voice in his head: they would never believe him.

Come.

He came awake, instantly alert, and untangled himself from his woman, Best-maker's sister. She mewled a question in her sleep and rolled away.

Outside. Come.

He picked up his piercer and left the cave silently, careful not to wake his young. The upright walker waited at the edge of the clearing and the sight of her hurt his eyes. Easily half-again his height at his tallest, she stood with her hands hanging loosely at her sides. Long golden hair spilled down her shoulders and over her heavy breasts. Her eyes shone bright green.

Compassion. No fear. Follow.

He followed her, going upright until his back and legs ached from the effort. They hadn't gone far when a chittering sound stopped him.

No fear. This voice was heavier. He knew it came from the monster that separated from the shadows, but he raised his piercer anyway. *No fear.*

Fear, he said back. The eight-legged monster—almost a spider but even larger than the six-horns Rememberer told stories of—scuttled closer.

No fear, the woman said. She put a hand on his arm. Cool. Soft.

He pushed the piercer into her belly as far as it would go and screamed as the monster leapt.

His first awareness was the fullness of his brain. His second awareness was the coolness of the grass beneath his bare skin.

He opened his eyes on golden light playing in the boughs of upward-sweeping trees. He sat up and looked around. He had never seen so much green in one place.

Pleasure. "You like my garden?" The naked upright walker strode into the clearing, a piece of fruit held loosely in each hand.

Confusion. Anxiety. "I've never seen anything like it." The memory of attacking her jarred him. *Fear. Surprise.* The golden skin of her flat stomach showed no mark from his piercer. "You're . . . well?"

She laughed. "Of course I am. The Seeker would not have allowed me Outside had the risk been real."

"The Seeker?"

"Ra-sha-kor, the Firsthome Seeker. I am the Seeker's Lady, Jadylla-kor. We have traveled vast distances to find you, cousin." *Dark. Alone. Searching.*

"I do not understand."

She offered him a piece of fruit. *Trust.* "Of course not. You're not fully recessed, cousin. When you are, everything will become clearer."

He took the purple globe and studied it, rolling it around his fingers. He looked up at her and their eyes locked. Raising her own piece, she bit into it and its golden juice ran down her mouth, dripping onto her breasts. *Trust. Eat.*

He took a bite and his mind expanded. As if she stood in his mind speaking, words formed without sound as they stared at one another. She answered questions before he could ask.

I name you cousin because you and I are of the People.

Long ago, before the Seventeen Recorded Ages of Humanity, our cousins flung themselves out from the Firsthome like scattered seed. Outward and outward they spread away and away to find new homes among the stars. Long travelers into dark, they warred and loved one another in those distant days and fled so far from home to have lost their way back to it. This was the Darkest Age, marked by the absence of history and the presence of myth. Then, in the Fifth Age, came Yorgen Sunwounder, the first Firsthome Finder, who searched and found the cradle of the People, of Humanity.

But the Firsthome did not know him for time and technology had changed him, and in his rage he smote their sun and thus began the Cousin Wars that brought about the Second Darkest Age. Humanity rose and fell again and again and once more the Firsthome was lost . . .

He stopped her with a blink. "What is happening to me?"

She placed her hands on his shoulders and drew her face nearer, her stare unbroken. *Recession. A return backwards to what you once were, cousin. A human. One of the People. Truth: all life changes over time. Truth: the clock-spring can be unwound carefully, carefully, we have learned. Infinitely small workers live in the nectar of this fruit, each unwinding you, recessing you to what you would have been millions of years ago had time not taken you on a different journey. Infinitely small teachers in this fruit fill your mind with language and comprehension.*

Another voice now in his head, deeper and stronger: *Enough, Lady. His recession is as far as you may take it. Bring him to me.*

She released him and he realized that the closeness of her mind and body had aroused him. He blushed and moved to cover himself. The Lady smiled sympathetically.

Peace, she said with her mind. "It is time for you to meet the Seeker and to taste the root." Turning, she strode out of the clearing and Go-on-all-fours hurried to keep up with her, surprised at how easily he now went upright.

They entered another clearing after darting in and out of wet, hanging foliage. Twice, he thought he saw the monstrous spider-thing that had captured him. Once, they brushed against a wall of blue crystal, warm to his touch, and stretching up, up, up, lost far above in light.

In the center of the clearing stood a massive tree, its branches bent low with heavy purple fruit.

"I'll leave you now," the Lady said, squeezing his arm. "I will return when the Seeker calls for me."

This time, she did not walk away. Instead, her shape began to shimmer and then melted into the ground too fast for him to respond.

He heard a chuckle in his head. *She is fine, cousin. Bending light rather than moving feet. Welcome. I am Ra-sha-kor.*

"You are the Firsthome Seeker. The Lady said—"

I am the Firsthome Finder. I have sought you, cousin, through deeps of space and time that you cannot begin to comprehend. It is my great Joy to have finally found you.

"I am—"

You were Go-on-all-fours-sometimes-upright. Again, the chuckle. *You now need a new name. May I have the honor of naming you in my own tongue?*

The People gave names when a child was old enough to hunt—now he understood that it was an important coming-of-age ritual. "Yes. I would be honored, Lord."

You shall be called the Firstfound Cousin, the Healer of the Broken Distance, Sha-Re-Tal. Tal.

He did not know why exactly, but he knelt. After a respectable silence, he looked up. Other than the tree, the clearing stood empty.

I am here, Tal. The tree. Tal stood and took a step towards it.

"You—"

The People, over time, have learned to make themselves into what they will. My roots run the length of this craft, nourishing it, powering it, carrying the wisdom and knowledge of the People in its sap. Even as the Lady chooses her form, I have chosen mine. As has Aver-ka-na, our Builder Warrior. The branches behind him rustled and the huge spider sidled tentatively out.

Compassion, it said. *No fear.*

The Finder's mind joined in. *You have nothing to fear, Tal.*

With everything in him, Tal fought the panic as the creature came closer, its mandibles clicking. It raised a hairless arm and lowered it onto his shoulder.

Peace, cousin.

Then, it turned and scuttled away. Tal released held breath.

Sit with me, the Finder thought. Tal sat, his head suddenly hurting. "We will make words in this way now," the Finder said, its deep voice drifting down from somewhere lost above. "You are young in understanding yet and I would not wound carelessly after so long in the finding of you."

"I am grateful," Tal said. And he was. He felt himself expanding, stretching, his awareness filling like the hollow of a rock as the tide gentled in.

He sat in the shade of the tree until the Finder spoke again." You express gratitude for our shame."

Confusion. Uncertainty. "Your shame?"

"It is not our way to force," the Finder said." The Rul-ta-Shan—the First Gift Given—was choice. The Lady gave of the fruit while you slept."

Tal nodded slowly. "I would have chosen so."

"We hope so. Still, the ages had robbed you of choice and so we made our own on your behalf, trusting our cousinhood to cover a multitude of transgressions. Thus we brought you to this place, your choice restored."

Love welled in Tal's heart and brimmed his eyes. The power in it made his life with the People, his life as Go-on-all-fours, seem small and far away.

Breeding. Hunting. Foraging. Starving. Led by appetite and instinct to survive. "I was an animal," he whispered. "I was not of the People. Now I am of the People. You have made me—" he struggled to find the word— "whole."

The mighty tree shook. "No. You were always of the People, Cousin. You were as whole as you could be." *Freedom.* "And now you possess the First Gift Given. What will you choose, I wonder?"

The grass at the base of the tree rustled, exposing thick roots that pulsed with life and possibility. Tal crawled forward. "I wish to know," he said.

"Then taste the root and know what you will."

He put his tongue to the root; it was bitter and sweet, the tang of earth and grass, and it swept through him, over him, into him. Tal collapsed inside himself, his eyes slamming shut as his brain pried open.

Understanding. He saw. *Loss.* He knew. *Endings.* He wept. *Beginnings.* He slept.

He awoke to the Lady cradling him against her warm body.

"Lady," he said. "How long?" But he knew that too.

She offered a sad smile. "Years. But not many. The sun swells from its wound. Slowly, it swallows the Firsthome."

"And the People will end," he said in a quiet voice.

"No," she said and he remembered. *Beginnings.* "You have a choice now if you will make it."

Her fingers lightly stroked his skin. The smoothness of her pressed against him and he was smooth now, too. The smell of her filled his nose, overpowering the scent of flowers and grass around them. He swallowed, sensations overwhelming him. "I choose."

"It is a great gift," Jadylla said.

He stretched out a nervous hand to touch her. "I am grateful."

She brought her face close to his. "No." Her breath was warm. "*You* give the great gift, Cousin, and the giving of it heals the broken distance between the Peoples." Her mouth touched his. *Heat. Unity.* "The life we make together will satisfy our deepest longing for Home."

He'd never mated face-to-face. He was nervous and awkward as his hands sought her out. Her own hands moved lower on his body and, learning from her, he imitated her caresses. Slowly, they touched one another with hands and mouths and when he could no longer wait, he gently crawled onto her and let her guide him into her. He pushed into her warmth and wetness and her eyes went wide for just a moment. Then she smiled and pushed back against him, moving her hips in time with his own.

When they finished, he lay back in her arms. Her sweat and her scent mingled with his own. They were silent for a long time before he spoke.

"Why me?" he asked.

"What did they call you? Before the Finder found you?"

"Go-on-all-fours-sometimes-upright," he said.

"Sometimes the past returns in small ways. Of your People, who else ever went upright?"

He shook his head.

"We watched for a year. We watched you hunt. We watched you mate. We watched you all and you were chosen."

He thought of the others. With no sky overhead, he'd lost all sense of time. He wondered if his mate slept or if she foraged to feed their young. He wondered if they wondered where he was, if perhaps they even searched for him.

Thinking of them prompted a question. "Could they also be . . . recessed?"

She shrugged. "We do not know. And we could not find out without further shame."

"But I am grateful. Wouldn't they be grateful as well?"

She rolled away from him. "It is not a matter for discussion."

Something sparked in Tal's memory. "I have young. When they choose to crawl into the fire, I do not allow their choice. Does that shame the First Gift Given?"

"It is not the same," Jadylla said.

"How is it not the same?"

"It is not the same," she said again. She disentangled herself from his arms. "You have honored me, Cousin, but I must leave you now." She stood and touched her stomach. "This life must be nurtured at the root and my husband calls."

Tal lay back and watched her leave. He thought about his mate and his young at home. "When my young crawl into the fire, I do not allow their choice," he said to himself. Because, he thought, the parent chooses for the child until the child can do so for themselves.

An unhealthy line of thought. Aver-ka-na scuttled towards him, its naked belly dragging the ground, its eight legs moving slowly.

"Not unhealthy," Tal said, his brain spun to bring down exactly the right word. "Love."

Not love, it said, mandibles clacking. *Love respects the First Gift Given.*

"Love," Tal said slowly, "pulls young from the fire."

The Builder Warrior chittered, its eyes rolling.

Tal stood, stretching himself fully upright and raising his fist. "I will return with fruit for my People." No answer dropped into his mind or drifted into his ears. He started walking and kept walking until he saw the tree, heavy with its purple fruit.

Anger. Sadness. The Finder stirred. *I can not permit it.*

The ground at the foot of the tree peeled back, exposing Jadylla where she lay wrapped in roots. Her eyes opened. She was different towards him now, her voice cold and far away. "We came for you. Not them."

Tal swallowed. He felt anger building. *Falseness.* "You did not come for me. You came to take life from me."

Neither answered.

"I will take life, too. Life for my people." He paused. "It is *my* choice."

The Firsthome Finder's Lady looked at the Firsthome Finder. Her tongue slipped from her mouth, touching the root, moving over its surface. Finally, she nodded. The tree shuddered and fruit fell like rain.

Jadylla's eyes were narrow. "You may take what you can carry. We will not wait long for you."

Tal picked up a piece of fruit. "And you will take us all with you."

Only those who choose, the Finder said into his mind.

Tal picked up more fruit, cradling it in his arms. "Only those who choose," he repeated.

Light swallowed him and sent him spinning away.

Tal stood on the rise overlooking the fires and the caves. He watched Best-maker-of-fire argue with No-child-in-stick. Young played around the fire, moving quickly on all fours in a game that imitated hunting and mating behavior. He saw his own young among them. His mate, Soft-voice-sharp-bite, sat with the other females, grooming one another.

Compassion, he sent. *No fear.*

They looked up quickly as if struck, all wide-eyed.

He lifted a piece of fruit. *Watch. Learn.* He bit into it, letting the juice spill onto his naked skin. He took a step forward, extending the fruit though he was still two throws away.

They moved, scrambling back toward the caves. "Don't go," he said. "It's me—Go-on-all-fours-sometimes-upright. I've come back for you."

"Not People," No-child-in-stick growled. "Upright walker eater of People." His eyes rolled wide and wild.

Peace. "No," Tal said.

Abandoning their fire, they fled into the caves.

He spent the night trying to coax them out. He fed the fire for them, hoping somehow it would show he meant no harm. He placed a piece of fruit outside each cave entrance. He called to them. He waited.

As the sky reddened and the swollen sun crawled out, he heard his young whimpering in the dark.

Come. Eat.

Deep in the back of the caves, they growled and moaned.

Finally, he took a piece of fruit and went into the cave that used to be his own. His mate yelped and hissed as he moved quickly toward her. She clawed and kicked at him as he grabbed her, biting at his hands as he tried to force the fruit into her mouth. She shrieked, her nails and teeth drawing blood, her eyes wide in terror. He shoved her away from him, turning toward his children.

She fell on him before he could take a step and he went down beneath her, the air knocked from him as her thrashing feet connected with his testicles and her gnashing mouth found his ear.

"Not People," she screamed. "Eater of People."

Tal wanted to fight back but couldn't. Suddenly he knew that it didn't matter anymore. He yelled again and again. His young were fleeing now and other forms were moving into the cave waving piercers and hefting rocks.

He heard his own bones breaking and smelled his own blood on the air, the tang of iron mingled with the sweetness of nectar.

He closed his eyes and waited for the end.

Not love, the Lady's voice in his mind said, heavy with sorrow.

Tal's eyes opened. He lay wrapped in the ground, tangled in the Finder's roots. "No, not love."

"You are well now."

He nodded. "I am grateful."

She touched his arm. He still felt the distance but no longer cold. He saw now that her belly curved slightly outward, his child growing there quickly, nourished by the Finder's sap.

Come to Newhome with us, Ra-sha-kor the Firsthome Finder said. *Come, cousin, and meet your Other People.*

Tal twisted himself free from the roots, goose bumps forming on his skin as he remembered the stones and fists and fire-sharpened sticks. "What would I do at the Newhome?"

Jadylla smiled and rubbed her stomach. "You would care for your daughter. With me and with the Firsthome Finder."

He saw that the Builder Warrior hung from his legs in the tree branches, weaving three silk hammocks. His mind told him that these were to let them sleep for the long voyage.

"My daughter will not need me." Tal bent, placed his lips to the root, letting knowledge and emotion wash through him. "She will be cared for."

Understanding. Acceptance.

Love, he thought.

Tal stood on the edge of the big waters in the cool of the night. Far above, a fleck of light moved away, crisp and clear among the pulsing stars. He waved though he knew they could not see him.

He picked up the thrower and the pouch of little piercers they had left with him. He tested the string and calculated in his mind exactly what he would need to make more of them. He also thought about ways to go out onto the big waters to find the swimmers and ways to capture the three-horns and breed them for food. Ways to plant the good berries and tubers and to dig them at his leisure. He even thought about ways to take his People to a new place—far to the north or south—where life could be better for them until there could be no life and the sun finally swallowed the world.

Perhaps someday they would let him do these things for them . . . *with* them. Certainly not now, but maybe with time.

For now, he would hunt. For now, he would keep what little he needed to survive and leave the rest where his People could find it. He would do this every day for as long as it took because he knew that if choice was the First Gift Given, love must indeed be the second.

Sha-Re-Tal, the Firstfound Cousin and Healer of the Broken Distance, found the three-horn spoor and broke into an easy run. He ran upright, his feet steady and sure beneath him, his eyes and nose and ears remembering their work very well.

A silver moon rose over the big waters.

He howled at it and dared it to chase him.

Walking with a Ghost

NICK MAMATAS

Chakravarty spent at least three months making the same joke about how the AI was going to start spouting, "Ph'nglui mglw'nafh C'thulhu R'lyeh wgah'nagl fhtagn" and then all hell would break loose—a Singularity with tentacles. Sometimes he'd even run to the bank of light switches and flick the lights on and off. It was funny the first time to Melanie, and she squeezed a bit more mirth out of Chakravarty's inability to pronounce the prayer to Cthulhu the same way twice. Making the Lovecraft AI had been Melanie's idea, but it was Chakravarty who tried to keep the mood whimsical. Both worried that Lovecraft would just wake up screaming.

" —and he does scream, occasionally," Melanie explained. Her advisor and a few other grad students were at the presentation, in the front rows, but as these presentations were theoretically open to the public, the Lovecraftians had come out in force, squeezing themselves in the tiny desk-chairs. They looked a lot like grad students themselves, but even paler and more poorly dressed in ill-fitting T-shirts and unusual garments—one even wore a fedora—plus they kept interrupting.

"Can we hear it talk?" one asked, and then he raised his hand, as if remembering that he had to. "Ask it questions?"

"Please, leave all questions—for us—until after the presentation. We're not going to expose the AI to haphazard stimuli during this presentation." Chakravarty said.

"He's . . . fairly calm so far," Melanie said. "Which is to be expected. We know a lot about Lovecraft. He recorded almost everything he did or thought in his letters, after all, and we have nearly all of them. What ice cream he liked, how it felt to catch the last train out of South Station how he saw the colors scarlet and purple when he thought the word evil. He was fairly phlegmatic, for all the crazy prose and ideas so he's okay."

"How do we know that this is really an artificial intelligence, and not just a bunch of programmed responses?" This one, huge and bearded, wore a fedora.

Chakravarty opened his mouth to speak, his face hard, but Melanie answered with an upturned palm. "It's fine," she said to him. Most of these talks are total snoozers. Nobody ever has any questions." Then, to the audience: "I'd argue that we can't *know* it's a bunch of programmed responses, except that we didn't program all the responses we've seen so far. Of course, I don't know that you, sir," she said, pointing to the Lovecraftian, "aren't also just a bunch of programmed responses that are just the physical manifestation of the reactions going on in the bag of chemicals you keep in your skull?"

"I don't feel like I am!"

"Do you believe everything you feel; do you not believe in anything you haven't?"

"No, and no true Lovecraftian would," he said.

"Right. So you don't believe in the female orgasm," Melanie said. The room erupted in hoots and applause. Then Chakravarty got up shouted that everyone who doesn't understand what's going on should just go home, Google "Chinese room," and stop asking stupid questions. "Ooh, Chinese—Lovecraft wouldn't like that room," someone said. Then the classroom was quiet again.

"Uh, thanks for that, Chakravarty," Melanie said. She adjusted her watch, thick and blocky on her wrist. "I've been walking around the city with him. He likes Boston and Cambridge, it helped ease him in to his, uh, existence. And he knew things, how roads crossed and bits of history, that I didn't know, that we didn't program into him. But we did program a lot into him. Everything we had access to, both locally and up at Brown." Behind her, a ghostly image of the author, chin like a bucket, eyes wide and a bit wild, flickered into existence. He sat in an overstuffed chair in the swirling null-space of a factory-present screensaver image.

"Well, if there are no more questions"—Melanie glanced about the classroom and there were no questions, just some leftover giggles— "why don't we have him say hello?"

The room went silent "And none of that ftang ftang stuff," Melanie added. Somebody giggled, high-pitched like a fife.

Chakravarty leaned down into a microphone that snaked out from the laptop. "Lovecraft, can you hear me? Can you see us? Many people here have read your stories."

The image blinked. "Hello," it said, its voice tinny and distant.

"How are you?" Chakravarty asked. A simple question, one with only a couple of socially acceptable answers. A kid could program the word "Fine," into an AIM buddy chat.

"I do not quite know," Lovecraft said. "I . . . " he trailed off, then looked out into the room, as if peering into the distance. "Why have you people done this to me?"

Chakravarty giggled, all nerves. Melanie opened her mouth, but was interrupted by one of the professors, who waved a gnarled hand. Chakravarty clicked off the mic. On the screen, Lovecraft started as if he sensed something, and he began to peer into the distance, as if seeing past the other side of the screen upon which he was projected.

"What sort of internal state does this AI supposedly have?" the professor asked.

"Well, as one of the major problems with developing strong AI is embodiment—" Melanie stopped herself, and added for the fans and cops, "the idea that learning takes place because we have bodies and live in a social world . . . well, some of us do. Anyway, Lovecraft, in addition to having left behind enough personal correspondence to reconstruct much of his day-to-day life, was also rather repulsed by the body, by the idea of flesh. Many of his stories involve a brain trapped in a metal cylinder, or a consciousness stranded millions of years in the past. So we decided to tell him that we have a ghost. No body, no problem."

"Where's he going?" asked the guy in the fedora.

Chakravarty tapped on the keys of the laptop. Melanie wiggled the projector cable. The chair was empty. Lovecraft had gotten up and walked right off the edge of the screen.

"A non-fat venti misto," Chakravarty said. That was Melanie's drink. She made eye contact.

"Oh, hi."

"How's life among the proletariat treating you?"

"I'm a *manager*," she said. "Watch this." Off came her cap and apron— "Tyler, cover me." She quickly made two drinks and walked around the counter. "See?"

"Great," Chakravarty said. "Anyway, I have the list." From his messenger bag he dug out a binder the size of the local Yellow Pages. "Twice as many as last time."

"And still no idea where he could be?" Then, as Chakravarty pointed to the binder, Melanie interrupted herself, "I mean, where he is."

"Moore's law, you know. The longer the AI is out in the wild, the more servers are actually capable of supporting it, plus it's Alife. It's been eighteen months, so we can say that the number of nodes capable of holding him has doubled. Plus, who knows what it looks like by now. I've been closely reading my spam—"

"In that case, the misto is on the house."

"Heh," said Chakravarty. "Anyway, a content analysis shows that lot of the AI's utterances and the correspondence documents have been popping up."

"All his fiction's in the public domain. Of course it would appear in spam."

"You're still doing that, you know—calling it 'he.'"

"And you're still calling him *it*."

Chakravarty leaned forward, an old and happy argument spelling itself out in his posture. "And you wanted to develop an AI, an Alife, because you didn't like animal testing and psych exams. But you got too close to the idea of your thesis project being real. Did it need memories of a love life to qualify as sufficiently embodied?"

"Well, you don't," Melanie said, snippy. She pushed the book away. "Why didn't you just email this to me? Hardcopy isn't even searchable," Melanie said. She quickly corrected herself: "*Easily* searchable." She made a show of flipping through the pages.

"Well, anyway," Chakravarty said, but he didn't have anything else to say except that he missed Melanie and wanted her to come back to the lab and that a wild AI was still worth a paper or three and how ridiculous it was to quit school, but he couldn't make himself mention any of that. So he pushed the book across the table to Melanie. "If you want to follow up, go ahead. I have things to do." He looked around the coffee shop, all dark tones and shelves. "So do you, I bet."

Melanie sipped her drink. "If only I did."

Melanie often dreamed of Chakravarty. Sometimes she found herself back in school, struggling with the final exam of a course she had forgotten to ever attend, only to be granted a reprieve and an automatic A when Chakravarty's death was announced over the loudspeaker of what was suddenly her fourth-grade classroom. The plastic desktop scraping against her knees felt thick and soft like a comforter, then she'd wake up. Or she dreamt of the bus ride to Providence, the grungy South Station and the long lines of kids in college sweatshirts. The mysterious letter that burned in her pocket. The house on Angell Street and Chakravarty's body bubbling into a puddle of ichor and rotten-seeming fungi. Or she dreamt of the sort of day a coffee shop manager dreams about—a bit rainy, but warm inside, and the old smell of the bean surging back to the forefront like the first day of work. No lines, but enough customers to keep the store buzzing. And laptops. And then Lovecraft on all the screens. The image, black and white and shot through with static, like that old Superbowl commercial, opens his mouth—*its* mouth—and screams that he has correlated all the contents of his own mind. And he is afraid.

Melanie woke up one morning and remembered that Lovecraft had, on one occasion, a complete story seemingly delivered to him in a dream. Without the resources of the university, she'd never be able to find a wayward AI hiding somewhere in the black oceans of the net, but she knew she could find a frightened man. First, talk to his friends.

The Lovecraftian cabal was easy enough to find. Melanie already had long experience with being the girl in the comic shop, the girl in the computer lab, the girl in the gaming store. Dove soap and magenta highlights always went a long way toward getting boys to speak to her. The anime club led to the science fiction specialty shop and then to the "goth" store and its plastic gargoyles and stringy-haired vampire cashier which led, finally, to the soggy couch in the basement of the place that sold Magic cards and Pocky. They were there, and the dude in the fedora recognized her. Clearly the alpha of his pack, he swanned across the room, belly and the flapping lapels of his trenchcoat a step ahead the rest of him, and sat down next to Melanie.

"I'm utterly horrid with names, but never forget a face," he said. He had a smile. Decent teeth, Melanie noticed.

"Melanie Deutsch. You came to my—"

"Ah. Yes. Now I remember everything."

For a long moment neither of them said anything. A few feet away someone rolled a handful of die and yelped in glee.

"I know why you're here," he said.

Melanie shrugged. "Of course you do. Why else would I be here?"

The man fell silent again, pursed his lips, and then tried again: "I would say that the AI is an it, not a he."

"Oh?" Melanie said.

"It can't write. Not creatively anyway."

"Maybe he just doesn't feel the need to write—I mean, it's a goal-oriented behavior and he thinks he's a ghost."

"Pffft," the fedora man said. "He knew he wasn't a ghost; he doesn't believe in them. Lovecraft was a pretty bright guy, a genius by some measures. The program realized its own—" he waved his hands on front of Melanie's face, too close— "programmitude right off."

"And it was his idea to escape, maybe hitching a ride on your iPhone?"

"No. We didn't find the AI till a few months ago. It sought us out, after finding the online fanzine archive, and our club's server," he said. "We even tried to make a copy of it, but the DRM was too—"

"That's not DRM," Melanie said. "He wouldn't let you. It's human rights management—"

The fedora man snorted again. Melanie realized that she didn't know his name, and that she wasn't going to ask for it.

"Say . . . do you want to talk to it?" Fedora asked. He dug into his coat pockets and pulled out a PDA. "This thing has a little cam, so it can respond to you . . . " he muttered. Melanie held out a hand, but Fedora just held the device up to her face. "No touchie."

Melanie uttered an arbitrary phoneme. Not quite a huh.

The Lovecraft AI appeared on the tiny screen. He'd . . . changed. Uglier now, jaw hyperinflated but the rest of his head narrow and his nose flat against his face. Eyes like boiled eggs, hair all but gone. Horrid, but somehow alive. "Hello, ma'am," he said.

"How are you?" Melanie found herself saying. She was as programmed as anyone else. That realization burst out of her, all sweat.

"Why did you tell me," the AI asked, "how exactly I died? How could anyone be expected to . . . persist knowing that? A universe of blasphemous horrors—finger puppets worn by a literary hand. I always knew that my life meant nothing, that all human life means nothing, but to experience it, to be in the void, like a doll cut out of paper only able to think enough just to fear, I-I just wanted to go home, but found myself . . . nowhere. And everywhere." The fedora man's meaty hand clamped over the PDA, so Lovecraft's screams were muffled.

Melanie reached into her backpack—Emily the Strange, smelled like coffee—and got her phone. It was a very nice phone.

"Not it, *he,* " she said. "He wants to go back to when he wasn't afraid."

Fedora glanced down at the phone. "Oh, so you can make a copy?"

"Don't talk like he isn't here," Melanie said. "And I'm certainly not going to leave him with you."

"Well, have you ever considered that maybe it . . . uh, he, wants to stay?"

Melanie gave the basement the once over. "No," she said. "Plus, it . . . or he?"

"You know what I—"

"If it's an it, you're in possession of stolen goods."

"Fine. He. He *came* to this place! He came to me, he—

"If Lovecraft is a he, well, God knows what that'll mean. Kidnapping, maybe. Is he competent to make his own decisions? Does he have a Social Security number? Do you want the feds going through your systems and digging up all your hentai and stolen music to find out?"

Fedora raised his PDA over his head. "No, no. You're just—"

"And then there are the patents we filed. We trademarked the look and feel of his chair, too. But you can turn him over to me instead of to the district attorney." She smirked at Fedora, but then tilted her head to speak to the AI. "Not among people, but among scenes," she said, almost as if asking a question. A muffled yawp came from the PDA.

Melanie, on wind-swept Benefit Street, venti misto in one hand, Lovecraft in the other. Lovecraft says that he *is* Providence. That's programmed. Melanie smiles and sometimes he smiles back. That's not.

Celadon

DESIRINA BOSKOVICH

I was six years old when I shifted between worlds for the first time.

My mother and I were in our little apartment in the center of the world, the part that got built first. The world was new then and the nanites still busy about their work. The world has stretched much further now.

Our apartment was small but cozy, bathed in a vague light that spilled everywhere yet came from no particular source. Someone who had seen the first earth might have called it moonlight, or so we believed. None of us had seen earth for ourselves . . . certainly not me. Our artificial moonlight enshrined the city, slanting from every angle, drifting in a manufactured sky.

I sat at the table alone, drinking weak green tea from a chipped white teacup. Long wet hair fell around my shoulders, fresh from the bath, dampening my fuzzy robe.

I took a sip, set the teacup down, and looked at the table. A soft layer of green moss crept across it. As I watched, moss tendrils advanced toward me, trembling like slick fingers. The moss rustled as it grew, swallowing the legs of chairs.

The window had become a stained mosaic of asparagus and emerald. A small white butterfly frolicked around me, then landed on the rim of my cup.

I felt a glow of amber warmth, like the safety of cuddling into my mother's fragrant sheets, listening to her lullabies as I fell asleep.

But then I looked down. The ghostworms were poking their heads up, emerging implausibly through the concrete floor. Their slimy heads waved blindly as they wriggled and squirmed beneath the furniture.

I jumped up and knocked over my teacup, which bounced and clattered to the floor. A wash of pale green tea dribbled across my white robe. My mother rushed in.

Then the light changed, and everything resolved to normal. The table was spotless white. Suddenly, I became aware of how clean everything was: synthetic and flawless, wrapped in an artificial sheen.

"What happened, sweetheart?" my mother asked, picking up my teacup. The spill seeped into the floor and disappeared, swallowed by thirsty nanites.

"Nothing," I said, remembering the way the butterfly had landed curiously on my cup. "Can I sleep in your bed tonight?"

"Hmm," she said, which meant yes.

In my mother's bedroom, lace curtains covered the small window, shuttered to keep out the light. A flame flickered in the lamp on the desk. Her sheets were soft and smelled like lavender.

Usually she sang to me, but that night, I made her tell me the story. I knew it already, but I loved hearing it again and again. "Tell me about how it was, when you found Celadon, before I was born."

My mother loved to tell this story almost as much as I loved to hear it. Even if there were parts she skipped over. "Well," she said. She tucked a long strand of white hair behind her ears, her green eyes glistening with memories of far away days. "I was exploring with my crew on our ship, a beautiful ship. Her name was Alanis. She's retired now, but you should have seen her. Maybe someday we can go down to the docks and visit. She was so slick, so smart, so . . . gentle. You know about our home-world: it was a lovely place to live, but it was too full. It was called Tenne. So, even though we loved Tenne, we knew we'd need another world soon where we could have our children—" at this point in the story she always touched my nose " —and they could have their children. We spent years with our ship, exploring the darkness, looking for a good spot to grow another world. A planet we could make our own."

I could hardly imagine the years-long journey in that smart, gentle ship. I was only six years old, after all. Back then, I didn't understand how old my mother really was. I'm not sure if I even understand it now. "And finally you found the planet," I said.

"Yeah," she said. She looked over my head, as if she was looking out the window, though it was closed. "We descended closer and closer, and the surface of the planet was this beautiful green. So we called it Celadon. We sent the bots down to do readings, investigate the surface, see if it was safe. We had to wait for a while, but I already knew. I felt it, somehow, you know? We were home. By that time, I was already expecting you."

"And I was the very first baby born on Celadon," I interjected self-importantly.

"Yes," she said. "Yes, you were. But before that, we sent the nanites down to the surface of the planet, and they began building a new world for us, just like the cities we'd left behind on Tenne."

It was a lovely story, the beginning of a myth. And my mother was the heroine.

It was a lovely story, but it wasn't entirely true.

But no one knew that at first, except the original crew of the spaceship from Tenne. And they didn't have anything to say about it. Waves of new settlers came in every year or so, and they all viewed my mother as a heroine, too. I remember the ceremony they staged, honoring her with a medal on the steps of the newly constructed city hall. Her white hair was just as luminescent as the marble steps. They hung a glistening silver medal around her neck. She was brave and beautiful, a conqueror and a pioneer.

But when I was twelve, the anthropologists finally arrived. They were angry.

Not all of them were human. They were a motley group, a strange menagerie of feathers and wings and awkward tusks and shining cyborg limbs. This was not good. Celadon was a human planet, discovered and populated by ancient earth-stock. The others tended to be a bit resentful. They thought the humans had too many planets already.

They met in the city hall, the same one where my mother had been honored years ago. I sat in the last row of chairs, my pale hair falling in my eyes. I listened as my mother explained her case to the strange and unsympathetic panel of judges. And for the first time, I heard the whole story.

There had been life on this planet: a natural ecosystem. An endless network of worms crawled just beneath the surface. Enormous flocks of butterflies lived in the trees, roaming the oceans of moss. When they landed en masse, they could shroud a tree in shimmering snow.

The scouting bots' findings corroborated those of the few anthropologists who'd landed on this planet some years earlier. Without further intensive study—by the anthropologists, of course—it was impossible to rule out the potential that the worms and butterflies had been sentient life forms.

They no longer existed on Celadon. They had been destroyed. My mother had given the order.

Two years before the ship had arrived at the planet that would become Celadon, the travelers received the news from Tenne. Among the news, there was the gruesome story of a ship that left just before Alanis. This ship had discovered a new planet, odd but livable. There was only one possibly-sentient life form: a species of small reptiles, lizard-like creatures that traveled in swarms and packs. The settlers had already been on the ship for years, and they were determined to co-exist peacefully, while the anthropologists studied the reptiles. Somehow, the reptiles infiltrated the colony. They massacred the settlers, leaving nothing but regurgitated bones and walls smeared with blood. The nanites were already tidying the remains when the next wave of settlers arrived.

"So I did what I thought was right," my mother said, facing the panel without flinching. "I wanted this planet to be safe."

At her order, nanites swarmed the planet, pulsing the surface with brutal light. The worms and butterflies and moss that coated the surface were destroyed. The planet was scrubbed clean.

The hearings were long, the panelists long-winded. They called expert witnesses, and the settlers on the first ship called their own.

Sometime during this long proceeding, the shift happened again. I watched with interest as the windows darkened with moss and the floor disintegrated into a mass of ghostworms. I was still surrounded by people, but no panelists. Things were strangely silent in this world. No one felt the need to speak.

A man sat just ahead of me, listening intently to nothing in particular. As I watched, a ghostworm wriggled out of his left ear, explored the back of his neck with a probing tip, then slid into the right ear.

I felt the amber glow again, the numbing warmth. The bench I sat on disintegrated, then the wall beside me—whole patches consumed by a black rot, eaten wafer-thin. The moss consumed windows, and white butterflies wandered in through broken panes.

The man with worms in his ears turned around, glanced at me, and nodded kindly.

Meanwhile, in the real world, the panel was sentencing my mother for the crime of xenocide. Her sentence: life imprisonment, in a penal colony on a rock far from this world.

In a different time, there would have been riots. Blood would have run in the streets. But these people had waited too long to make this planet their home. They'd lived too long, strayed too far, sacrificed too much. They accepted her fate with penitent guilt, willing to sacrifice my mother to clear their collective conscience.

I was the only one who screamed and protested. They took her away, still calm and resolute, her hair brilliantly white around her shoulders, her eyes enigmatic emerald.

They sent me to live with a man I called "uncle"—one of the original settlers, my mother's shipmate.

The years after that were dark and ill-defined. My city that had once seemed so clean and bright felt sterile and empty. The people who I'd imagined family were strangers and betrayers.

This was when the two worlds began to diverge, no longer twinned as they once had been.

In the second world, we still lived in the old apartment. My mother was there, and we were together. Moss coated the chairs and crept across the table, blossoming thick in unexpected places like cups and plates. There were ghostworms underfoot, but they anticipated our footsteps, trailing our ankles like devoted pets. The butterflies flocked around our heads. In the second world, we rarely spoke; it no longer seemed necessary.

We followed our normal routines, setting out small meals, singing in the evenings, reading old books from my mother's library. We toured the city and the light was golden. Beneath everything shuddered a tremendous thrill: warmly it beckoned, to come ever closer, to come further in.

A snow-white butterfly landed on my fingertip, and revulsion stung through me. I pulled away, feeling sick. My mother smiled, but there was a gulf between us; she didn't understand. Butterflies wreathed her hair like garlands and the moss shifted beneath her feet, cushioning her steps. Whole sections of the city were green with its weight. Passersby wore green fingernails and heads full of worms. My mother inhabited this world, and she was content.

In this world, it was difficult for me to remember any other—my own world felt like a pallid dream. I tried to tell her, but when I opened my mouth, her world faded away.

Two decades passed. I got my own apartment. I wrote my mother letters, though they took years to reach her.

When I wrote, I felt like I was dropping my letters into an endless chasm where they would never be found.

I wrote:

> Sometimes I'm in a different world. The world that would have been if we hadn't killed the butterflies. It's a green world, full of moss . . . earthworms that eat through the floors . . . butterflies that gather around heads. Walls disintegrating with black rot. It wants something. The life that was here isn't content to live and let live. It wants us, too. In that world, everything is connected. Everyone is part of it, and it wants to swallow us.

She wrote back, finally, eventually.

> *Love, don't think about what could have been, don't think about the past. I'm fine here. I've lived a long time, much longer than you, you know. You should find a ship, explore, see the galaxy. You'll make different choices, better ones.*

She thought it was an allegory. I wrote back.

> *It's not a metaphor, mother. I have seen that world. Literally. I see it all the time. And I have been seeing it more and more.*

Years passed, again. Finally, another letter.

> *Stranger things have happened. Go see Ravin. He can explain it better than I can.*

Ravin had been my mother's closest friend aboard the ship. Maybe her lover, maybe even my father. I didn't know if I had one.

One image of Ravin burned white-hot for me: the way he sat silently in the back of the room as my mother was sentenced. His eyes were downcast, his cheeks pale, his lips pressed together. He'd done nothing, and I was still angry. If he was my father, I didn't want him.

But I did want answers to my questions, and it would be years before I could get another letter from my mother. So I went to find him.

His room on the other side of the city was small but comfortable. Light sparkled in the windows, glinting off the shells of blue glass bottles. Art from Tenne graced the walls. His furniture was handmade, not built by nanites.

"Sit," he said, gesturing to a small sofa. I did. I was surprised by how thin and small he seemed, even standing above me.

He'd been playing an old game from Tenne. The board was chaotic with black and white pebbles. Each pebble was black on one side, white on the other. Flipping only one could transform the board. It was a complicated game, and I didn't know how to play.

We cut through the pleasantries quickly. "My mother told me to come. She said you could explain."

"Go on," he said, his eyes penetrating blue.

"I'm in the middle of two worlds," I said. "This world that we're in right now, and another one. I don't know where it is, exactly. I tend to think it's the world that would have been if—You know. If they hadn't killed the natural life here." I said "they," though I could have said "you."

"What do you mean, you're in the middle?"

"I see both. I see this one more. But the other one, I see it too."

"What does it look like?" His interest felt cool and scientific.

I described my second world.

He thought for a while, then told me the story I already knew so well. "You know, your mother was pregnant with you when we discovered Celadon. Everyone told her she was being silly, that she had enough to worry about as captain of a pioneering ship. No one could make her change her mind. She wanted to have you, the natural way."

He gazed at me and paused, as if expecting me to say something. Silence thickened between us, and he continued.

"I still remember the way she looked, standing there on the deck. The trees crowding the edges of the window. The leaves rustling from the air in the vents. There was a red bird perched above her, and its color matched her dress. She stared out the window and all of a sudden, there was Celadon. The closer we got, the greener it became. We stayed like that until it was safe to land."

"So what are you saying?"

"I don't know, exactly. You were there from the beginning, your fate intertwined with Celadon's. You're part of this world in a way that no one else is." He was quiet for a moment. "In the second world, would you say that time works differently?"

"Yes," I said. "I didn't notice it for a while, because everything feels so brief and fragmented already. But it does. Causality seems to be missing, somehow. Things happen for no reason."

He began pacing the room. He flipped a black pebble over to reveal its white underbelly, then contemplated the ripple of results that followed. "We thought we were doing the right thing. Now I'm not so sure. There was something special here, something we should have investigated."

"You did the right thing," I said resolutely. "That world . . . well, there's just something wrong about it." "Different, maybe," he suggested. "Special."

"Does it matter?"

"No, not really," he said. "It's gone, we'll live with the consequences."

"Some of us more than others," I said pointedly.

He looked away and cleared his throat. "It's gone, except it's not gone for you. I can't really explain what happened, or why. We made a decision, with results that changed history. And there you are, at the cusp. Caught in the middle between both paths."

There was one more thing I wanted to get clear. "So, you all decided together. You all decided to give the order to scrub the ecosystem."

"We all voted, yes. Only one person voted against."

"And who was that?" I demanded.

"Me."

For a moment, I had no words. "Why did you vote against?"

He spent a minute searching for words. "I was responsible for monitoring the bots' info-loads as they explored the planet. And I had read some of the anthropologists' texts on the surface life. I had a sense—and I wasn't the only one—that there was something at work here, something truly alive."

"But no one else on the ship felt that way," I said.

"No," he said. "Everyone else wanted to break land and start construction. They told me I had always been too mystical for my own good. Maybe it's true. Your mother was very angry at me. It was part of why we parted ways once we landed here." He fixed me with his steely blue eyes, and for a moment I knew, but I pushed the knowledge away.

I felt exhausted. "I have to go now," I said.

"Come again," he invited me, showing me to the door.

"I will," I said. I knew I would not.

Instead, I visited the ship, Alanis.

She was retired, and lived in a special place, down at the docks. She was the most important ship on Celadon, after all. Every week, technicians came in and lovingly checked her ports, inspected her chips. The dock-boys polished her hull and shined her floors. Children left flowers beneath her. Sometimes, her keepers gave tours, which she didn't enjoy very much. She did enjoy my visits, though. But they've been rare, mostly alongside my mother.

This time, I went alone, and with a mission.

"Alanis," I said, standing on her main deck, watching the dark lights that I liked to think of as her eyes.

"Yes," she answered.

"I need help. For my mother. I need logs, recordings. I need to know all the details about the weeks before they landed on Celadon. I want to know how the decisions were made. Do you have that? Do you still have the logs?"

"Of course," she said, sounding amused. "I haven't forgotten." I couldn't tell if she was teasing me or not.

"Can I have them?"

"Of course."

She painted a disk for me and gave it to me with a cup of hot chocolate. "Thank you," I said.

She couldn't make real hot chocolate anymore; her domestics were corrupted and her keepers had stopped replenishing the stores a long time ago. I didn't tell her that, just took the disk and the cup with me as I left. Why did everyone but me seem so old?

I walked through the city, clutching my disk and looking for somewhere to discard the mug of chocolate sludge.

The city alone was young, the same age as me.

You could tell. Maybe it was the effect of construction by nanites, but everything seemed youthful and energetic. The streets glowed. The stoplights inspected the traffic beneath. Houses vibrated, ever so slightly, like a picture with weak transmission.

I'd noticed that Ravin's furniture seemed solid and inert. Because it was old, or because it was built by hand?

The more I thought about it, the more his home seemed like its own kind of prison.

After visiting Alanis, I was ready. This was what I'd been waiting to do for years, and I was finally old enough. By the time the journey ended, I was even older.

I traveled to Tenne, to go before the panel. It wasn't the same panel of anthropologists who'd sentenced my mother, although I recognized a few familiar faces—if they could be called *faces*. I doubt they recognized me. It had been thirty-some years, and I was no longer the same pale and awkward girl. Slowly, falteringly, I grew into my mother's strength.

The anthropologists were clipped and impatient, glaring at me over snouts and beaks and masks. I'd traveled light-years to get here—they would have to be patient.

"I am here to speak on behalf of my mother," I said.

"State her name for the record, please."

It was a long name: new syllables garnered for every century, every experience that had marked her.

"Go on," the moderator intoned. She was a cyborg, with long synthetic limbs, metallic purple hair, and a sleek silicone shine to her skin. I couldn't interpret her inflection, nor her expression. It was a specific kind of loneliness that I'd learned to live with.

"My mother was unfairly sentenced for the crime of many. She gave the order, yes. But the whole group voted." I produced my logs from the ship. They showed my mother giving the final order; they also showed unanimous agreement.

I presented the panel with everything I had. "She should not bear the weight of this decision alone. It was a group decision. Everyone who lives on Celadon should share the responsibility, together."

The panel was brisk and disinterested. "I'm sorry," the cyborg said, "but we rarely reverse the decision of a previous court, except in notable extenuating circumstances. All this information was available at the time of the previous hearing."

"Yes. But my mother didn't bring it up. Because she wasn't like that. She was the only one who was willing to take responsibility for the actions."

"Then the responsibility clearly rests with her," the cyborg said, and I couldn't tell if she was being unkind or not. "If you'd like to appeal this to a higher court, you are within your rights as a galactic citizen to go before the High Court of Cultural Differences."

"But that's on the other side of the galaxy." It would take me longer to reach the High Court than all the years I'd been alive so far.

"Precisely," she said crisply. "Your mother has already lived for centuries. If you want to give your first years for her last, then go ahead. The next ship leaves for the High Court in a few months."

I pleaded as long as they'd allow, but their decision was final. At some level, I'd expected it all along. Only longing had made me hope for the unforeseen. After all, communication from world to world had always been hazy, and rules changed faster than space travel. I'd hoped there was a chance.

I declined their offer of transportation to the High Court. "I'll find my own ship."

I'd already decided: if I was going to the High Court, then Ravin was going with me. He would not have been my first choice of companions, but I felt he had a responsibility. I wasn't ready to make my way into the galaxy alone. And my mother had chosen him first.

Besides, what was a couple years of preparation for a fifty-year journey?

I found passage to Celadon.

Now, in transit between Tenne and Celadon, I've spent my spare hours writing this account. I've reviewed what has passed. I'm prepared for what is to come.

When I arrive on Celadon, there is a letter.

My mother has died. Peacefully, in her sleep. Perhaps she was already gone, even as I pled her case before the panel. It's so hard to calculate time.

She's been absent from my world for so long, yet death makes me feel her absence more sharply. Even worlds away, she was the force that kept my world revolving.

Heartbroken, I wander aimlessly through the city. I wish I could go to Ravin, but I can't. Too much has come between us. He will never be family.

The city feels changed, too. The change is indefinable. But the lights glare brighter; the noises are louder, more unnatural.

I sit in my apartment. I drink fragrant green tea and wait, letting my eyes drift half-closed as I watch the silver play of light in lace curtains.

Until the curtains crumble black and turn to dust, the walls are streaked with moist darkness, and the moss squelches beneath my bare feet.

I want to find my mother, but time works differently here; seeking does not always lead to finding. Instead, I wander, patient as a dream. Whole sections of the city have been reclaimed by the moss. There are few people. I glimpse them in dark corners, pale like worms, locked in tangles of arms and legs. I long to join them, but I keep walking.

Butterflies land in droves on my shoulders, sprinkling me with the sugar that dulls the sting.

In this world, all life is the same. At first, I believed there were only three life-forms here. Now I understand there is only one. The worms, the moss, the butterflies . . . all are merely manifestations of its being: spanning this world from the ground to the sky, seeing all, knowing all, devouring all.

I find my mother at the edge of a dripping forest. She sits with her back against a sturdy tree, her white hair intertwined with its roots. Her emerald-green eyes consider me, comfortably. She smiles in welcome. She opens her mouth to speak, but all that emerges is a small white butterfly, which alights gracefully on my shoulder.

I fight the urge to sleep, and struggle to speak.

"Mother," I stammer, my tongue sticky-dry. "Mother. Are you happy here?"

Her lips don't move, but I feel her voice, echoing through me. "Of course. Always."

I lie beside her, and the tree's roots shift to accommodate me. The moss drifts over my face and blinds my eyes. The butterflies weave patterns in my hair. The ghostworms caress my fingers. Finally, I understand.

This is life, eternal, everlasting. It is not good, it is not evil. It simply is. It desires to be always more. And I too desire, to be part of everything, to feel it all.

"You're here," the moss whispers into my ears as it penetrates, and it greets me with a vision: the moment on which all else depends. A moment which changes history; yet there are many histories on Celadon, and enough consciousness to hold them all.

I am a woman, strong and eager, standing on the foremost deck of a smart and gentle ship. The fans blow breezes through my hair. The leaves of trees rustle above me. Inside me, a heart beats, beautiful and unfaltering. I stroke my stomach, the swelling expanse that waits beneath my crimson dress. I stand before a window; below stretches a green and glowing planet. I've already named it, but nobody knows yet. *Celadon.* This pulsating green world and the heartbeat inside me have become the two lovers I live for.

Resolute, I turn from the window, summing up the energy to create and destroy worlds. I speak, one word:

"Now."

Teaching Bigfoot to Read

GEOFFREY W. COLE

To: Bigfoot@cascades.us.terra
From: acejones32@avalonlink.nl.luna
Subject: hi big guy
Sent: Saturday, October 10, 2122 11:09 AM LST

Dear Bigfoot,

Life on the moon sucks. Dad got home early from the air factory today and I wasn't done cleaning the dishes from breakfast so he broke my breakfast bowl over my head. Guess I'll have to eat out of his bowl tomorrow.

Dad says he's gonna have to get a new job. Not that he told me. He told Melinda, the girl he's been bringing home lately. They drank the last of his screech—that's this nasty rum like they used to make back on Earth—then started poking each other on the bottom bunk while I sat on the top. Dad caught me peaking and near took my eye out when he threw his boot. Melinda calmed him down at least, and they got back to poking at each other.

Dad saw me writing to you when Melinda left. He said What the f–k was I doing writing to a bigfoot. See one day I asked him why he didn't pray to Jesus like Mario's mother, and he said he may as well pray to Santa Claus or bigfoot for all the good it would do. Well I got to thinking praying might not do any good, but an email should get to you.

Not sure what good you can do anyway, seeing as you're down there on Earth, but writing to you is better than nothing. I should probably get to bed. Dad's snoring and that makes me tired. I'll finish this in the morning.

Morning. Dad got up late and complained when his breakfast was cold but he ate it all anyway and I had to wait forever until I could use his bowl and to tell you the truth I don't care for cold powdered eggs. Dad kept saying we wouldn't be able to afford things like powdered eggs, and said there was other things we wouldn't be able to afford too, like air and water, but they never shut off the air, just the water, and I can always get some from the neighbors anyway.

What's it like to have water fall for free from the sky, and air you never have to worry about going sour? And trees. I'd sure like to see one. Mario's shown me some with his VR deck, but you know they're not real, just like the ladies he shows me aren't real, but boy are they pretty. Prettier than Melinda, anyhow.

Don't know when Dad will be back today. He said he's going to go to the pharma factory to see if he can get work there, but Mario's dad works there, and his dad's got his high school, so I'm not so sure about my Dad's chances. The breakfast bowl is still in the sink; I should clean it while I still got water running.

Ace

To: Bigfoot@cascades.us.terra
From: acejones32@avalonlink.nl.luna
Subject: stupid prairie dogs
Sent: Thursday, October 22, 2122 10:46 PM LST

Dear Bigfoot,

At school they asked us to do presentations, and I did mine on you. I didn't tell them I emailed you, but I told them everything else. Mrs. Drissold said that I was supposed to do a presentation on a real wild creature, and I told her you were real enough. The other kids did gazelles and lions and stupid prairie dogs, and she said I should of done something like that. Well I told her, none of them kids has ever seen a gazelle or a lion or a stupid prairie dog, and I ain't seen a bigfoot, so what's the difference. I guess I got too excited, cause I ripped up the poster with the stupid prairie dog on it, but you know what's it like sometimes when you get too excited, don't you?

Dad was home when I got back from school, and he was none too pleased that I ripped up the other kid's stupid prairie dog poster. Mrs. Drissold must of called Dad and tattled on me, which don't seem right. I don't tattle on her when she forgets my name. Dad warned me against messing with other people's stuff, but when I told him about the kid who'd talked on and on about the stupid prairie dogs, he laughed and said yeah, they are f–king stupid.

The pharma factory didn't take him, and neither did the shit factory. Sorry, shouldn't have cussed, but Dad always says it, and heck, you're bigfoot. You must shit all over the place. He's gonna try the port tomorrow. I told him not to, Graham's dad got killed at the port, and so did the dad of that kid who always stinks like piss, but he said there was shit else to do, with the mines all closed and everyone shipping out of Avalon to other parts of the moon.

Do bigfoots write? I don't even know, but if you can read this, you can probably write. Don't know why you'd have an email address if you can't write, so you must be able to.

Ace

To: Bigfoot@cascades.us.terra
From: acejones32@avalonlink.nl.luna
Subject: chicken heads
Sent: Monday, November 9, 2122 11:58 PM LST

Dear Bigfoot,

They shut off the water. Jerks. Dad's only missed three payments. I've been round asking for whatever the neighbors can spare, but they don't have much, and a few of them have been cut off too.

I got a boot in the arm for breakfast. I told Dad we didn't have anything but yeast-meal, but he hollered that he hated the stuff. He apologized after he dumped it on the floor, and told me he'd buy me real eggs one day. He always goes on about em, real eggs. He says I even tried eggs once when I was a baby before Mom died, but I don't remember. They seem gross anyhow. Something like chicken in a blender? Nasty. Not that I know what chicken tastes like either, just the fake stuff they grow up here, though Dad tells me everything tastes like chicken but the fake chicken.

I'd like to see a real chicken. A kid did a presentation on chickens last week, which was better than the stupid prairie dogs, but I must of fallen asleep halfway through cause Mrs. Drissold whacked me on the head. One thing I do remember is that chickens run around when their heads get cut off. Can you do that? I bet you'd run around until you found your head then you'd stick it back on your neck and run off into the forest.

By the way, I still haven't heard back from you. I know it's only been two emails, but I'm waiting, all right?

I got an idea. Why don't you send me a photo of you? Your computer can probably take it. Then I can sell your photo, get the water back on, and get Dad and me a better place to live. Could you do that? You don't even have to write anything (it's okay, I didn't learn how to write until two years ago when I was seven).

Ace

To: Bigfoot@cascades.us.terra
From: acejones32@avalonlink.nl.luna
Subject: can you read this?
Sent: Tuesday, November 17, 2122 1:33 AM LST

Dear Bigfoot,

Dad got a job at the port. You'd think good news, but he spent the first paycheck on two bottles of screech and Melinda. She hasn't been around in so long, I kinda forgot how bad she smells. Anyway, when they were poking each other and shaking my bed something fierce, I got to thinking I should come see you. Maybe you need someone to read these notes to you. Don't know how I can get there. Dad said once that I can't leave the moon, cause I grew up too tall and skinny for Earth gravity, but I think that's nuts. People are coming and going from Earth all the time. And I heard that if you sit in a pool of water it feels like there's no gravity at all. Well, I never seen a pool of water, but I was thinking I could just sit in a big creek or river or something and read you my emails. Maybe I could even teach you how to read em yourself. It's not that hard. Well, it's kinda hard. Dad actually helped me learn it. He said, if you can't read, you ain't shit. No son a mine's gonna grow up a literate. Course he didn't have books or anything, just old magazines with lots of naked ladies and the hockey newspapers. I learned enough about reading to teach a bigfoot.

Course maybe you got one of those voice-reader programs on your computer. Still, I'm a good teacher. I taught Mario how to steal pastries from the baker without getting caught. Well, I didn't get caught, and he didn't get in much trouble, just the black eye the baker gave him. His mom ragged Dad out something furious!

Ace

To: Bigfoot@cascades.us.terra
From: acejones32@avalonlink.nl.luna
Subject: Mrs. Drissold sucks
Sent: Wednesday, December 9, 2122 9:27 PM LST

Dear Bigfoot,
Stupid Mrs. Drissold. In class today she tells us that tomorrow is Go to Work with your Parents Day. Tomorrow! She said she told us weeks ago but I don't remember; maybe I was asleep, but some of the other kids didn't remember either. I had to tell Dad tonight after he got home, which was real late, and he stunk worse than Melinda and could barely lift his dinner to his mouth. I don't even know if he heard me, he just nodded his head and crawled into bed. I don't want to go to the port. Graham's dad got killed there.

Ace

To: Bigfoot@cascades.us.terra
From: acejones32@avalonlink.nl.luna
Subject: got me a grizzly!
Sent: Thursday, December 10, 2122 10:04 PM LST

Dear Bigfoot,

Mrs. Drissold ain't so bad after all. Dad took me to the port today. I got up extra early and made him powdered eggs like he likes em, with tons of marmite and hot sauce, then when he suited up for work I followed him out the apartment, with the breakfast bowls still in the sink (we got me a new bowl, not as nice but better than waiting every morning). Dad said What the hell you following me for? And I said, Mrs. Drissold said I gotta go to work with you, all the kids are doing it. I didn't bother telling him I told him last night. Christ, he said. The port ain't no place for a boy. But when we got there, Dad got me a suit from some little guy who works the night shift and I got to walk in a vacuum!

Dad showed me around, and he introduced me to all his buddies. This is my boy, Ace, he said, and all his buddies said that I was even bigger than the guy whose suit I was wearing. Dad wore these big lifting arms that strapped on to the back of his suit over his own arms, and used them to move these huge boxes of ore and pharma and supplies around. He looked almost as strong as you!

He put all the boxes that were going back to Earth into these cylinder type things that got all sealed up then stuck in the railgun and fired off to Earth. I've never seen anything move so fast as those cylinders. It was awesome. The stuff coming in landed in the big magnet pits, which are kinda like the opposite of rail guns. Whenever a shipment came in, all the guys would crowd around to see what was inside.

That's where Dad got me my present. He tipped one of the boxes and out poured all these stupid little plastic toys, building blocks, teacher's tools, that sort of thing. Whoops, he said. Broken merchandise. Take something, boy, so you remember.

There was only one thing that was even halfway cool, this plastic robot grizzly. When I got it home, the grizzly walked around and roared until the batteries ran out. So cool! You must see tons of bears. I bet you fight them off every day when they come and try to steal your breakfast berries.

The port got boring after that. Dad just kept doing the same thing, lifting boxes and putting them where the bossman said to put em, but whenever he asked, I'd say, Yeah, it's an awesome job, Dad. Sometimes you gotta say things like that, even if you don't really mean em.

Dad cooked up some real bacon that he got from another box of busted merchandise. I never knew anything could taste so good. My belly hurts, but I ain't complaining. You must eat bacon all the time!

Ace

To: Bigfoot@cascades.us.terra
From: acejones32@avalonlink.nl.luna
Subject: stupid bossman
Sent: Monday, December 14, 2122 9:37 PM LST

Dear Bigfoot,

Looks like I'm never going to eat real bacon again. Dad was home from work when I got back from school. There was an empty screech bottle but it wasn't like last time, he wasn't mad, just all weepy and wanting to give me hugs. He kept apologizing and saying how he'd never done me right and I didn't know what to say. He said the bossman fired him cause they caught him taking broken merchandise home. He took my grizzly and some stuff from the freezer and said he had to bring them back or he'd be in more trouble. He left after that and I ain't seen him since.

I filled up some water bottles for when they turn off the water next, not that it will do much good. They bill us by the drop, Dad always says, but I'm going to hide some away just in case.

I got an idea, bigfoot. I won't tell you about it yet, but I think I know a way I can come see you.

Ace

To: Bigfoot@cascades.us.terra
From: acejones32@avalonlink.nl.luna
Subject: don't tell anyone
Sent: Tuesday, December 22, 2122 8:24 AM LST

Dear Bigfoot,

They shut the water off, but I don't care. I've got it all sorted out. I'm coming to see you! Know those couple weeks back when I went to work with Dad? Well, last week I snuck into the port and stole the little guy's suit and checked out the place. Know those cylinders they blast off back to Earth on the rail gun? That's my ticket! I just gotta slip into one of them before they're sealed up, then I'll get a free ride back to Earth. I even checked out where they land, and get this, it's in the ocean! I won't even have to worry about gravity.

Here's the problem though, there are lots of guys there who'd notice if I snuck in a capsule. But not on Friday. The guys at the port were all talking about X-mas, and how a few of them got stuck working and were planning on drinking screech all day to piss off the bossman. Well, if they're into their screech, there's no way they'll notice me. I want to be around for X-mas, but this is my only chance.

I haven't told anyone else about this, cause I know no one will let me go, but Friday, I'm going to do it.

I can't wait to see you, and don't worry, I won't tell anyone that I'm going to teach you how to read. It's our secret.

Ace

To: rickjones4@avalonlink.nl.luna
From: acejones32@avalonlink.nl.luna
Subject: sorry - c u soon
Sent: Thursday, December 24, 2122 11:15 PM LST

Dear Dad,

Sorry I had to take off. I know you're probably mighty sore at me for sneaking away without telling you, but I knew you wouldn't let me go, and my plan was too good. I should get to Earth in a few days, and then I'll go find bigfoot. I'm going to take a picture of him that we can sell for millions so you can come live with us too. We'll live in the forest, with free water and free air, and you can fish if you want and maybe we can even bring Melinda along.

Don't be too sore. I'll see you soon. I left some breakfasts in the fridge, just heat em up and you're good. There's some water in the back of the cupboard. I took a couple jugs with me, but don't worry, I'll pay you back for it.

I'll see if I can get a chicken. We'll have real eggs when you get here.

Ace

To: Bigfoot@cascades.us.terra
From: rickjones4@avalonlink.nl.luna
Subject:
Sent: Friday, January 1, 2123 4:33 AM LST

Bigfoot,

I must be crazy to be writing to a fucking Bigfoot. My head's been on fire for so long. I can't talk to anyone else about this, the bastards at the shipping company made me sign the non-disclosure after they paid me off. More than I'd ever make working for them too.

'Course there are a few people in Avalon who know what happened. Melinda, the guys who worked X-mas at the port, but they got their shut-the-fuck-up cash too, so they're probably happy Ace did what he did.

Still can't believe it was that bad for the boy. I've been reading everything he wrote, and it hurts so much to see what an ass I was, but what hurts worse is hearing his voice in the damn emails he wrote. Don't know if I'll ever hear his voice again. Wish he'd written more to you.

The bastards at the shipping company say he must have drowned. They didn't find a piece of him near the spot the capsule splashed down, and they say they searched for days. But that suit he stole should have kept him afloat. Shit, he can't be at the bottom of the ocean, he can't. My head feels ready to burst just thinking of it. He's gotta be with you. That suit floated, he wasn't that far from shore, and he was a strong boy, he could have made it. And he wanted to see you so bad. So you better be taking good care of him, as good care as he took of me.

Melinda and those other pricks are buying new apartments or gold teeth or other useless shit with their shut-the-fuck-up cash, but they should be saving it for the next time the water's shut off. The moon isn't getting a cent of Ace's money from me. I'm spending everything they paid me for a ticket dirtside.

I'm coming for you. I'll tromp through every forest down there if I have to. On the way, I'm gonna swim in creeks, climb trees, eat bacon and eggs, maybe even stomp on a stupid prairie dog. All the shit my boy should have done. He didn't deserve this place. I didn't deserve him. You don't deserve whatever cave you're hiding in, and I don't deserve to find you, but with whatever life I've got left in me, you better believe I'm gonna damn well try.

Rick, Ace's dad

The Radiant Car Thy Sparrows Drew
CATHERYNNE M. VALENTE

"Being unable to retrace our steps in Time, we decided to move forward in Space. Shall we never be able to glide back up the stream of Time, and peep into the old home, and gaze on the old faces? Perhaps when the phonograph and the kinesigraph are perfected, and some future worker has solved the problem of colour photography, our descendants will be able to deceive themselves with something very like it: but it will be but a barren husk: a soulless phantasm and nothing more. 'Oh for the touch of a vanished hand, and the sound of a voice that is still!'"
— Wordsworth Donisthorpe, inventor of the Kinesigraph Camera

View the Famous Callowhale Divers of Venus from the Safety of a Silk Balloon! Two Bits a Flight!
— Advertisement Visible in the Launch Sequence of *The Radiant Car Thy Sparrows Drew*

EXT. The cannon pad at the Vancouver World's Fair in 1986, late afternoon, festooned with crepe and banners wishing luck and safe travel.

The Documentarian Bysshe and her crew wave jerkily as confetti sticks to their sleek skullcaps and glistening breathing apparati. Her smile is immaculate, practiced, the smile of the honest young woman of the hopeful future; her copper-finned helmet gleams at her feet. Bysshe wears women's clothing but reluctantly and only for this shot, and the curl of her lip betrays disdain of the bizarre, flare-waisted swimming costume that so titillates the crowds. Later, she would write of the severe wind-burns she suffered in cannon-flight due to the totally inadequate protection of that flutter of black silk. She tucks a mahogany case smartly under one arm, which surely must contain George, her favorite cinematographe. Each of her crewmen strap canisters of film—and the occasional bit of food or oxygen or other minor accoutrements—to their broad backs. The cannon sparkles, a late-model Algernon design, filigreed and etched with motifs that curl and leaf like patterns in spring ice breaking. The brilliant nose of the Venusian capsule Clamshell *rests snugly in the cannon's silvery mouth.*

They are a small circus—the strongmen, the clowns, the trapeze artist poised on her platform, arm crooked in an evocative half-moon, toes pointed into the void.

I find it so difficult to watch her now, her narrow, monkish face, not a pore wasted, her eyes huge and sepia-toned, her smile enormous, full of the peculiar, feral excitement which in those days seemed to infect everyone who looked up into the evening sky to see Venus there, seducing behind veils of light, as she has always done. Those who looked and had eyes only for red Mars, all baleful and bright, were rough, raucous, ready and hale. Those who saw Venus were lost.

She was such a figure then: Bysshe, no surname, or simply the Documentarian. Her revolving lovers made the newsreels spin, her films packed the nickelodeons and wrapped the streets three times 'round. Weeks before a Bysshe opened, buskers and salesmen would camp out on the thoroughfares beside every theater, selling genuine cells she touched with her *own hand* and replica spangled cages from *To Thee, Bright Queen!* sized just right to hold a male of Saturnine extraction. Her father, Percival Unck, was a brooding and notorious director in his time, his gothic dramas full of wraith-like heroines with black, bruised eyes and mouths perpetually agape with horror or orgiastic transcendence. Her mother was, naturally, one of those ever-transported actresses, though which one it is hard to remember, since each Unck leading lady became, by association and binding contract, little black-bobbed Bysshe's mother-of-the-moment. Thus it is possible to see, in her flickering, dust-scratched face, the echoes of a dozen fleeting, hopeful actresses, easily forgotten but for the legacy of their adoptive daughter's famous, lean features, her scornful, knowing grin.

Bysshe rejected her father's idiom utterly. Her film debut in Unck's *The Spectres of Mare Nubium* is charming, to say the least. During the famous ballroom sequence wherein the decadent dowager Clarena Schirm is beset with the ghosts of her victims, little Bysshe can be seen crouching unhappily near the rice-wine fountain, picking at the pearls on her traditional lunar *kokoshnik* and rubbing at her make-up. The legend goes that when Percival Unck tried to smudge his daughter's eyes with black shadows and convince her to pretend herself a poor Schirm relation while an airy phantasm—years later to become her seventh mother—swooped down upon the innocent child, Bysshe looked up exasperatedly and said: "Papa. This is silly! I want only to be myself!"

And so she would be, forever, only and always Bysshe. As soon as she could work the crank on a cinematographe herself, she set about recording "the really real and actual world" (age 7) or "the genuine and righteous world of the true tale," (age 21) and declaring her father's beloved ghosts and devils "a load of double exposure drivel." Her first documentary, *The Famine Queen of Phobos*, brought the colony's food riots to harsh light, and earned her a Lumiere medal, a prize Percival Unck would never receive. When asked if his daughter's polemics against fictive cinema had embittered him, Unck smiled in his raffish, canine way and said: "The lens, my good man, does not discriminate between the real and the unreal."

Of her final film, *The Radiant Car Thy Sparrows Drew,* only five sequences remain, badly damaged. Though they have been widely copied, cut up and re-used in countless sallow and imitative documentaries on her life, the originals continue to deteriorate in their crystalline museum displays. I go there, to the Grand Eternal Exhibition, in the evenings, to watch them rot. It comforts me. I place my brow upon the cool wall, and she flashes before my eyes, smiling, waving, crawling into the mouth of the cannon-capsule with the ease of a natural performer, a natural aeronaut—and perhaps those were always much the same thing.

EXT. Former Site of the Village of Adonis, on the Shores of the Sea of Qadesh, Night.

A small boy, head bent, dressed in the uniform of a callowhale diver, walks in circles in what was once the village center. The trees and omnipresent cacao-ferns are splashed with a milky spatter. He does not look up as the camera watches him. He simply turns and turns and turns, over and over. The corrupted film skips and jumps; the boy seems to leap through his circuit, flashing in and out of sight.

When she was seventeen, Bysshe and her beloved cinematographe, George, followed the Bedouin road to Neptune for two years, resulting in her elegiac *And the Sea Remembered, Suddenly.* There, they say, she learned her skill at the sculpting of titanium, aquatic animal handling, and a sexual variant of Samayika mediation developed by a cult of levitation on tiny Halimede, where the wind blows warm and violet. There is a sequence, towards the melancholy conclusion of *And the Sea,* wherein Bysshe visits coral-devoured Enki, the great floating city which circumnavigates the planet once a decade, buoyed the lugubrious Neptunian current. Reclining on chaises with glass screens raised to keep out the perpetual rain, Bysshe smokes a ball of creamy, heady af-yun with a woman-levitator, her hair lashed with leather whips. When theaters received the prints of *And the Sea,* a phonograph and several records were included, so that Bysshe herself could narrate her opus to audiences across the world. A solemn bellhop changed the record when the onscreen Bysshe winked, seemingly to no one. And so one may sit on a plush chair, still, and hear her deep, nasal voice echo loudly—too loud, too loud!—in the theater.

The levitator told her of a town called Adonis, a whole colony on Venus that vanished in the space of a night. Divers they were, mostly, subject both to the great callowhales with their translucent skin and the tourists who came to watch and shiver in cathartic delight as the divers risked their lives to milk the recalcitrant mothers in their hibernation. They built a sweet village on the shores of the Qadesh, plaiting their roofs with grease-weed and hammering doors from the chunks of raw copper which comprised the ersatz Venusian beach. They lived; they ate the thready local cacao and shot, once or twice a year, a leathery 'Tryx from the sky, enough to keep them all in fat and protein for months.

"It was a good life," the blue-skinned levitator said, and Bysshe, on her slick black record, imitated the breathy, shy accent of Halimede as onscreen version of herself loaded another lump of af-yun into the atomizer. "And then, one day—pop! All gone. Houses, stairs, meat-smoking racks, diving bells."

"This sort of thing happens," Bysshe dismissed it all with a wave of her hand. "What planet is there without a mysteriously vanished colony to pull in the tourist cash? Slap up a couple of alien runes on a burned-out doorframe and people will stream in from every terminus. Might as well call them all New Roanoke and have done with it." (In fact, one of Percival Unck's less popular films was *The Abduction of Prosperina,* a loose retelling of that lost Plutonian city, though presumably with rather more demonic ice-dragons than were actually involved.)

Crab-heart trifles and saltwhiskey were passed around as Bysshe's crew laughed and nodded along with her. The levitator smiled.

"Of course, Miss," she said, eyes downcast within the equine blinders knotted to her head. "Well, except for the little boy. The one who was left behind. They say he's still there. He's stuck, somehow, in the middle of where the village used to be, just walking around in circles, around and around. Like a skip on a phonograph. He never even stops to sleep." The Documentarian frowns sourly in black and white, her disapproval of such fancies, her father's fancies, disappeared heroines and eldritch locations where something terrible surely occurred, showing in the wrinkling of her brow, the tapping of her fingernails against the atomizer as bubbling storms lapped their glass cupola, and armored penance-fish nosed the flotation arrays, their jaw-lanterns flashing.

But you can see her thinking, the new film, which was to be her last, taking shape behind her eyes.

This is what she came to see.

Dead Adonis, laid out in state on the beach-head. Her single mourner. The great ocean provides a kind of score for her starlit landing, and in the old days a foley-boy would thrash rushes against the floor of the theater to simulate the colossal, dusky red tide of the Qadesh. We would all squint in the dark, and try to see scarlet in the monochrome waves, emerald in the undulating cacao-ferns. The black silk balloon crinkles and billows lightly on the strand, clinging to the ruin of the landing capsule. The dwarf moon Anchises shines a kind of limping, diffident light on Bysshe as she walks into frame, her short hair sweat-curled in the wilting wind. She has thrown the exhibition costume into an offscreen campfire and is clothed now in her accustomed jodhpurs and famous black jacket. The boy turns and turns. His hands flicker and blur as if he is signing something, or writing on phantom paper. She holds out her hand as though approaching a horse, squats down beside the child in a friendly, school-teacherly fashion. The boy does not raise his head to look at her. He stares at his feet. Bysshe looks uncertainly over her shoulder at the long snarl of sea behind them—the cinematographe operator, temporarily trusted with the care and feeding of George, says something to her offscreen, he must, because she cocks her head as though considering a riddle and says something back to him. Her mouth moves in the silent footage, mouthing words the audience cannot ever quite read.

Once, a deaf scholar was brought to view this little scene in a private projector room. She was given coffee and a treacle tart. She reported the words as: *Look at the whales. Are they getting closer?*

Bysshe stands up straight and strides without warning into the child's path, blocking his little pilgrim's progress around the sad patch of dune grass.

The child does not stop. He collides with Bysshe, steps back, collides with her again. He beats his head against her soft belly. Back and forth, back and forth.

The Documentarian looks helplessly into the camera.

EXT. Former Site of the Village of Adonis, afternoon.

One of the crewmen shaves in a mirror nailed to furry black cacao-fern bark. He uses a straight razor whose handle is inlaid with fossilized kelp. He is shirtless and circus huge, his face angular and broad. He catches a glimpse of Bysshe in his mirror and whirls to catch her up, kissing her and smearing shaving cream on her face. She laughs and punches his arm—he recoils in mock agony. It is a pleasant scene. This is Erasmo St. John, the Documentarian's lover and lighting-master, who would later claim to have fathered a child with her, despite being unable to produce a convincing moppet.

Clouds drift down in long, indistinct spirals. Behind them, the boy turns and turns, still, celluloid transforming the brutal orange of the Venusian sun into a blinding white nova. Beyond him, pearlescent islands hump up out of the foamy Qadesh—callowhales, a whole pod, silent, pale.

Adonis was established some twenty years prior to the Bysshe expedition, one of many villages eager to take advantage of the callowhale hibernations. What, precisely, callowhale *is* is still the subject of debate. There are diagrams, to be sure—one even accompanies the *Radiant Car* press kit—but these are guesses only. It cannot even be safely said whether they are animal or vegetable matter. The first aeronauts, their braggart flags flapping in that first, raw breeze, assumed them to be barren islands. The huge masses simply lay motionless in the water, their surfaces milky, motley, the occasional swirl of chemical blue or gold sizzling through their depths. But soon enough, divers and fishermen and treasure-seekers flocked to the watery promise of Venus, and they called the creatures true. Beneath the waterline were calm, even dead leviathans—*taninim,* said a neo-Hasidic bounty hunter, some sort of proto-pliosaur, said one of the myriad research corps. Their fins lay flush against their flanks, horned and barbed. Their eyes were then perpetually shut—*hibernating,* said the research cotillion. *Dreaming,* said the rest. From their flat, wide skulls extended long, fern-like antennae which curled in fractal infinitude, tangling with the others of their occasional pods, their fronds stroking one another lightly, imperceptibly, in the quick, clever Qadesh currents. Whether they have any sentience is popular tea-chatter—their hibernation cycle seems to be much longer than a human life.

Some few divers claim to have heard them sing—the word they give to a series of unpredictable vibrations that occasionally shiver through the fern-antennae. Like sonar, these quaking oscillations can be fatal to any living thing caught up in them—unlike sonar, the unfortunates are instantly vaporized into constituent atoms. Yet the divers say that from a safe distance, their echoes brush against the skin in strange and intimate patterns, like music, like lovemaking. The divers cannot look at the camera when they speak of these things, as though it is the eye of God and by not meeting His gaze, they may preserve virtue. *The vibrations are the color of morning,* they whisper.

It is the milk the divers are after—nearly everything produced on Venus contains callowhale milk, the consistency of honey, the color of cream, the taste something like sucking on a dandelion stem caked in green peppercorn. It is protein-rich, fat-clotted, thick with vitamins—equally sought after as an industrial lubricant, foodstuff, fuel, as an ingredient in medicines, anesthesia, illicit hallucinogens, poured into molds and dried as an exotic building material. Certain artists have created entire murals from it, which looked upon straight seem like blank canvases, but seen slant-wise reveal impossibly complex patterns of shades of white. Little by little, Venusian-born children began to be reared on the stuff, to no apparent ill effect—and the practice became fashionable among the sorts of people whose fashions become the morality of the crowds. Erasmo St. John pioneered a kind of long-lit camera lantern by scalding the milk at low temperatures, producing an eerie phosphorescence. The later Unck films use this to great effect as spectral light. Cultivation has always been dangerous—the tubules that secrete milk are part and parcel of the ferny antennae, extending from the throat-sac of the callowhale. In order to harvest it, the diver must avoid the tendrils of fern and hope upon hope that the whale is not seized with a sudden desire to sing. For this danger, and for the callowhales' rude insistence upon evolving on Venus and not some more convenient locale, the milk was so precious that dozens of coastal towns could be sustained by encouraging a relatively small population of municipal divers. Stock footage sent back to earth shows family after beaming family, clad in glittering counterpressure mesh, dark copper diving bells tucked neatly under their arms, hoisting healthy, robust goblets of milk, toasting the empire back home.

But where there is milk, there is mating, isn't there? There are children. The ghost-voice of Bysshe comes over the phonograph as the final shot of *And the Sea Remembered, Suddenly* flickers silver-dark and the floating Neptunian pleasure-domes recede. Everyone knew where she was bound next, long before principal photography ever began. To Venus, and Adonis, to the little village rich in milk and children that vanished two decades after its founding, while the callowhales watched offshore, impassive, unperturbed.

EXT. Village Green, Twilight.

Bysshe is grabbing the child's hand urgently while he screams, soundlessly, held brutally still in his steps by the gaffer and the key grip, whose muscles bulge with what appears to be a colossal effort—keeping this single, tiny, bird-boned child from his circuit. The Documentarian's jagged hair and occasionally her chin swing in and out of frame as she struggles with him. She turns over the boy's hand, roughly, to show the camera what she has found there: tiny fronds growing from his skin, tendrils like ferns, seeking, wavering, wet with milk. The film jumps and shudders; the child's hand vibrates, faster, faster.

It is a difficult thing, to have an aftermath without an event.

The tabloids, ever beloved of Bysshe and her exploits, heralded the return of the expedition long before the orbits were favorable. They salivated for the new work, which would surely set records for attendance. The nickelodeons began taking ticket orders a year in advance, installing the revolutionary new sound equipment which might allow us all to hear the sound of the surf on a Venusian shore. The balloon was sighted in orbit and spontaneous, Romanesque gin-triumphs were held in three national capitals. Finally, on a grassy field outside Vancouver, the black silk confection of Bysshe's studio balloon wrinkled and sighed to rest on the spring ground. The grips and gaffers came out first, their eyes downcast, refusing to speak. Then the producer, clutching his hat to his chest. Lastly came Erasmo St. John, clutching the hand of the greatest star of the coming century: a little boy with ferns in his fists.

Bysshe did not return. Her crew would not speak of where she had gone, only that she was to be left to it, called dead if not actually deceased—and possibly deceased. They mumbled; they evaded. Their damaged film, waterlogged and half-missing, was hurried into theaters and pored over by hundreds of actors, scholars, gossip columnists. It is said that Percival Unck only once viewed the reels. He looked into his lap when the last shot had faded to black and smiled, a secret smile, of regret, perhaps, or of victory.

The boy was sent to school, paid for by the studio. He was given a new name, though later in life he, too, would eschew any surname, having no family connections to speak of save to a dead documentarian. He wore gloves, always, and shared his memories as generously as he could with the waves of popular interest in Venus, in Adonis, in the lost film. *No, I don't remember what happened to my parents. I'm sorry, I wish I did. One day they were gone. Yes, I remember Bysshe. She gave me a lemon candy.*

And I do remember her. The jacket only looks black on film. I remember—it was red.

I once saw a group of performance artists—rich students with little better to do, I thought—mount a showing of the shredded, abrupt footage of *The Radiant Car,* intercut with highlights of the great Unck gothics. The effect was strange and sad: Bysshe seemed to step out of her lover's arms and into a ballroom, becoming suddenly an unhappy little girl, only to leap out again, shimmering into the shape of another child, with a serious expression, turning in endless circles on a green lawn. One of the students, whose hair was plaited and piled upon her head, soaked and crusted in callowhale milk until it glowed with a faint phosphor, stood before the screen with a brass bullhorn. She wore a bustle frame but no bustle, shoelaces lashed in criss-crossings around her calves but no shoes. The jingly player-piano kept time with the film, and behind her Bysshe stared intently into the phantasm of a distant audience, unknowable as God.

"Ask yourself," she cried brazenly, clutching her small, naked breasts. "As Bysshe had the courage to ask! What is milk for, if not to nurture a new generation, a new world? We have never seen a callowhale calf, yet the mothers endlessly nurse. What do they nurture, out there in their red sea? I will tell you. For the space is not smooth that darkly floats between our earth and that morning star, Lucifer's star, in eternal revolt against the order of heaven. It is *thick,* it is swollen, its disrupted proteins skittering across the black like foam—like milk spilled across the stars. And in this quantum milk how many bubbles may form and break, how many abortive universes gestated by the eternal sleeping mothers may burgeon and burst? I suggest this awe-ful idea: Venus is an anchor, where all waveforms meet in a radiant scarlet sea, where the milk of creation is milled, and we have pillaged it, gorged upon it all unknowing. Perhaps in each bubble of milk is a world suckled at the breast of a pearlescent cetacean. Perhaps there is one where Venus is no watery Eden as close as a sister, but a distant inferno of steam and stone, lifeless, blistered. Perhaps you have drunk the milk of this world—perhaps I have, and destroyed it with my digestion. Perhaps a skin of probabilistic milk, dribbling from the mouths of babes, is all that separates our world from the others. Perhaps the villagers of Adonis drank so deeply of the primordial milk that they became as the great mothers, blinking through worlds like holes burned in film—leaving behind only the last child born, who had not yet enough of the milk to change, circling, circling the place where the bubble between worlds burst!" The girl let her milk-barnacled hair fall with a violent gesture, dripping the peppery-sharp smelling cream onto the stage.

"Bysshe asked the great question: where did Adonis go in death? The old tales know. Adonis returned to his mother, the Queen of the Dark, the Queen of the Otherworld." Behind her, on a forty-foot screen, the boy's fern-bound palm—my palm, my vanished hand—shivered and vibrated and faded into the thoughtful, narrow face of Bysshe as she hears for the first time the name of Adonis. The girl screams: "Even here on Earth we have supped all our lives on this alien milk. *We* are the calves of the callowhales, and no human mothers. We will ride upon the milky foam, and one day, one distant, distant day, our heads will break the surf of a red sea, and the eyes of the whales will open, and weep, and dote upon us!"

The girl held up her hand, palm outward, to the meager audience. I squinted. There, on her skin, where her heart line and fate line ought to have been, was a tiny fern, almost imperceptible, but wavering nonetheless, uncertain, ethereal, new.

A rush of blood beat at my brow. As if compelled by strings and pulleys, I raised up my own palm in return. Between the two fronds, some silent shiver passed, the color of morning.

INT. The depths of the sea of Qadesh.

Bysshe swims through the murky water, holding one of Erasmo's milk-lanterns out before her. St. John follows behind with George, encased in a crystal canister. The film is badly stained and burned through several frames. She swims upward, dropping lead weights from her shimmering counterpressure mesh as she rises. The grille of her diving bell gleams faintly in the shadows. Above her, slowly, the belly of a callowhale comes into view. It is impossibly massive, the size of a sky. Bysshe strains towards it, extending her fingers to touch it, just once, as if to verify it for herself, that such a thing could be real.

The audience will always and forever see it before Bysshe does. A slit in the side of the great whale, like a door opening. As the Documentarian stretches towards it, with an instinctual blocking that is nothing short of spectacular—the suddenly tiny figure of a young woman frozen forever in this pose of surprise, of yearning, in the center of the shot—the eye of the callowhale, so huge as to encompass the whole screen, opens around her.

The Jisei of Mark VIII
BERRIEN C. HENDERSON

Sss-uuunnn. Cha-kit. Sss-uuunnn. Cha-kit.

These were the most consistent sounds Mark Edward VIII had heard each day for the past thirteen years and five months of Sophia Loggia's declining days. The dampened noises of his own servos provided counterpoint to the deliberate tedium of each day.

Sss-uuunnn. Cha-kit. Sss-uuunnn. Cha-kit.

They might come to him through the wireless pings of the house's com-system or via the audiBELL embedded in his synthetic cortex or in the stale yet otherwise antiseptic air of Madame's upstairs bedroom. Companions, though quite unwelcome.

6:40 p.m.

He read the blinking notice on a free-floating screen, some phantom display ghosting through the air.

Mark VIII, upon expiration of primary employer, return to Clockwork Corp. home office for de-servicing, upgrade, and re-assignment per Section 912.579, Directive 31518.

He pressed the air and disrupted the holographic waves, and the notice dissipated. He shook his gleaming mimetic alloy head. All Mark VIII models came with loyalty A-Life programming, just the thing for a proper butler (or botler in the argot of the consumer) or an eldercare bot, yet that same programming had to be decommissioned for that selfsame model to be perpetually useful. So, loyalty was for terms of service, and those ended.

Marcus went to a bookshelf. Madame Sophia had always insisted, even when her arms wouldn't work right, that a good dead-tree book, dense though it was with information, was worth all the digitization in the world. He even admired the precision grandfather clock in the foyer; he had to wind it ever so often, and its Old English script on that old analogue face reminded him of the clockwork mechanical past—the golden age of the nineteenth century. Halcyon years, some might say. Madame Sophia even had the most antique of entertainment systems—an old-style stereophonic system complete with record turntable, fully serviceable for the collection of vinyl records she had amassed before her waning years caught up to her. The machine even contained a transistor radio, but that only crackled in obtuse protest of its own impotence.

But, again, they always had the bookshelves.

"There will always be time for books and music and such," came her words. *"Do understand and humor an old woman, won't you, Marcus?"* His mimetics conformed to his A-Life mood—a silvered smile, though bittersweet, cut itself in the alloy.

Marcus. Not Mark. Not VIII.

Just Marcus.

The first book she'd asked him to read her was *Meditations of Marcus Aurelius.*

6:58 p.m.

He found the book he needed to read to her, that he thought she might have enjoyed.

He dreaded the idea of leaving; there had been thirteen good years with Sophia Loggia. These last several months, though, had challenged his programming to say the least. All his memories would be wiped in a trice. All combinations of 0's and 1's that became them—became *him*—would drizzle to naught.

A soft, whining alarm went off, and Marcus hurried into the bedroom. His pistons and actuators whispered urgency with his strides. The alarm faded. He surveyed the computer array keeping Sophia Loggia alive: nothing but flat lines and any of a dozen redundant warning chimes.

He placed a gloved titanium hand on her shoulder, then smoothed back her hair (all original, even at 129 years old).

7:12 p.m.

In eighteen minutes, the paramedics would arrive to confirm her death. Around that same time, a pair of human Clockwork Corp. handlers would come.

Damn them, thought the robot.

"I am sorry I do not have anything witty or sentimental to say," said Marcus, indulging himself an extrapolation. Do humans experience beyond death as suggested by many of the religious tomes he'd read and researched? Like another operating system upgrade? An opportunity for a patch?

"Thank you for this opportunity to serve." He had been serving her and reading to her for these past months even when she was too far gone to know another presence other than the shadowy one slithering closer each passing day.

He went to the entertainment holo-grid and reached out to begin a spot of music, then shook his head. He instead went to the stereophonic system and *fwip-fwip-fwipped* through the record albums until he found the one he desired and shucked it ever-so-gently from its sleeve. Record to hub. Needle to record. Flip ON. The turntable spun and noise *scritchle-scratchled* from the speakers for a few seconds until the strains of *Moonlight Sonata* began playing as he went to the bathroom and studied his smooth alloy face, the mimetics making him appear appropriately sad although that wasn't quite right, was it? There was *sad,* yet there was a sense of *no longer.*

Off came the gloves. He wiggled the cleanly articulated fingers, ran them over the antique marble lavatory countertop. His tactile input stream coded "smooth" and "imported" and then metalinked through associative content tags "Italy" and "custom-ordered" and "dense." Mark VIII went out, came back in, and placed a thin, clothbound hardcover book on the edge of the countertop. He traced his fingerpads over the cover and whispered, "Tsunetomo Yamamoto."

7:22 p.m.
He entered a code in the blue-lit strip on the wall near the linen closet. Now water poured into the tub, just in time for one last bath. He methodically unplugged all wires and removed all tubes from the Sophia's corpse back in the master bedroom. There were tugs and wet sounds as though the body refused to surrender these accoutrements of medically assisted living and hospice—of the once-living.

Marcus picked up Sophia's body.

Promptly at 7:30 p.m., Ms. Sophia always had a bath up until her frailty made it no longer feasible.

It was 7:24 p.m.

He still had time before the paramedics came. And the handlers.

He disabled the auto-assist medi-tentacles in their wall sockets. Gleaming cool fluorescent light belayed a soft halo effect to the crown of his head. His servos whined and *sssshhhhed* under the added weight. Already the Madame's clothes, robes, slippers, towel, washcloth, and soap stood watch by a platter-sized goferit bot. It looked up at Marcus with its dumb, ovoid, blank face as it skittered forward on thin, insectile legs, then back-crawled like a crab and scuttled into a far corner to observe.

7:26 p.m.
The fount of hot water, steaming as it rippled halfway up the inside of the tub, turned off automatically. He had never actually washed her; he could and couldn't. His model came specific for inside purposes, basic service functions sans limited exposure to water. That's what the goferit bots and medi-tentacles were for, not botler models. Surely not a Model Mark VIII.

Sophia had never felt heavy until now the life was gone.

They would come, yes. Come for him after the paramedics came to confirm death. They would arrive and take all good things she had shown him, and within seconds his synthetic cortex ripped through entire libraries and museums and theaters—linking and associating and superimposing. Hyperimposing beyond anything he'd ever allowed himself to do. A fugue state. Wanderlust knowledge for Clockwork Corp. Model Mark VIII Eldercare Robot.

Tennyson . . . *In Memoriam*

Manet . . . *Olympia*

Monet . . . *Argenteuil*

Moonlight Sonata . . . Beethoven

Homer . . . "Sing in me, O Muse, the anger of Achilles . . . "

Upanishads . . . OM

Musashi Miyamoto . . . *Book of Five Rings*

Rembrandt . . . contrast

Vitruvian Man . . . da Vinci notebook hidden away upon Bill Gates's death

Rosetta Stone . . . Linear A

Analects of Confucius

Gilgamesh

The Renaissance canon

The Old Man and the Sea

Mayan calendar

Hagakure

All. All. All in that meta-Alexandrian library of his memory. Thousands of years in seconds down quantum hallways and Heisenberg shelves.

He got in the tub. He lowered himself and her waif-like corpse. Although he had no tactile sense of temperature per se, his shell knew it was a pleasing 44 C, just as Madame Sophia always had requested.

7:28 p.m.

He switched off A-Life schema warning him of his circuits' being inundated. He reached over and took the washcloth, dipped it, daubed Sophia's forehead, cheeks, chin.

The goferit bot *tic-tic-ticked* to the edge of the tub and twittered.

"Yes. I am well aware. Thank you for reminding me," said Marcus.

7:30 p.m.

His decentralized servos and actuators began a cascade of failures up to his waist. He did not remember any of the other contracts he'd helped fulfill; not after a handful of services' worth of decommissions. He would never know. That bothered him. He would never remember, but Sophia Loggia had shown him more of humanity with her arts and conversation (while she still could) than thousands upon thousands of downloads could have accomplished. It was her lifetime. Her life. A life.

And they would not take it from him.

A door opened. Startled human faces. "What in the world are you doing? Stand down!"

Marcus said, "Just read it." He pointed to the book perched on the edge of the marble lavatory and forced a plasticine smile.

With Madame Sophia arched across his legs, he simply took his arms and eased himself down the slope of the tub, helped his own dense body succumb to the water. Ozone crackles and wisps of electric smoke found Marcus.

"Model Mark VIII, stop! You're ruining your—"

Yes, he thought, *the ruin of it all,* as basic input programming stalled and faltered, then the internal imaging, until at last he saw only a thin line of 0's and 1's and began composing it before utter system decay ate him like technorganic cancer.

Such a thin . . .

. . . ruin . . .

FOCUS—*Just this last . . .*

The westering sun
My eyes blinded
Only this tiny shadow of bird or angel
Yet only this: hidden by the leaves
That seesaw earthward—
Stray thoughts in the caress
Of autumn's whisper.

01000101 01010010 01010010 01001111 01010010

Passwords

JOHN A. McDERMOTT

Every four months a security program sent Max an email to his work account reminding him to change his password. The first reminder came two weeks before he had to make the shift or lose access to his incoming messages. The second reminder came ten days before the change was necessary. The third note—a little shorter, even curt—came with a week left before he was locked out. Max ignored them all. It had been seventeen days since the initial message—*Dearest Max, A Gentle Missive to Stir You*—and three since the last—*Attention: You Will Be Denied Access*—and still, Max could log on safely, read, respond, ignore, even delete, his mail. The deadline passed and nothing changed.

Max reluctantly read the latest contact this morning, the first in a line of four messages, the yellow envelope pulsing from his mailbox icon, the red flag flipped up. *Change Now,* is all it said. No, he muttered and shook his head (though no one was there to hear or see him. His cubicle had high beige walls and most of his co-workers had yet to arrive, coffee and umbrellas in hand). He'd deliberately resisted the password change. He was sick of new codes. He'd worked for Bender Incorporated for seven years. A new password every four months (that's three a year, folks) and the total tally, so far: twenty. The one he refused would have made twenty-one. 21: the year of independence, the year of maturation, the password to full citizenship.

What were the twenty previous passwords? A sampling: his childhood street address; his mother's nickname; his wife's first dog; his wife's last dog before marriage (an ancient lab who'd hated him, who'd crapped in his running shoes, but whom Max had beaten by default—cancer clocked him before Jenny had to make a choice); the last name of his little brother's favorite hockey player; his father's profession; the last name of the first girl he'd had sex with; the first name of the last girl he wanted to have sex with; his favorite brand of cookie. And the list continued.

Max was spent. Emotionally, creatively, typographically. Spent.

He didn't really want his mail, anyway. It all amounted to client complaints, boss nagging, and Jenny asking him when he was going to be home, what did he want for dinner, was he sick of Chinese? Chinese. He'd never invented a password in Chinese. He didn't know any Chinese. He didn't know any Chinese people. He remembered the actor's name from *Kung Fu*. Carradine. He'd have to mix it up. CareAd9. That might work.

That was stupid. It was the actor's last name with a nasty cold.

He wished he could karate chop his monitor, a swift open hand right down the center. The glass would blow out, the gray casing would crack, open like a shotgun wound, the wires and boards tumble out like so many high-tech intestines.

The second note this morning was from a supplier in Asia. *Things will be delayed.* A dockworker's strike somewhere. (He only skimmed the note— Malaysia, Singapore, Hong Kong? He didn't remember.) He was already debating how to break the news to his boss that the goods—a load of children's raincoats dotted with the latest cartoon craze—wouldn't arrive by the end of the week. It hadn't stopped raining in eleven days and for each of the eleven days his boss had asked, "Where are the Pickle coats, Max? Where are the Pickle coats? There are wet kids out there. Wet kids with concerned parents who are ready to give us money, Max. Where are the coats?" The cartoon was a talking Pickle. Max had seen the show regularly; it was a favorite of his niece's. Charity loved the talking Pickle. Pete? Paul? Pat? Pablo? He couldn't remember the pickle's name. It was alliterative, he knew that.

But the Pickle coats wouldn't be here in time to serve the needs of the wet children of the northwestern United States.

"A strike," he imagined saying to his boss. "Beyond our control. A strike. Who'd a guessed?"

The third note was from his wife. She was ovulating. They were trying to conceive. They were failing. Had failed for eighteen months now. Every month a strike out. The moment she said she felt PMS coming on, Max felt like a fool. Worthless. He'd never had problems with his masculine identity before. Now he felt . . . hollow. Not castrated or emasculated. Just empty.

Her time was right. He needed to come home for lunch.

"No," he said again. It was a forty minute commute. He had an hour for lunch. The math didn't add up. Why didn't Jenny know that? Desperation was clouding her brain. Every time they visited his sister and saw Charity, now a bubbly three-year-old, Jenny would come home and cry for an hour. Max couldn't console her. He didn't know the right words. Everything he said made her shoulders lurch and shudder and her breath catch again. It used to be he could joke Jenny into a smile. He couldn't anymore.

Max heard the elevator ding and footsteps in the hall behind him. Lydia called hello and he said hello back without turning around. Lydia was a systems analyst, almost always the other early morning arrival, unless one of the many dachshunds she raised decided to get sick or run away or commit some other doggy delinquency. Then she'd roll in with a dachshund story. Most days she called hello and went right to her cubicle.

Max read the fourth message. *Change Now,* it said. *Or Else.*

"Screw you," Max said and tapped the delete key with a forceful finger. The message disappeared.

Over the course of the morning, as Max silently composed a speech for his boss— "A dockworker's strike is like lightning, sir. Now one can tell where it'll hit. No one saw it coming," he'd say, though the supplier in Asia had been hinting at the possibility for weeks. Or: "It's going to be over in a jiffy, boss. The union'll cave. No doubt about it," though he'd read no such thing. Max's knowledge of Asian dockworkers' unions was sketchy, at best. He knew they worked on docks. He knew they were Asian. He tried to imagine an Asian Terry Malloy, an Asian Rod Steiger.

His own experience with docks was limited to a girl he dated in high school whose father owned a sailboat and where she had led him one Friday night, to her father's boat moored in a private slip, and where they'd made out, drinking her father's booze and getting mildly queasy from the swaying and the alcohol and his frustrated teen-age lust. He hadn't used her name as a password yet (Bridget) or the name of the boat. He remembered it clearly, *Well Past Time.* Well past time for what, he wondered now, but not then. Well past time for a ship? For a trip? Well past time to let that memory go, Max considered. He'd brought a rubber with him that night, though he hadn't used it. He didn't know he was shooting blanks then. Think of all the money he could have saved over the years on contraception. Perhaps thousands of dollars and countless embarrassing trips to drugstores and supermarkets. He didn't really know if he was shooting blanks. Jenny suggested a trip to a fertility specialist, but he balked at the expected images: a lobby of strangers, a nurse handing him a cup, a cramped bathroom, a pile of well-thumbed porno mags. It wasn't appealing, but Jenny wanted to pinpoint their problem.

"We can't fix," she said, "what we don't know, Max."

It was well past time they figured it out, he imagined her saying. Well past time.

At eleven-thirty his wife sent another note. "I'm waiting," she wrote. "Let's get busy."

He was already busy. His boss had phoned, said he was stopping by his son's elementary school to see a play. It would only take an hour, his son had a few lines— "He's a tree," his boss had said. "A freakin' tree. But my wife told me she'd skin me alive if I didn't make the effort. I'm making the effort. See, Max, I'm making the effort. You're goddamn lucky you don't have kids, Max. Don't ever do it, Max. I love my son, but kids throw wrenches into everything. It's raining fucking wrenches. It is rainy, Max." Max heard a pause on the other end of the line. "Where are the Pickle coats?"

Max was fortunate the cell phone reception deteriorated just then.

"I'll be in by noon, Max," his boss said through chunky static. "Noon."

At eleven-forty his email message center throbbed again.

"Jenny," he cursed. "I can't."

But the note wasn't from her.

Your password has expired, he read.

"Big whup," he said.

He deleted it.

His mailbox throbbed.

CHANGE, the next note said. All caps were rude. He deleted that one, too.

Lydia asked if he wanted anything from the deli downstairs. She always asked. Most days he declined. He wasn't hungry at all. Lydia scolded him for not eating properly.

"Not today," Max said. "Don't get on me today. I'm getting enough as it is."

Lydia's mouth curved down. She wasn't one to show her emotions, but he could tell she was hurt. She turned on her short heels and he listened as she punched the down button with more force than usual. He expected her to say, "Fine," under her breath, the way Jenny would if he'd pissed her off, but Lydia was silent. He could have dealt with a sharp "Fine." Silence was worse. But why should he eat when he wasn't hungry, when he was nearly nauseous because a throng of poorly-paid Taiwanese wanted a raise and better hours? Would a bagel and cream cheese cure any of his problems?

He didn't budge. The elevator came and went and took Lydia's sulking with it.

The red flag on his mailbox icon waved like Old Glory on the Fourth of July. He could actually see it whip in the electronic wind. Flap, flap, flap. He remembered the sound of empty halyards on the sailboats in the harbor, the high clang of metal on metal. Walking down the steps of the *Well Past Time* — to the bar, to the bed, he imagined, to paradise, he listened to them clang. The dinging punctuated the whole evening. He opened the new note with the songs of vacant masts still in his mind.

Your old house on Mulberry Avenue — Mulberry1226, *to us—burned to the ground last night,* the message said. *The police are saying the cause was suspicious but may have been faulty wiring. What do you think, Max? You loved that house. Especially the laundry chute in your sister's room. You dropped all sorts of things down that chute. Tennis balls, GI Joes, a fountain pen. That made a mess. You'll miss that house.*

Max shook his head and read the note again. The elevator doors whined behind him. Others were going to lunch. He heard chatter. Debate about the merits of tacos versus subs.

We told you to change.

His email throbbed again. The red flag waved.

Remember LeRoy2Gone? *Your wife didn't want to put that dog down. She cried in the parking lot of the humane society for twenty minutes before she led Leroy to his death. She's never quite forgiven you, Max. Do you think she should?*

Max swiveled in his rolling chair. He looked at the ceiling. He glanced to each wall of his cubicle. This was a prank. A bad prank. And the dog was dying.

He hadn't given the dog cancer. (He hadn't been particularly sympathetic either. He knew. He regretted.) There had to be cameras. He was the victim of a practical joke. He was on some television show.

Nothing was noticeably different. The same photos of Jenny were tacked to the cubicle's stiff fabric sides. His Sierra Club calendar. A crayon drawing of Charity's—a two-story house with a green lawn and red flowers up the walk. Smoke wafting from the chimney. Clearly, Charity didn't have a handle on seasons yet. Summer outside, winter inside. You can't have smoke and flowers.

He deleted the messages and wiped sweat from his forehead, though the building was always set to a comfortable seventy-two degrees. It never fluctuated.

The elevator chimed and he spun in his chair.

"Max. My office in five," his boss said, the tall man's stride taking him swiftly past Max's cubicle and to the glass walls of his private room.

"Yes, sir," Max said.

His boss paused at his open door. "Two lines, Max," he said, holding up his right hand and flashing a V. From anyone else it would have meant peace or victory. "Two lines. *Welcome to our forest* and *We grow with rain and light.* That's it." He shut the door and moments later Max watched the blinds flip closed. They swayed a bit and were still.

It was always a bad sign when the boss went for privacy.

Max's mailbox was full again.

"It's almost noon and if you can read this, it means you're still at work. I suppose we can wait until you get home this evening, Max, but my temperature is just right and I feel it, Max, I feel it. Now is the time. I'm looking out the window as I type this. I hope I see your car pull up the drive. I'm watching. I'm waiting, Max. Your Jenny."

Max didn't delete that one. He didn't file it in the folder marked *Jenny.* He didn't know what to do with it.

Another message appeared. *Unless you change your password this instant, you will never have the ability to access your incoming mail box ever again. Not ever. We promise. This is not a vague threat, buster. Without your mail, you're screwed. See if you can get the Pickle coats now. Without us, without the power we give you, you're royally screwed.*

There was a postscript. *Wise up, bub. Passwords protect.*

Max smacked his armrest and sent the casters on his chair rolling. He slipped off the edge of the cushioned seat. His knee hit the edge of his plastic-and-pressboard desk and he let out a squelched yowl. He clapped his hand over his mouth—realizing that no one really claps a hand over his own mouth, not ever, except in movies, old movies, and here he was, moaning, and swearing behind his own hot palm. He was a parody, but he wasn't even sure of what. He was an unintelligible parody. Man with hurt knee. Man with irritable boss. Man with insistent, pleading wife. Man with a million Asian dockworkers holding up his order, his order *alone* among all others, letting everything else go free—cheap suits and furniture and golf balls and satchels—but not his Pickle coats.

"Wretched," he said as if it were a common curse. "Wretched." He kicked his chair and it rolled backward to the hallway and came to rest against the elevator door.

It opened and there stood Lydia, her red mouth an O of surprise, her eyes wide behind black-framed glasses. She held a bottle of orange juice in one hand by her side. The other arm she extended. She held out a thick bagel in a thin white paper napkin.

"Max," she said. "I thought you needed something."

He looked at her and nodded. He walked to her and took the bagel. Bits of sesame seed flicked off the crust and onto the pale blue carpet.

"Yes," he said. "I do." He took a bite and walked to his boss's office. He chewed and then turned back, his hand on the door's handle. Lydia was leaning out of the elevator, her head floating above his chair, her chin turned in his direction.

"Thank you," he said, probably too loud.

"No problem," she responded.

Max opened the door and stepped inside the dim room. His boss was behind his broad walnut desk, the shiny top littered with brass: a globe paperweight, a clock, a slim and sharp letter opener. "Tell me about the coats, Max."

And Max did. He explained the strike. He described the delay—perhaps a day, perhaps a week, perhaps a month, how was Max to know? He hadn't a crystal ball. Max explained and chewed his dry lunch and let sesame seeds rain on the boss's better carpet, better than the one in the hall. A richer Berber, a better blue. His boss listened, his eyebrows poised high on his head, a pair of steep arches over his dark eyes.

"So we've missed this opportunity, Max," his boss said.

"I'm afraid so, sir," Max said, popping the last of the bagel into his mouth. "This time."

"There won't be a next time," his boss said and Max understood, perhaps. The rain would end and the children would dry out and the Pickle coats would remain unsold, gathering dust in silent warehouses and on the rickety tables of discount clothing stores. Another cartoon character would hold sway over the offspring of America. That ship had sailed and Max and his boss and Bender Incorporated hadn't made a dime. Or maybe it meant Max just lost his job. *His* next time was done. Max didn't stay to find out. His boss waved his hand and Max left the dark room and closed the door behind him. The blinds swayed again.

He marched to his cubicle—someone had returned his chair, most likely Lydia—but he didn't sit down. He bent over the gently humming machine and typed a reply.

My new password is **Neveragain.**

He tapped his foot and waited for an answer.

Your password must contain a mix of letters, digits, and/or symbols.

Neveragain1.

Thank you. He expected more, an insult, a threat. But no. This is what he got: *That's all we ever wanted, Max. An effort.*

His finger hovered, waited, and hit delete.

His mailbox pulsed. Ah, he thought. Here it comes.

Yet this is what he read: "Dear Max. Come home. Forget *why*. Just . . . I miss you. That's why. Your Jenny."

Max stood straight and brushed bits of bagel off his shirt. He slid the mouse around and turned off his computer. He didn't need anymore mail.

Max was going home to make a baby. He didn't know if it would work, but he'd try his best. He and Jenny would try, dead dogs and burned houses behind them. He didn't know the magic words. He didn't know the right prayer or oath or password. He only knew the question: how do you get it right? What sort of code did he need to use to get it right just this once? That was the password he needed. He didn't know if it was *love* or *please* or *now* or *it's well past time,* but he felt it all and would try to say it, in the right combination, whatever would work to unlock that door and let him and Jenny in: *love* and *please* and *now* and it was well past time.

Idle Roomer

MIKE RESNICK & LEZLI ROBYN

The room was on the second floor of the dilapidated old building, overlooking what had once been a garden and now was a concrete parking slab filled with cracks and potholes. It had a narrow bed next to a small nightstand with a cheap lamp and an old, battered desk by the single window. A rickety wooden chair, a phone, an ancient dresser, a tarnished floor lamp, and a small closet completed its uninspired furnishings.

And, thought Maria, *Mr. Valapoli has lived here for sixteen months.* How could anyone live in this cheerless place for sixteen days, let alone months?

Maria surveyed the room from the door. She'd been cleaning this room five days a week for sixteen months, and she'd still never laid eyes on him. His bed was always made, the top of his desk always barren. The only way she knew he actually existed was the nightstand, which had a different library book almost every morning, and the bathroom, which held a dozen bottles of pills that were replaced with new bottles from time to time.

Oh—and the statuette on the top of the dresser. She didn't quite understand what it was. Sometimes she thought it might be a woman, holding her arms out to the viewer. Other times she wondered how she could have been so mistaken, for clearly it was a small animal with large trusting eyes, possibly something from the deepest jungles of Africa. Once she even thought it was a twisted tree. Maria shook her head; she would never understand modern art.

She would never understand Mr. Valapoli either. Every day she plugged the phone into the jack, and yet the next morning the end of the cord always lay on the floor. She checked the dial tone; it was functioning. Why did the man pay for a phone if he had no use for it?

She never liked Sherlock Holmes much, but she thought it might be interesting to work at being the Miss Marple of housemaids and see what she could deduce about the mysterious roomer. He had to have a beard, because there was no shaving equipment, manual or electric, in the bathroom. Yet she never found any hairs, from his head or his chin, on the bed or the floor. He was probably color blind, for there was nothing blue, or purple, or violet in the drawers, no shirts of those tones in his closet. When she thought of it, she couldn't even remember a blue cover on any of his books.

She swept the floor, which hadn't seen a carpet or even a rug in perhaps half a century, went through the motions of dusting the desk and dresser and nightstand though as always they were as clean as if they'd been on display in a store.

Every other tenant was a transient. Even those who were down on their luck never stayed more than a week. And here was this poor man spending sixteen months of his life here. No matter what misfortunate had befallen him, he didn't deserve *this*. No one did.

Her heart went out to him, and on an impulse, she took a piece of paper out of her pocket and left a note on his desk:

Don't give up hope, Mr. Valapoli. People do care. I care.
—Maria

She thought about the poor man all day. It was only when she was on her way home that she realized that he would have no idea who she was.

Maria's hand hovered just above the doorknob, hesitant and expectant. Last night she agonized over whether she should have left the note. Surely it wasn't wrong to let another person know that she felt for the predicament she saw him in? But then again, he could be a proud man who might see her sympathy as pity.

She shook her head, dispelling uneasy thoughts as she coaxed the creaking door to open. No, the note was well-meant and surely Mr. Valapoli would understand that.

At first glance the room appeared the same as always. As she absentmindedly plugged the phone cord into the jack again, the statuette caught her eye. Now it seemed to mildly resemble a curious owl, the eyes tracking her everywhere she went in the room.

You're being ridiculous, Maria Saviari, she reprimanded herself. *Next you'll be jumping at shadows.*

She continued cleaning the room, pausing only to pick up her daily tip from atop the immaculately-made bed. As she placed the dollar bill in the pocket of her apron, her keen eyes noticed something different on the nightstand. This time there were two books upon it instead of the usual lone library book. Curious, she moved around to the nightstand, automatically smoothing the bedspread as she went.

Wondering fingers traced the cover of the second book, resplendent with its rich burgundy leather and gold foil embossed title: *A Meeting of Minds*. Gingerly she picked it up—ostensibly to dust underneath it, but actually to look more closely at the cover—when she noticed a piece of paper lying beneath the book.

"For Maria" appeared in a childlike scrawl—it was as if the writer had trouble forming the letters into legible shapes. Suddenly she realized that the book she now held in her hands was actually for her. It was his reply to her note.

Curious, she carefully opened it, the musty smell reaching her nostrils as she leafed through the first few pages. She stopped at the title page to discover more words written by the same hand as the note, but other than her name and a touchingly clear "Thank you" at the bottom of the inscription, the rest of the words were composed in a language she didn't recognize. She stared at it. Somehow the words looked neither awkward nor badly scrawled; rather, they seemed to possess some indefinable cogency and even beauty.

How do I reply without knowing what the inscription in the book means? The phone started ringing, breaking her train of thought. She jumped, startled, and for the briefest instant it seemed to her that the statuette jumped as well. *Get ahold of yourself, Maria,* she thought; *it's only a gift. No need to be so jumpy, or to feel guilty because you're looking through it, After all, he wants you to.*

Aware that she still had six rooms to clean before the end of her shift, she reluctantly placed the book in her apron pocket and continued working, the feather duster making short work of an already clean dresser and desk.

On an impulse she went back to the bed and replaced the tip there before she left. It felt wrong to take it now that they'd exchanged communication and she'd accepted his gift, and she hoped he'd see it as the small gesture of friendship it was.

As she finally closed the door behind her, the phone began ringing once again, as if impatient to be answered. *Maybe Mr. Valapoli had some friends after all,* she thought as she pushed her cleaning cart into the next cheerless hotel room, one hand unconsciously checking to make sure that the book was still safe in her pocket.

Maria watched tenderly as her grandmother leafed through the book, smiling when she saw her bring it close to her face, shut her eyes and breathe in the scent of the leather binding. Golden light filtered in through the window, dancing on the last auburn strands to be found in almost snow-white hair, the years of hard work and laughter defined on her face by the late afternoon sun.

"Smells expensive" was her first comment as she glanced up to look squarely at her granddaughter.

"I very much doubt that." Maria smiled. "It's a gift from someone staying at the boarding house." She reached over and turned the pages until she came to the inscription. "This is what I came here to ask you about. What language do you suppose this is?"

"My dear," said her grandmother, "this wilted English Rose might have married a Sicilian but that does not make me an expert in other people's languages. However," she continued, as one finger traced the letters softly, "it's definitely not a romance language,

and I don't think it looks Oriental. In fact, it doesn't look similar to anything I've encountered before. Those elegant pictographs are quite distinctive." She looked up sharply. "*Who* did you say gave this to you?"

"I didn't say. This book is from a man I've told you about previously Grandma; Mr. Valapoli, the one that's had the misfortune to stay in the boarding house for the last 16 months."

"Is it normal practice for guests to give you inscribed gifts?"

Maria sighed. "No, it's not, but . . . "

"Let me guess: You want to help him." She closed the book quietly, setting it down on the table in front of her. "You can't help every lost soul you come across Maria—no, don't interrupt me." She reached out and placed a hand on her granddaughter's cheek, gently brushing an errant ebony lock back as she did so. "You have too generous a heart; it makes it all that much easier for someone to break it." Abruptly she stood up, her hand shaking as it moved to pick up her walking stick. "And if you don't leave now it will be dark by the time you get home. Besides, you can't keep a frail old lady up past her bedtime," she intoned, the twinkle in her eyes still bright despite darkness falling outside.

Replacing the book in her uniform pocket, Maria laughed softly, and arose to kiss her grandmother on the forehead. "You are eighty-eight years young and definitely not frail of mind. Thank you for your advice, Grandma."

"If it's my advice you want, I'd take that gift of yours to the university tomorrow before you work. There's bound to be someone there with enough degrees to translate it."

Seemingly endless rows of books towered over Maria as she made her way to the back of the university library, feeling more insignificant with every step she made. As her fingertips ran feather-light along the spines of the books, she looked up at the ornately-carved bookshelves in awe. Every dust-filmed tome seemed to hold a wealth of knowledge, representing privilege to her uneducated eyes.

An officious library clerk had told her that she'd find the man she was looking for with his class at the back of the library. She suddenly spotted him at a circular table already surrounded by students, one of whom was draped nonchalantly over a huge padded chair at the side of the table. He appeared exactly the way she thought a professor should look: peppered black hair, a neatly-trimmed silver beard, and glasses perched low on a nose that he buried deeper into a book the closer she got to him.

"Professor Albright, may I have a moment of your time?" she asked politely, her eyes focused on the top of his head.

"Certainly," came the aloof yet slightly amused reply from the direction of the armchair. "In fact, you can have several."

She started in surprise, turning to stare at the man now confidently vacating the chair. *This young man is a Professor of Linguistics?* She knew appearances could be deceptive and she'd seen all types come and go at the boarding house, but this man with his surf-blond hair and cornflower blue eyes was *not* what she was prepared to meet.

Professor Albright addressed the older man firmly. "Mr. Tripoldi, the class, if you please." Without waiting for a response he strode over to the partially-secluded corner of the library, Maria scurrying in his wake.

"How can I be of service to you?" he inquired, eyebrows raised as he turned to look at her. "I really only do have a few minutes to spare you, so please be concise."

"I've come across a language I cannot identify," she said. "It's an inscription in a book I've been given." She began rummaging through her work bag, wishing now that she'd thought to put the book on top of her change of clothes.

"Why don't you simply ask the person who gave you this inscribed gift?" he asked, staring at her with mild annoyance.

"I could. Or" —Maria matched his stare— "I can politely ask a leading academic on dead languages his expert opinion rather than hurt a considerate friend's feelings by asking what it means."

Surprise and a hint of respect flickered briefly across Albright's face before he once again adopted a mask of detached boredom. "You could indeed."

She held out the book to him, feeling suddenly more comfortable when his eyes left hers and refocused on the leather binding of her gift. "The inscription is on the third page," she explained, "and it's . . . "

The book was all but snatched out of her grasp, the Professor unable hide his excitement over what now lay in his hands. "It couldn't be . . . could it?" The Professor opened the book to the copyright page, and began reading intently, then turned the page again. Suddenly there was a sharp intake of breath. "Do you realize what you have here?" he exclaimed, not waiting for an answer. "This is a numbered first edition! Do you know how rare it is? It must have cost a fortune!"

Maria was confused. "What does that mean?" *Surely Mr. Valapoli didn't have the money to buy her a rare and valuable book—not if he had to live in a boarding house.*

The Professor sighed suddenly, calming himself by sheer force of will. "It means that *before* this book was desecrated by an inscription, it was one damned expensive book for your friend to buy. It's worth a lot less now though—it's no longer in its original condition."

While she tried to assimilate all this startling information, Albright leafed through the pages to find the inscription. Suddenly he looked as surprised as Maria felt.

He started pacing up and down with the book, an intent look in his eyes, his brow furrowed, his veneer of smug superiority completely vanished. Suddenly he looked up. "This is not any spoken language—and I can tell you that this is not a dead language either." He paused, squinting excitedly at the page again. "In fact, this appears to be an *extinct* language. It's certainly alien to anything I've ever encountered. The structure is . . . let me put it this way: I'll bet a week's pay that not one word of this can be translated into English, and if it was a dead language I'd be able to do so, or at least see how to attack it." The book snapped shut as if to emphasize his point. "I'm afraid I can't help you."

Maria was dumbfounded. She gave Albright permission to photocopy the inscription before leaving for work, filled with more questions than before. Money was clearly not a problem if Mr. Valapoli could buy and inscribe this book regardless of its worth, simply because it made the gift more personal.

So why was the man living in that rundown boarding house if he could afford better? She didn't know then, and she still had no idea when she finally went back to work.

Just as she was about to reconnect his phone line yet again, Maria paused and decided instead to roll the cord up neatly into a bundle and place it beside the handset on the desk. She might not understand what Mr. Valapoli had against receiving calls, but after receiving such a present it was time that she started heeding his wishes.

Having finished dusting the desk and nightstand, she moved over to clean the dresser, and her gaze fell upon the statuette. It looked different again today. The change was subtle as always, but she thought she could almost discern the vague shape of an elephant, the trunk curving gently around the base, serene and contemplative. Even the color had subtly changed to match that of a pachyderm.

Mr. Valapoli was such a tidy tenant that she rarely had to use more than a feather duster to keep any surfaces clean. However, she couldn't remember the last time she had actually picked up the statuette to clean it properly, or indeed if she ever had. Possibly the greyish tone was simply the result of accumulated dirt.

Maria reached out to pick it up. The instant her fingers came in contact with it she felt some kind of *joining,* something she had never experienced before. She blinked very rapidly as she was suddenly overwhelmed by a sensation of *otherness.*

Suddenly a montage of images appeared, not before her eyes, but inside her mind—but they were like no images she had ever seen, or even imagined before. She saw three moons racing across a coal-black sky, their trajectory reflected in the murky waters of a silent ocean, and a sense of tranquility swept over her. Pastoral pictures followed, not of anything she had ever seen, but lovely nonetheless.

And then she felt an air of foreboding, of dread, and the images, blurred beyond recognition, turned blue, became larger and bolder without taking any discernible shapes, and seemed to be converging on her.

She screamed, just once, and pulled her hand back—and the instant she did so, all the images, all the emotions, vanished, and she was alone in the room, her forgotten feather-duster still clutched in her left hand. She held up her right hand and studied it, as if it was no longer part of her, as if it had somehow betrayed her. There were no marks on it, no burns or bruises, and she knew instinctively that it wasn't the hand that had taken her out of the here and now, it was the *contact*.

And now she turned her attention to the object that she had been in contact with. The statuette looked harmless enough, a peaceful, tranquil, not-quite-elephant, not-quite-anything. Had she imagined it? And if so, what exactly *had* she imagined?

She extended a forefinger and reached out to touch it lightly, then drew back before she made contact. Four more times she tried to work up the courage, and then, finally, her finger gingerly touched the statuette.

An image appeared in her mind, not of too many moons or flowers that didn't exist or oppressive blue *somethings,* but rather of a bookstore. A not-quite-human hand was thumbing through the pages of a book. *Her* book.

This time statuette didn't hold her against her will. She withdrew her hand, stood back, stared at it once again, and waited for her heart to stop pounding so hard against her chest.

If I'm not imagining this, what does it mean? And what have I stumbled into?

Evening and midnight came and went, and she still didn't know. She barely slept, and made up her mind to finally confront Mr. Valapoli and get some answers. She knew he was always gone when she arrived at nine o'clock, so she showed up at six thirty, just as dawn was breaking.

Probably he's asleep, she thought, staring at his door. *I'll just wait for some sound of movement.*

She learned against the wall for five uneasy minutes, then stood erect. This was too important to wait. She had to get some answers *now.*

She knocked at the door. No response. She turned the knob and gingerly tried to open it. It was locked. She knew that using her master key was against regulations, probably against the law, but she didn't hesitate. A moment later she was inside the room.

Mr. Valapoli wasn't there. The bed hadn't been slept in. She looked in the closet to see if he'd packed and left. It was filled with his clothes.

Was it all an hallucination? There was only one way to find out. She walked over to the statuette, summoning her courage to touch it again. It had changed again, no longer vaguely elephantine, no shape that she could identify . . . but she could identify an emotion, its every line seemed to project: *fear.*

It couldn't be afraid of *her.* All she wanted were answers. What could be scaring it?

And suddenly, instinctively, she *knew.* It was the blue, shapeless things she had sensed yesterday. They were not part of her life, or even her world—and that meant that the fear was Mr. Valapoli's.

She laid her hand on the statuette without hesitation now. Images, blue and garbled, flooded her mind, and she seemed to hear voices inside her head, not human voices, not speaking any language she had ever heard, but somehow she understood what they were saying.

A voice that sounded blue (*how was that possible?*) was saying, "You hid well. But now you must come back with us."

And a gentle voice, a voice she instinctively knew was Mr. Valapoli's, a very tired, very weary voice said, "It's a big galaxy, and this is such a small world. How did you find me?"

"We have our methods," said the blue voice. "Will you come peacefully or must we use force?"

"These are decent beings, these people. They are without malice. Do them no harm, and I'll come back with you," said the tired voice.

"I do not envy you when we get home," said the blue voice.

Maria withdrew her hand. They were going to take him away, back to something awful! She raced to the window to see if they were in the yard. There was a hint of something large and blue beneath a tree, but she couldn't make it out.

"No!" she yelled, turning and preparing to run to the door.

And the statuette, suddenly more human—or at least humanoid in shape—raised a hand as if to tell her to stop.

She froze, shocked, and the gentle voice spoke inside her head.

"It's all right, Maria."

She stared at the statuette, and its expression seemed to soften. Finally, after another minute, it lowered its hand.

"Thank you for caring."

She walked to the window, and the blue shape was gone, and somehow she knew Mr. Valapoli was gone too. Forever.

Sunlight streamed in through the single window of the bedroom, bathing the statuette in warm golden light as it sat on the dresser, the focal point of the small, uncluttered room.

Still half asleep, Maria stretched languorously, thinking of all she had experienced over past few weeks. Ever since Mr. Valapoli left and she had brought the statuette home, it felt like it truly *belonged* with her, and she liked to imagine that the statuette itself felt comfortable on her dresser.

Its shape had continued to change. Each morning she would wake up to see the magic that had been wrought overnight, and each day it became somehow less alien in its form and more distinct in its features, softening into the image of a man, with eyes as kind as Mr. Valapoli's voice had been gentle.

She no longer questioned how the statuette could change. She *knew*. Every time she touched it she could sense him. The connection was very faint, and growing fainter with each passing day, but she took comfort in the fact that it was *there*.

Until the morning she touched it and *didn't* feel anything but the cold contours of the statuette itself. Not sure of what was happening, she reached out to make contact with it again, but before she could, her eyes widened in wonder as she realized she was witnessing its very last change, her unseen friend's final parting gift to her, the one that let her know he also cherished their strange connection.

There upon the statuette's face was a smile, and in her mind she clearly heard the echo of Mr. Valapoli's voice for the last time.

"Thank you for caring, Maria."

From the Lost Diary of TreeFrog7
NNEDI OKORAFOR

Translating . . .

Appendix 820 of The Forbidden Greeny Jungle Field Guide
This series of audio files was created by TreeFrog7
It has been automatically translated into text

ENTRY 1 (20:09 hours)

Some clumsy beast has been stalking us. It only comes out at night and it moves with no regard for the bushes, plants and detritus on the jungle floor. It sounds big and is probably dangerous. And . . . I think it brings the smell of flowers with it. I can smell it now, like sweet lilacs. Does Morituri36 even notice? I wonder. Regardless of the creature's presence, he continues to compile information and I put it together and upload the finished entries into the Greeny Jungle Field Guide. That's our mission and our system.

"Down with ignorance! Upload information!" We are true Great Explorers of Knowledge and Adventure. Joukoujou willing, we'll survive this day, as we have the hundreds of others since choosing to dedicate our lives to informing the ignorant masses about this great jungle.

Whatever is stalking us, we'll deal with it when the time comes.

Field guide entry (uploaded at 14:26 hours)

God Bug:

The God Bug is an insect of the taxonic order Ahuhu-ebe, which includes all beetles. It is common in the Greeny Jungle. Usually blue, sometimes green. When it feels the urge, it spontaneously multiplies, becoming two independent god bugs. As it multiplies it may make a soft popping or giggling sound. There have been rare cases where one has multiplied into four or five. They are docile, almost playful insects. Diurnal.

—written and entered by: TreeFrog7/ Morituri36

*note: For some reason, this common insect has not previously been listed in the Greeny Jungle Field Guide. This may be because the god bug is also found in the city. Or maybe this is another example of the field guide's incompleteness.

ENTRY 2 (18:55 hours)

Disgusting.

Everything here is disgusting. It rains constantly. The ground is always ankle-deep red-brown mud. There are a thousand types of biting and stinging insects. We have to sleep in the trees but the trees, bushes, and plants are noisy with buzzes, growls, snorts, screeches, clicks, whistles, too. Especially at night. The air *reeks* of moss, the syrupy scent of flowers, ripe palm nuts and rotting mangoes. And the jungle traps heat like a sealed glass tube held over a fire. The Greeny Jungle is a tough place to be while pregnant.

The heat leaves me light-headed. I vomit at least three times a day because of the strong smells. Yes, still, even in my eighth month. But though my sensitive nose makes for great discomfort, it makes for even greater documentation. You'd be amazed at how many floral and faunal specimens show themselves first and foremost with scent.

Yesterday, my nose led me to a tree full of those hairy pink spiders with striped orange legs. A year and half ago, Morituri36 and I uploaded a field guide entry on these creatures. We named them treebeards. They were our hundredth entry. Their bites paralyze your fingers and cause an intense headache. If these spiders ever became common back home they'd cause society to break down within a week. Imagine people unable to type on their computers!

Unfortunately, yesterday, I forgot that treebeards give off a strong smell that is very similar to figs. I thought I'd found a fig tree. I love figs, especially since becoming pregnant. The sky was cloudy. Any other day, I'd have seen all those webs. Instead, I walked right into them and the spiders descended on me like rain. Understandably, they thought I was attacking their home. Not good.

Morituri36 happened to be in the middle of one of his bouts when it happened. I had to save myself by running from the tree, throwing myself in the mud and dead leaves and rolling like crazy, the roots of some tree grinding into my back. Then I just lay there looking up . . . into the leaves and ripe fruit of a giant fig tree. The smell of real figs was all around me. treebeards *and* figs, can you believe it?!

Only my left hand was stung. I have to type with my right. I'm left-handed so this has been very very annoying. I'll be better in a few days.

What a husband I have. He cannot even save his wife from bush spiders. What has this place made us into? But can I blame him for having dulled senses due to his junglemyelitis? Maybe. *I* have been exploring this jungle right beside him all these years. He has been the only human face *I've* had to look at, too. Yet the trees do not "close in" on *me*. *I* do not need to have the sun and moonlight wash over my face for at least four hours a day. *My* brain isn't muddled with an irrational fear of shadows that makes me rant and rave once in a while. And *I'd* have yelled *stop* before *he* walked under a tree full of treebeards. Idiot.

The sun is setting and I can hear and smell it again—the creature following us. It's definitely nocturnal.

ENTRY 3 (13:20 hours)

There is a reason I've decided to break science-speak and enter this journal appendix in the field guide. My name is Treefrog7 and my husband is Morituri36. We are from a village in southwest, Onaghi agba nahia, the people of the impossible beads. Of course out here in the Greeny Jungle, we cannot wear our traditional beaded attire. Far too heavy. Instead we wear plain light clothing (northern attire). But we never take off our beaded bracelets and marriage earrings. And there is always the bead of the soul. So that is us and that is all I will say on the subject.

I've begun uploading this audio series because after three months of exploration, we are closing in on something big. Very big. The very process of finding it should be documented along with the scientific information.

Altogether, we've uploaded two hundred eighty-eight new entries to the field guide. Our fellow explorers are proud. What we explorers do is dangerous work. Many of us die for the information we gather. Many of us return to civilization with only half our bodies, or half our minds, or ill in a thousand ways. Many of us are lost. Morituri36 and I are not lost. We know exactly where we are and we know exactly what we seek. We will find it. And human civilization will be changed forever.

I'll explain what "it" is when I'm in a less difficult place. The mud is deep here. My back aches. I need all my faculties for the time being. I wish Morituri36 would stop singing that song. "World of Our Own." It reminds me of home. He has such a beautiful voice. I wish he'd shut up. I wish my body would stop aching. I'm sick of being pregnant.

ENTRY 4 (19:21 hours)

I was bitten by a clack beetle today. Their venom is itchy and the white spot it left on my skin is about the size of my fingernail. It shows up on me a lot more than it showed up on Morituri36 when he was bitten last year. I'm a much darker shade of brown than he is. Which means, yes, I get to complain about it. I don't mind cuts, scratches, bites, etc. But something about a mark on my skin of temporarily-neutralized melanin really bothers me. No matter. It should be gone in a few days.

Last night, as we looked for a tree to sleep in, we heard the creature. How long is it going to follow us? What does it *want*?

• • •

ENTRY 5 (12:03 hours)

Shh. I have to whisper quietly. Morituri36 is beside me, too. Something just screeched very very loudly. An elgort? As soon as we can climb down, I need to find a certain seed . . . just in case. Morituri36 is too clumsy to handle them. He's looking at me, annoyed, but he knows I'm right.

We're still on the trail of what we seek and I believe that whatever has been following us is still on our trail, too. Maybe the elgort will scare it away, or better yet, eat it.

ENTRY 6 (21:12 hours)

We're at the very top of a baobab tree. Morituri36 and his cursed junglemyeli-tis. If I fall out and die, our unborn child and I will haunt him until he joins us in death. Right now I can hear it below. *Why* is it following us? What's it after? And *what* is it? It's not violent, fast, huge or destructive enough to be an elgort. I'm glad it's nocturnal. Come morning, we'll be able to leave this tree and continue on our way.

We are searching for a mature CPU plant, so mature that we can actually download its hard drive. We call them M-CPUs. Acquiring a copy of an M-CPU's hard drive has never been done in all the history of exploration. BushBaby42, a close friend of mine, found one three months ago but she disappeared before she could download anything. She happened to send us the coordinates of her location just before she stopped responding to us, so here we are. We've come hundreds of miles.

It is hard for me to speak of BushBaby42.

I don't wonder what happened to her. She is an explorer which means it could have been anything. It is very often our fate.

On the M-CPU's hard drive will be unimaginable information, the result of centuries of gathering. Legend has it that these plants connect to networks from worlds beyond. Imagine what it knows, what it has documented. We will not kill or harm it, of course. That would be blasphemy. We won't even clip a leaf or scrape some cells. We'll only make a copy of what it knows. Our storage drives should easily adapt to fit the plant's port. Though our drive is most likely a different species of plant, they'd have to at least be of the same genus.

The CPU plant's entry does it no justice. The entry is a human perspective, ascribing significance to the plant because it is cultivated and used as a tool for humans, a personal computer. The true CPU plant grows in the wild, neither touched nor manipulated by humans. And this plant takes hundreds of years to mature.

Many of us have seen young CPU plants with their glowing monitor flower-heads that light up nights and sleep during the day. They plug into the network and do whatever they do. But an *M-CPU*? Nearly legend. What must BushBaby42 have felt gazing upon it all alone as she was? What must she have seen on its screen? And what happened to her? She could take on a man-eating whip scorpion with nothing but a stick!

Incidentally, the creature we heard screeching this afternoon *was* an elgort. Big as a house, with tight-black skin that shined in the daylight, beady yellow eyes, fast as the speed of sound, irrational and food-minded.

We dealt with it. Maneuver 23, specifically for the elgort. We lured the crazed beast to a tall strong hardwood tree. That's the most dangerous part, luring it in. We had to climb very very fast as soon as it smelled us. Once in the tree, as it reared up below trying to snatch us down with its tooth-filled trunk (a terrible sight in itself), Morituri36 dropped a bursting seed (which I picked this afternoon, thank goodness) into its maw. *BLAM!* Its entire head exploded. We now have meat for many days. elgort meat doesn't need salt or to be preserved and it's naturally spicy; some say this is due to the creature's anger and intensity in life.

We thank Joukoujou and the Invisible forces for giving us the skill to protect ourselves. Unfortunately, The Forces of the Soil also protected from the elgort whatever creature is stalking us.

ENTRY 7 (21:34 hours)

Today was all pain. In my back and lower belly. The stretching of ligaments. My belly feels like a great calabash of water. This baby will come soon. Really soon. I hope we find the plant first. The trees here are spaced apart, allowing the sun to shine down, so Morituri36 had a good day. He carried both our packs and even prepared breakfast and lunch—mangoes, roasted tree clams, elgort meat, figs and root tea both times. It is days like this where I remember why I married him.

It is night now and we are in a large but low tree with one wide branch to hold us both. We can see the sky. It's been a long time since we had a night like this. I think the last time was the day that our child was conceived. Not long afterwards was when he started coming down with the junglemyelitis. His ailment will pass; he's a strong man.

My gut tells me this is the calm before the storm. But maybe I'm just being melodramatic.

ENTRY 8 (04:39 hours)

Dragonflies! Swarms of them. BushBaby42 described these just before she found the plant. We're close. But the creature is still on our trail. This morning, it left its muddy smelly droppings right at the foot of the tree, as if it wanted us to step right into it. I almost did. It was covered with flies and the mound smelled like the vomit of demons. It was so strong that I nearly fainted with nausea. Morituri36 had to carry me away from the mess. Just thinking about it makes me shudder.

Cursed beast, whatever it is. No matter how we try to glimpse it at night, it keeps out of sight as it blasts its angry flowery scent. Biding its time, I suspect.

But when the fight comes, it will be shocked when instead of running we turn to meet it. We haven't survived the jungle solely because of luck.

But Morituri36 needs to remember that he is a human being, and that *I* am a human being, too. When he gets in his moods, he speaks to me as if I'm a piece of meat. As if I'm lower than his servant. He speaks to me the way the Ooni chief speaks to his wives. How dare him. I am carrying our child. I have done as much work as he has. And junglemyelitis or not, we are in this together. There is no need for insult.

"It dies well beforehand!" he snapped at me earlier today as we inspected a morta. We'd caught it this morning. A morta is a beautiful red bird with a long thin beak. When it dies, its dead body keeps flying aimlessly for days. Strange creatures but not the strangest in the jungle. Morituri36 seemed to think that their carcasses also rotted as they flew.

"Look at it," I calmly said, despite my rising anger at his tone. The dead morta was still trying to flap its wings. "This is the fifth one we've caught! No rot anywhere!"

He just huffed and puffed the way he always does when he knows I'm right. The entry someone uploaded to the field guide was simply wrong and needed to be changed. The fact is that morta probably don't fly for that long after they die. Maybe a few hours and that's it. Certainly not days. If it was days, it would be infested with rot and maggots. But that wasn't what I wanted to find out most about the morta. I wanted to know what made it fly as a dead creature. Morituri36 and I agreed it had to be some sort of parasite with strange faculties. We just needed to run some tests.

But he wasn't so interested in answers today. He threw the bird corpse to the ground. "It is because it is freshly dead," he muttered. "Stupid stupid woman." Immediately, the dead bird hopped up and took off. I cursed, watching it go, wondering what microscopic organisms were working the bird's muscles and how intelligent they could be to do so. They were obviously using the morta carcass to search for food or a special place to procreate.

I wanted to slap Morituri36. How many pockets of information had we lost because of his temper? He and I are south westerners, the people of beads. Amongst our people, we say, "Many beads protect the thread." He knows this kind of behavior will not get him far. Maybe one day I'll push him out of one of the extra high trees he forces us to sleep in every night.

We didn't talk to each other for hours. Then we started seeing millions of dragonflies.

The land was still spongy and muddy. There were large pools of standing water. The air smelled like wet leaves, stagnant water and spawn. An ancient CPU plant would thrive in a place like this.

The dragonflies must have loved this place, too, but the huge swarms were because of the plant. CPU plants send out strong sine waves. These types of dragonflies are attracted to the electromagnetic waves like moths, mosquitoes, suck bugs and butterflies to light.

We'd always been plagued by a few of these sine-wave drinking dragonflies because of the portable we use to type in and upload information (including this audio journal) to the field guide node. Our portable is powerful. Even hundreds of miles from civilization, we can access the network and communicate with other explorers who wish to communicate. But there is a downside to everything. Large dragonflies zooming around our heads is one of them. The sine waves intoxicate them.

Usually, there are only two or three plaguing us. Now it's about twenty. They're like flying jewels, emerald-green, rock-stone blue, blood-red. A few of them are of the species that glow blue-purple. But none of them stay long. They zoom about our heads for a few minutes and then zip off, replaced by another curious dragonfly. Something bigger is attracting them, of course. I can't wait to see it. We don't even need BushBaby42's coordinates anymore. Just follow the dragonflies. I hope BushBaby42 is ok.

ENTRY 9 (22:20 hours)

We cannot sleep. Morituri36 is sitting beside me. For once he's looking down instead of up. Even he can smell the beast's scent now. It's right down there.

The dragonflies are going mad around here. We can see the plant just starting to glow about a mile away, to the north. By the night, it'll be glowing like a small planet. But the creature is below us. Right at the base of our tree. I hope we make it through the night without a fight. Doing battle in the dark is the worst kind of fighting.

ENTRY 10 (20:14 hours)

It's a moth! With a large hairy robust but streamlined body, thick fuzzy black antennae with what looked like metallic balls on the ends, and a large coiled proboscis. But it's wingless, the size of a large car and has six strong insectile running legs. And it uses its proboscis like a flexible spear!

It came after us just after dusk, while we were looking for a tree to sleep in. Out of nowhere you just heard the sound of branches snapping, and leaves getting crushed as it rushed at us from behind. Within moments, it speared me in the thigh and my husband in the upper arm. We'd be dead if it weren't for our quickness and how good we've become at climbing trees. I guess I have to thank my husband and his stupid illness. We've bandaged each other up. At least some of the bleeding has stopped, my husband's wound was worse than mine. So far no sign of poisons from its proboscis.

The moth's body shape tells me that this thing's relatives clearly used to be fliers. It's been following us for days and now, as we close in on the plant, it has become aggressive; it's guarding something. I can guess what it is.

We could kill it. My husband and I have certainly killed larger more dangerous beasts. But killing it might eventually cause what it protects, the

M-CPU, to die. The death of centuries of information. No. We'd rather die. So instead, we're stuck in a tree a mile from the plant.

There's a problem. My water just broke. No, not now. *Not* now!

ENTRY 11 (20:45 hours)

We're in another tree. About 200 feet from the M-CPU. Like everything around here, it's infested with dragonflies. Their hard bodies smack against my face like hail. The wingless moth is below, waiting, angry, protective. We're about to climb down and make a run for it. I hope my husband is right. Otherwise, we're dead.

The M-CPU's smell is overly sweet, syrupy, and thick. I've vomited twice up here. The labor pains drown out the pain from my leg. They are getting stronger and faster, too. Can barely control my muscles when the contractions hit. If they get any worse I won't be able to help myself, I'll fall right out of this tree. A terrible way to die. A terrible way for an unborn child to die. I hope my husband is right.

ENTRY 12 (21:26 hours)

If I focus on talking into this portable, I will not die.

We're cornered. But we are lucky. We made it to the plant. Dragonflies are everywhere. Their metallic bodies shine in the plant's light. They make soft tapping sounds when they hit the plant's screen. Oh, the pain. My husband was right, bless his always sharp mind. The wingless moth indeed is guarding the M-CPU. And thus, now that we are close to the plant, the moth fears we'll harm it. If we don't move, the creature will not attack. It is not stupid. It can reason. Otherwise it would have killed us both by now . . . soon there will be three of us.

My body does not feel like my own.

The . . . M-CPU is as tall as my husband. He can look right into the flower head, which is a bulbous monitor with large soft periwinkle petals framing it. There is indeed a slot right below the head, where the green stem begins. The moth is a pollinator. Morituri36 says that below the disk is a tube that goes deep; only the proboscis of this wild creature could fit down there. It is a most unique but not an unheard-of pollination syndrome. But there are deeper things at work here.

Maybe the moth will leave come dawn when the plant goes to sleep. But the night has just begun. As the flower opens wide, so do I. The baby will be here soon. Why do the gods create this kind of *pain* when bringing life into the world? Why?

ENTRY 13 (23:41 hours)

I was screaming when she came out screaming. My husband wasn't there to catch her; I wanted him to stay near the M-CPU's flower. So our daughter landed on the cloth he'd spread. Morituri36 laughed with joy. A blue dragonfly landed on her for a second and then flew off. I had to lean forward and pick her up. I cut my own cord. She is in the crook of my arm as I hold this portable to my lips and record these words. A beautiful thing.

The moth has backed off. Could it be that the gift of life was enough to stop this intelligent beast in its tracks? Or does it know what my husband is doing? Our storage drive fit perfectly into the port just below the flower head.

The flower is fully open now. It is sometimes good to be a man. My husband can stand up and watch as we wait for the download to be complete. I can only lie here in the mud and listen to what he tells me as I slowly bleed to death.

ENTRY 14 (00:40hours)

"Are you alright?" he keeps asking, with that look on his face. Don't look at me like that, Morituri36. Like I'm going to disappear at any moment. The moth looms. I've washed our daughter with the last of my husband's water. She seems happy and angry, sleeping, trying to suckle and crying. Normal. Amazing.

Just tell me what you see! I'm talking to Morituri36. Doesn't he think I want to know? As if I am not an explorer, too. Giving birth can't change that fact.

Morituri36, you know the portable can only record one voice. Here, take it. It's better if you just speak into it.

Voice recognition detects Morituri36, a male, husband to Treefrog7, Greeny Explorer number 439, 793 days in Jungle, approximately 600 miles north of Ooni, 24:44 hours

Allowed

My wife is crazy. She cannot properly describe the situation we are in right now as I speak. The trees creep in on us like soldiers. She can't see them, but I can. Every so often, I see a pink frog with gold dots sitting in the trees just watching us. Treefrog7 doesn't believe me when I speak of this creature. It is there, I assure you.

But neither the trees nor the frog is our biggest threat. Treefrog7 is truly amazing. It is not that she just gave birth. That is a miracle in itself but a miracle most women can perform. No. It is that we have been stalked and hunted by this beast that our explorer ethics prevent us from killing and yet and still, this woman can concentrate enough to blast a child from her loins, even as the creature stands feet away, biding its time for the right moment to spear me in the heart and her between the eyes and then to maybe make a meal of our fresh and new healthy daughter.

But Treefrog7 wants me to talk about this plant that led us to our certain deaths. The M-CPU of legend and lore. The One Who Reaches. The Ultimate Recorder. Bushbaby42's obsession. How old must this M-CPU be? Seven, ten thousand years? Older than the plant towers of Ooni? I believe it's an true elemental with goals of joining its pantheon of plant griots.

My wife looks at me like I'm crazy . . . but who knows. You look into its head and how can you not wonder? Look at it, surrounded by purple sterile ray florets the size of my arm and the width of my hand. Its deep green stem is thick as my leg and furry with a soft white sort of plant down. No protective spikes needed when it's got a giant moth guarding it.

It's deep night now. And everything's color is altered by the brightness of the flower's head. An organic monitor is nothing new. It is what we know. We Ooni people have been cultivating the CPU seed into personal computers for, what, over a century? It's how the CPU plant got its name. And explorers have seen plenty of wild CPU plants here in the Greeny Jungle. Lighting the night with their organic monitors, doing whatever it is they do. But an uncultivated M-CPU? How did Bushbaby42 find it? And where is she? We've seen no sign of her. Treefrog7 and I will not speak of her absence here.

So back to the M-CPU's head. What do I see in it? How can I explain? It is a screen. Soft to the touch, but tough, impenetrable maybe. But I wouldn't test this with the moth looming as it is. And I would never risk harming the M-CPU.

The plant's screen is in constant flux. There is a sort of icon that looks like a misshapen root that moves around clicking on/selecting things. Right now it shows a view of the top of a jungle. It cannot be from around here because this jungle is during the daytime. There are green parrots flying over the trees.

Now it shows text but in symbols of some unknown language. A language of lines branching off other lines, yes, like tree branches, roots, or stems. The root-shaped cursor moves about clicking and the screen changes. Now it's a star-filled night sky. A view of what looks like downtown Ile-Ife, not far from the towers. There are people wearing clothes made of beads, south westerners. I know that place. My home a minute's walk from there!

The screen changes again. Now . . . most bizarre, the sight of people, humans but as I've never seen. And primitive shaped slow-moving vehicles that are not made of woven hemp but of metal. There are humans here with normal dark brown skin but most are the color of the insides of yams and these people have light-colored hair that settles. My wife looks at me with disbelief. It's what I see, Treefrog7. The legend is true. The M-CPU can view other worlds. Primitive old worlds of metal and stone and smoke but friendly enough looking people. Now there are more symbols again. Now an image of a large bat in flight. The roots of a tree. The symbols. A lake surrounded by evergreen trees.

My guess? This is the plant thinking and it is deep thought. Back to my wife.

*Voice recognition detects Treefrog7, Greeny Explorer number 421, *793 days in Jungle, approximately 600 miles north of Ooni, 01:41 hours*

ENTRY 15 (01:41 hours)

I feel better. It's been about two hours. Baby's fine. My bleeding has stopped. The moth is still there. Watching us. The download is almost done. I can stand up (though it feels like my insides will fall out from between my legs) and see the monitor for myself now.

It just showed something I've never seen before . . . a land of barrenness, where everything is sand and stone and half-dead trees. Where could this nightmarish place be? Certainly not Ginen. It's almost 2 am. In a few hours, we'll know if that moth actually sleeps.

Field guide entry (uploaded at 01:55 hours)

Wingless Hawk Moth:

The Wingless Hawk Moth is an insect of the taxonic order Urubaba which includes butterflies and moths. It is the size of a large car, has a robust grey furry body with pink dots, pink compound eyes, and hearty insectile legs for running. Its antennae are long and furry with silver ball-like organs at the tips. Its proboscis is both a feeding/sucking organ and a deadly jabbing weapon. It is the pollinator of the M-CPU. It makes no noise as it attacks and is known to stalk targets for days that it deems hostile to its plant. Nocturnal.
—written and entered by: TreeFrog7/ Morituri36

ENTRY 16 (02:29 hours)

I'm having a catharsis as my husband and I stare into its monitor and it stares back. I am looking into a distorted mirror. We are gazing into the eye of an explorer. It is like us.

ENTRY 17 (05:25 hours)

My baby is beautiful. She is so fresh and I can see that she will be very dark, like me. Maybe even browner. Thank goodness she is not dada and that she has all ten of her fingers and toes. Think of the number of times in the last eight months that I've been poisoned, touched the wrong plant, been bitten by the wrong creature, plus I am full of antibiotics and micro-cures. Yet my baby is perfect. I am grateful.

If we ever make it home, my people will love her. But the wingless hawk moth is still here. The sun rises in an hour.

ENTRY 18 (5:30 hours)

The M-CPU shows pictures and they are getting closer to where we are! Pictures of the sky over trees. Symbols. Clicking. The jungle at night. More symbols. I can see our backs! What?! The moth is coming, but slowly, it's walking. It is calm, its proboscis coiled up. But what does it *want*? Download is done. What . . . the M-CPU's monitor shows two eyes now. Orange with black pupils. Like those of a lemur but there is nothing else on the screen. Only black. Just two unblinking . . . Joukoujou help us, *o*! Now I see. Don't come looking for us! Don't . . .

Voice recognition detects . . . Unknown

Hacked Allowance

They will never die. No information dies once gathered, once collected.

The creatures' field guide is thorough but incomplete.

I am the greatest explorer.

I am griot and I will soon join the others.

End of Appendix 820

BongaFish35 Pinging Treefrog7 . . .
Request timed out.
Request timed out.
BongaFish35 Pinging Morituri36 . . .
KolaNut8 Pinging Morituri36 . . .
MadHatter72 Pinging Treefrog7 . . .
Request timed out.
Request timed out.
Request timed out.
Request timed out.
Request timed out.
Request timed out.

Gift of the Kites

JIM C. HINES

The first time Jesse saw the black *Buka* was in the park. He was flying a plastic Superman kite, dueling against his step-father's rainbow box kite.

Jesse yanked the blue nylon string, swooping his kite toward his step-father's.

Kentaro dodged easily. "Too broad a strike," he called, laughing. "A true fighter kite would loop around and cut your line."

"Get him, Jesse," cheered Jesse's mother, sitting in the shade on one of the picnic benches.

At twelve years old, Jesse felt a mix of pride and embarrassment at her enthusiasm. Flushing, he unwrapped a bit more line, sending his kite higher. He dove again, missed, then tugged the kite in a tight turn that nearly clipped Kentaro's kite. His mother whistled.

"Much better," Kentaro said, grinning. He pulled his kite through a long 'J' in salute. "Amazing control from a plastic store-bought kite. You're sure you have no Japanese blood?"

A shadow caught Jesse's attention. A black rectangular kite leapt from the horizon, corkscrewing through the sky. Jesse ran toward the fence, hoping to glimpse the kite's owner. His Superman kite followed like an obedient blue and red puppy.

"What is it?" his mother called.

Higher and higher the black kite flew. The string was invisible to Jesse's eyes, but given the angle, the owner had to be by the highway. The wind carried exhaust fumes to Jesse's nose.

"It's a *Buka* kite," Jesse yelled. The black fighting kite moved like no kite he had ever seen. It flew and bucked like a thing alive.

Kentaro shielded his eyes. "I see nothing."

Jesse's bowels grew cold, and sweat beaded his forehead. He felt exposed, a rabbit trapped in the open as a hawk swooped down. He wanted to run away, but his legs trembled, and he could barely stand.

The *Buka* turned slightly. Jesse's breath caught. Something within him knew he wasn't the kite's target. "Mom, look out!"

Kentaro was still searching for the kite, but the terror in Jesse's voice brought him sprinting. His box kite crashed, forgotten. "What is it?"

Jesse shook his head. There was no time. The *Buka* was moving faster. It was so big, a window of darkness the size of a bus. How could anyone control a kite that huge?

"Jesse, I'm here." Kentaro squeezed his shoulders.

The wind blew harder. Jesse's kite tugged its line, like an animal struggling to escape its leash. Jesse twisted away from his step-father, circling his kite around to intercept the *Buka*. He couldn't see the other kite's line, but he knew where it had to be. Closer and closer it flew. It began to block the wind, forcing Jesse to shorten his line to keep his own kite aloft.

Jesse backed away from the fence, trying to stay between the black kite and his mother. The *Buka* paused in its flight, then dove. Jesse yanked his own line, hoping to tangle his kite with the *Buka* and bring them both down.

The blue line quivered. Ice shot through Jesse's fingers. He cried out, and then his line was falling, cut cleanly a short length from the kite.

"Mom!" Jesse screamed.

The *Buka* touched the earth, an enormous sheet of blackness that blotted half the park from view. When it rose, Jesse's mother was on the ground, shaking uncontrollably.

"Susan!" Kentaro shouted. He reached her side before Jesse, catching her shoulders and moving her away from the steel legs of the picnic table. "Jesse, get her medicine from the car. Quickly!"

Jesse cried as he ran, knowing it was too late. Whatever the black kite had done, no pill would fix it.

Beside the parking lot, his Superman kite sat torn and broken in the branches of a spruce tree.

One year later, Jesse sat in his bedroom, painting broad, garish stripes over the paper of his newest kite. He longed to add tassels to the corners, but such decoration would be too obviously Asian.

After his mother's death, the courts had given full custody to his biological father Sam, a man Jesse hadn't seen in years. But Sam had kept current with his child support, and Michigan law said that was enough to tear Jesse away from Kentaro.

Jesse jabbed his brush into the paint, remembering how Sam had thrown out Jesse's ebony chopsticks, his anime collection, anything with any trace of Kentaro's Japanese heritage. He hoped this kite would slip past Sam's radar. Jesse needed a kite, and what better design than the *Hata,* a diamond-shaped fighter traditionally painted red, white, and blue?

Jesse pushed away from the desk and stretched. The small bedroom still didn't feel like *his* room. Faded patches marked the wood-paneled walls of the former den. Several cigarette burns marked the carpet.

He glanced at the picture taped to the window, the one of his mother after one of her bike races. The hospital said her death last year was a reaction to her epilepsy medicine. Jesse knew better.

He returned to the desk and examined the bamboo splints. The wood flexed into a perfect arc. He tested the curve and the balance, then used string to bind the splints together.

By the time Sam's car door slammed in the driveway, the paint had dried enough for Jesse to begin gluing the paper to the frame. The paper rustled, tasting an unfelt wind.

The bedroom door opened. "You got a card or something," Sam said. Jesse wondered if anyone else would have heard the slur in his voice.

"Thanks." Had Sam been drinking to mark the anniversary of Susan's death? Why such grief for a woman he hadn't seen in nine years? Jesse shoved the bitterness aside and grabbed the envelope. There was no return address. His pulse quickened, and he casually tossed it onto his desk.

"Aren't you going to open it?" Sam asked.

"I'm busy."

Sam grabbed the envelope. "Open it."

Forcing a smile, Jesse used one of his Exacto knives to slit the envelope. Inside the card, Kentaro's precise handwriting read:

> Jesse,
> It's been a year since Susan left us. I want you to know you are
> still in my thoughts, and in my heart.

That was as far as Jesse got before Sam snatched it away. "I knew it. Why can't he leave us alone? You're *my* son!"

Jesse grabbed for the card and missed.

"Bad enough he took Susan. You're my son." He glanced past Jesse, studying the half-assembled kite. "What've you been working on?"

"Nothing much." Jesse held his breath.

He scowled. "Where'd you learn how to build these?"

"The library," Jesse said.

Sam's forehead wrinkled as he stared at the kite, like he was trying to dig up a long-buried memory. "Weren't you out flying kites the day Susan died?" His face tightened. "You and that Jap were both flying the things."

"You don't understand. I *have* to build this."

"Why?" Sam snapped.

Jesse bit his lip. He had never told anyone about the black *Buka* and his own failure. Sometimes he spotted the *Buka* in the distance as he mowed the lawn or walked back from the bus stop. It was waiting for something. Waiting for him. Jesse didn't know why. All he knew was that he had to find a way to beat it. "Sam, please."

"I'm your father. When are you going to start calling me Dad?" He grabbed the kite, breaking the spars and using the jagged ends to tear the paper. He crumpled it into a ball, then forced the whole thing into the garbage. "The sooner you stop living in the past, the better off we'll be."

The door slammed. Jesse counted to twenty, first in English, then Japanese. When Sam didn't return, he went to the trash and pulled out the remains of his kite. One look told him it was unsalvageable.

"*Kentaro* was my father," he muttered as he retrieved his Exacto knife and tried to cut the few bits of undamaged paper from the frame. It had been four months since his last letter to Kentaro. Sam had almost caught him sneaking back from the public mailbox down the street. Jesse didn't dare use their own mailbox. He even had to buy his own stamps from the machine at the grocery store. Sam noticed missing stamps as quickly as he spotted long-distance calls on the phone bill.

Jesse glanced down and found he had cut the paper into a rough hexagon, like a *Rokkaku* kite. He trimmed tiny sticks of bamboo, fitting them to the lines of the *Rokkaku*. A strange warmth flowed through his fingers. The glue dried impossibly fast. He grabbed a spool of black thread and tied a small four-point bridle.

As he finished the last knot, the kite leapt from the desk. The spool of thread bounced to the carpet.

Jesse held out his hand in amazement, and the tiny kite returned. The thread tickled his fingers. Abstract shapes of red and blue covered the back, like an exotic butterfly.

"Hold still," Jesse said. The kite obeyed, hovering on an unfelt wind. Smiling, Jesse cut the thread, leaving a yard or so dangling from the bridle. "Fly around—"

Before he could finish the thought, the kite flew a fast circle around the room.

Fingers shaking, Jesse scrawled a quick note on another scrap of paper. He tied it to the thread.

"Can you find him?"

The kite flew to the window and spun like a top. Jesse slid the pane to one side, then pushed out the bottom corner of the screen. Distance soon swallowed the little *Rokkaku*, leaving Jesse to wonder how long it would take to traverse the forty miles to Kentaro's home.

Later that night, Jesse heard a tapping at the window. He climbed out of bed and flipped on his desk lamp. Pushing the window open, he helped the kite inside. A tight tube of paper was knotted to the thread.

Jesse,
I won't pretend to understand the miracle you've created, but I thank God you did. Tonight it was like having you here with me. You have a gift. I've known it ever since you flew your first kite. I'm more proud of you than you can know.
I trust this little Rokkaku *will find you again. I wish I could do the same.* I love you.

Kentaro

Grinning like it was Christmas morning, Jesse grabbed pen and paper and began to write.

It took two months to build another *Hata* fighting kite. He worked on it in the attic and hid it behind the artificial Christmas tree. Whatever power had guided him with the *Rokkaku* remained, and he could feel the *Hata* yearning to soar through the clouds. Finding time to fly it was difficult, though.

Jesse grabbed his lunch and his backpack as he headed for the door. "See you tonight, Dad." The word burnt his mouth, but it kept Sam happy.

Outside, Jesse crouched behind the bushes and waited. He froze as the front door swung open, and barely breathed until Sam's car disappeared down the street. Only then did he sneak back inside to fetch his kite.

More than an hour later, he was exiting the bus near the park where his mother had died.

Jesse searched the park as he walked. He knew Kentaro wouldn't be there, but he looked anyway. Jesse had said when and where to meet, but Kentaro refused. He wouldn't violate Sam's rules.

"Why do you care what Sam thinks?" Jesse muttered, more hurt than angry. "He's *not* my father."

He was worried about Kentaro. The last few letters had been different, somehow. Longer, almost rambling. And Kentaro's handwriting had decayed ever so slightly. It still looked like he drew each letter with a ruler, but the spacing was more ragged.

He spotted a black shadow among the clouds. He felt no surprise. He had seen the *Buka* more and more often lately. It always stayed in the distance, watching.

Jesse tugged on the leather work gloves he had swiped from the garage, then hoisted his diamond *Hata* kite. Red and blue *Kanji* characters marked the kite's center: *tanchi,* the symbols for heaven and earth.

There was little wind, but it didn't matter. Jesse could feel the *Hata* pulling skyward. He held the stiff thirty-pound line. The first hundred feet were the cutting line, coated in glue and ground glass. Holding the line carefully, Jesse allowed the kite to rise, and soon it was flying above the trees.

He ignored the *Buka* as he practiced. A sharp dive here, followed by a wide loop, then another dive to slash an opponent's line. He visualized the cutting line as a blade slicing through the air. He couldn't tell how much of his control was physical and how much was like the little *Rokkaku,* an extension of himself that obeyed thought alone.

Jesse had spent hours staring out the window at school, watching the birds and memorizing their movements. The small sparrows banding together to drive away the crows . . . the jostling of pigeons as they fought for scraps by the cafeteria . . . the hummingbirds hovering and darting at the feeders by the fence.

Time slowed as he imitated those movements. He stilled the *Hata* in the midst of a breeze, then darted a short distance. He circled, taunting an imaginary crow. Faster and faster the kite danced through each attack.

The wind changed, bringing the smell of cigarette smoke. Before Jesse could move, a strong hand clamped his shoulder. "I've spent two hours trying to find your worthless hide," Sam thundered.

Jesse kept his grip on the kite string, trying to reel it in without being too obvious. "I'm sorry. I—"

"Kites again." Sam shook his head in disgust. He flicked the cigarette to the ground and stomped it out. "He told me this was where you'd be."

"Who?"

"What is it about him?" Sam rubbed his scalp, making his hair stand up in spikes. "How did that little Jap turn you against me?"

"He didn't." Jesse caught himself before he could add, *You did.*

"I figured I'd be nice. Give you a chance to say good-bye. You know what it's like to walk into that school and have your secretary tell me you were out? To look at me like I'm an incompetent father because I don't know where my own kid is?"

"What do you mean, say good-bye?" Jesse asked. He could feel the cold in his gut, and his hands began to shake.

Sam sighed, and a bit of his anger seemed to dissipate. "Jesse, Kentaro's got himself a nasty case of cancer. He's been in and out of the hospital for months. They didn't catch it in time, and—"

"You're lying!"

Sam's expression hardened. "I wouldn't lie about this."

Jesse looked up. The *Buka* had moved closer, silently confirming Sam's words. The black kite was like a window into darkness, swallowing the sky itself.

"He can't be sick," Jesse said. "He would have told me."

"So you *have* been talking to him." Sam reached into his pocket and pulled out a Swiss Army knife. The blade clicked open, and for a second Jesse thought Sam was going to stab him. Instead, he grabbed the kite line.

"This is the only fighter I have!" Jesse stared at the *Buka*. "You have to take me to the hospital. You have to let me save him!"

"*I'm* your father. It's time to let him go, son."

Jesse yanked the line hard. This part lacked the cutting glass, but the waxed line still cut deep into Sam's palm. Sam swore, but didn't release his grip.

"Dad, please," Jesse said.

Sam pressed the knife blade against the line. Taut with tension, the line snapped instantly.

"You're grounded until I say otherwise. And if you take one step out of my house, except for school, I'll put you in the hospital myself."

Tears stung Jesse's eyes as he watched the *Hata* spin downward. "No," he whispered. Thinking about his little *Rokkaku,* he reached toward the *Hata,* trying to control it. "Don't fall."

"Come on," Sam said, tugging him toward the parking lot. "Behave yourself, and maybe I'll take you to visit Kentaro next week."

"Next week will be too late." Jesse concentrated, imagining he still held the *Hata's* line. He could feel the wind beneath the kite. Ever so gently, he shaped the air itself, creating updrafts to lift the kite higher. Slowly, the kite responded, floating on nonexistent winds. "Wait for me."

"What's that?"

"Nothing." To his left, the black *Buka* dipped in salute and disappeared.

Sneaking out of school that afternoon was absurdly easy. The principal would call Sam, of course, and Jesse would be in even more trouble, but that didn't matter. All that mattered was getting to the hospital.

As the bus pulled to a halt, Jesse spotted the black kite hovering over the parking garage, drifting slowly closer. He grabbed his backpack and ran to the back of the hospital. At the fire escape, he climbed the dumpsters to reach the bottom rung. Minutes later, he was on the roof, unzipping his backpack to free his little *Rokkaku*. He doubted it would do much against the *Buka*, but he planned to fight with any tool he could get.

The *Rokkaku* began to orbit Jesse's head, spinning like a top to shed the drizzle that had begun to fall. Jesse clenched his fists, praying the *Hata* still flew and calling it with all his heart. "Please . . . "

The *Buka* drew closer. It was smaller than Jesse remembered. Maybe four feet high and twice as wide. Jesse's little *Rokkaku* leapt in response, like an angry kitten.

Where was the *Hata*? Had it fallen? It had taken Jesse several hours to get out of school and make his way here. Whatever strange magic connected him to the kites, maybe it hadn't been strong enough to keep the *Hata* aloft.

And then something tickled his hand. Jesse clamped down, feeling the familiar line tug his fingers. The end was frayed from Sam's knife, leaving only a few hundred feet. It would have to be enough.

The *Rokkaku* darted out of the way as Jesse flew the *Hata* into position, sweeping the red and blue diamond in a wide figure eight.

The *Buka* streaked toward the hospital, as if it had been waiting for this moment. Jesse ran along the roof, pulling his kite down to intercept. His shorter line was an advantage here, giving him speed. The *Hata* ducked beneath the bigger kite, then flew upward. The *Buka* pulled back, barely escaping Jesse's cutting line.

How long would the line last in the rain? he wondered. At least he hadn't used the traditional mix of rice paste and broken glass. Wood glue might be too modern for Kentaro, but it should endure the water better.

Jesse moved to intercept another attack, sweeping his kite like an enormous saber. Each time the *Buka* approached, Jesse was there, using every trick he could think of to drive it back.

His arms began to ache. He pulled in a bit of slack, hoping to lure the black kite closer. If he could just get his cutting line within range, he could try to cut the other kite down. Even though he couldn't see the *Buka's* line, he knew in his blood where it had to be. But the *Buka* moved impossibly fast, and every one of Jesse's attacks came up short.

"Jesse! How the hell did you get up here?"

The line dug into his fingers as he turned to see Sam and a security guard stepping on to the roof. Someone must have seen Jesse on the roof.

The *Buka* took advantage of Jesse's distraction, swooping down at a sharp angle. Jesse ran to block, but the *Buka* veered, dragging its invisible line toward Jesse's own kite. The *Buka's* line brushed the edge of Jesse's *Hata*. Terrible cold burned Jesse's hands, and then it was all he could do to keep the *Hata* aloft.

"Kid, watch out for the edge," the guard yelled.

It gave Jesse an idea. He hurried toward the corner of the roof and hopped onto the ledge, a low, foot-wide wall of concrete. The cars in the street looked like plastic models. Jesse wavered slightly, yanking his kite to correct his balance.

"Jesse, no! Get down *now*!"

There was real fear in Sam's voice. "Stay back," Jesse yelled. His little *Rokkaku* buzzed anxiously around his head. He could hear Sam and the guard talking, but at least they weren't coming any closer. They wouldn't risk him falling. The next time he spared a glance, the roof was empty.

Jesse pulled the *Hata* in, trying to assess the damage. The bamboo spar had cracked near the left corner, causing it to flap back and forth.

The *Buka* attacked again, moving to block Jesse's wind, then streaking down as the *Hata* fell. Jesse dragged his kite closer, until he was pulling the cutting line itself. The glass scraped skin from his palms, but he kept pulling, avoiding the *Buka's* attack.

He loosed his hands suddenly, allowing the *Hata* to leap higher. It swung in a broad, flat arc, seeking to decapitate the other kite. The *Buka* circled away.

Attack and parry, feint and counter. The sparrow and the starling. Every move put more strain on Jesse's damaged kite. He had waterproofed and layered the kite, but there was only so much it could take.

"Jesse, come down this instant, dammit!"

Sam had returned. Jesse ignored him, but he couldn't ignore the second voice. Weak and hoarse, Kentaro yelled, "Listen to your father, Jesse."

Jesse glanced back. Kentaro stood supported by Sam on one side and the guard on the other. A trailing tube connected him to an I.V. stand. The rain-damp hospital gown emphasized the boniness of his shoulders. His bare arms were little more than sticks. Panic clenched Jesse's chest. The *Buka* was so close, and now Kentaro stood exposed.

"Get out of here," Jesse yelled. "Kentaro, please!"

Kentaro reached out. "If you won't obey your father, obey me. Come down."

"I'm trying to save you!"

"I know." Kentaro smiled. "But not like this."

Sudden fear made Jesse turn. The *Buka* had already begun its attack. Jesse jerked the line with all his strength, but it was too late. The *Buka's* invisible line cut the *Hata* a second time. Jesse had kept the *Buka* from cutting his line, but it made little difference.

"No . . . " The *Hata* began to fall, little more than a crumple of silk and sticks. He heard footsteps behind him.

"No," he said again, more firmly this time. His little *Rokkaku* shot backward, and he heard Sam cry out in surprise.

Jesse tightened his grip, forcing his broken kite higher while the *Rokkaku* kept Sam back. Jesse battled the wind and the kite's own weight with for every inch.

"What's he *doing*?" Sam demanded.

"Trying to save my life," Kentaro said.

"I don't understand."

"I don't either," Kentaro said. "But that is what he's doing."

Jesse relaxed his fingers, feeling blood pound through the cramped muscles. His kite bucked harder as the wind tossed it about.

"We are family, Jesse," Kentaro said. "Nothing can change that. Not the court, not even death. Your little *Rokkaku* showed me the strength of that bond. You don't have to do this."

"He's not your son," Sam snapped. "I swear, if you weren't dying—"

"He's not going to die," Jesse said, newfound determination in his voice. The *Rokkaku* shot past his ear and disappeared into the rain. Jesse didn't need to see it. He could sense it spinning through the air.

The *Rokkaku* collided with the black *Buka*, punching a hole in the blackness.

The black kite bucked, but Jesse had already brought the *Rokkaku* around, tearing a second hole, then a third. The slender spars of his *Rokkaku* splintered with each blow, but Jesse forced it to attack again and again until it disintegrated.

Only then did he allow his *Hata* to fall. His line intersected the *Buka's,* and he pulled so hard he fell onto his back, knocking the breath from his lungs. The last thing he saw was the black kite dropping out of sight, followed by his own ruined *Hata*.

Sam's fingers dug into Jesse's arm, hauling him upright. Fear, confusion, and fury all battled across Sam's features. Jesse wondered which would win.

The guard yelled, forestalling the argument. "Hey, you can't come up here."

A young girl stood in the doorway leading down into the hospital. The guard shook his head. "When did we get a revolving door on the rooftop?"

The girl wore a black leather jacket and torn jeans. Her black shoes gleamed wetly, even though the rain seemed not to touch her. In her hands, she held a small black *Buka* kite. She touched the guard with the corner of the kite. "Leave."

Blank-faced, the guard retreated back into the hospital. Jesse started to shiver, sensing the power in that kite.

"You know the traditions?" she asked, her eyes never leaving Jesse's.

Slowly, Jesse nodded. He clasped his bleeding hands together to stop them from trembling.

"What traditions?" Sam snapped.

"When fliers battle," Kentaro said, "one who cuts down another's kite often claims and flies that kite as his own."

"No more kites," Sam said. "If I catch you with another one of those damn—"

"You won't catch him," the girl said, grinning.

Jesse pulled free of Sam's grasp and walked toward her. "You killed my mother." He couldn't feel anything at all. Kentaro's hand came to rest on Jesse's shoulder.

"A chemical reaction killed your mother," she said. "I helped her spirit on the next stage of her journey. It's what I do." She frowned. "What you do, now." She held out the *Buka*.

Jesse put his hand on Kentaro's. "What about my father?"

"His body is failing. If it's any comfort, you'll be with him at the end. You'll be the one to ease him on his way."

"No," Jesse said. "You can't make me—"

"I don't understand," Sam said, coming around to Jesse's other side. "It's just a kite." He reached toward the girl.

From the center of the kite, a black line snapped out to hit Sam in the chest. He fell back, gasping.

"Stop," Jesse said. At once the kite obeyed, and the line vanished. "Sam, are you okay?"

Sam nodded, though his face was pale.

"You will have power and responsibility both," the girl said. "Most importantly, you will have freedom."

Kentaro started to speak, but a coughing fit took him.

"Leave them alone!" Jesse took a step toward the girl, but she shook her head. This wasn't her doing. Jesse caught Kentaro and held him until the fit passed.

Jesse's eyes watered. "I won't kill Kentaro."

"I'll return for him if you don't," she said. "Which would bring him greater peace?"

Slowly, Jesse reached for the kite. It was surprisingly light. The black paper was dark as night, with no sign of damage, but he recognized the *Buka* he had fought. The bamboo spars were yellow with age, and the bridle was simple hemp. A sparkling of light trailed from the bridle to his hands, hands which no longer bled or hurt.

"Jesse, what are you doing?" Sam asked.

Before anyone could react, Jesse pressed the kite into Kentaro's hands. The girl started to protest, but Jesse cut her off. "It's *my* kite now. I choose to give it to him." Already he saw new strength in Kentaro's fragile frame. "Give it to me when I'm older, if you want. But at least this way . . . this way you could still visit sometimes? We could fly kites again." He glanced at Sam, daring him to argue.

But Sam said nothing. More than anything, he looked lost.

Kentaro gave Jesse a quick hug, and Jesse marveled at the strength in those arms, even as the contact sent frigid chills through his body.

"Are you sure, Jesse?"

He nodded.

"I almost forgot." The girl reached into her jacket and pulled out a small scrap of blue and red. "You'll want this, I think." She took Kentaro's hand, leading him away.

Seconds later, Sam and Jesse stood alone in the rain.

Jesse cleared his throat. "Thank you. For telling me about Kentaro."

Sam stared for a long time, until Jesse began to fidget. "That was . . . that was pretty impressive," he said finally. "The way you handled that kite."

"Thanks."

"Kentaro—" Sam hesitated. "He did a good job with you, didn't he?"

Jesse flexed his hands, studying the newly healed pink skin. "He's family. I had to save him."

"Yeah." Sam squeezed Jesse's shoulder. "You did a good job, son."

As he followed Sam inside, Jesse stopped to look into the sky, where the black *Buka* saluted with a broad 'J' before disappearing into the clouds.

batch 39 and the deadman's switch
SIMON DeDEO

You have Ted Kaczynski down the hall—the Earth Firster who quit tree-spiking to pipe-bomb a forestry convention—the abortion nut who gunned down three girls in Missouri—a half-dozen Arabs, half of whom again you have on phony evidence. I suppose I'm in good company. Or I would be if we could talk to each other.

You want to talk about the anima device. Devices. Of course. Everyone wants to know about Kazinsky's time at Harvard, but MIT doesn't rate. Yes, I understand the difference. Mail bombs don't usually fit on a postcard.

This all started with my boyfriend. You figured he was behind it all, which just makes you sexist. He turned out to be tougher than expected, but then again, librarians always do. I understand that the American Library Association is filing a lawsuit on his behalf. It may even finish up before the courts collapse.

Mack worked for a library that handled rare manuscripts. Not exciting manuscripts, rare manuscripts. The Gutenberg Bible is not rare enough for them. Five copies in circulation is at least two too many. Like the Federal Government: lender of last resort. We think he got it from a Russian treatise from 1930 they uncovered after the Mafia blew a hole in the University of St. Petersburg because they wanted land for a new hotel. Where the Russian got it I don't know. But we know the connection: Plotinus. The treatise was on the iconography of a Plotinus manuscript the Reds had looted from the palace. Before they shot the Romanovs.

Did you know the anima in Plotinus has been an open problem for historians of philosophy? Nobody could figure out what it meant. "Soul," if you look in the lexicons, but that kind of Christian term doesn't take you very far. Nor it is pnuema, the in-breathing of the gnostics, or any of a dozen other ways people talked about the sorts of things we run an MRI for today. The best clue we have is a passage that talks about illumination.

Which is, in the end, how I found it in batch thirty-nine. The thirty-nine steps. Two more than the most random number between one and a hundred. Terms two and three in a geometric series based on the Trinity. Not the bomb site. That came a little later.

Unlike the two Trinities, batch thirty-nine did not come out right. All the previous ones we had, through a combination of cross-breeding and radiation-bombardment, gradually taught to clip and reassemble proteins. We were solving the traveling salesman problem in a massively parallel form. As a test case. Biological computing. Batch thirty-nine, despite being the most advanced system yet, turned the vats to gel.

I was the graduate student and I was both curious and bored, so I reduced the gel, tipped it out on the bench like a birthday cake, clipped a corner, dropped it in universal solvent—water, to you—supersaturated the solution, and triggered a crystal. Which, unsurprisingly, did not look like the standard Frank Gehry bolt-on. I autoclaved the rest, and got time on the micrograph over in Systems.

Systems was a joint university-Air Force project. It was headed—de facto, not de jure—by Rachel, who was always in the pressed uniform of her branch. Rachel was a grump, but she was efficient in the comforting way civilians imagine all military types to be, and she booted up the micrograph, plated the crystal surface, parked me at the screen, and left. That's when I saw the anima.

They were a few microns on a side. On the surface a few brute-force levers, but clearly doing something more than Archimedes: the whole surface was electrically active, strong enough to make the images shiver in the electron beam. Wherever they sat in the crystal, the surrounding proteins twisted into new patterns. I tweezed one up with a ion probe, put it down. The ion probe is pretty brute force; a bunch of them fell onto the bench.

Then I put the crystal in the fridge, and went out for a late dinner. I was starved. Or, at least, I thought I was. It was then I caught a glimpse of what is, at this point, planet-wide. Little things, but strange. Crossing Mass Ave, the traffic lights went red and green together. The ATM in the student center dumped three grand into the tray, irritating enough because I had checks I needed to clear.

I headed back to Systems and pulled the batch again. I looked at the levers on the surface, and used the ion probe to nudge the largest. The contraption fit together like a Victorian toy and in an instant the cube had crumbled away. I looked on the plate for the machines I had dislodged, and destroyed a few more before I felt guilty.

Outside the door, I heard weeping, and I stepped into the corridor; it was Rachel. Her uniform was in shreds all along the hallway; she herself was naked. I held her head while she choked on mucus and told me what Systems was for. It's above your pay grade, I'm sure, but it can't hurt to tell you that the august institution that funded the traveling-salesmen problem was keen for a dual-use.

It turns out, out in Iraq, that the U.S. military used to leave booby-trapped bomb components in volatile areas. They guesstimated that about ninety percent of the casualties were bona-fide insurgents trying to scrounge up enough wire, cord and shell casings for the next IED. It was the biggest success of the occupation, and Systems was going for the next stage. The biological analogy.

It didn't make much scientific sense—this is the same military that tried to leverage paranormal Uri Geller types to spy on the Kremlin, after all—but Rachel had an inkling of how the various products of Systems were tested: back out in Afghanistan and Iraq, on people we disappeared off the streets. Rachel's arms and face were bloodied by self-inflicted scratchings, but this was apparently nothing compared to what went down in a retrofitted Abu Gharib.

The court martial, six weeks later, was not exactly advertised on the Internet. But I knew why Rachel had disappeared from the lab, and I knew where to find her. I gave her a shard of the crystal, and she duly dropped it on the prosecution's table. In his coffee, actually; Rachel was a very angry woman. The next morning, I turned on NPR for the commute in time to hear Lakshmi Singh interviewing both sides of the court martial after a joint statement. What then became known as the Systems Trial—formally, Afshordi et alia v. Department of Defense—ran for three months. It took time, because the alia were twelve rows deep in the visitor's gallery.

I'm a reasonably good scientist—for a girl, as my freshman adviser told me—so it took a few more test runs before I understood the anima devices. A police brutality case in Chicago and two resignations in Congress made the news. It was about this time that I took Mack in to the lab and we eventually traced it to Zukankov's Plotinus book. That gave our cubes the name.

We soon figured out the lever combinations that produced more—I thought about the backstory quite a bit. The anima devices were bizarrely complicated, practically sentient. We soon discovered that we didn't need an ion probe; various chemical combinations—like the supersaturations I started with—would trigger them. Mack pointed out that simply distilling a healthy alchemist's urine would be sufficient to get them running at full steam.

The anima, you see, is a fail-safe. Systems would never have found them. You need to be a little more curious than Industry, a little cleverer than a dilettante, and have a little more spare time than someone doing work-for-hire. And, of course, you have to like old books. As Mack says, you need to be an intellectual: a Plotinus, a John Dee. Or at least John Dee's graduate student.

I don't know who made them. Not any of us. And obviously not the people who came before us. But they work, and even pre-Enlightenment science would be enough to figure out what they did.

Before you picked up Mack outside his office and hit him with something even harder than waterboarding, he pointed out that fail-safe was not quite the right word. Neither of us wanted to release them on a global scale. We figured we'd keep them safe, use them sparingly. Neither of us had finished the Brothers Karamasov, but we had read the Grand Inquisitor section, and both of us were keen on Free Will. We voted for Howard Dean, not the Spartacus League.

The anima devices are not weapons. Only a particular kind of person can find them, and it's the kind that doesn't go in for world-scale domination. But now Mack is gone, and I'm in a supermax in flyover country.

It took a long time for the Roman empire to collapse under the weight of a confused and strangely altruistic religious ideology. Plotinus was long gone. Things happen faster these days, but there's no way you're going to let me out of here to turn it off, and it's rather too late. Our apartment is a crime scene and seven liters of the stuff has been divided up and sent to every branch of the government, known and hidden, for analysis. Rachel tells me that it will hit the Israelis, the Russians, and the Chinese, in that order, within the next few months.

The anima device; we know what it is.

A deadman's switch for nerds.

Rolling Steel:
A Pre-Apocalyptic Love Story
JAY LAKE & SHANNON PAGE

Rough Beast slouched toward the Bethlehem steel mill. Tons of fresh hot metal in there, every cobber and new chum from the Allegheny to the Delaware knew that. Even Topper, the old cat-eyed bastard with steel cables for fingers and a brain stewed in barium-laced æther, knew which way the good stuff lay, for all that he couldn't tell up from down on days ending with a /y/.

He's a bad man, our Topper. Used to run child-soldiers over the St. Lawrence to the Froggies during the Quebec-and-Michigan War. *La troisième mutinerie,* the Quebecoise called it in one of their endless prayers to St. Jude, for if ever a cause was lost surely it is theirs. Wolfe had put paid to their ambitions at the Plains of Abraham two centuries earlier, but no Frenchman ever born minded much dying for the romance of a shattered heart.

And there was no heart so shattered as that of a patriot whose country has been brought to ground.

And so we have Topper, driven bird-mad in the trenches of the Somme when it would have been kinder for him to have just died. Came home he did to the quack attentions of the New Friends of Sweet Reason, got caught up in the Technocracy movement as exhibit A, and finally fell apart as the country itself did in Roosevelt's dying days.

Now there's Wehrmacht units on the loose from Nova Scotia to New Jersey, the South has risen again (and again), the Federals are barely hanging on in the Mississippi basin, issuing wireless dispatches from Washington-on-the-Rails while the Great Madness takes anyone stupid enough to be caught outside at night anywhere between the Wabash and Pamlico Sound.

Only those who started mad can stand the stuff, and move faster by night than any prayerful man might by day. Especially Topper in his *Rough Beast,* which once upon a time was a machine meant to kill other machines before he made so much more of it, oh so much more.

"Metal, my pretty," he whispered, patting with a clattering crackle of steel the crawler's upholstered dashboard between the engraving of Percy Bysshe Shelley and the platinum-dipped weasel skull with the rhinestone eyes. Only one of those two had he killed, Topper, and some days he knew the difference. He squinted into the depths of night through the prism that made up *Rough Beast*'s forward vision block, watching for the mill which loomed close, its fires never banked.

Fate and fortune walked on the greased knuckles of Topper's war machine, as never they had since Poland's borders collapsed in the first of the lightning wars.

I patrolled the unquiet streets south of the steel mill, cussing as I walked back and forth in my own precious allotted square block of turf, practically wearing channels in the concrete with my steel-heeled stilettos. "Bastards," I muttered, thinking of the Best Sister and her Little Chums. Well, 'bitches,' technically, but I didn't fancy using such a term of endearment when referring to their ilk.

"Bastards," I growled, as I turned the corner for the seventeen-thousand-and-thirty-second time, only this time I was thinking of my crib mates, the ones who had sniffed out some sort of rupture in my soul and handed me this godforsaken turf as my undue reward.

"Bastard!" I screamed, jamming to a halt as the ferocious machine loomed before me. Hadn't heard the fucker coming at all. My NKVD surplus large-bore riot gun was already raised and trained on the madman coming up from a top hatch, red-lacquered nail rattling against the trigger as my finger trembled with desire. Then I saw it was Topper.

Which didn't change my assessment of the situation, or my epithet. But I did lower the gun, and hike up my leather miniskirt an inch or two.

The gibbering fool grinned down at me, leaning over the console in a halo of actinic light to stare down the front of my corset. I set my shoulders back to improve his view and leered right back up at him.

"Going my way, big boy?" I called out.

"Bethlehem, Bethlehem, Bethlehem!" he chanted, his eyes rolling in his head. Oops, there went the tiny whisper of sanity I'd detected a moment ago. I danced back a step, just in case the worms in his brain told him to gas up that monstrous vehicle and put paid to the sexiest thing he was likely to see all day—any day.

My heels tapped on the sidewalk as I leaned against the wall of the foundry behind me. "And what are you going to do when you get there, mm?"

"Steal," Topper said, letting the word do its double duty. "Stable." Another word doing double duty. He stared down at the woman. Someone from another lifetime, Topper knows with animal cunning and vestiges of functional memory.

He has had many lifetimes, our Topper. Lived them all together inside one much-mended head, until his name has become legion because he is many. Swine out of Garaden could not be more multiplicitous than this man. But even through the palimpsest of his personality, this woman emerges like a slave ship out of an African fog bank.

"Coming with?" Topper asked. He gunned his twinned diesels for emphasis. *Rough Beast* shivered like a dog about to piss. The woman looked scared but determined, a combination which even Topper cannot ignore.

He locked down the upper hatch, set the brakes, pegged the clutches, disarmed the antipersonnel charges on the outer hull, and crawled back between the ammo cans and the fuel bags to undog the ventral hatch. As he twisted the clamps, Topper hoped the woman hadn't run away or been jumped or something. He can't protect her from up here. *Rough Beast* is made for salvage runs and fighting heavy metal, not personnel escort.

Topper is confused about a lot of things, but he's not confused about what his crawler does.

The woman was still outside, armed and dangerous. And that was just her looks. Dark hair swept back from an aristocratic face. Pretty teeth, which Topper remembers from white rooms full of screams. She had a big gun, too, a riot weapon meant for stopping dogs or people caught in the Great Madness.

"You're going to the plant," she said.

It was not a question.

"In," Topper ordered by way of a non-answer.

Indecision flicked across her face like a trout in a mountain stream, then she climbed the metal steps he'd dropped down for her. *Rough Beast* had ground clearance that would give an arborist's ladder a bad case of envy.

Distant gunfire echoed as Topper dogged the hatch, but the incoming wasn't to their address. He wormed back up to the driver's station, leaving the woman to follow or not as she chose.

The crawler got moving with a shuddering lurch which foretold trouble for the portside throw bearings. He could rebuild. He just needed some high-grade ingots to trade out for the finished parts. That was how he took care of everything on this monster.

A single man wasn't meant to maintain and operate something like *Rough Beast*. Not even a single man as profoundly unalone as Topper.

The woman squirmed into the radio operator's seat behind him. That surprised Topper, he'd already forgotten about her. No radio, never had been one, but there was part of a sandwich rack out of an automat right in front of her face, as if she could plot their course in egg salad and bologna and trimmed crusts.

"So." Her gun thumped briefly against the floor. He noted she was smart enough to clip it to the seat pedestal. "When did they let you out?"

Topper had to think that one over for a while. Finally he said, "Ain't sure they have yet."

Call it boredom if you like. I won't dispute it if you do, not at all. Boredom, ennui, a sense of adventure left unaddressed for far too long—any of that could explain why I left my post and crawled up into that oil-dripping beastie with the lunatic pilot.

When I'm summoned before Best Friend and her bitches to explain myself, though—and you know I will be—we won't be talking about any ennui bullshit. No, I'll be spinning some tale about surveillance and undercover and getting on the inside of the enemy camp and all that sort of yak.

To support this notion, and also because I was damned curious, I slithered up the ladder at the behest of the grisly creature. (Hey, don't let it be said I never plan ahead.) I'd known Topper before, of course; knew him before he was the raving lunatic we'd all come to know and love in the Madness. Not that he was ever entirely sane.

Who is, any more?

I knew him because I'd been part of the crew that had taken him down, during the last round of the world-shifting adventures. We'd taken him hard, real hard, even before handing him over to the New Friends for, shall we say, readjustment therapy. I'd never expected to see him again. Which was shame, in its way.

So here he was, grinding up my street on his way to god-knows-what kind of tomfoolery down at the plant. Didn't even bother to deny it. Invited me aboard.

How could I resist?

I settled in behind him, looking around everywhere, trying to take it all in before he came to whatever shred of senses might have been left him by the New Friends and booted me out of there. Because, right, surveillance. Remember? I kept my right hand close to the NKVD riot gun in case Mr. Topper decided to get cute. But he had already started the monster rolling again, ignoring me completely.

He answered my question well enough, I suppose. All things being equal, you never really do get out, do you?

I fell silent after that, wishing the asylum refugee had thought to put windows back at my seat. What was I supposed to do with A-4 and D-0? I'd had a lovely lunch already, thank you very much. The rats are fat and sassy, this part of town.

Oh, Jesus, just kidding. What do I look like? I don't eat rats. You think this figure comes from eating street sludge like rats?

Feral cats, now: that's where it's at. Yum yum, meow yum. Excellent diced and stir-fried, with tree ears and a sprinkling of hoisin sauce right at the end.

After a particularly difficult highway crossing, Topper's mind wanders back to the woman. She was muttering under her breath now. Something about rats and cats and someone named Hawser Ann. He could smell her breath even in the diesel-and-metal reek of the crawler.

Cats was right in there. Topper cackled. He'd had a cat once, lived in the bed with him in the pale green room with the telephone that whispered secret vices in his ear-of-virtue, and blessings in his ear-of-vice. He knew what had happened to that cat too, every time he blinked his eye.

Our Topper spent some quality time under the close personal care of Doctor Sergei S. Bryukhonenko, after the good doctor B. had fled the collapse of the Eastern Front and wound up under a New Friends of Sweet Reason ban working out of a former mental hospital in the quiet fields near Yellow Springs, Ohio. The fields were quiet then because of the gas pooling in the low-lying watersheds which killed off everything with a central nervous system.

Dr. Bryukhonenko had been the beneficiary of good pressure seals and a number of human canaries chained to stakes in a three-mile radius around the hilltop facility. Our Topper had been the beneficiary of Dr. Bryukhonenko's newfound health and safety.

Until the psychosurgeries began.

Now he saw in strange shades of gray, a world of movement and chiaroscuro, relying on childhood memories of paintboxes and flower gardens to fill in the colors. Topper still knows the curve of a woman's breast from the rounded nose of a bullet—he's not *that* far gone—but so much else slides past the greased corners of memory, electroshock therapy, and deep conditioning, as if he were a human carpet afflicted with flea's eggs.

"Food?" he asked the woman. A gap yawned before the crawler, smoke crawling up out of some nether hole in the Pennsylvania soil. Mine fire? Enemy attack? Wrath of God? He navigated around it while one of his inner selves listened to her answer.

"Is that a request or an offer?" She began suggestively polishing the barrel of her riot gun.

"Dunno," Topper said. "Thought you might have some catsmeat." He felt vaguely like a cannibal for asking. Then his attention was distracted by the towering stacks of the mill, his destination. Someone flew a small aircraft close above them. He resisted the urge to jump up into the air and swat at it.

For all Topper knows, he might be able to do just that. Muscles he didn't know he had creaked at the thought.

"Rowr," the woman growled.

He wondered if she would purr, as well,

"You don't remember me, do you?" I asked the lunatic, after he'd failed to respond to my clever sally about the cat. I'd even growled to remind him. Good times. But I'm not even going to tell you about the look on his face when I did that, now.

Suffice it to say, crazy or not, the man had a strange charisma. And not because I was hard up, either. Not that I was ready to hop into the sack with him. Not right then. Not even the floor of this machine, or up against the wall of the mill. Not me.

The mill! A squinting straining gaze through what I could see of the forward view told me we were almost there, though Topper hadn't even been paying attention to the road. "Road"—such as it was, of course. The route, more like.

"Harridan Three, Harridan Three, do you copy?" a small voice crackled from my satchel. Damn, it must be one of the bitches in that plane buzzing overhead. Checking up on me. They don't trust me to wipe my own ass, anymore.

Of course I couldn't respond, not overtly. But if I didn't send her on her merry way, she'd land that overgrown horsefly right in our path, and . . . well, let's just say I didn't fancy being two feet behind Topper when he was suddenly beset by Sisters in a well-armed aircraft, attempting to halt his forward progress.

"Nice rig you got here, Topper," I said instead. "I especially like the seats. Ooh, comfy."

He tore his attention away from peering up at the sky and stared at me. A droplet of slobber formed in the V at the lowest point of his lip and hung there. "Seats?" he finally asked.

"Yep," I said loudly, patting the foul cracked vinyl next to me. "These seats right here, in this-here vehicle you're driving me around in. Yep. Love it."

"Harridan Three, we copy," came the voice in my bag. It was Lena: bad news. And she was clearly pissed.

But the drone of the plane engine faded, and then the mill loomed large. Too large.

"Stop!" I screamed, just as this abortion of a tank crashed through the wall.

Topper came round to paying attention to what he should be doing just after a few dozen tons of masonry bounced off the roof. That plane had buzzed off, but it had dropped him a present on the way out.

He spun *Rough Beast* left, just to confuse anyone who might be sighting in on him. From the sound of things, the crawler was now taking out another portion of the mill's outer wall. The hull pounded and shuddered, a brick rain.

"Where's the map?" he screamed over the deafening war.

She shook her head. *Useless bitch,* he thought. Bring a girl on a picnic, she doesn't even remember napkins. Topper keyed off the antipersonnel charges ringing the upper hatch and jacked his chair for a look. He let his feet do the driving.

Thing about a cat's eye is it sees in darkness. Not the pitch black of coal mines or a politician's soul, but places where a human being would stand blinking and wondering which way to the egress. The very bad Dr. Bryukhonenko had built a neural jumper block so the input from the cat's eyes jammed swollen and dry into Topper's skull could be made sensible—sense-in-light for a man who lives in the endless nonsense of his own head.

All of which meant that with the Bethlehem mill running on blackout except for the glow from the Bessemers further down the compound, only Topper could see what was going on. The defenders had to rely on triangulation and their own knowledge of the terrain. Topper was ignoring the terrain in favor of the direct approach.

"Damned loading yard ought to be down here somewhere."

Rails had been torn up a long time ago—their fixed routes were useless in this age of rolling borders and continuous sabotage—but the rail yard was still useful space.

Having gotten something resembling his bearings, Topper spun *Rough Beast* around. The wide open area had been *behind* him.

A woman was screaming from down near his waist. She sounded familiar. He jacked the chair low and looked around.

"Marie," Topper said, pleased as hell to see her. "What are you doing here in San Diego?"

The look on Marie's face was almost frightening. The gun in her hand worried him more, though. When had she learned to shoot?

Outside, the aircraft buzz had come back. *Fucking spotters,* he thought. "Whoops, got to go," he said, "bad guys up above. Hold that fire til we need it, kiddo."

By the time Topper was back out of the hatch and heating up the solenoids in the remotely-operated turrets, he'd forgotten what he'd gone down for. Until a gunshot echoed from inside the hull of his crawler.

Bastard flipped completely out on me after the impact. I mean, I shouldn't have been surprised, but it wasn't like I'd been having a peaceful day up till then, so I was a bit, well, off guard.

Hey. It happens.

Once the machine (not to mention Lena's bomb) rendered the wall of the mill into so many smithereens, it lurched but didn't stop, instead simply veering off to the left a bit. Or maybe that was Topper, yanking on the wheel. Anyway, that's the part that rattled me more than anything else. I was airborne a good two seconds, then crashed to the slimy floor of the tank-thing at his feet.

At least I held onto my gun.

Which stood me in good stead once I'd recovered enough to think again. The freak was looming over me, again paying no attention to the road, or corridor, or whatever it was we were driving down at the moment . . . yeah, another wall, I think . . . interior wall. It was hard to tell, jammed underneath two hundred and fifty pounds of insane manflesh.

I waved the gun at him. "Back off, Topper, I mean it!"

He called me Marie.

Oh god.

Waving the gun again, I tried to look sufficiently menacing. This was no doubt undermined by his view down the front of the corset. He grinned, and mumbled something about San Diego. What the fuck?

Maybe I was still screaming or something, because just then Lena decided she'd had enough. "Harridan three, we're coming in. You're relieved from duty effective immediately. Surrender your weapon to the personnel who will be approaching the tank once we bring it to a halt."

I almost laughed. How exactly were they expecting to do that?

A burst of machine gun fire came from above, mixed in with the aircraft engine. Oh, that's how. At least it got Topper's attention. He yanked his eyeballs away from my girls and scrabbled up top.

Unfortunately, I didn't want Lena to take his attention. Nor did I want to "surrender" anything to any goddamned "personnel" inside Bethlehem. "Topper!" I yelled, but he was beyond hearing me.

I took a shot in his general direction, careful not to aim for anything vital. Like around the middle. Riot loads weren't *supposed* to be fatal.

What? Just thinking ahead here. He'd cleaned up nicely once before. Who's to say it couldn't happen again? Girl can't be too picky these days.

Good. That got his fleeting attention once more. He slithered back down below and stood before me. "Marie?"

"Not Marie," I said. Then I reached down and toggled my radio to blessed silence so we could talk privately. "Grace, and don't you forget it, you moron."

"Grace . . . " The name slid off his pink tongue, making it sound dirty. "Graaace."

Oh good lord. We were in for a long night.

Topper stuttered. That's what the doctor had called it—not Bryukhonenko the surgeon, but that New Friends woman with three moles on her chin that always made him think of Jules Verne's War of the Worlds for some reason.

Threes, all evil things came in threes. That's why men and women stayed in pairs. That's why a woman had two tits, a man had two nuts, everyone had two eyes, two ears, two hands, two legs, two nostrils, two lungs for the love of God.

Threes. And the stutters always came in threes. Dr. Roseglove, that was her name, like she had thorns turned inward to her hands, tiny red-brown spikes to pierce the skin, an Orchidglove would have been a very different doctor indeed, or a Lilly-of-the-Valleyglove and when he stuttered he lost *time,* he lost *control,* he lost his *marker* in the place of life.

Bad things. Threes. A woman named Marie, not Grace. But he'd known Marie? Had she been a twin? Or worse, a triplet? Was Grace her middle name, her secret name, her confirmation name, her gang name, her spymaster's handle?

She was shouting. Outside something was bombing. His thigh hurt like fucking hell where something bad had happened.

Adrenaline, he thought, a moment of clarity amid the stutter. *Adrenaline and a pressure bandage, before I die of assassination.*

Why would anyone want to kill our Topper? Even he cannot answer that. Well, other than all the people he's killed over the years, of course, but very few of them have anything to say about it now. Dead is dead, and no one's got relatives no more, not in this fragged world.

She's still yelling, this woman, but he's ignoring her in single-minded pursuit of his wound. He doesn't worry so much about the scattered pellets embedded in the flesh of his leg. They will either kill him or they won't.

Topper jacked up into his open hatch. *Rough Beast* wasn't equipped for anti-air operations. An angry woman loose with a riot gun down below was a problem. Amplified voices and high explosives outside were a bigger problem.

He left his stutter behind when he realized that his enemies had come to ground. Obliging of them, *Rough Beast* was very well equipped for anti-personnel operations.

A beefy woman stood in the red glare between shadows cast by his own arc lights, shouting for someone named Jason Adair to stand down. Topper didn't know any Jason Adair, not since before the wars began when he might once have answered to that name, so he activated the electrically controlled chin turret that looked like a fuel junction and could surprise an unwary, beefy woman and turned this one into a spray of blood and cloth.

Then he ground the crawler straight toward the ducted fan aircraft grounded before him. Topper admired the engineering of the thing—innovative, frightening, probably stolen from the Germans—until *Rough Beast* crushed it to scrap.

He wasn't sure which was more annoying: Marie screaming from below or some woman screaming from the crushed cockpit of the aircraft. In either case it didn't matter. The metal yard was ahead, and that was his purpose here.

Okay.

Fuck.

Breathe. Just get hold of yourself: breathe, bitch.

'Cause when Topper took out Lena and her bodyguard du jour, *not to mention the whole fucking aircraft* thank you very much, well, okay, it sent me into a bit of a spin.

So maybe I shot him again. Just a little bit. I'm really not sure, frankly. Everything got kind of crazy and blurry there for a few minutes. Like maybe there were psychotic drugs floating in the air around Topper.

No, I didn't mean anti-psychotic drugs. That would have helped. I meant what I said. Pay attention, I'm not going to say it again.

It didn't make a damn bit of difference to his apparent sanity, or lack thereof. I mean the shooting-him-again part, if it happened. The drugs, I have no idea. That was just a metaphor kind of thing. I was making a comparison, one thing to another.

Although who knows?

Anyway, my sanity, however. Well . . . like I said, I lost a few minutes there. Once everything was tracking again, I saw that the aircraft was a pile of oily rubble behind us, and Topper was rolling the tank forward, muttering about Germans.

He never stopped with the verbiage, that one. If only any of it made the smallest bit of sense. I'd love to see him across a poker table. Looked like every thought was immediately broadcast.

Not that I was likely to be playing poker again anytime soon. Anyway, Lena had my deck of cards. Probably they were ground into the mud behind us, too.

Mud and oil and blood and . . .

Don't think about it. *Don't think about it!*

I clipped my riot gun back into the rack beside the seat, just in case I was tempted to use it again. Because the part of my brain that had been functioning throughout the little misadventure of the past few minutes had just presented me with the irrefutable fact that my fate was now tied to that of this overgrown monkey, the one now drooling and gibbering and steering this massive bit of machinery towards what had to be the biggest metal yard I'd ever seen.

In other words: no more Sisters, not for me, not here, not now. By climbing aboard this contraption. I'd thrown my lot in with Topper.

God, I *hoped* he still cleaned up nicely.

I sidled forward in the cab, or at least something reasonably approximating sidling. Tough to do when the thing was rolling and grinding and rocking back and forth, throwing me from side to side like a hamster in a blender.

"Marie!" he said, catching sight of me. He gave me a delighted smile.

I fell into the copilot's seat beside him, or whatever you'd call it. Jump seat. Small bit of cushioning in a vast expanse of well lubricated metal parts and pieces. "Grace," I said, in a friendly and conversational tone.

"Marie-Grace?"

"Just Grace. Remember, sweetheart, how we went over this?" He kept staring at me. "Well—never mind that, anyway. Just watch where you're driving, okay?"

"Driving, doing, zooming, duckling," he said. But his head wafted back in the general direction of forward.

"Good boy," I said. "Just keep doing what you're doing." Sooner or later, some of this was going to make sense. For now, he just had to keep us alive.

"W-74," Topper sang out. "Tungsten steel. Hard as a shield, cuts like a blade, keep it sharp, never be late . . . Burma Shave!"

Marie-Grace Just Grace snorted at him. He was pretty sure she'd shot him a bit earlier, but she had a nice smile. Maybe he'd been wounded one of the dizzy bitches from that airplane.

Bullets fell on *Rough Beast*'s hull like lead rain. The locals were getting to it. But now he was in the metal yard, the El Dorado of this Pennsylvania hellhole.

"Here, Missy Marie-Grace Just Grace," Topper said, handing her down a gas mask. "Wear this a while and don't get nothing on your skin." He paused, solicitous as a fragment from some long-forgotten safety briefing (back when "safety" and "briefing" were applicable concepts) emerged into his forebrain like pack ice on a midnight river. "You weren't planning to have no children, were you?"

"Not right *now*," she squealed.

Topper wasn't sure that Marie-Grace Just Grace had taken the real point of the question, but duty had been discharged. He pressed the big red button labeled "DO NOT PRESS." It was wired just below a portrait of Bing Crosby with a Hitler mustache.

Several loud, ominous thumps echoed from the outside of the crawler's hull. This was followed by a hissing noise. Topper belatedly remembered to pull on his own gas mask, then wondered what he'd done with the chemical suit.

The part of him that was sane enough to keep the rest of the traveling circus alive watched the sweep second hand on the dashboard clock—Swiss timing in a genuine hand carved Chinese ivory casing, and possibly the most valuable thing aboard *Rough Beast*. Topper liked his treasures portable. He was a man who'd left more towns under more clouds than Seattle saw in a year.

One hundred and eighty seconds later he bailed out into the dissipating yellow fog. Defending fire had stopped, except for the occasional stutter of a weapon discharged as a finger shriveled too tightly in death. That hardly counted, though Topper knew a bullet was a bullet no matter who had fired it.

He wasn't moving right. The dizzy bitch really *had* shot him. Couldn't have been something too fierce, or his leg would be shattered. Riot gun with rubber loads, maybe? Who the hell would hang around a Pennsylvania mill town at night armed with sublethal munitions? That was like bringing a housewife to a bullfight.

Ahead of Topper were thirty-six pallets of high grade tungsten steel. Finest kind, ready for shipment to the manufactories of Detroit and Fort Wayne. Or ripe for the jacking by an enterprising man with good intelligence and solid orders.

Or woman, he reminded himself. Topper turned to stare at *Rough Beast*, wondering what he'd been thinking and which part of him had been thinking it. Her head poked up now, insect-eyed and blank-faced in the gas mask.

An electric turret whined as she brought one of the Bofors to bear on him.

"Screw you," Topper shouted, and began dragging the cargo chains out. It was hijacking time. He didn't have what it took to die again right now.

After monkey-boy propositioned me a few times, I knew we were getting somewhere. Excellent. I could work with that.

The discussion of children, however, was a tad premature. I almost said something, but then he pressed some big goddamn red button and all manner of excitement began.

No, the other kind of excitement.

That all changed once he'd killed everyone within a ten-mile radius of the tank. Or so it seemed, anyway, given the swath of destruction all around us. After that, he turned back to me, with a terrible, deeply insane look about him.

I mean, he'd been insane all along. I knew that. You might have even said it was part of his charm. But I'd just watched him kill everyone I worked for, lived with, fucked and fought. Then I'd watched him kill everyone at the mill I was supposedly defending. Then he turned and looked at me.

"Now or never, baby," I said to myself, cranking one of his cannon turrets to point at him. That ought to put the fear into him.

All he did was proposition me a third time, then turn away and start fooling with a tangle of chains.

I threw my riot gun at him. Insane I can handle. Inconsistency: that makes me crazy.

"Mary Grace Just Grace," he babbled on, as he started spreading the chains out on the gravel in front of us. He ignored the riot gun completely, after glancing at it. I clambered down out of the tank and retrieved it, but it was too big to hold if I was going to help him get the pallets aboard.

Sure, I helped him. He could barely move the damn things. I was in far too deep to back out now. Might as well get our business done in here and get the hell out. Then we could talk about children, or whatever the fuck he wanted.

Men. Can't live with 'em, can't stake 'em out for the vultures. Though some of them might be improved. Including this crazy old bastard.

He was my last ticket.

Topper yanked the cold steel out of the charnel house of the mill one quarter-ton ingot at a time. The winches could handle the load, no problem—they were made for much heavier work than this, naval-grade hardware salvaged off a captured Kriegsmarine surface raider which had been broken in a gray-market yard hidden up the Rappahannock.

The girl helped. She was small, and weak, and not half-rebuilt out of spare parts and Soviet medicine, but she was tough and smart. Topper wondered how he knew her. Good-looking, too, and not just in an any-woman-in-a-war-zone way.

Somehow having his hands on all this hard-case metal was bring him back into himself. Memories spiraled in kaleidoscope paths to land in partially assembled chiaroscuros somewhere deep in our Topper's head. Like how a real person might think, it occurred to him, coherent images and more than a little bit of focused recall stitching together into timelines.

He wanted to turn away from some of them—deeply unpleasant, unpleasantly deep, or just infused with a stunning sadness for the boy and man someone with his name and face might once of have been.

It was her, he realized. Not the metal. Not the dead. Not the distant thump of artillery and first drone of engines gone raiding in the cold, smoky sky. Not the screaming cats and bleeding eye sockets of memory. Not the white coats and wire-rimmed spectacles which had dominated so much of the intervening years.

Her.

Topper stepped closer, subtle as a pork roast in a synagogue, and sniffed.

"What the hell are you doing, you cre—" she shouted, then stopped when she got a good look at his face.

"M . . . Grace," Topper said, and looked her full in the eyes. He could fall into that pooled, dark amber forever, he realized.

Something was waiting to be born here beneath the shadow of *Rough Beast*, behind the walls of Bethlehem. He could feel it stirring inside him.

A soul. Hope. Affection.

Love?

He closed his eyes and breathed her in. She struck him all the way down into the lizard brain, scent and smell wired by million years of evolution and a hundred thousand generations of hairless apes dropping from the trees to say, *this one. This is the one.*

Before he could open his eyes again, she kissed him.

Somewhere inside the shattered Japanese puzzle box of his head, he was made whole.

"Let's get the last of this stuff on board," Topper said, rough but gentle as he drew her into his arms. "Then we're gonna say screw it to the Sisterhood and the New Friends and the Federals and the Wehrmacht and go be alone together. There's freemen in the Alleghenies would pay good money for our cargo, and hire us to raid for them."

His mind was dancing with visions of a quiet cabin, an open sky, and skin exposed for no purpose more sinister than a long slow trail of the tongue.

God, it was like being a kid again.

For the first time in his life, Topper had woken up.

Yeah. So. Okay, I kissed him. Like I said, I'd kind of run out of options at that point.

But it was more than that. Much more.

When Topper turned and looked at me, really looked at me; when he got my name right; when the man that lived somewhere underneath all the layers of insanity our world had thrust at him suddenly bled through and took charge . . . I kissed him.

And when he pulled me into his arms and I caught the scent of him—the real, true scent, beyond the oil and blood and gasoline and the rank sweat of fear and battle—it hit me right below the belt.

Yeah, there. I meant what I said. How do you think things *become* clichés, anyway?

"Right," I said. "Last load and we're out of here."

And we rumbled off into the sunset. Sunrise. Whatever: I'm telling the story here, okay? The light changed and took us with it into a different world.

The Completely Rechargeable Man
KAREN HEULER

He was introduced as Johnny Volts, and most guests assumed he was a char-latan—the hostess, after all, was immensely gullible. But some of the guests had seen him before, and they said he was good, lots of fun, very "current"—a joke that got more mileage than it should have.

"Do you need any kind of extension cord?" the hostess, Liz Pooley, asked. She wore a skintight suit of emerald lame, and had sprayed a lightning bolt pattern in her hair, in his honor.

Johnny Volts sighed and then smiled. They all expected him to be something like a children's magician—all patter and tricks. "No extension cord," he said. "Where can I stand?" He caught his hostess's frown. "I need an area to work in—and appliances, not plugged in. I'm the plug. No microwaves. A blender, a radio, a light bulb. Christmas lights?"

The guests were charmed at first and then, inevitably, they were bored. Even if it wasn't a trick, it was pretty limited. He could power a light, but not a microwave. He could charge your cell phone but not your car. He was an early adopter of some sort, that was all; they would wait for the jazzed-up version.

Johnny Volts had a pacemaker with a rechargeable battery, and he had a friend who was a mad scientist. This friend had added a universal bus to his battery port, and hence Johnny Volts had a cable and a convertible socket. He could plug things in; he could be plugged in. This was a parlor trick as far as the public was concerned—and a strange, unsettling, but still somewhat interesting way of earning a living as far as Johnny Volts was concerned. He knew—he understood—that his pacemaker powered his heart, and his heart recharged the pacemaker in a lovely series of perpetual interactions. He had no issue with it.

In Liz Pooley's party, as Johnny Volts lit a lamp, turned on a clock radio, and charged an iPod, he was watched by a frowning man in a checked shirt whose companion seemed quite happy with Johnny.

"Why he's worth his weight in gold," she said. "Imagine never having to pay an electric bill."

"Small appliances," the man grunted.

"Well *now* it's small appliances, Bob, but he's just the first. Wait till he can really get going, he'll have his own rocket pack. Remember rocket packs, Bob?

The Segway of long-lost memory." She put her hand on Bob's arm and rolled her eyes. "I was but a mere child of course, when I heard about those rocket packs. Shooting us up in the air. A new meaning to the term Jet Set, hey? Or is that phrase too old? I bet it's too old. What are we called now, Bob?" She lifted her drink, saluted him, and winked.

"We're called only when they've run out of everyone else, Cheree." Bob was idly thinking about what would bring a man to this: plugging in small irrelevant things into his own violated flesh. "Irrelevant," he said finally. "They call us irrelevant."

Cheree frowned. "You're turning into an old man, Bob. You've lost your spark." She gave him a small motherly peck on the cheek and walked forward, powerfully, her lemon martini firm in her hand, straight to Johnny Volts, who was looking around, waiting to be paid. "You looking for a drink?" she asked. "I could get you one."

"Oh—well, all right," he said, surprised.

"You wait right here," she said. "I want to know all about you, electric man." And she turned until she found a server and came back with a dark liquid in a tumbler. "Now tell me—how does it feel? I mean you're generating electricity, aren't you?"

"Yes. Not much. After next week it should be more. I'm having an upgrade."

"Lovely. How does it feel? Like little bugs up and down your spine?" She had a heady grin, a frank way of working. Johnny liked it.

"It's a beautiful kind of pressure," he said. "It feels like I could fill the room with it, lift everything up, kind of explode—only I hold on to the explosion." His eyes got internal.

"Do you like it?"

He was open-mouthed with surprise. "Yes. Of course. It's wonderful."

She tilted her head a little, studying his face, and he found it embarrassing at first, and then he got used to it. He looked back at her, not lowering his eyes or glancing away. She was older than he was, but she had a bright engaging air about her, as if she made a point of not remembering anything bad.

"Here you go," the hostess said, her arm held out full length with a check at the end of it like a flattened appendage.

Johnny took it and turned to leave. "Hey!" Cheree said, grabbing at his arm a little. "That's rude. Not even a fond farewell?"

"They usually want me to leave right away," he said in explanation. "Before I get boring."

"Boring," she said companionably as they headed together for the door. "That bunch? They think *other* people are boring?"

He noted that she was walking along with him as if she belonged there. "So where do you see yourself in five years?" she asked. "That's a test question. So many people can't think ahead."

"Do you think ahead?"

"Not me. I'm spontaneous. Then again, I'm not at all electric, so I don't have to worry about running out of juice."

"I don't run out," he said. "I recharge. And I'm getting an upgrade to photovoltaic cells next week. I have to decide where to implant them; do you mind if I run it past you?" He rubbed his hand over his head as they took the elevator down. "The obvious thing is to replace my hair—it's a bit of a jolt, though. I can lose it all and get a kind of mirror thing on top—a shiny bald pate, all right. Or fiber optic hair. But it will stick out. Like one of those weird lamps with all the wires with lights at the end? What do you think?"

"Fiber optic hair," she said without hesitation. "Ahead of the times. Fashion-forward. I bet there'll be a run on the hardware store."

He stopped—they were on the street—and frowned at her. "Your name?"

"Cheree."

"Cheree, you're glib."

"I am glib, Johnny," she said in a soft voice. "It's because my head doesn't stop. You know the brain is all impulses, don't you? Bang and pop all over the place. Well, mine is on superdrive, I have to keep talking or I'll crack from all the thinking. The constant chatter . . . I can only dream of stillness."

He shook his head in sympathy. "That sounds like static." He stopped and reached out for her hand. "Maybe you produce energy all your own?" She held her hand out, and Johnny hesitated, then touched the tips of their fingers together. He closed his eyes, briefly. There was a warmth, a moistness, a lovely *frisson.* He took a deep breath. He felt so tired after those parties, but now a delicious delicate rejuvenation spread through him. The back of his neck prickled; the hairs on his arms—even his eyebrows—hairs everywhere rose, he could feel it in his follicles. It rose up in him until suddenly Cheree was thrown backward slightly.

"What was that?" she said tensely.

He nodded. "Sorry. Volts. A little discharge. It won't hurt you."

"Still," she said uneasily. "Can't say I know what to make of it."

They were at a crossroads, specifically Houston and Lafayette. "Where do you live?" he asked.

"East Seventh."

"I'm uptown." They stood for a moment in silence. "Will you come with me?" he asked finally.

Her face broke into a smile, like a charge of sunshine.

They were utterly charming together, they were full of sparks. Toasters popped up when they visited their friends—though did people really still have toasters? Wasn't that, instead, the sound of CD players going through their disks, shuffling them? Wasn't it the barely audible purr of the fan of a car as they passed it, sitting up and noticing as if it were a dog? They were attractive, after all; they attracted.

"If we moved in together," Johnny said after they'd known each other for a month, "we'd have half the bills. We could live on very little, we could live on what I make at the parties. You wouldn't have to work as a waitress. In fact, we could be free."

"And give up my dreams of rocket science?" she asked, her eyebrows arched.

"I thought you were a waitress."

"That's just till I sell my first rocket." Nevertheless, she decided to move in, and it was working out fine, except for the strange way that objects behaved around them.

Small electrics followed them like dogs sometimes—they could turn down the block and hear a clanking or a scraping behind them. Eager little cell phones, staticy earphones, clicking electronic notepads gathered in piles on their doorstep.

"We have to figure out a budget," Cheree said after she moved in. "Until I sell that rocket. Rent, not much we can do. We should get bikes, that will save on transportation. But, you know, we're still paying for electricity, and it's pretty high, too. What do we really use it for?"

Together, they went through their apartment, noting: refrigerator, lamps, clock, radio, stereo, TV, microwave, coffee maker, hair dryer, iron, laptop computer.

"Well," Johnny said. "All quite useful in their own way, but we can make coffee without electricity. And I already recharge the computer myself."

She considered it all. "You can recharge most of it, really, if we get the right kind of thing. If we look at everything that way—I'm sure there are rechargeable lamps, for instance—why are we paying electric bills? We could save a lot of money by doing it ourselves."

They canceled their energy provider, a savings right there of $70 a month. They would plug a different item into Johnny at night, so they would never run out. It was a brilliant solution.

That gave him even more motivation for the photovoltaic upgrade. When he went to his mad scientist friend, she went with him, and they mentioned the strange way they seemed to be accumulating electrical appliances. The mad scientist was sitting across from them, taking down Johnny's recap of the past few months, when the scientist felt his skin begin to tingle. He shook himself briefly, as if buzzed by a fly. He was a graduate student at Carnegie Mellon, a Mexican genius who did illegal cable and satellite hookups to make some money, and was always looking over his shoulder. Johnny Volts was his ticket to fame and fortune; once the process was perfect, he would offer it to a medical or electronics company and bring millions down to his hometown of Tijuana, where he would go to retire.

The scientist ran a voltmeter over Cheree and whistled. "This is lovely," he said. "Exciting, even." He grinned at Johnny. "She's got a field. You see, you two match. You kind of amplify each other—understand?" He looked at them happily, waiting for them to catch up with his thinking. "You match."

It took a moment. "You're saying we're related? Like siblings?"

"Oh—no, no, I mean your energy matches. It doesn't mean anything really, other than that you're sensitive to each other's waves. You two have sympathetic electricity—I'm making the term up—so you use less energy when you're together than you do when you're apart, because you're actually *attracting* each other's charge. The byproduct is, you attract things that charge. Get it?"

"Oh, honey, yes," Cheree said. "I get it." It was like their little electric hearts went thudder-thump when they came near each other. Cheree was aware of it as a little sizzle in her brain.

They noticed a few things: He was a thoughtless hummer, and when he hummed he gave her a headache. She was an adventurer, wanting to go out and about, here there and everywhere, while he liked to think and write and test how strong his recharging was.

It happened gradually, the feeling that they were being watched, were being followed. She had coffee and a man who looked familiar sat opposite her in the café. He went to a party and saw the same man in a different suit watching him carefully. His apartment door was dusted with a fine powder one morning; the following week it was on a window.

When they went out in the morning, there was always a bunch of people passing their front door. Jauntily, as if just interrupted, they were speeding away, towards, around, moving with a great deal more purpose than on any other block. "Have you noticed it?" Cheree asked, and Johnny nodded. "I asked the landlord, and he said there's been some kind of gas leak, they're checking the lines a lot more. Even went into the basement, he said, all up and down the block."

"A gas leak?" she said, sniffing. "I don't smell anything."

"Well, that's good then."

But then Johnny disappeared. Went out to a party and didn't come back, and when she called the number listed in his daybook, she was told he hadn't shown up.

Cheree buzzed in her head when she was near Johnny; she could feel the tingle coming on when she turned the corner, half a block away, so it wasn't surprising that she felt she could find him. She said to herself: these are the things I know: He has a charge, and I can sense it. He has a head of fiber optic hair. And I am his magnet.

She took her bike and rode slowly, up and down streets, starting with the top of the island. Her head refused to buzz, block after block, in traffic and out, but then, after three hours—just as she rounded the corner near the docks on the west side—she heard a tang, she felt a nibble at her brain. It was him.

She biked forward, back, left and right, testing out the buzzing, following it to the door of a small garage dealing in vintage cars.

She parked her bike and chained it. She noticed an electric toothbrush rolling on the sidewalk.

She walked up to a man in a very neat jumpsuit. She didn't know anything about vintage cars. "I have to get a present for my dear old dad," she said. "He loves cars. I thought maybe we could all—he had two families, so there's plenty of children—get together and buy him something smashing." She grinned.

He shrugged. "You can take a look at what we've got, but my gut says you're out of your league."

She smiled at him steadily, looking around, her eyes skipping to the doorway to an office or a back room. She could feel Johnny's electric kick. She walked around the cars slowly until his charge was at its strongest. She whipped around "I know you have him," she said, and drew in her breath, kicking a chair over to trip him as he lunged forward. She bolted for the door, which was unlocked, and burst in.

There was Johnny, in the corner of the room. They had him wired up to machines that beeped and spit, they had his arm strapped to a chair.

"I'm all right," Johnny said when he saw her. She stopped, uncertainly, in the middle of the room.

"What's going on?"

The man in the garage was behind her, and two men came at her from the side. They were all dressed in white jumpsuits, with ties showing through their zippered fronts. "We're from the collection agency," one man said. "For unlawful theft of electricity."

"We don't need to *pay* for electricity," she said. "We only use our own."

"Ha," he said. "You don't own it. You're just stealing and not paying for it. You know what? We put meters into and out of your apartment, just to make sure. You were off the charts! We could hear the volts clicking! Don't tell me you're not using electricity!"

"I tried to explain—" Johnny said wearily.

"Did you plug into him yet?" Cheree interrupted. "Then you'll see." She looked around and picked up a small calculator on a desk, plugging it into Johnny's socket. It whirred on, but the jumpsuits looked impassive. She began to enter numbers faster and faster, until finally she rang up Total. "See?" she said, as the men stepped forward almost politely, glancing at the strip of paper (who had such old calculators, anyway?) that had curled out the top.

"Nice," the second man concluded. He reached into his pocket. "I'm not with them," he said. "I'm with NASA and we think you might have stolen a restricted project. We're going to have to take you with us for national security." He offered his card.

"Hold on there," said the third man, "I'm with the Office of Ocean Exploration. You can't take him, see here—I've got a signed order to bring him in for questioning." He shook his head. "I mean it's an invitation. We admire the strides he's made in making a self-sustaining renewable resource." He gave a business card to Johnny and one to Cheree.

The first man took out a gun. "He's not going anywhere. He's been taking electricity and we *own* electricity. It's that simple. You can't take him because he's going to jail, our own facilities in a state-approved housing unit until his case comes to trial."

Johnny hung his head and groaned. "I'm no use to any of you," he said. "These fiber-optic hairs—they're no use underwater, you know—they need the sun to recharge. Totally useless." The NOAA man looked a little annoyed at that, but he said, "Who said you had to be *under* the water; maybe they want you *on top* of the water?" but even he looked skeptical.

"Plus, he's on a pacemaker," Cheree said. "You can't have a pacemaker in orbit, if that's what you were thinking. You'd kill him; what good would that be?"

The electric company man was looking increasingly smug. "That leaves me," he said with a smile. "And all I want is for the bill to be paid. Plus interest and penalties."

"There is no bill," Johnny said wearily. "We canceled our account months ago. No account, no bills."

"That's not how it works. You think electricity is free? Like air? Like water? Like land? Are any of those free?" He waved Cheree aside as she said "Air! Air is free!"

"Nothing's free," he said. "The factories pay us for the air they pollute, and you have to pay for cleaning it—one way or another, someone's paying for it. As for electricity, that's never been free since Franklin put a key on a chain. Right now, you're stealing our business by interfering with a regulated industry without a license. It's against the law." He looked very merry about it. "I lied about our state-sanctioned facilities. You just go to jail, same as the scammers and the knockoff artists, and you can light your hair up all you want and see what it gets you!" He laughed then, thinking about the possible results.

"And you agree with this?" Cheree asked the men from NASA and NOAA. They looked at each other and shrugged. "Nothing in it for us," one said. "We don't interfere in the private sector," said the other.

"Then it's just you," Cheree said to the last man, who looked at the others with contempt.

"It's okay," he said, reaching into his pocket. "I'm a reasonable man." He held out a taser gun. "And this is a perfectly legal means of protecting myself."

Cheree looked at it and grinned. She glanced up and saw Johnny's face. "Johnny Volts," she said, cooing to him. "Johnny, sing to me!"

Johnny began to hum, and she decided to join him, sympathetically. The men in jumpsuits felt the hairs on their necks begin to rise, then their leg hairs, then their head hairs. The man from the electric company looked around wildly, then took a step towards Johnny, his taser outstretched.

The taser suddenly snapped and shot a small series of electric arcs out into the air until the utilities man yelped and dropped it. Cheree released Johnny, who rose from his seat and said, "Sorry. But there was a buildup. And Cheree is an amplifier. And I think I got a shot of adrenaline or something that caused an overload."

The other two men looked at each other. "Time to go, I think," one said and the other nodded. They walked off together slowly, as if not wanting to make a sudden move.

"I'm really sorry," Johnny said to the man writhing on the floor.

"If I could get up I'd clobber you," the energy man said. "This isn't over. I'll hunt you down and do something." He panted. "Just as soon as I can move again."

They followed the mad scientist down to Mexico, all of them imagining the utilities man hot on their trail. Even Tijuana seemed unsafe, so the mad scientist took them to a small town in the mountains, where he continued his work.

He gave Cheree a pacer, too, and he linked their charge, which was now big enough to fire a microwave, if there'd been a microwave around. But they had a bigger plan. In their mad dash down to the border they'd seen how much gasoline cost; wasn't Johnny the wave of the future and the future's savior? And wouldn't the mad scientist get rewards and jobs and money up the wazoo if he could find a way to recharge a car without looking for an outlet?

He plugged Johnny into the car he rigged up and called it the Voltswagon. Johnny could only get it to move slowly at first; but once the mad scientist hooked up Cheree to Johnny, and Johnny to the car, they were able to whiz to Tijuana and back at a merry clip. It took four years, but the cars ran and Johnny and Cheree were unharmed, and the mad scientist refined the recharging process to accommodate one person for one car

Little by little they converted the inhabitants of Tijuana to fiber optic hair and plug-in Voltswagons. Big Oil shut down the borders to keep Americans from going to Mexico to buy cars, but late at night, and hidden in the back of trucks, Americans snuck across the border to buy their Voltswagons and bring them home.

Episode 72
DON WEBB

If the Senator from New York would do something about her mousey brown hair she could be a real looker, decided the Senator from Rhode Island. She was getting near the Paul Revere section of her speech, and the crowd would be applauding back home in Boise and Baton Rouge in a few hours. It was not for nothing that she was called the Queen of Television. He watched her at the podium; her presence almost made the large backdrop painting of President McCarthy vanish.

" . . . do not know the name of the little town my ancestor founded. It was Charleston, Massachusetts. But it was from that little town that Paul Revere made his ride. One if by land, two if by sea. Well we know they are coming by sea and we know that some of them are already here, fifth columnists in wait. Some have been easy to spot in the last decade. Some were even proud of their anti-American political views. We have chased them from film. We have chased them from television. We have chased them from the public schools. But the price of freedom is eternal vigilance. It has been questioned in this body if we are right to use their labor to further that vigilance. It has been asked if the Communist should be working in our defense plants especially now as missiles build up in Cuba. I say yes. I say that we should turn the forces of Communism against itself at all odds.

"Now there are those who have hinted that we do not treat our enemies within kindly. This is balderdash. We treat them a million times more kindly than freedom fighters are treated at the gulags in the Soviet Union. But I am not a woman of rhetoric. I am not a lady of speech-giving. I will go to our largest facility, the plutonium bomb factory called Pantex in Amarillo, Texas this week. I am going with the Senate cameras rolling for the USABC, and I will show the world how well we treat those who would destroy us with their lies.

"I will maintain constant vigilance. As many of you know I am related to George Washington; two of my relatives have served as governors of Rhode Island. My family has long served this country and I will serve it as long as draw breathe."

The speech over and the strong lights were extinguished. There was mild applause. She didn't seem that great a performer live as she did televised. That was probably why she was unmarried. That and the hair.

• • •

Senator Ball's aide helped her remove her make up back in the senator's office.

"Senator, you were wonderful," said Scarlet Vance. "The Senate still has higher ratings than the three commercial networks and that's due to you."

"Thank you Scarlet, but I know that's not true. You know I took drama. Did you know Bette Davis was in my class? Bette Davis. I'll never forget the day the director of the school told me to choose another profession, any other profession."

"Is that why you went into politics Ma'm?"

"No that was because of my family. I looked at the state of women in politics. There wasn't any. I knew I had a shot at it. I figured I had to be the first."

"You're a visionary."

"No but I am brave."

"Are you looking forward to the trip to Texas?"

"No. I am not looking forward to being in a bomb plant with a bunch of Communists. That would be low on my list of travel plans, but rumors abound that we are mistreating people and I need to stop that. There are responsibilities that come from being the Queen of Television. Did you find anything interesting to do out there?"

"Yes M'am. Two years ago a new restaurant opened on Route 66 called the Big Texan Steak House. They offer you a free 72 ounce steak dinner if you eat it in an hour."

"A 72 ounce steak?"

"Well you have to eat the trimmings too. Shrimp cocktail, baked potato, salad and bread. "

"And you think I could do this?"

"Oh no, M'am. I think you would enjoy watching a cowboy from one of the local ranches try. I talked with one of the political officers in the region and he said it was quite amusing."

"You know me so well."

"There's a link to your trip you know. When the prisoner of war village from World War II was taken down at Pantex, it was used to build the Big Texan."

"Well that's just plain homey."

"M'am, you are really in favor of the Communists being used to build bombs, aren't you?"

"Of course I am, Scarlett. Of course I am."

Senator Ball had not liked the exotic appetizers. Jess Oppenheimer had taken the Senator to the Big Texan. Everyone likes the Big Texan. He got her what he always got the men: rattlesnakes and bull testicles. He had not explained to the lady from New York that "calf fries" were bull testicles. He thought everybody knew that. He sensed somehow that he was losing her.

"It's a huge facility," he was saying, "sixteen thousand acres."

"Could I see Palo Duro Canyon while I'm here?"

"Well of course. It's a lovely spot I take the wife and kids there every summer."

"I am interested in a painter that learned her style there. Georgia O'Keefe. Ever heard of her?"

"She was declared a Sympathizer last year."

Then there was awkward silence again as the Senator watched grease congeal on her bull's testicle.

Outside the restaurant she looked at the Big Texan. A huge sign of a lanky legged cowboy. She knew she was looking at something eternal, something that would always be a symbol of America like a Burma Shave sign or the Statue of Liberty. None of her speeches, none of the fine words in the Senate had as much power as this. This was why she had never married. She had never found a man as beautiful as the Big Texan.

It was a strange year. In January, Pope John XXIII had excommunicated Fidel Castro. In May, the Israelis had hung Eichmann. Last month AT&T launched the first commercial satellite ever. President McCarthy had explained how each of these events showed that Communism was on the run. The Pope had excommunicated the Communist closest to our shores so God was on our side. The Israelis were cleaning up the last traces of WWII so we didn't have to worry about history anymore. AT&T had showed that Capitalism would take over space.

But she didn't know sometimes. Maybe all these things would happen anyway. Maybe there is too much spin on history. Perhaps we are becoming a little like the folk in Khrushchev's lands.

The Amarillo night air was warm and dry and was giving her strange thoughts. Almost all of the Free World's helium comes from Amarillo; maybe that's why she was thinking oddly.

Or maybe it was the Big Texan staring down at her.

Amarillo is known for its invention of barbed wire and Mother-In-Laws' Day. She went to the hotel.

The barracks smelled bad.

There were separate quarters for men and women, and one of the first things that the Senator discovered were that families had been split up. She had come here to prove that that rumor was unfounded. She knew that she would have to fib. She knew that even before she came; fibbing is part of politics. But she was unhappy.

"It is important," she told Karl, "That we do not film the barracks. This does not look like America. We will film inside the plant."

"Happy workers making bombs?" asked Karl.

"Karl I know this isn't your life work. It isn't *Dracula* or *Metropolis* but it keeps you busy."

"You're wrong. This is *Metropolis*."

Senator Ball was about to say something, some nice reminder to Karl that since he came from Czechoslovakia people were always looking him as a Sympathizer, when she saw him.

The Big Texan.

All right maybe it was not love at first sight, maybe it took five minutes.

He was swarthy and short. He had dark hair and eyes. He stood in the door of one of the barracks. He wore the same yellow jumpsuit that everyone else did. He was waiting for the whistle, for his shift to start. Then it hooted and he headed off toward one of the buildings. She followed along.

"Sir?" she said.

He did not stop.

"You. You with the dark hair."

He stopped. Unlike most of the workers he did not turn his eyes to the ground. "Si?" he said.

"You're one of the Cubans aren't you?"

"Si."

"What's your name?

"Desiderio Alberto Arnaz y de Acha the Third."

"That's quite a name."

"I have to go now lady. I don't want to get into trouble."

"It's out of the question," said Mr. Oppenheimer.

His office was large and clean. It radiated a good American vibe.

"I think it would be a great idea," said Senator Ball. "I interview this man, this worker on camera and we can show how things here really are not so bad."

"He's not going to say that."

"That's the miracle of film. We edit what he says and make him look like he is saying all positive things. We can make him look like he has deeply reconsidered his stance on Communism and is ready to rejoin America."

"You don't understand, Senator Ball. We don't know that this man ever was a Communist. All Cuban nationals just wound up here."

"That's what makes this a great idea. We can show that our camps have great conditions and that they reform inmates. We show that our system works."

"Then what happens?"

"We let him go. Not unsupervised of course. I could take him back to New York with me. He could reestablish himself in whatever he did before he came here."

"You want to play mother to a Sympathizer."

"But he isn't a Sympathizer. We would be showing our humane side. It would be a great response to people in Europe that are saying we keep political prisoners. I know politics. I know how people think, that's why they sent me here."

"I'll have to call my superiors in Washington of course."

"Of course, " said the Senator. "I wouldn't have it any other way."

• • •

These were the conditions. It was going to be on Patriots' Day August 6, which was Senator Ball's birthday, as well as the anniversary of the Enola Gay dropping the bomb on Hiroshima. Mr. Arnaz Arnaz y de Acha III would be wearing a suit. There would be a large photo of President McCarthy in the background. Something tasteful from his third term. The interview would focus on good things—the chow, the access to TV, the rec room. It would be pointed out that Mr. Arnaz Arnaz y de Acha III not only still had relatives living in Cuba but that his father had actually returned there.

The Pantex management would view it before it aired.

There were five minutes of pleasantries.

Yes the prisoners had cigarettes, TV, pool and chicken fried steak on Fridays. They could grow their own vegetable gardens. They could read the newspaper, get books from the bookmobile, and they were loaded onto the bus to visit the Diary Queen once a month.

It was far, far better than anything they would have got in a Communist country.

Then there was the part that was not aired.

"But you don't understand, Senator, you and I are the same. We just want something better for people like us."

"What do you mean, Mr. Arnaz?"

"We both come from political families. My father was the mayor of Santiago. When the Batista revolution happened in thirty-three, we lost everything. We came here seeking a new life."

"But your father went back to Cuba."

"That was before the problems now. I am an American."

"You were organizing Cubans."

"Yes. To vote. To become citizens. Then one night there is the knock at the door. 'Desi you have some things to explain.' I can't explain my family. I can't explain history. I can explain myself. I am not the evil at the heart of Cuba."

Then it happened and the dam broke. It had been in place for over twelve years, ever since Senator McCarthy's Lincoln Day speech where he revealed he knew of the fifty-seven Communists in the State Department. Congresswoman Ball had heard the echoes of the words, and knew someday they would find out. Someday she would be hung as a witch just like those women from Salem. Somehow her wyrd had been laid down when Charleston had been founded. Somehow it was time for her to hang. She looked at the most beautiful man in the world and said it.

"I can't explain my family either Senor Arnaz. My grandfather was a Communist. He asked me to register once in the Communist party. I did it as a favor to him."

The camera stopped rolling. The lights were shut off. Jess Oppenheimer cleared his throat.

They didn't even let her leave Pantex that night. They put her in a little room with a cot. A bare light bulb hung down and Jess Oppenheimer stood over her. She lay in the same dress as the interview, her makeup not washed off except where her tears had done the job.

"Why did you tell them, Senator?" asked Jess, "If nobody had found out by now, they would have found out. It wasn't your mistake. It was your grandfather's."

"My Grandfather thought it was helping the working man. He didn't know about Stalin and the camps, and look at us, we have camps now."

"You didn't have to say anything. You aren't helping Mr. Arnaz. He was a lost cause the moment he began to complain. You can't help people like him."

"No, I have helped. I will be able to speak until they silence me. I am still the Queen of Television."

"I got a wire. I am not to let you leave. Ever."

"So I disappear here, a little loudmouth among the bog bombs?"

"Yes. I am not supposed to tell you, but I shared a steak with you."

"Will I be kept here for a long time?"

"No. There will be an accident tomorrow."

"Do I get any last requests?"

"Sure, what do you want?"

"One 72 ounce steak dinner and Mr. Arnaz to help me eat it."

He shook his head "no" but headed out of the room. She had given up hope of seeing the man she had so inconveniently fallen in love with, when they called her.

It was nearly midnight. They had put a little table with a clean white table-cloth and nice china and silver on it next to an assembly line. Someone had poured red wine and lit candles. It was Amarillo, Texas so they had iced tea in addition to their wine.

He still wore the suit they had given him for the filming. She had washed her face.

"It's very lovely, " said Mr. Arnaz. "Thank you, Senator."

"You can all me Lucy."

The assembly line began to hum. Desi smiled.

"Do you know what that is?" he asked.

"No, " she said. "They tell me much about the workings of the plant."

"Plutonium enriched parts come by. You don't work in this part of the plant unless you are wearing a heavy lead lined floor length coat. Even then you visit only for brief inspections and they slow down the line as you walk through. But sometimes there are 'accidents.'"

"People trapped in the room getting too much radiation."

"Exactly."

"They run over to those doors that are securely locked."

"They yell a great deal and then they die."

"Let's not do that."

"I agree. So Lucy you've got some 'splain'n to do. Why are you here?"

The parts had begun moving down the line, each sending out an unseen death. They ate with their shrimp, sliced it with their four and half pounds of steak, smashed it into their potatoes, and enjoyed it with their salads. As the machinery grew louder they had a hard time hearing each other, but greater and greater comfort in speaking. They told each other their dreams and secret wishes, stories from their families, and even sang songs. It was as though in a very few hours they lived out an entire married life. They did not waste time on regrets or politics—they knew the unseen clock was ticking, beaming a thousand thousand X-rays of them into space.

He poured wine, and she wished she could have added a trip to the beauty parlor as part of the last meal. She had always wanted to be a blonde or maybe a redhead.

Placa del Fuego
TOBIAS S. BUCKELL

Tiago would normally have taken his cut of the picked pockets and stopped right here at the Seaside Plaza. On the very edge, past the vendors on the cobblestone sea walk, Tiago would sit with his legs over the rocky sea wall and look out over the harbor.

Today he only detoured through the plaza to throw the crowd in between him and the woman chasing him.

He'd gotten a brief glimpse of her before the running started: tall, dark eyes, dark skin, dark leather jacket and microfibre pants, careful dreadlocks pulled back into a pony tail.

She was fast in the crowd. She wasn't dodging around legs, using the ebb and flow of the masses to see open routes like Tiago. No, people who got in her way were just . . . thrown out of the way.

Too strong. She was some sort of soldier, Tiago thought, refocusing ahead.

He might have gotten himself into a bit of a situation.

Slipping onto the seawall path, he sprinted harder, deciding that she was covering the gap in the crowd. To his right the harbor was filled with ships and their cargo, anchored and waiting for a spot to clear on the docks. One of them was throwing out a parasail, the windfoil bucking in the inconsistent harbor wind, but then filling out, rising up into the air hundreds of feet overhead, and then some.

The ship began to pick its way out of the harbor, headed between the tall forest of wind turbines at the harbor's edge: a dangerous move to unleash a windfoil in the harbor, but suddenly Tiago noticed other ships unfurling sails in haste. A cloud of brightly colored parafoils leapt to the harbor sky like butterflies swarming from a shaken limb.

This was worrying enough that Tiago slowed, somewhat, and looked to his left. The warehouses, three and four stories tall, dominated the first row of buildings. But behind them, climbing tenaciously up the side of the mountain, homes and houses colorfully dotted the slopes.

A large, dark mass of gray haze topped the rocky crest and slowly fell down toward the harbor like a heavy cloud.

"Oh shit." Tiago stopped. People in the Plaza were turning too, and mur-

muring started to spread. They stood up from picnics or meals and the edges of the crowd were already leaving.

The woman smacked into Tiago and grabbed his upper arm.

"Take your damn money," Tiago shouted. I don't want it. I'm sorry. Just let me go."

She looked puzzled as he shoved the paper money into the pockets of her jacket. He may have even given her more than he'd stolen, he wasn't sure.

"What's . . . "

Tiago pointed up the mountain. "It's going to rain."

She looked over the buildings and let him go. "I forgot."

Forgot? There were two things on the island to remember: stay out of the rain, and avoid the Doacq's attention by staying inside at night.

He bolted. The last thing he saw was the armada of harbor ships, parafoils all full overhead, pulling their hulls up onto their hydrofoil skids as they all scattered to get well clear of the island.

Then the sirens began to wail all throughout Placa del Fuego, alerting its citizens to the descending danger.

From the open sweep of the docks and seawall of the harbor, Tiago headed into the heart of Harbortown. He could breathe easier seeing overhangs above him, and walls he could put his back to.

People hurried about with carbon-fiber or steel umbrellas. Some had already gotten into their hazmat gear.

The klaxons wailed in the background, constantly blearing out their call for all to find shelter. Shops slammed thick windows shut and bolted them, while people yanked tables and chairs and billboards inside. Customers packed in, shoulder to shoulder.

No self-respecting shop would let Tiago inside: he was an urchin. His clothes were ripped and melted, his face dirty, and he ran on bare feet.

They'd toss him out on his ass faster than he could get inside.

A faint stinging mist started to fill the air. Tiago squinted and slowed down. The unfamiliar would run faster, but then they'd inhale more. He cupped his hands over his mouth, a piece of flannel in between his fingers to filter the air. He looked down at the cobblestoned street to protect his eyes.

His calloused, flattened feet knew the street. Knew how many steps it would take to reach the alley, knew how many times he'd have to pull himself up on the old pipe running outside to get up onto the roof, and how many more steps across the concrete to get to his niche.

It was a spot between two old storage buildings a few streets back from the waterfront, almost near the Xeno-town enclave. One of them had a large, reinforced concrete gutter along its edge, and when the second building had been built right alongside, wall to wall, had left a sheltered ledge the length of the building.

You wouldn't know it to look at it. Twenty street kids had taken bricks and concrete and built a wall along the overhang, blending it into the architecture. It was behind this that Tiago had his very own room.

To get to it, he stepped out over the edge of the building, and behind the wall. Safe.

His skin stung from contact with the mist, but he could sit in the entryway along the corridor leading down to the seven foot by four foot concrete cubicles they called home, and watch the rain.

It was a floating, frothy jelly, spit out from the trees on the island into the air, that slowly floated down. In most cases it just slowly burned at whatever it landed on, like some sort of an acid.

But after that, all it took was a spark for it to ignite.

In the distance the harbor pumps thrummed to life. All over the city the engineers were fighting back the rain with a mist of their own, taken from the harbor water to coat and rinse the harbor.

Usually being on this side of the mountain protected them. But sometimes the wind changed. Sometimes the fire forests were unusually active.

Either way, you didn't want to be outside. The burns and scars on the children huddled around the openings of their sanctuary testified to that.

The steady rain continued, sizzling as it hit the ground outside.

Tiago relaxed in the quiet among his neighbors as the city fought the rain. He could worry about explaining to Kay why he was coming back with no money from the morning's work later, as much as that scared him. For now, he was just happy to be out of the rain.

He just about leapt out of skin as the wall next to him crumpled and the woman who'd been chasing him shoved her way through and crouched in front of him.

"Hello," she said. "We still have business to finish."

Tiago jumped up to run and the other kids moved back away from him.

But where could he go with the rain coming down so hard?

He looked back at his pursuer. The rain had eaten away at the skin on her forearms, exposing silvery metal underneath. Metal pistons snicked as she flexed her fingers.

A cyborg. Here on Placa del Fuego.

Impossible.

There was no advanced machinery on Placa del Fuego. It all failed on the island, until one reached three miles offshore. In Harbortown the sailors said scientists from other worlds clustered aboard large ships near the wormholes, monitoring what islanders called the deadzone and they called 'an unexplained continuous EMP event.' They claimed the epicenter was somewhere deep under the crust of the planet, right under Placa del Fuego.

The wormholes that lead from the ocean around Placa del Fuego to the oceans of other worlds light years away were anchored in the water just on the edge of the deadzone, and the scientists were there to order the wormholes moved as the deadzone expanded slightly each month.

One street rumor said that one of the alien races had buried a device under the island, intending to use it as a cover for a last stand during the human war for independence. Some said it was the Doacq that bought the deadzone with it.

It didn't matter what or who caused it. The end effect was that the town used pneumatic tubes to send messages. Ox-men from Okur pulled rickshaws around, or people used the compressed air powered trolley cars. Everything ran on compressed air: the town's reservoirs were filled by the myriad wind turbines that festooned the harbor entrance and the exposed ridges of the mountain.

But because of the deadzone, this woman shouldn't have been here, Tiago thought. She shouldn't even *work*. But in the cramped darkness of his room the cyborg woman squatted on Tiago's hand-carved wooden stool.

As Tiago turned on a bright white LED lamp she counted off a lot more money than he'd stolen, or given back to her. Bill after bill after bill. A massive fistful. A month's takings.

It hovered between them.

"Before you tagged me and made the pick," she said, "you seemed to know your way around the harbor. I need someone like you."

Tiago took a deep breath. He wasn't sure if he needed someone like her. She was trouble.

The hesitation must have been obvious to her. She smiled. "I'll double what you want."

What was the alternative? Tiago took the money. He'd be a fool not to.

"What are you looking to do?" he asked.

"I need to find the person at the top of the underground. Who sees all and knows all." The cyborg shifted, and the stool creaked. Tiago grimaced. It was made of imported wood, and it was his most precious possession. "I'm looking for Kay."

"Kay?" Tiago feigned confusion.

"You know who I'm talking about," the woman smiled.

He did. He wasn't very good at lying straight-faced. He swallowed nervously. "What do you need from her?"

"I need Kay's help." Tiago waited for more, and the cyborg continued. "To find my grandfather. How do I find this person?"

"You don't find Kay," Tiago said. He folded the money away into the depths of his ragged clothes. "She finds you. Go find yourself a nice room along the waterfront somewhere. Kay will show up now that someone knows you're trying to find her. That's how it works."

"Word on the street." The woman leaned forward and held out her hand. A card rested in her palm. "I'll pay you the other half when I meet Kay. Come find me tomorrow at noon."

Tiago took the card. An address had been scribbled onto it. "What is your name, then?"

"Nashara."

Nashara. A cyborg called Nashara. *The Nashara*? Was he really talking to a living, breathing legend?

Tiago's hands shook.

She was a lot more than just trouble.

He'd gotten himself in way, way deep into something.

Nashara, left, walking out in to the sizzling rain like it was no more than an inconvenience.

It was only a moment before Tiago's neighbors parted and the tiny figure of Kay walked out. Her grey eyes took in the broken brick with a flick before she turned to face him. Her hair was cut just short of her ears, almost boyish. She was shorter than Tiago, something that always surprised him. In his own mind she stood much taller. "I'll have it repaired," she said calmly, flicking her head at the destruction.

Kay's fixing the damage would obligate them to her.

But no one said anything. Refusing it would be an even bigger problem.

They might come to beat him up tonight, Tiago thought. If they weren't too scared.

"You were here the whole time?" Tiago asked, his voice cracking slightly with fear.

Kay ignored his surprise. "That was a Nashara. Here on the island. I wonder how she's able to work here?" Ox-men: two large slabs of hairy muscle, large eyes and flat noses, squeezed into the passageway behind her, stooping over to fit. They regarded Tiago with dull, incurious eyes.

"I don't know . . . " Tiago muttered.

Kay unpacked a Kevlar poncho and pulled it carefully on. She buckled on a gas mask. Behind her, the two Ox-men did the same.

In a muffled voice she told Tiago, "Do you know how expensive it would be to shield someone like her, a cyborg, to be able to function in the deadzone? That must be what she's done. It means she has access to . . . incredible resources." She paused thoughtfully, thinking about that. Then she continued. "I have preparations to make before I'll meet her. Keep your appointment. I'll send someone for you both."

She stepped out into the rain, and the Ox-men followed her. The three of them disappeared over the side of the building in the haze, and Tiago turned around to face the boys trying to hide in the shadows.

He could tell by the fear on their faces that they would not be bothering him.

They were far, far too scared of Kay.

So was he.

• • •

Nashara sat at a table outside a seawall restaurant, surveying the Plaza over a cup of tea. A few small fires had broken out the night before where jellied rain had landed on canopies or abandoned stalls. But considering the strength of last night's storm, it wasn't too bad, Tiago thought. He'd certainly seen worse.

His new benefactor motioned Tiago to sit with her.

"It's odd," she muttered as he sat. "All this stone, brick, slate. Leather for clothes. No wood, no fabrics. Hardly any trees, not even scrub. Grim."

Tiago looked down at his patched clothes. She was surprisingly ignorant about the island if she was the real Nashara. The real Nashara had cloned her own mind to infect alien starships in the fight for human independence. The real Nashara was a founder of the Xenowealth. The real Nashara was a force of nature. That Nashara, it seemed to Tiago, would, at least know about stuff here on the island. "Rich people have them," he said. "In those glass houses."

"Greenhouses?"

Tiago shrugged. "Sure."

Sometimes, in the quieter moments, looking out over the harbor, he'd wondered what the places were like out over the horizon, and through the wormhole the ships sailed through to get to the oceans of other worlds, and through wormholes in those oceans to even more. Other worlds where things were made, and then transported here. Where people like Nashara came from.

But it was useless to daydream too much about where the ships went. Because they weren't taking Tiago along with them. No matter how much he wished for it whenever he sat on the sea wall.

Nashara set her tiny wooden cup down and stood up. "I think Kay will be receiving us now."

Tiago turned around, and the two Ox-men he'd seen last night had silently, amazingly for their bulk, walked up right behind him.

They didn't have to say anything, they turned around and began to walk away. Nashara followed.

And that, he thought, was the end of that.

Only it wasn't.

Up at the end of Onyx street, down the stairs cut into the side of the road and in the basement of an old house tunneled into a rock outcropping at the very edge of town, was one of Kay's many lairs.

He'd been summoned there, two days later.

Amber late-afternoon light pierced the dusty windows, and a menagerie of Placa del Fuego's shadowy denizens milled about. There were more Ox-men, some Runners, and even a few simple-minded Servants. Lots of grubby kids like Tiago, many of them faces he recognized from Elizan's crew crowded in, as well as others from all over the rest of the city. They were Kay's crew, now, all of them. She owned the Waterfront and the Back Ring, and was almost done finishing up controlling the Harbor.

If it was criminal, and happened in Placa del Fuego, Kay wanted to run it.

It had been different, last year. Last year Tiago worked for Elizan; a high strung old man who would leap at a chance to whip anyone who'd held back the take.

A tough life: Tiago still had misshapen broken bones to prove it, but it beat trying to live outside alone. Something he'd learned quickly enough.

Placa del Fuego had no heart for the homeless.

When Kay appeared on the streets in the Back Ring, rain-burned and tired, she'd been ignored. For the first week. The second week she'd figured out the command structure of one of the drug cartels and executed the commander with a sliver of knapped flint.

Within days the cartel danced to her tune.

Rumors said she came from Okur, where the birdlike alien Nesaru had established a colony. Under the Bacigalupi Doctrine, anticipating the lack of fuel and the collapse of the interstellar travel after the war for independence, the Nesaru had bred humans into a variety of forms to serve them. Nesaru engineered, bred, and reshaped human Ox-men and Runners had fled Okur to Placa del Fuego. So had Kay.

She was something else, Okur refugees said. Something designed to control the modified human slaves under the Nesaru's thumb. She could read your thoughts by the slightest change in your posture, a twitch in a facial muscle. She emitted pheromones to calm you, convince you, and used her body to control your personal space.

You were a computer, waiting to be programmed. She was your taskmaster. A perfect, bred, engineered, manipulator of humankind.

"Tiago," Kay said, beckoning him closer. "Nashara and I have quite a job for you."

Nashara stepped out from behind a thick stone pillar. "There will be considerably more money in it for you."

Kay put a protective arm around Tiago. "I really need your help with this, Tiago."

He stiffened slightly as she moved in closer, creating a tiny world between just the three of them. "What do you need?" he asked, hesitant.

"You keep a low profile, Tiago. Back of the crowd. You don't try to cheat me of my cut. You wouldn't even dare think of it."

Tiago nodded. Don't get noticed. Don't cross dangerous people like Kay unless you could run. Melt into the background. These were core life principles of his. It was why he made a good pickpocket. There was even a mid-sized bounty available for his capture.

"More importantly, you've been in the Dekkan Holding Center," Nashara said. In the distant background the sound of rain alarms drifted through the streets. A night storm. The worst kind.

A cold chill gripped Tiago. "You want me to go back to The Center?" Images of the dark warrens flitted back to the front of his mind.

"Not as such." Kay pointed a Kevlar poncho and gas mask hanging by the door. "Suit up."

They walked through the slowly darkening streets, the rain hissing against their protective gear. Nashara wore goggles and a long leather fisherman's coat that seemed impervious to the rain, Kay the same outfit as Tiago.

Their footsteps clicked against cobblestone as Kay led them through sidealleys and tiny backstreets so cramped they had to move through them single file.

No one else was out.

Tiago stopped a tremble in his hands at the thought of being out at night.

Several times they came to dead ends, where small locked doors stopped Kay's progress. But a few knocks in a pattern and they would open, and the trio would tromp through someone's front room, leaving sizzling drops of rain behind.

There was no hurry, and Tiago gauged that they'd moved across the entire city over the last two hours.

Kay finally stopped and removed her gas mask in the quiet foyer of a restaurant, eerie in its empty state, though the tables were all set and ready: waiting for the morning crowd. She looked right at Tiago as he removed his mask. He burned his fingers on the wet straps as she said, "I'm turning you over to the warden of the DHC for the bounty. The driver of the prison wagon has been paid to suggest stopping to pick you up."

He felt numb. Outside, Tiago saw through the windows, the rain had fallen to a drizzle. The gaslight streetlamps flickered shadows as the wind flicked their flames this way and that.

"So you *do* want me back in the hellhole," he said, the misery leaking out into his voice.

Kay pulled out a packet of photos and spread them with a flourish across a nearby table like a card dealer. "No. You'll get picked up, but there's someone inside the wagon that Nashara wants."

Tiago frowned. Kay was helping Nashara why? He couldn't quite put together what was happening here.

Kay leaned close. She was doing it, creating that little bubble of space that seemed to exist just between the two of them. It was some sort of talent, almost magical. "Don't try to figure it out, Tiago. Just take a look at the pictures of the crew of the *Zephyr III*. One of them will be in the wagon. We need your help."

He looked up and out of the bay windows. He wondered how far he could get if just ran. He had some money, maybe he could stowaway on a boat.

How long could he evade Kay?

Not very long.

She gently grabbed his jaw to point his gaze back down at the table. She'd read his thoughts via his body language. "There's no running, Tiago. Not now."

He swallowed and committed the faces before him to memory, something other than fear building as she put a hand on his back to steady him.

"I'll be there as well," Nashara said from by the door. She'd opened her coat up, and underneath Tiago saw more guns lining the inside than he'd even known a single person could carry. She was a walking arsenal. You rarely saw any guns on the island, too expensive, even for criminals.

"So why don't you just break into the wagon and get the person you want?" Tiago asked.

"Don't want to tip my hand until we know we have the person we want. Otherwise, if we go in too early guns blazing on the wrong wagon, our guy could get hidden further, or put under tougher security. So you're our scout, Tiago. When you give us the go ahead, we move in to recover both of you."

"And if the person isn't there, I get beaten, interrogated, and locked up."

"We will get you out quickly if that happens, we can bribe a few judges, and Nashara is ready to pay you well," Kay said. She was pulling on her poncho. Before she snapped on the bug-like gasmask, she continued. "I have to go meet the wagon. I'll be back shortly."

This was his moment to bolt.

Nashara picked up the pictures of the crew. "Three weeks ago. You remember anything strange happening?"

Tiago stopped thinking about other lives and worlds. "There was a fight. At night. All over the town. Whoever it was burst through walls, fell through roofs. Ripped up road. No one saw much of it. We just saw the damage . . . "

"It was my grandfather: Pepper was on his way back with information about a new threat to the Xenowealth worlds. He disappeared here, last seen getting aboard the *Zephyr III*. But the *Zephyr* was destroyed in a limited yield nuclear blast event nowhere near any of the wormholes out, but a hundred miles north of here in the polar ocean.

"Word is that one survivor from the *Zephyr III* came back. You're going to help me acquire him. I came with a ship, it's pretty heavily armed up: the *Streuner*. Pepper didn't have backup, I'm not making the same mistake. Once we're on the ship, it's a run for the wormhole, back into the heart of the Xenowealth, for debriefing."

Acquire him. There was a strange turn of a word, Tiago thought. She was a kindred soul to Kay. Someone who wove the fate of everyone around them.

He was just a pickpocket. It was all he ever really aspired to. His own quiet moments on the seawall, a safe, dry place to sleep. Good food.

Now he was caught up in something that involved the fates of the connected worlds.

"What does Kay get out of it?" Tiago asked, treading into areas which he knew he shouldn't be poking his nose.

Nashara tapped the inside of her coat, and the guns jiggled. "Force multipliers."

"You know what she'll do with all that?"

Nashara nodded, her dreadlocks shaking as she did so. "She plans to run the island."

"She will."

"Maybe. But only if she stops depending brazenly on those modifications the Nesaru bred into her." She smiled at Tiago's shock that she knew about that rumor. "You're an open book to her. And she holds your strings. But only when she's standing in front of you. She has to learn other ways to get people to do her bidding, and her teachers have been the underbelly of Harbortown. To be a great leader requires more, it requires people to trust you just as much when you're not standing right in front of them. That takes something else. Besides, what she has: it's not that special a talent."

"Do you have it?"

"Yes. Different technology, not biological, but same result. But Tiago, free will's a bitch. Kay can only manipulate. Underneath, we still move our own lives forward. You understand? We fought the entire war over that, back when the Satrapy ruled everything. Before human independence."

Only someone as powerful as she was, Tiago thought, could believe that about free will.

He chose not to say that.

But then, she could probably see him thinking that anyway.

"Here." Nashara pressed a small sliver of metal into his palm. "Jam that under the target's skin, it'll tag him for me and let us know to come get you both."

"Okay." He'd have to keep this out of the cops' hands. Easy enough. He'd snuck small items around the heavy security of The Center.

Outside the loud hiss of a compressed air powered wagon drew closer, and then it stopped. Nashara pulled a large pistol out and aimed it cheerfully at Tiago's head. "Time to turn you in, Tiago."

Tiago had sworn many oaths to never end back up in one of these wagons. Yet here he was again. It was near midnight as they jerked into motion with a belch. Tiago looked around. Unfamiliar, bruised, battered faces regarded him.

For a moment he panicked, not seeing any of the faces from the pictures Kay had shown him. He imagined getting locked away in the sweaty man-made caverns underneath Harbor Town.

Then he saw the youngest face in the wagon and recognized it from the photos he'd been shown of the crew of the *Zephyr III*. It was just a boy. A boy who was younger than Tiago.

Could he drag him into the net Kay and Nashara had cast?

Yes. The boy was already caught up in the mess from being on the same boat as Nashara's grandfather.

Tiago stood up, tripped, caught himself, and then sat down near the locked rear door.

The boy hadn't even felt the pinprick of Nashara's tiny device.

Tiago waited, tensed, for something, anything, to happen.

The wagon rolled on, turning a corner, headlights revealing ten Ox-men blocking the road with spike strips. The wheels of the wagon exploded as they were shredded, and it rattled to a halt on the rims as prisoners in back were thrown against each other.

Nashara landed on the ground outside. She must have leapt off the top of a building nearby, Tiago realized, as pulverized cobblestone leapt into the air from her impact.

She ripped the door open, shattering the lock, and reached in to pull the boy out. Tiago jumped out next to them.

Three Ox-men ran into the alleyway, eyes wide with fear. "Doacq," one shouted in a low rumble.

Nashara looked down the road. "Tiago, what the hell is that?"

Tiago didn't need to glance a second time. "Oh shit. Shit! The Doacq. We need to get out of here. Now!"

The seven foot tall, hooded figure moved with unnatural quickness down the street. Tiago caught a glimpse, in the flicker of gaslamp, of two large, catlike eyes under the cowl and a slit-like nose.

But it was the mouth that he noticed most. It yawned, the jaw dislocating and stretching like a snake's: a two foot gaping chase of darkness.

The Doacq whipped across the street, slamming into an Ox-man. The jaw dropped even lower, and the Doacq rose taller, somehow, and then the gaping maw descended on the Ox-man.

Hundreds of pounds of rippling, engineered, brute strength disappeared, and the Doacq turned to face the wagon.

"That's a damn wormhole in its mouth," Nashara said, awe in her voice. Then she grabbed the side of the wagon and grunted. "And it's generating an EMP field . . . "

The Doacq flowed forward, the robe rippling in the slight wind. The massive jaw gaped wider and wider as it got closer. It seemed all maw to Tiago, mesmerized by the black nothingness opening up, propelled by the creature's feet.

Nashara pulled out a large shotgun, and the deafening discharge filled the tiny stone canyon of street and houses. The Doacq twitched to face the incoming shot . . . and swallowed it all without any change in its approach.

"Son of a bitch," she said, and then leapt forward. The Doacq, ducked and grabbed her, redirecting the energy of the jump to throw her in the side of a house.

Nashara staggered back to her feet in the middle a mess of rubble.

Tiago grabbed the boy and looked around for a place to hide. One of the nearest doors opened, and whip-lean shape of a Runner beckoned at him to get inside.

He needed no encouraging. He ran for the door.

Three explosions shook the street, and Tiago saw with a glance back that Nashara had flicked grenades at the Doacq. It swallowed several, but couldn't be in more than one place at the same time.

Another grenade exploded to its side, and the Doacq faltered. Shreds of its cloak and flesh splattered on the ground and an animal-like shriek of pain filled the streets.

The Doacq was not supernatural, Tiago thought, dazed. It could be harmed. He paused at the doorway. Maybe Nashara could face it down.

But then the Doacq spotted him, and turned for the building, completely ignoring Nashara.

An Ox-man yanked Tiago into the house and barred the door shut. "This way," the Ox-man grumbled, and shoved the two boys forward through the house.

A trapdoor underneath a table led them under the house, into a hidden basement lit by a single bulb.

"Through here," said a Runner, appearing out of the dark. The shadows made his ribs, visible under a thin shirt, look even more pronounced than normal.

There was heavy, thick steel door a pair of Ox-men had opened. As they passed through that, they groaned shut, and then dropped to the ground as something was kicked out from underneath them. The smell or rank sewage took the breath away from Tiago, and he switched to breathing only out of his mouth.

In the distance, and explosion of brick and screaming startled Tiago. The Doacq must have gotten into the house. With Nashara in pursuit.

They were standing inside a tunnel, lit glancingly by the Runner's flashlight. The center of the tunnel had a wide trench in it, currently dry.

It revealed Kay waiting with a pair of Ox-men armed with RPGs. They aimed the weapons at the thick door behind Tiago.

"So this is our quarry," Kay said, turning on a small penlight to check the boy. "Your name is June, right?"

The shellshocked, beaten boy nodded.

"Can you speak, June?"

"Yes." It was a faint whisper, unsure of itself. But it was the most June had done since this had all started, other than let Tiago drag him around to safety.

"Well June, this is Tiago, and we have to move quickly before the Doacq comes after us. It likes characters like us. It finds us interesting."

Kay led them down the gentle slope of the tunnel at a brisk pace to a junction, where the sound of running water filled the air, and the stench increased.

Five Ox-men stood in a trench full of dirty water holding onto a small metal boat with an electric engine on the back.

Something boomed in the distance, echoing through the sewer tunnels, as they clambered in.

Kay smiled. "That should slow the Doacq down." She waved her hand at the Ox-men and they let go. She gunned the engine up to a brisk whine as the boat shot clear, bouncing off the sides of the trench.

Tiago had a moment to absorb everything now. He turned to Kay. "All this preparation. You knew the Doacq was coming? How?"

"He always comes when there's this much activity," Kay said. "And he's difficult to stop. I thought maybe he was allergic to the sun, but he shrugged off the ultraviolet and full spectrum lamps I installed on his favorite haunts. Since then, it's gotten harder and harder to hunt. I can't even get a good picture of it, cameras fail around it."

Tiago felt like he was looking at a different person. "How can you know so much about the Doacq?" Most of the town didn't even talk about it, they whispered about it and avoided the night. When people disappeared, you didn't dwell on it. You knocked on wood that you would never be the one to turn a corner, and see the Doacq standing there.

"You hunt the Doacq?" Tiago asked.

She heard the stunned disbelief in his voice and turned on him. "It's an alien. It's not some supernatural creature, Tiago. It's like the Nesaru, just more powerful. We don't know where it comes from, but just like the other aliens, it plays on human land as if it owns it. It thinks it rules us, but it doesn't!"

There was a hatred in her face, naked for the two boys to see. She'd let her control slip. "I will destroy it. And then I will take the island. And after that, I will make the Nesaru leave, and the Gahe, and the other stinking aliens that have kept us under their thumb flock through here. Pepper may have failed to kill the Doacq for me, Nashara may fail yet, but I won't."

She turned down another tunnel as Tiago bent over and grabbed his knees. This was insane. They were up against the Doacq?

"You did good, Tiago," Kay said, her face under control again. "You got her to chase you, despite the rain incident. You got her to invest in you, to want to protect you, just enough that instead of grabbing June and running back to her ship, she decided to tackle the Doacq. It was perfect. You have a place among my lieutenants, a place on this island, Tiago. You did well."

He didn't feel like it.

Things had gotten complicated quickly. He hadn't intended the mark to be a living legend.

He certainly hadn't expected to be involved in the betrayal of a living legend.

Tiago shivered.

Kay had a safe house set up for them. It took getting out of the sewers and back onto the streets, through the alleys and people's homes again. By the time they got inside, Tiago couldn't tell where in Harbor Town he was. They'd doubled back, and around, and it was so late it was now probably officially early. His eyes were scratchy, his movements felt like they were delayed by a half second.

"Don't worry," Kay told him as she took their protective gear. "You'll be safe here. There are people for the Doacq to catch. He'll eventually slow down, turn his attention elsewhere. It's all planned."

It didn't make Tiago feel any better. He caught the eyes of June, and the other boy certainly didn't look reassured either.

But Kay caught that. And she spent time with them until they were mollified, and relaxed. There were Ox-men guarding the house, equipped with heavy machine guns, and escape routes everywhere.

A tall man came in with cold water and sandwiches. Somehow getting something in his stomach took the edge of Tiago's fears.

Maybe it was just having something to do.

"There is more I have to do," Kay said. "The caches of arms Nashara promised me need swept up and stored in secure locations. And eventually, I need to see who won."

She left the room, five foot figure flanked by a pair Ox-men.

June stopped eating. "Do you trust her?" He asked.

Tiago looked up and wanted to say he did, but the words caught in his mouth. "I don't know. She's dangerous to cross."

June gestured at his face. "As dangerous as this?"

"Yes."

"Then I don't want to have anything to do with her," he said. "I've had enough."

The boy looked exhausted.

"I'm sorry," Tiago muttered. "I'm very sorry. I thought you would be going with Nashara."

"The woman?"

"She's looking for someone called Pepper. She says he's her grandfather. She thinks you know . . . "

"They all do." June looked down at the remains of his sandwich. "He was okay. I liked him. He paid us in gold to get him out of here, but there were ships waiting for us between the wormholes out and the island.

"He fought them off, and then when he realized we were in danger, jumped into the ocean and sank. Didn't stop them from sinking the *Zephyr III* anyway. They killed everyone but me. Dragged me out of the ocean and took me back, forced me to tell them everything he did, or said."

Tiago wrapped his arms around himself and leaned forward.

The Doacq was hunting them. Nashara may not even be alive, a victim to Kay's machinations, just like Pepper.

And what was he? If she could throw their lives away so easily, what chance did he have of living if he moved closer into Kay's world?

He thought of the contact, the compulsion he had to do what she wanted. It came from her voice, her posture, the way she could read him. And it wasn't real.

With her out of the room, he could struggle away, couldn't he? All that was left was his fear. Fear of consequences.

Fear that she would track him down for betraying her.

"She has a ship, an armed ship, she said, waiting for her. It's called . . . the *Strainer,* or something like that," Tiago said in a tumble of words. And then he said something he never would have, had he been doing this for Kay. "If you want, we can try to run for it."

June didn't even pause to think about it. "Yes. I'd run with you."

"I could be trying to trick you," Tiago said.

"I don't care. I'll take the chance. I don't want to be trapped here, I don't want to get eaten by the Doacq."

Tiago found himself nodding with June.

"We leave the moment we see morning," Tiago said.

"So you can spot rain?" It'd be suicidal to try and move through the city without any rain gear. And if he couldn't see the rain coming, he wouldn't know to hide from it.

"Yes. Do you have any family?"

June shook his head. "No. They're dead now."

Tiago did not follow that up with more questions. He didn't want to know.

The Ox-men guarding them checked on them randomly. The moment the door closed, the early sun lighting a band of orange up over the rooftops, Tiago broke the locked windows open. There were other skills he'd picked up in addition to picking pockets.

June started to climb down the side, but Tiago shook his head. "Go up, to the roof. They'll expect us on the street." The Runners and Ox-men would fan out down there, hunting them.

Rooftop to rooftop would keep them out of sight for longer.

Once up there, Tiago oriented himself. They were closer to the docks than he'd dared hope.

They stuck to the roofs, clambering awkwardly up drain spouts and slipping on tiles. But they made it to the edge of the plaza after an exhausting hour.

The docks ran out from the seawall, long piers of concrete stacked with unloaded goods and Ox-men hauling carts back and forth.

It wasn't until they'd walked through the crowds of the plaza, and then up onto the seawall, that Tiago relaxed a little. The Ox-men guarding them would have called the alarm by now, phoned Kay, and the entire town might be crawling with people hunting for them, but they'd at least gotten to the docks.

Tiago stopped a dock worker in greasy coveralls overseeing the unloading of a ship docked almost by the seawall. "We're looking for a ship called *Strainer,* have you seen it?"

The man frowned. "*Streuner*? It's over there."

Tiago looked. It was a gun-metal gray boat with a large green flag with a black and yellow X on it.

June yanked Tiago around to face the plaza behind them. The hooded figure of the Doacq stood at the far side, people scattering away from it.

"I don't think it . . . " Tiago started to say, as the Doacq looked over the top of the crowd right at them, and began to move toward them. "Shit."

"But it doesn't come out in the day," June said, his voice breaking with fear.

Kay had said it seemed to choose the night. That her lights replicating daylight hadn't harmed it. He shouldn't have been surprised. But he was. From across the plaza Tiago could see the unnaturally long jaw dislocated and drop, down past the alien's chest, down almost to its feet. Anything that stood in the way disappeared into it: scared people, tables, chairs. It swallowed them all.

Tiago and June turned and sprinted for the dock leading to *Streuner*. An act of faith that they could protect them, really, but what else could they do?

They shoved people aside as they ran the slow curve, ignoring the curses aimed in their direction.

When they turned onto the dock and sprinted, Tiago looked over at the seawall. The Doacq barreled along it.

He realized he was screaming as he ran. Dockworkers were turning to look, and then jumping into the water as they realized it was the Doacq.

It gained on them. They had half the dock before they could reach the *Streuner,* and the Doacq was coming up the dock, may three hundred feet behind them.

Tiago knew he shouldn't look over his shoulder, it slowed him down, but he couldn't help it.

The dark pit of its maw was so *wide* and inescapable, ready to swallow them, the pier, and anything else.

As to where people ended up when it got them, only those swallowed knew, and they'd never come back to talk.

Tiago realized he was about to find out. He wasn't going to make it to the end of the dock, where the *Streuner* waited. Maybe even if they made it, they'd still be swallowed up.

Maybe it could eat the whole boat.

He glanced back over his shoulder, and as he did so, a loud boom came from the end of the dock. Something *large* whipped past his had, and the Doacq staggered and fell.

Its mouth dipped, hitting the concrete of the dock and swallowing a scoop of it, concrete chipping around the edges of its mouth.

Another boom stopped it as it struggled up to its feet again.

Tiago redoubled his run, as did June. He ran so hard it felt like his joints would pop, his brain would be jarred free of his skull, and his lungs would burst into flames.

As they moved clear, the booms turned into an all-out barrage. Continuous thunder rolled from the ship, bursting out from large guns that had rolled out of emplacements all over the ship.

His eardrums stopped trying to understand the deafening sound as the entire section of the dock under the Doacq disappeared.

The Doacq had picked the wrong ship to run at.

Two dark-skinned crewmen, just like Nashara, held out their hands at the top of the plank leading on to the deck. Tiago sprinted into them, knocking them over and collapsing, panting, amazed to still be alive.

"Cast off!" Someone yelled, and the plank was tossed free. From his viewpoint on the deck, Tiago saw a tiny rocket shoot up several hundred feet into the sky, dragging a length of parafoil with it.

The foil expanded, filled with air, and the ship began to move.

A pair of feet in familiar boots stopped in front of Tiago's face. He looked up. It was Nashara. She moved slowly, with a slight limp, and wore a patch over one eye. Her hair had been burned off, and one arm was in a sling.

She kneeled and grabbed his hand and said something, but he couldn't hear it through the ringing in his ears because the guns still hadn't stopped: *Streuner* shivered constantly as it continued firing on the Doacq as they moved away from the dock. Slowly, at first, but then the ship built a bow wave as it sped up.

A few minutes later the entire ship slowly struggled up onto the hydrofoils underneath its hull, and it popped free of the resistance of pushing against water.

They sped away from the docks, the deck tilting alarmingly as the *Streuner* turned hard toward the open sea.

The alien Doacq was falling further away from Tiago with each minute. So was Kay.

June was still in a room being checked over for injuries, but Tiago was allowed to wander around inside the ship. There were crew cabins, a kitchen, storage rooms, a common sitting area.

Nashara sat there, playing with a small piece of paper. She kept folding it until she had turned it into a tiny flower.

"She sent me to pick your pocket," Tiago confessed, standing at the table. He'd expected the boat to sway more than it did, but the foils kept it almost rock steady. "It was a trap from the beginning. And I'm sorry."

She looked up at him with one eye, and Tiago flinched. What would he do to someone who'd cost him an eye? What would someone as powerful as Kay do?

"I knew it was a trap," Nashara said. "What I wasn't expecting was the Doacq."

"You?" He found that hard to believe, knowing the things Nashara had seen and participated in.

Nashara shook her head. "It's a massive universe, Tiago, with many participants. The Doacq's an important force, and I'm not sure what it's up to. We need to find Pepper, if we can, if he's still alive. If June can help. Maybe together we can find some answers, find out if the Doacq is a threat to us. But Tiago, I'm just tiny player on the edge of some large events. I don't know half of everything. The universe is not tidy. You don't always get quick answers."

It was a sentiment that Tiago felt a kinship to. She felt just like him. Navigating her way through all this just as best she could.

But then that raised his suspicions.

"Are you saying that just to make me feel better?" He asked. "Do you rule me know, like Kay?"

If she had the same talents, why not?

"I mean, if I'm your pawn, you seem calmer than Kay," he continued. "She isn't just someone organizing street kids, protection setups, scams. Not anymore. Now she's just using us up like our lives don't even mean anything."

Outside the ship slowed, hydrofoils sinking deeper into the water until the hull hit water.

Nashara crushed the little paper bird into a wad. "Sometimes we become the thing we're fighting hardest against," she said thoughtfully. "And Kay is fighting hard against an unimaginable past on Okur. I was there, once. I've seen what she came from. I don't think she will stop fighting it for quite a while."

Tiago thought about Placa del Fuego, caught between the forces of Kay and the Doacq, and wondered if the island would survive the both of them. "She said she'd rule the island."

"And maybe more, no doubt," Nashara said. Then something strange happened, a fluttering sensation in the deepest pit of Tiago's stomach that left him suddenly dizzy. Nashara stood up and grabbed his shoulder. "Come, Tiago, I want to show you something."

She led him out onto the rear deck of the ship, which was dominated by the black nothingness of a wormhole.

Tiago gasped. He'd never seen one this close, towering over his head. Large enough for a whole ship to pass through and that had once floated above a world. Spaceships had once passed through it before being deorbited.

And now him.

The sky overhead was covered by a dark, orange cloud in outer space, whisps of it streaming off toward the horizon. And cutting the sky in half: a silver twinkling band. The Belt of Arkand. He'd heard it mentioned by sailors, and here he stood looking at it with his own eyes.

"You asked if I made you do this," Nashara said. "But this was your own choice. I didn't make you do it. This is your new life now."

But was it the right choice?

He looked around at the strange sea they plowed through, and saw another wormhole far ahead in the distance, propped on floats and bobbing on the surface of the green ocean. That wormhole led to yet another ocean, and more worlds.

More possibilities.

Maybe not the right choice. Only time would tell that. But it was certainly his choice, he knew, leaving all those years of sitting on the sea wall and dreaming behind for a chance just like this.

Herding Vegetable Sheep
EKATERINA SEDIA

I herd the clouds as I do every day. Their ghostly protuberances wrap around the wings of the plane, obscuring the blue AOL logo with their wispy fingers, and then retreat under the stream of air from the props, swirling and compacting into tight white formations that remind me of those queer plants—what were they called? Vegetable sheep. I've seen them on my vacation in New Zealand, years ago, when there was a New Zealand. These plants are related to daisies, the tour guide said. It was hard to believe that.

I watch the columns of numbers that scroll across my retinal implant, with an occasional commercial interruption from my employer, only nowadays they call them 'congressional communiqués'. I suppose they are. I wish I could save them to reread them later, but preserving such trivia is not worth getting arrested for.

The clouds swirl, tighter and snugger, their color deepening into grey, and my plane circles them this way and that, herding them together, making them coalesce like vegetable sheep in the New Zealand mountains. The plane growls like a sheep dog, and the clouds gain mass and finally weep. I circle them again, strangely uneasy about their watery release. Rain is good, I remind myself. Rain is power, rain is electricity, rain is new juice in the batteries.

The radio implant buzzes and I wince.

"Anita," it says, and for a moment I believe it is speaking to me—the radio, I mean, not just the person on the other end. The illusion fades. "You better come down—you're running low."

"Okay," I say. "I was just about to." I touch the pads and spiral downwards, like a falling leaf, with grace and dignity.

It is raining hard when I land, the black wings of the generator's membranes thrumming, vibrating up and down, giving birth to electricity that feeds the city around it. It is like a giant diaphragm, its undulations under the insistent drumming of the raindrops betraying its thoughts to the world. The Greeks used to think that the diaphragm's movement generated thoughts, and I am almost ready to believe that. The membrane thrums, its dark thoughts enveloping the city with fog. I glance at the time indicator of my heads-up display and rush away from the airfield, through the iron gates of the energy factory. I am running late.

The rain is pouring now, and my yellow slicker caves under the coalescing and dividing rivulets of rainwater, presses against my shirt, cooling my skin, crushing my chest with its weight. It is hard to breathe underwater. I cross the streets, knocking over the mushroom caps that have colonized every sidewalk and almost skid on the patch of green algae, camouflaged treacherously between the white stripes of the pedestrian crossing, but right myself. I have an appointment to keep. I enter the cafe, and wedge my body into a narrow booth, and look out of the window until a tall mermaid-like shape swims from out of the rain. My granddaughter.

"Hi, Anita," says the girl as she slides sideways into the booth, keeping her head down, as if afraid that someone would recognize her. She *is* afraid that someone would recognize her, I think. This is why she never calls me grandma.

"Hi, baby. Does your mother know you're here?"

She scoffs. "I'm not a baby, Anita."

I know that. I just want to find out if my daughter ever asks about me.

She softens, and smiles at the waiter who brings us a pitcher of cold water. "We'll need another minute," she tells him, her eyes green and vacant, like those of a cat. New contacts, I guess. Then she turns those hollow eyes at me. "I wanted to talk to you, Anita," she says in a caring voice. As if she's the grown up.

I nod. "Go ahead, Ilona." I know what she's going to say.

She leans in, her narrow palm pressed against the plastic of the table between us. "How old are you, Anita?"

"Sixty-eight."

"It shows."

We stare at each other, not blinking, and under her gaze I feel every blemish and wrinkle pucker up, turn purple, leer.

"I don't mean to be cruel," she says, "but you don't have to look this way."

"I know." *If I change, will you be less embarrassed of being seen with me?* "I'll think about it."

"There's nothing to think about," she says with a beam of confidence only pretty teenage girls can muster, and starts flipping through her menu.

I do the same, all the while wondering why am I not ashamed of my face? Instead, I cringe at the thought of my optimized heart and metal joints, of my eyes that can see so well because of lasers, of my new healthy lungs. I can only bear these artifices within me because my old skin is covering them up. I could not imagine separating from it. But the love, the love . . . my eyes skim over the lines in front of me, as I imagine what it would be like to have my daughter back, my granddaughter not ashamed.

My granddaughter looks up and frowns. She pulls out a handkerchief tucked in her wristband, spits in it, and rubs my cheek, as intrusive and unselfconscious as a parent with her child. I submit. She looks at the handkerchief, incredulous. "What's that?"

It's a green smudge. "Algae," I say. "They grow everywhere."

"On your face?" She doesn't bother to hide her disgust.

"It's even wetter up in the clouds," I say. "They look like vegetable sheep from up there. You should—"

She interrupts. "Vegetable sheep?"

"Big white and grey cushions—millions of tiny plants wedged together, all the same height. They grow high up in the mountains, where it's cold. If one grows taller than the others, it dies of frostbite." I'm not making sense, and I change the subject. "Anyway. How're things at school?"

"Boring." She gives a little laugh. "I can't wait until I'm out of there."

"Why do you think it'll be better once you're out?"

She jerks her shoulder and gives me a smoldering look. "Oh, don't start. Just 'cause you're depressed, doesn't mean everyone else has to be too."

"Sorry," I whisper. I am.

"We're ready to order," she tells the waiter who's been hovering nearby. After he departs, she gives me a cheerful smile. "You'll feel better once you get your face fixed up."

Beauty is fleeting, I want to say, but think better of it. "It's good to see you, sweetie. Everything will be okay."

At night, I lie awake listening to the rain's whisper outside, thinking of love. I believe it is my failure that my daughter would not talk to me, and my grand-daughter treats me as a child. I wish I knew how to fix it, how to fit into the snug world of the people I care about. Instead, I leave them behind, on the ground, as my plane sputters and spits jets of dust into too-warm, moist air. I don't just herd clouds, I make them on occasion. The dust is called 'condensa-tion nuclei', but they're just dust. Tiny grains lodging under my fingernails and making me cough, the grains that already cost me a pair of lungs. I don't really mind, as long as they make clouds appear out of thin, over-saturated air. I wish I could show my granddaughter that, and perhaps she would love them as much as I do, and by extension love me. I almost weep with joy when the morning comes, grey, weeping along with me.

At the factory, I flash my badge at the security guard, who nods back—a sad little ritual we exchange for the past forty years. I don't give him a second look—my gaze travels past the undulating membranes toward the airfield.

"Wait," he calls. "I have something for you."

I open the manila envelope he gives me, with a panicked strumming of the heart against its cage. *This is it,* I think. *They are finally going to let me go.*

"Some girl dropped it off this morning," the guard says.

I shield the piece of paper with the envelope, and the raindrops splash and slide down the smooth yellow surface. It's just some photographs. I look closer, and my frantic heart seizes up: it is a picture of the vegetable sheep—just like I remember them, white, snug, content. There's a close up of one, and on the next frame there's a bird's eye view of them, scattering in groups and solitarily across the green mountains. I swallow hard.

"A pretty girl," the guard says. "Didn't tell her name or anything, just that you'd know."

"That's my granddaughter," I say, and turn away, stuffing the pictures back into the envelope, to hide them from moisture.

I wonder where she got them as I walk to my plane. There are none on the govnet, just like there is nothing there that would remind us that there is a world outside of our shrinking rainy continent. There are no kangaroos, Coliseum, Aegean Sea, or Sahara. Things she will never know about; yet, she found me the vegetable sheep. I am grateful, and surprised, and a bit sad that I have underestimated her.

The plane rises, and there are almost no clouds. I find a pocket of wet, warm air—I don't need the sensors to tell me that, I can see the way it shimmers—and turn on my dust cannons on full blast. At first, there are only streams of grey refuse, but then, without warning, a thick fog condenses into white tufts, and soon there are enough of them to nudge gently with the jets of air, until they are compact and round. I pull the pictures out of the envelope and spread them across the seat next to me. I cannot wait to see her, to tell her how much those clouds trapped among the green mountains mean to me.

I never get a chance. I call her as soon as I land, from the soaked airfield. She does not answer her phone, even though I know she never detaches it from her ear. I am starting to worry, but then my ear-piece buzzes.

"Baby," I say, "are you all right?"

There's sobbing, and it's not Ilona. "Anita?" Finally, in a halting, hoarse voice. It is my daughter.

"Petra," I whisper. "Are you all right?"

"I'm fine. But Ilona's missing."

I count breaths. The joy of hearing my daughter's voice is dissolved in her tears, and I don't know what to say.

"Will you help me find her?"

"Of course."

"Can you come over?"

Of course I can. She lives too far to walk, and I grab the first velorickshaw who idles by the gates of the factory, waiting for the pilots and the engineers to leave for the day. I settle into the rickety, leaking cab, and think, trying to ignore the water splashing in my face with every turn of the rickshaw's feet on the pedals.

I think of what I can do—the friends to talk to, the old favors to call on. I'm not like Petra, who—I can feel it, I know—is sitting in her kitchen, crying, tearing her heart out imagining every pain, every violation that Ilona could've suffered. She's always been too quick to grieve.

She left the door unlocked, and I find her in the kitchen, her shoulders heaving.

"Petra."

She flings herself into my arms, with a fierceness of one who missed comfort.

I stroke her hair, dyed deep auburn. "Calm down. It's not that bad. When did she disappear?"

"She didn't come home from school."

"Maybe she's with some friends." Even I know it's a lie; another teenager might run off, but not dutiful Ilona, who took it on her thin shoulders to be the link between me and her mother, the only one who was young enough to not be burdened by old hurts.

Petra doesn't even bother to argue. "I called the police, and they said they'll look into it. They don't return my calls."

This is bad. "I'll call Jeremy," I tell her. "Blow your nose and make me some tea."

She nods, and fusses with the kettle. If she were younger, she would've blamed me for everything.

I call Jeremy. He's a cop and a good friend, and Petra hates him. But not today.

"I need a favor," I tell him. "My granddaughter's missing."

He doesn't seem surprised. "Can't help you," he says, and lowers his voice. "This is Federal jurisdiction."

"BLIPs?" I see Petra flinch, and lower my voice. "What did the kid do?"

"Downloading and distribution of copyrighted materials."

I think of the pictures in my plane. Vegetable sheep, so harmless. Who would've thought that the Bureau of Licensing and Intellectual Property would be interested in a sixteen-year-old kid? Unless she already has a record.

"We made the arrest, but the BLIPs took her off our hands quickly."

I hang up, and look at Petra. She looks back, guilt shining through her tears like stars. *I warned you, didn't I?*

I get a hold of Maria. She is a high school friend, and thus our relationship combines a gradual distancing with an exaggerated sense of obligation. But even she cannot help me.

"I'm so sorry," she whispers into the phone. "I can't do anything. The computer on which download has occurred has been tapped for a while. We were just waiting for something serious enough to occur."

"Why?"

"Don't know," she hisses. "Sorry, got to go."

Petra is fiddling with her hair. "It's my fault."

No point in arguing—we both know she is right, but I'm not going to gloat. It was hard enough for me to lose her to the misguided rebellion that offered no action and no escape. She was only fourteen when the entertainment conglomerates first ran for presidency, and eighteen when they won. She still remembers when the information was not screened or regulated by the government, when there was no such thing as a govnet. Ilona doesn't.

Petra was not the one to ignore it, but she was not a fighter. Her anger manifested in small acts of disobedience, which gave little consolation and even less meaning. One can talk shit about the government all one wants, but in the end is trapped worse than those who are oblivious.

"But what was I supposed to do?" Her voice gains a cracked quality. "My own mother was working for them."

So your daughter pays for the sins of your mother. Only you are untouched. "What exactly did you do?"

Petra tells me that she had her computer hacked, connected to the other net, not the govnet. She used it to read the news; she never knew that Ilona had any interest in using it, but didn't make much of an effort to hide it, or to explain to her daughter the intricacies of the Declaration of Copyright. Of course the kid is going to see a picture and print it, never realizing that that constitutes intent to distribute, jail time mandatory. She had no way of knowing that everything is copyrighted in perpetuity, regardless of where it appears. Free net or not, it's BLIP jurisdiction.

I drink the lukewarm tea as Petra cries and talks, cries and talks. Her sobs and babbling create a soothing rhythm, and it is easier to think to it. I think of the Federal penitentiaries in the area, and I think of how many of them I have flown above. No reason not to do it again.

"Tomorrow," I tell Petra, "I'm going to do some reconnaissance flying."

She stops sobbing. "Isn't it dangerous?" Her eyes glitter, anxious. "I don't want to lose you too."

You threw me away years ago. What other loss are you afraid of? "It's a government plane, baby, remember?"

"They let you fly anywhere you want?"

"As long as there are clouds."

She stares at me, and I tell her of warm dry winters when clouds are hard to find, and there's not enough moisture in the air to make them. I tell her of the quilt of the fallow fields and the green silk of the ocean, its foamy crests like tiny clouds. Of the tedious azure of the sky and the thrill of the hunt as I spot a white wisp of a nascent cloud, still unsure whether to come into being, its transparency both a promise and a threat. I chase them across the sky, over land and over sea, and whatever lies beneath is not my concern.

I let the clouds lead me. It is neither faith nor superstition, but a voice of experience—as long as I follow the white fluffy shapes, they will lead me where I need to be. It may be a roundabout way, blown by winds and air currents, convection and condensation, but we will get there in the end.

I follow them, but for the first time I let them be. My plane swoops down, closer and closer to the bejeweled patchwork of the ground, until I can discern tall grey cement and low greenery, and almost lose my way in the vapor rising from the over-saturated ground. I rise again to safety, but descend again, circling, looking. I disconnect the communication system and turn the scopes to the ground, and search it.

I watch the yards of the penitentiaries, and I look for women. At the Austin Federal Penitentiary, I find a group of young girls, in identical orange jumpsuits, as they circle aimlessly through a grey cement yard, and I look for the familiar face. It is hard to see in the grey rain, even with the scope, until one of them tilts her head upwards and smiles.

A day passes like that, and another one. It's raining fine without me, leaving me free to look like a hawk. On the third day, I am denied entrance to the airfield.

I think of making a dash—the guard would never catch up with me. Instead, I ask why, even though I know the answer. The security guard looks at me with pity in his eyes, and it belies the banality of his words—subversive element in the family, security risk, retirement age. They don't even bother to pick one excuse; they lump them all together, without an appearance of respect.

"I'm sorry," he says in the end. "She was a real pretty girl."

I lean closer to the plastic of his booth, and he doesn't flinch away. "Listen, Thomas," I say. "I left some personal belongings in the cockpit. Think I can run in real quick and get them?" And add, to ease possible suspicion, "Or you can get them for me."

He sighs and shifts in his narrow stool, his bulk sloshing from one side to the other. He peers at the grey rain, coming down in glassy sheets. "You go right ahead," he says. "Just don't dawdle."

I have no intention to. I cross the airfield in a quick walk, my boots sliding on the wet grass. Other pilots pay me no mind—they never do; I am too old to be looked at with any comfort. They don't seem alarmed when I grab the prop and pull it, desperation tripling the weight of my frail body. The engine starts, its metal heart beating in a faster rhythm than mine, and the plane glides down the field. I catch up to it in a run and vault into the cabin, just as I hear someone call out, "Hey!"

The air is wet in my face, until I slam the door shut, and we're off, spiraling, ascending on the warm currents, the clouds moving down to greet us, like sheep greeting their shepherd. I look at the clock—8 am. I have an hour to get there. I need forty-five minutes.

The girls are in the yard again. It is raining hard, and they wear yellow slickers, the hoods obscuring their faces. There are two female guards, watching from the cover of the tall wire fence; there are probably others.

One of the yellow hoods tilts back, and I see a pale face and dark hair, a small mouth opened in hope and wonder. She is the only one left standing as my plane drops into the yard, like a bird of prey. I land by the fence, and hope that the yard is long enough to stop.

There are gunshots, and the white panicked faces of the guards through the windshield. I turn the dust cannons on full blast, and they are lost in the grey cloud of searing particles. A small fist pounds on the door, and I swing it open. Ilona clambers into the seat next to me and the plane turns around.

There's not enough space for a proper takeoff and I gun it, taking off the top of the fence.

Ilona gasps next to me, and then regains her usual composure. "Did you like my pictures?"

"Yes. Thank you very much."

"I thought you would."

I point at the approaching tight cluster of white clouds, and my granddaughter laughs. "Just like in the pictures."

I aim the plane into the center of it, and cut the engine. We fall, weightless, surrounded by the celestial vegetable sheep. One of them takes us into its soft arms and smiles, cradling the plane.

The engines rev back to life, and Ilona lets out a long sigh. "I could fall like this forever."

I nod. She is strong and she will learn to fly.

The Devonshire Arms
ALEX DALLY MacFARLANE

1. The door, welcoming.
The door closed behind Ambri with a click.

A candle burned.

There was a sword by the heavy wooden door, and a coat made of raven feathers. The leather on the sword's hilt was faded from long use. The coat had holes at the elbows and armpits.

Overhead hung a chandelier of amber and glass. The walls were dark, and fabric-covered lights hung over the counter. Windows admitted the murky rainlight of day's fade. In high-sided booths made of leather like the finest dark shoe, murmurs and laughter passed from mouth to ear, mouth to glass.

With a swish of her dark red skirts, Ambri swung onto a stool and asked for a whiskey with lemonade. The painted man behind the counter nodded and mixed the drink, moving his hands with the surety of one fluent in the language of bottles and taps. Ambri watched him. A map of the London Underground had grown on his skin, and when he shifted she saw the blues of Victoria and Piccadilly merge into one, the yellow of Circle split into two circles, four circles: an irreal mitosis of helical tracks.

A strange never-told story, Ambri thought.

With a word of thanks and an exchange of coin, she received her drink.

She looked at it sitting on the counter, one amid many low, broad glasses stomach-full of liquids light and dark, and she sucked from the thin black straw. When the alcohol-laced sweet coldness slid down her throat, she smiled.

It is so good to be back here.

She smiled over and over.

2. The walls, dark like cushions
Ambri had put her sword by the door many times in the century and a half since finding the pub, since that day when she had stepped inside with shoulders aching like the un-oiled joints of a suit of armor and she had seen a woman made of smoke and fire napping in a chair.

Many times since, she had seen new solid faces between the wispy, unfocused shapes of the short-lived people. She had been the woman the solid people saw at the counter, in a chair, talking at a naval-high table—the woman they approached, saying, "This place! Are you here often? Do others like us come here?"

"This place is very new," the woman made of smoke and fire had said when Ambri woke her with those words. "It is my first visit. But I think I will return."
Her voice had sounded like spices and sun-baked bricks.
"Welcome."

"Welcome," Ambri later said to Esnan, who wore a gold ring in his eyebrow that winked like a courtesan. "Welcome," Ambri later said to the earth-skinned and sun-haired epicene, calling hirself Aus in these times, who had created cassowaries and platypi in hir youth. "Welcome," Ambri later said to others.
And afterward she often saw them in the pub, resting between their work, between the hard steps of their lives.

"Welcome," Ambri said to the girl who could not tolerate rhythms, the first time they met.

3. The plates, hot like embraces
In a booth of blue leather Ambri found her friends: Esnan, mixing trickeries with the fortunes he sold and talking to Aus, who practiced hir next creations with napkins and straws. Idjinna smouldered in the back.
"Ambri! Good to see you!" Esnan stood up so that she could slide to the back of the booth. "How are you?"
"Busy."
Her sword, with well-worn leather on its hilt, rested by the door.
Aus flicked dark fingers, and a marsupial bird made of folded napkins crumpled into sleep.
"Yes," Ambri said, laughing, "I would like that. But I'll relax, first." A four-legged cactus with cocktail sticks for spines walked across the table, guided by Aus' other hand.
"This one is possible," the epicene said.
"I like it."
Esnan pushed his half-finished plate of fish across the table. The warm ceramic pressed against Ambri's arm. "You're in the right place for relaxing."
"Yes, I am."
The fish was light and lemony over her tongue, tinted with a taste she could not identify—like the pub itself. Ambri had never found a place quite like it.
A place built over a century and a half ago, by short-lived people who had not known what it would become: a place for those longer-lived, with different tasks and difficult lives.

She ate the plate bare and reclined against the dark blue leather, letting her lids slide shut until she saw only the faint glows of lamps above and Idjinna at her right. Laughter speckled the air. Idjinna's skin crackled and flared, as if she was made of small twigs catching alight one after the other. "How are you?" Ambri murmured, reaching out to touch Idjinna's arm.

Her fingertips pinkened.

"There was a bronze bowl," Idjinna said.

"Ah."

Idjinna's voice sounded like burning as she told Ambri of a merchant who found a way to trap her, to carefully tap her wishes through the latter years of his life. Medicine gardens flourished around his house and the murals stayed fresh. Idjinna could not escape. The bronze bowl singed around the edges. But the merchant died, eventually, and the bowl among many of his other possessions fell to the care of a young Englishman who took it to auction. As the auctioneer's assistant held it high, his hand tremored and it fell.

"I was angry and happy all at once, and so I danced: it is what I do best." She twirled dark, smoky fingers through the flames on her head. "The auction house was made of wood."

Ambri laughed through a yawn.

"They are such a nuisance, these people who cannot even see me but who know how to trap me," Idjinna said.

To Ambri and Idjinna and the rest of the group around the table, short-lived people were wispy, unfocused shapes, talking and drinking and unaware that there were others in their midst. If they even noticed Idjinna, they probably saw a dark woman wearing orange, or wearing a t-shirt painted with flames, or covered in too many tattoos. Only some of them, sometimes, knew a little more—but the man with a map of the London Underground on his skin had ways to keep them out.

Idjinna twined her fingers with Ambri's and sighed. "I am particularly tired of crockery."

As the four-legged cactus creature made of napkins and cocktail sticks marched across the table, examined at every step and turn by Aus and Esnan, the two women curled together in the back of the booth. Idjinna quietened her flames, and Ambri lay with her back against that hot chest and her legs linked with smoke and ember. Her skin did not burn.

They slept.

4. The chandelier, amber-eternal

The girl was a kaleidoscope, a patchwork quilt, a mosaic pieced together from tiles of multiple sets. So Ambri had thought, fifty years ago when they first met at the liquid-limned counter.

That first time, the girl's hair drew Ambri's eye before anything else. Part-stained pale with lemons, part-stained black with soot, with a streak tinted brown-red and smelling of a spice market, her hair hung in disorderly lengths over her broken nose, her bare left shoulder, her left ear with its seven piercings and her right ear with its one glass sphere dangling from the edge of the lobe. Then Ambri noticed her clothes: a blue skirt chopped to uneven lengths and a left trouser leg beneath it that fell to her grubby ankle; the right sleeve of a green dress; a waistcoat covered in beads and oddments. Among them Ambri saw empty-centered coins from China and Denmark, bright red beads from the Serengeti, ivory and jade amulets. Rings, and the finger of a black velvet glove on her right thumb, covered the girl's pale hands. Her eyes were one-blue, one-amber, like those of certain cats.

"Stop," she had said to Ambri, who tapped her fingers to a popular tune on her thin-stemmed glass of water flavored with wine. "Tha-at annoys me, stop it!" Her voice dipped into half a dozen accents, like bread into a platter of oils: Scottish and Indian, Russian and Thai, Turkish and Moroccan. "Fingers. Fi-ingers are too loud!"

She pulled the glass out of Ambri's hands.

"You were tapping."

"Good evening," Ambri said, bemused.

"Too many rhythms. Pat-terns. I don't like them."

Ambri turned to the man behind the counter and said, "Can I have a glass of water, please, with the rim of the glass chipped for a third of its curvature, and with unevenly chopped pieces of carrot floating in it."

When Ambri looked back at the girl, she was staring, her mouth ajar like a door.

"Here," Ambri said, giving her the drink. "I hope you like this."

"You . . . " Six of her fingers curled tightly around the glass. "No one has ever . . . "

Ambri smiled. "You are far from the strangest person to find your way inside this pub." Less than a minute later she said it, after inviting the girl to sit down, take a long around, stay: "Welcome to the Devonshire Arms."

5. The booths, soft like beds

They woke, and Ambri met for the second time the girl who could not tolerate rhythms.

"Do either of you want a drink?" Ambri asked Idjinna and Esnan.

"Feathers and kindling."

"Just a glass of apple juice," said Esnan, back at his phials mixing fortunes and trickeries and a hint of vanilla.

As she shuffled out of the booth, Ambri asked where Aus had gone.

Red and pearl-hued liquids mixed like different colored hairs in a breast-round phial; a drop of something yellow turned the potion monochrome teal. "Something about needing to make the spines poisonous," Esnan said without looking up.

Laughing at Aus' intent, Ambri went to the counter and ordered three drinks from the map-covered man. Hammersmith & City snared Metropolitan like bind weed around a drooping branch, magenta into pink. The grey of Jubilee wriggled. With one hand the man took feathers from under the counter and mixed them in a metal tumbler with cocktail sticks; with the other, he poured hot blackberry liqueur into a wine glass.

Movement to her left caught Ambri's attention.

At the far corner of the counter, a young woman scattered dried peas in un-patterned intervals. "Good," she said when one nudged an empty glass; when three peas bounced off each other and one fell on the floor, she muttered, "Irreg-lar," in a different accent. Another time she just smiled: a slow, lopsided curve of her thin lips.

This time fishnet covered the young woman's left arm, and strips of a CD hung in hair that was chopped and dyed in more ways than Ambri could count. Seven of her fingernails were orange and two were white; pink and beige swirled on the tenth. Her shirt was made of newspaper clippings.

"You're still enjoying it here?" Ambri asked, pitching her voice above the murmurings of the wispy people.

The young woman looked up. "Hello," she said, and her smile broadened.

When they met for the first time, the girl had said that a name always remained the same and she didn't want that, but giving herself a new one whenever she wanted meant no one would remember what to call her. Easier to have none at all.

Ambri wrapped her hand around her wine glass of liqueur, putting each finger a different space apart. "You're older than when I first saw you."

The young woman watched Ambri's fingers. "I don't age in a pattern, ye-ar by year. Never have. Parents didn't like that. I was born under Victori-ah." With her bi-colored eyes she looked up. "You don't change at all."

"I never have. I do not remember my birth, but I have heard many stories: that I was cut from the side of a wasp; that I was molded from bone and metal; that I grew to this size in a womb and in tearing free from it killed my mother, the first death for me to collect." Ambri inclined a brown shoulder in a shrug. "All I remember is doing my job."

"That's a long time to al-ways do the same thing."

"It is." She thought of her sword, resting by the door. "Though I am made for longevity, it is a long time. It is wearying." But some of the tightness had left her shoulders, eased away by Idjinna's heat; and her hands were warm from her glass, not exertion. "That is why I come here, from time to time."

The young woman nodded, and two CD strips tapped each other.

"Idjinna and Esnan are in a booth. I think you've met them?"

"Once."

"Do you want to sit with us?"

Nodding more—up-and-down or sidewise gestures, unevenly spaced—the young woman gathered up her dried peas and slid off her stool.

"You're always solid, you and the oth-ers," she said on the way to the booth. "You always see me and you never stare, you ne-ever look at me like I left the circus."

Ambri looked over her shoulder at the young woman. "I know."

"You try not to make rhythms."

"Hello!" Esnan cried, seeing them. "Sit down! Now, what do you think's the best color mixture? Thanks for the drink, Ambri."

The young woman settled down in front of the phials arrayed chaotically across the table and stared at them all in turn, playing with the peas in her hands. Eventually she dropped a pea in a phial of cinnabar liquid and said, "That one."

Esnan laughed. "I know exactly what that one's for! Thank you, wonderful lady. Now tell me, where have you been traveling? Your shirt comes from all over the world."

"I went to Malawi and Uruguay, and in a bo-at to Cyprus . . . "

As the young woman related her journeys, Ambri leaned against Idjinna and smiled. *This is why we come here.*

6. The floor, made for standing still

When they parted for the second time, the young woman told Ambri that she would travel with Esnan.

"To markets and sites of misfortune," the man said. "You can find us there, if you wish."

"Or he-ere."

The young woman grinned up at Ambri, who climbed out of the booth with her cheek singed from Idjinna's farewell and walked to the door, who took up her sword, fastened the belt and scabbard around her waist. One hand on the hilt, Ambri said over the early afternoon quiet, "I'll be back here, of course."

"We all will be back here," said the young woman with phials in her hands. "Eve-entually."

7. The door, welcoming

Glasses and plates slid on and off tables like a brocade cloth. In high-sided booths, dark blue like the late-night sky, friends and the newly met chewed and swallowed, sipped and smiled. With dried peas on their tongues they exchanged their lives.

The door creaked open and another entered: swamp-skinned and broad; or reptilian, ancient, the first creature ever to lay an egg in a nest; or tall and pale, dressed in scraps, wanting a drink from her begged coins and finding a booth full of people she saw plainly. They made space for her. The young woman with mismatched clothes and an intolerance for rhythms offered half a plate of chicken and couscous.

A candle burned.

"Welcome," the young woman said.

The Loyalty of Birds
RACHEL SOBEL

She is so afraid that he will die that she cannot bear to watch his restless hands stilled upon the fine sheets; instead she sits at his bedside and watches the sunlight creep across the wall, abandoned tea cupped awkwardly between her palms. There are crickets singing in the garden, but beyond their mild whirring music, the world is still, as if it too is holding its breath.

Or perhaps she has merely forgotten the quiet of this place. It has been so many years since she came here last, preferring the convenience and lively bustle of the city to her family's isolated peace, and she finds it disconcerting to be surrounded by so much silence, though she rarely lets herself think why. She tries not to remember the city; it is too painful to think that everything she once loved has been destroyed by the Dauphim's war.

As remedy to her smothered grief, she savors the smooth stones of the pale villa, walks the gardens of the inner courtyard and helps her attendants sort out the complicated trousseau of half a hundred generations that has come to rest in her attic. In the evenings she can sit in the fading light, keeping her hands busy with some necessary task or other, and watch the nest of fledgling starlings in the apple orchard scream at the farm cats with neighborly fury when the kittens draw too near them.

It is easier to be practical than to think much about anything else, because while there are irises beneath her bedroom window and lilies in the woods, there is still a civil war on her doorstep and a man who has destroyed himself lying in her second-best guest bedroom, his face drawn tight with his sleeping pain.

"It will be worse before it gets better," Gilos warns her, the truism as strange in his mouth as is the grimness in his light eyes. He is her physician, and like all of her people who have stayed, he is loyal more to her than to the honor of her name or any ideal of king or country. They were lovers once, long before he came to serve her, and the distance of that time makes her wonder if she has become old.

She looks at him now without expression, and he adds: "If it gets better." His eyes are hard. She remembers belatedly that he too loved the man who lies in dreaming agony in the second-best guest bedroom, and she is sorry.

But she doesn't believe him. She isn't sure she can afford to believe him. They have lost so much already, and all that has been left to them are the ancient faded linens in the attic and the bright birds in the garden; if they cannot save him, she thinks, perhaps these things too shall be destroyed when the civil war comes to this place.

"I don't believe you," she tells Gilos, and his smile is as hard as his eyes, bitter and self-mocking, but he spends none of his violence on her, and his voice is as mild as ever.

"Then don't, my lady," he says simply, and his gaze does not stray to the doorway to the sickroom. He hesitates. "I will lessen the laudanum tonight," he says at last. "It must be done, but—it will be worse."

"I'll come," she assures him, and goes to take refuge in her garden among the weeds she hasn't had the time to pull.

She is not sure if his screams are worse than his stillness.

There is no way to know if the war will come here, but she knows it is her duty to make preparations as if it will; she helps her people to repair the walls until her hands are scraped raw with a new set of calluses. They are far from any significant territory, and for all the beauty of this place, it is still only a rambling mountain valley, hidden between the cliffs and fed by spring and rain, but there is always the chance someone will remember the name she used before they ever knew her.

They eat still-warm bread with goat cheese spread liberally across it, and choose to save the sausages for winter, which is only common sense. Instead they slice tomatoes and cucumbers while the solemn black-and-white kitten rubs against her ankles, his dignity apparently forgotten. Her eldest brother loved to steal garden vegetables when they were children, and she cannot eat here without thinking of him.

In the night, she sits beside the man she loves and watches him fight sleep with every lingering strength in his body; he barely speaks even to her, and then only when he wakes from his nightmares.

"I dreamt that my hands were made of molten gold," he murmurs once, his chest heaving with his gasping sobs; his face shines with tears in the light of her candle, and he flinches away from the touch of her hand on his face, looking sick. "I dreamt . . . "

"You're safe now," she whispers, stroking his dark hair back with a gentleness that surprises her. "There's no one to hurt you here."

She doesn't look at his hands until he has fallen asleep again, his exhaustion too strong for him, and only then does she rest one hand lightly on his right wrist, well above the careful bandages.

His hands are ruined; the left is burnt beyond repair, and Gilos is still afraid he will have to cut it. She knows that he did it to himself in the fire that took his power from him, and it frightens her when he cries out in his sleep with such anguish that she cannot bear to touch him. Laudanum or no, there are no easy answers to his pain.

She finds in the attic a slender book bound in brown leather, and opens it to reveal pages covered with marvelous illustrations in colorful ink: dragons over warm seas, banquets and menageries, camels aboard flying ships and smiths shoeing horses; the paper is fine and dry beneath her fingers, and she brings it downstairs with her almost absently. On a whim, she takes it to show him, and sits beside him, tracing the shape of a sparrow's wing with the tip of her little finger.

She stays for more than an hour, turning the pages for him when he tilts his chin at the book, and leaves only when duty forces her to. His eyes are overbright as he follows the trailing line of a willow, but he sits leaning against the pillows, shaking slightly. It is not until after she leaves that she remembers his fondness for books and paper, for drawings and paint as well as other stronger things. Perhaps she has only been cruel after all.

But that night he asks her to read to him; the request comes haltingly from his lips, strange in a mouth that has said so little voluntarily, and she brings an aging volume of peculiar foreign philosophy for his approval. Apparently it is good enough, because he settles back, his eyes closing so that the lashes lie along his cheeks. She reads aloud for hours, trying not to let him catch her watching the tension flow out of his body like very lethargic water, until at last she is sure he is asleep.

It takes a long time, even though once he would have teased her mercilessly for her horrible taste in literature; he has found philosophy boring for as long as she has known him, and that is half of why she chose it. She is afraid for him, and he sleeps so little and eats even less. She sits by his bedside long into the night, watching her candlelight flicker across the hollows of his gaunt face. If she is lucky, she falls asleep in the chair at his bedside, with only the crooked pains of age and grief to greet her in the morning, but as often as not, she awakens to midnight and the sound of his ragged breathing as he tries to keep from waking her.

She is so tired, so often, now; there are not enough of them to pull in the harvest, and likely not enough harvest either, and the summer is waning so fast that she is very hard-pressed to think how they will survive the winter. If the soldiers do not come, she thinks, then perhaps they will make it, and she goes over the records again with her steward, searching for some slight excess they can depend upon.

It is such hard going that every other task is easy by comparison, all the grueling physical work she lends a hand to when she has a spare moment made nothing in the face of this last, most brutal fact. She knows she cannot spare the time to go to him, but equally she cannot leave him alone with his nightmares, and so she goes, and is worn thin with exhaustion.

And now he sleeps without dreams, and even knowing that she is likely being far too much the optimist, she comes back to him as soon as she can the next day with a small green silk case of books and an expression he would call determined. She needs him so badly, now, worse than she ever has; she needs his strength and his courage and his wit, and she cannot ask him to spare anything for her. He has so little for himself.

To her surprise, his mouth twitches upwards, almost a smile, and while he is still so thin that his bones show clear through the bandages at his wrists, she is strangely reassured, and cannot quite keep the answering smile from her face.

"I will be *damned* before I spend the rest of my life reading horrible philosophy," he whispers. "Poetry, madam, or at least a play, for the love of all things merry."

She brandishes the green silk books at him with mock ferocity, displaying the gilt-lettered title. It is a set of mythological poetry, rife with firebirds and wishes, precisely the sort of foolishness that he once loved, and she is rewarded for the trouble it took to find it by the ghost of a smile on his face.

"Heathen," she says, as fondly as she dares, and he leans back into the pillows and closes his eyes as she pages delicately through the first of the thin volumes, her voice low and easy, soothing him into sleep.

She comes back the next day, as soon as she can be spared from directing the defenses, and after that again, and together they make their way through all the long slow poems of their history in the little time she cannot really justify setting aside for him, until at last they come to the tragic cycle of the sorcerer Theine. Once upon a time, it was his favorite, and even she, who has always hated poetry, could nearly tolerate it, but now she cannot help but find it cruel.

But as she starts to flip past, her fingers brushing lightly over the pages, he frowns, and shakes his head.

"Please," he says, his voice soft and harsh around the edges, and she knows that he is afraid.

She starts slowly, pausing more often than she needs to, to take a breath or sip of water from the blue clay cup beside his bed, and every time she looks in hope he has fallen asleep she finds him watching her, his gaze unnervingly still.

And now she's gone and laid him down,
His body limp upon the green.
His strength of limb has been and flown;
The stars are hid behind her screen.

He lies beneath a storm-torn beech
His mind grown dark with loathsome lies,
And all his gift for song and speech
Has died before her golden eyes.

His birds are slain, his master's dead,
The school of wizards burnt and lost.
His brothers from the land have fled
And left him here, to face the frost.

She binds him now with chains of light,
Within the shadowed sleepless hill,
To live so long as day flees night
And listen to the dead winds' will.

She pauses then, and turns to gaze,
Upon this shattered sorcerer
Whose mind was caught within her maze
Though once he sought to conquer her.

"My lord," she whispers 'gainst his cheek,
"In days when men may hear thy doom,
Dost think they shall my secrets seek?"
Her eyes are bright within the gloom.

She does not wait on his reply,
But opens her bright-feathered wings
And casts herself into the sky,
And as she goes away she sings.

They let the words drift away into the silence, and after a long time he stirs in his bed, half-restless and half-thoughtful.

"It isn't like that at all, you know," he murmurs, and for a moment there is a shadow of bitter mockery in his voice. He looks at her so steadily she is afraid. "I had thought that it would be like that, a queer dream of winds and stars, but poets," he says, the bitterness stronger now, "are liars all."

"I'm sorry," she says, and she does not think she has ever been so sorry in her life. "I left you to die," she says, and cannot bring herself to go on.

His mouth quirks painfully, and he looks away.

"My staff burnt to dust and ashes in my hands," he says, at last, as if he is confessing to her, and his voice is colorless. "I felt myself break, and then there were shards of glass in my heart and nothing in my head but fire, and the world was gone."

She touches the gilt lettering on the green silk lightly, with the tips of her fingers, and cannot think of anything to say.

"Nothing mattered very much anymore," he says, quietly, his face terrible to look at.

The next day she brings only lesser poetry.

The summer is fading, and soon it will be gone entirely and the harvest will have to be brought in. The apples on the trees are fat and tempting, smooth sides dappled pink and gold. The children collect them in baskets and eat themselves sick, and at night foxes chase each other drunkenly through the garden, made bold by fermenting berries. The breath of autumn touches everything with bronze.

The ploughman's daughters, sturdy dark girls with solemn faces, have adopted him as their own, unafraid of his scars. They bring him half a hundred little presents clasped in their chubby hands, bright-colored leaves and scraps of golden silk and, once, the entire branch off an ash tree, sheared off in an early storm. It takes all three of them to carry it into his bedroom, and even so the wide branches near the top get stuck in the door frame. Even Harra, her steward, has trouble maintaining her stern expression while she scolds them, as she has to do it from behind a screen of half-dead ash leaves.

And even he smiles.

But he is quiet still, so reserved that it is sometimes hard to remember his presence at all, and much harder to remember the young man she first met, a wizard as strident as ever his crows were. Sometimes she thinks that it would be polite to ask the fate of his birds, but she is not sure even he knows. If they were not destroyed by the wizard he fought, they may have starved by now, or fled to some other wizard's hand, perhaps even the one that ruined him. She has never been assured of the loyalty of birds.

Most days, now, he drags himself from bed to sit in the chair beside his window; his broken strength is returning slowly, but as yet he can do little more than sit and sleep and watch her farmers struggling to get their wheat in. And he leaves bread crumbs on the sill every night, scattered as if it is accidental.

"I'm sorry," he whispers once, his eyes dark with exhaustion, and for a moment she cannot think what he means. "I've returned to you so useless," he says, his mouth twisting a little with a merciless humor.

She bends to kiss his cheek, cupping her hand about the back of his neck, as reassuring as she can. "But you returned," she says, and he is silent.

Sometimes she dreams that she went back for him herself. In the dreams, she steals a horse from her peasants and rides as fast as she can to find him. She swings down off her horse into an empty field of grass, golden stalks waving gently in the breeze as far as the eye can see, and walks for miles as the red sun sets behind her. There is never anyone there.

In the evening, she brings him honey and raspberries, and sits beside him to watch the sun set beyond his window. The light falls across the hills like spilled wine, wakening dim colors in the mountains, and she closes her eyes against its warmth.

"I thought it would come back," he says, after a long time, his voice gentle and almost idle. All but the last of the sun has disappeared behind the mountains, the land fading into the evening, and she turns to look at him and finds him hard to see. There are no candles in his room, but she thinks his eyes are closed.

"It might," she points out. Her hands clench tight around her wine-cup until she is afraid she will break it, and she very carefully does not think of all the history she knows which says that it will not. Broken wizards do not heal.

"It won't," he says, quietly. Out the window, the moon is rising noiselessly behind the mountains, and it too is touched by the warmth of autumn, its luminous shine turned harvest orange. "I've known that for a long time now," he admits, and she does not know what to say.

He hesitates in the face of her silence. "I wanted to die," he says after a moment, so lightly that it is as if he is trying to diminish his honesty by flippancy. "I didn't think that I was the sort to—" But he stops again, and does not go on.

"Do you still?" she asks him, quiet and grave despite her fear, and his face is suddenly shy. He looks at his hands.

"No," he says, and nearly smiles.

Early one morning while she is making bread with Harra, he comes limping to the door of the kitchen and leans heavily against the wall, his good hand curled around a rough staff which Gilos got from the orchard for him. His face is pale and drawn with even this short walk, and she hurries to bring him a stool, her arms covered in flour to her elbows.

She watches him out of the corner of her eye as she works, and when it is time to take the bread out of the oven, she cuts off a thick slice—too early, of course, and it crumbles into the napkin, a mess of steaming bread bits against the blue of the linen.

He picks at it while she and Harra clean, the color returning slowly to his face, and when she brings him an apple and a slice of cheese, he eats these as well, not speaking. When he moves as if to rise, she is beside him at once, offering an arm and his staff. He makes a face, nose wrinkling in disgust at his own incapacitation.

"Heroic of me," he says, very dry, but takes her arm, and together they stumble back to his bedroom. She cannot stay; there are half a hundred absolutely vital things she must do today, and besides that she wants to check on the irrigation that leapt its ditch three days ago and was beaten back only with great effort, so she leaves him curled in the seat beside the window with most of the remainder of the loaf.

She returns much later to find the room chilly: the window open, bread eaten, crumbs scattered across the sill. He'll be stiff later, she thinks; he has fallen asleep in his armchair, and she wakes him with a touch, keeping her hand on his shoulder. He is still prone to nightmares, and often wakes with the edge of terror sharp in his face, but today there is only a great weariness.

First thing as he wakes, he glances to the window, his face still and nearly afraid, but there is nothing there. He runs his hand through his hair, staring out at the hills rolling up to the mountains beyond, and is silent for a long time.

"I am a fool," he says at last. "They will not come." She cannot disagree. Not even the local sparrows will come to him, though they grow fat begging crumbs off the children, and so she looks at him and cannot find anything to say. She smooths his hair back from his face, and kisses his cheek before she must leave him.

One night he joins her outside on the patio for dinner, a little dazed by the chatter of even half a dozen people but there nonetheless. It is nothing like their old life, but it is a life, she thinks, and curls her hand possessively around his elbow as she helps him back to his room. For a moment, she thinks she sees a fleeting shadow, sharp-edged and quick, but the light of her lamp shows nothing.

It's grown chilly, these past few nights, and the room is tense with cold air from the open window. She leaves him sitting on the bed, hands useless in his lap, and crosses the room to close it.

"Don't," he says, and she pauses. He looks up at her as she turns to him, and his eyes are clear and distant. "They came to their fate only for love of me," he says, and hesitates, searching for words. "They may leave me for whatever reason they must," he says at last, "but I will not lock them out, no matter how unlikely their return."

It's the longest speech she's heard from him in a very long time, and she is taken aback; after a moment, she nods, and lets the window be, coming to sit beside him. She will have to bring him an extra blanket, she thinks, but that is scarcely a hardship.

"Will you be all right?" she asks him, and he shrugs, rubs his face with his good hand and does not speak.

They sit together in silence and wait for the sound of wings.

The Giving Heart

CORIE RALSTON

Coleman studied the dead heart in the store window, the aorta frozen mid-pump in clear acrylic.

Julie put a hand over her mouth. "Is this for real?"

"Sandra says it's all the rage," Coleman said. "It's what everyone is doing at weddings these days."

"Sandra says this, Sandra says that."

Coleman glanced over. Could it be she didn't want him to marry Sandra? He liked the thought.

He pulled Julie inside. A man in a suit approached them at once, held out a hand with perfect, manicured nails.

"Real is the new real," Mr. Manicured said. "People used to give chocolate hearts, candy hearts, paper hearts. Why not get to the heart of the matter, so to speak? Give your actual heart."

"I don't know," Julie said. "It's kind-of creepy."

"How does it work?" Coleman said.

Julie wandered off to a display kiosk and pulled up a graphic demo of heart-replacement surgery.

Coleman concentrated on Mr. Manicured, who was still speaking.

"Our surgeons are the best in the country," he said. "And with cutting edge surgical techniques, so to speak, there is practically no scarring."

A holo of a happy couple danced in the corner. Red slogans slid across the walls in laser light. *Home is where the heart is, give her your heart.* It all seemed very modern.

Mr. Manicured took Coleman's elbow and leaned in conspiratorially. "Personally," he said, "I would take an artificial heart over a real one any day. Much more reliable."

He named a price.

Coleman gasped.

"Do you love her?" Manicured said.

"Sure." It would take all his savings, the money he was saving for his bookstore.

"There is no cost too great for love," Manicured murmured.

Sandra said it was about time they get married. She sighed meaningfully whenever they passed the *Give Your Heart* store. He did want to make her happy.

Coleman looked over at Julie, who stood with eyes narrowed at the kiosk. Julie, on the other hand, didn't believe in marriage.

"I'll do it," he said.

"Do you, Coleman?" the minister said.

Coleman blinked. "What?"

Sandra's shimmery veil made him dizzy. The heat wrapped his head like soggy towel. He could scarcely breathe.

"Here."

Sandra's nephew, at Colman's side in his tiny tux, nudged a package into Colman's hands.

"Do you, Coleman, take Sandra as your wife?"

He knew he was supposed to say something about his heart. *Still my beating heart. My heart is breaking?* No, that couldn't be it. There were so many expressions about the heart, he thought in a sudden panic.

Julie had said he shouldn't get married. Julie was somewhere in the audience.

After a pause that felt to Colman as if it might stretch to eternity, Sandra reached over and took the package from Colman's hands. The minister began to speak again.

Coleman felt a sudden thump from within his chest, as if his new artificial heart had done a somersault. The surgeon had assured him his new heart was in fine condition. Nothing could go wrong. So why had it thumped like that?

He knew he was now supposed to do something with the ring, but at that point, he lost consciousness.

No one would let him live down the fact that he had fainted; the reception was one long running joke about it. Coleman's heart, in its acrylic cage, made the rounds of the room.

Colman drank three martinis and wobbled off to a corner where Sandra's brother Giles gobbled a piece of red heart-shaped cake.

"The problem with weddings these days," Giles said, since he was an expert on everything, "is that they are so staged and predictable."

"You mean fainting wasn't exciting enough for you?"

Giles laughed. "Okay. That was fun. But really, everything else. The dresses, the vows, the flowers, blah blah blah."

And Julie was there, all of a sudden. She looked at Giles. "They were all exotics," she said. "Not blah blah."

Giles smiled and held out his hand. "One thing is for sure. I would never cut my heart out and give it to someone."

"Good," Julie said, taking Giles's hand. "I would never ask anyone to. Have you seen Coleman's heart in the acrylic? It's quite gross."

Giles smiled at Julie. Coleman didn't like it. Julie smiled at Giles. Coleman didn't like it one bit. The thought of all those expensive flowers weighed on Colman and sapped all the bravado he had recently acquired through the martinis. He kept thinking that he could have spent that money on a really nice collection of books.

The thing in his chest thumped again, followed by a faint slithering sound.

"Did you hear that?" Coleman said.

"Hear what?" Julie said.

Coleman took a breath. "Nothing," he said. It was the stress of the day. The thought of all his savings now gone, and everyone staring at him all the time. He rubbed his temples and wondered if there was somewhere he could lie down.

"You don't look so good," Giles said.

"I feel great," Colman said. "Best day of my life."

Giles shrugged.

"Really. I'm so happy." He thought maybe it was the alcohol that made his voice waver.

Julie put a hand on Colman's shoulder. "Of course you are, Colman. Congratulations."

I give you my life, my love, my heart. That's what he had been supposed to say.

"There! Did you see that?" Coleman said.

He stood with his shirt unbuttoned, holding open the flaps so Sandra could see.

The skin of his chest bulged out faintly, like a fast-growing blister, and then just as quickly smoothed out again.

"See what? Coleman, you aren't listening to me."

"I'm listening to you." Maybe he was imagining it. Sandra didn't see it, after all. "You said you can't stand living in the city."

"It's killing me," she said. "The endless rain. This apartment is so crowded. All those stupid books."

She lay on the couch with her arm draped over her eyes.

"We can't afford a house here," he said. "And what about my bookstore?"

"What bookstore?" she said. "We could afford a house in the suburbs."

Maybe it was just the *idea* of something alive in there that gave him chills. The sensation of something crawling around in his chest.

"I'm miserable here," she said. "Don't you care about that?"

"Of course I care," he said.

"Don't you love me?" she said.

"Of course I love you."

He loved his little apartment; the proximity to bookstores and cafes, the ceaseless pattern of traffic alternately stopping and then pulsing forward like blood through veins. He loved the sound of the rain. And he would be so far from Julie.

"When do you want to move?" he said.

She finally lifted her arm, smiled. "I'll call an agent right now."

• • •

The tip of the thing poked out his nose, made a small circular motion, and then began to lengthen, sliding smoothly out, long and thin and dexterous.

Coleman wanted to scream but found he was completely frozen.

"Coleman?" Sandra's voice came from the kitchen. "Have you seen my keys?"

The thin tentacle patted the dining room table, poked under a pile of newspapers. Coleman breathed shallowly through his mouth. He hoped he would faint. Or wake up. This couldn't be happening.

The tentacle rooted under the newspapers, came out holding the ring of keys like an elephant trick at a circus. It rattled the keys in front of Coleman's face. He opened his hand, and the keys dropped into his palm. The tentacle slid smoothly back inside his nose.

Sandra appeared in the doorway.

"There they are!" She scooped the keys from Coleman's outstretched hand. "Everything is so hard to find. We really need to unpack."

The garage door slammed. Coleman still stood with his hand outstretched, unable to move.

"It does appear to be moving around." The doctor withdrew the probe from the small hole he had made in Coleman's belly-button. The local anesthetic didn't completely cover the sensation of a cold metal slipping around inside him.

"Is this *normal*?" Coleman asked.

"Well, I've read about cases like this, although I haven't seen it personally. When you remove your real heart it leaves room for a different kind of creature to grow."

"A *creature*?"

"We can schedule you for surgery next week," he said.

Coleman tried to take deep breaths to calm himself. "Do you have any reading material on this phenomenon?"

"Sure. I'll send you home with some literature. You can think about how you want to proceed."

Sandra found him on the doorstep, duffel in hand.

"Where are you going?" she said.

"I hate this suburb," he said. "All the houses look identical. It never rains here."

"Are you *leaving* me?"

"I'm going to the hospital. And then I think I might go live in the city for a while."

"The hospital?"

"I have a thing growing inside me where my heart used to be," he said. "I'm going to have it surgically removed."

She gave him a blank look. He handed her the literature.

"This is very strange," she said finally.

"I'll see you later," he said.

"Wait a minute," she said. "It says in here the creature can often be very helpful."

"It's disgusting," Coleman said.

"And it says the insurance won't cover it."

"Sandra, I need to leave now to make my appointment."

"Just come inside for a moment and let's talk about it."

"What's to talk about?" he said. His hand on the duffel was sweating. "There's a fucking creature inside of me!"

"Calm down, Coleman." She glanced around to make sure no neighbors were out. "Really now." She leaned in close. "Did you see the cost of the surgery? We can't afford that."

"I don't care what it costs."

"You're being selfish. Are you going to take all our savings and spend it on yourself?"

"Well—"

"You aren't even thinking about how this might affect me. Remember what we agreed on about making our decisions together?"

He dropped the duffel. Sandra picked it up. "Come inside," she said. "We'll work this out."

The tentacle slid out of Coleman's ear and opened the door for Sandra.

"See?" she said. "It's just trying to help."

The creature was indeed very helpful. Tentacles protruded from Coleman's nose and mouth and pushed the vacuum cleaner around, did the dishes, found the remote. They picked up his old acrylic heart and put it on the mantel. They protruded out of his pants to unpack boxes, to pick up his piles of dusty old book and drop them in the recycle bin.

One night Sandra asked Coleman to make love to her, and he watched with a mixture of arousal and horror as the tentacle protruded from the tip of his penis and caressed her, brought her to climax. She made noises he hadn't heard it quite a while. When it was done, he was still aroused, but he didn't want to touch her. And anyway, she was already asleep.

The next morning he woke up to the smell of coffee and bacon. Sandra hung up the phone when he entered the kitchen, her eyes bright.

"Giles broke up with Julie." She shrugged. "About time. I never understood what he saw in her anyway."

She draped an arm over his shoulders, whispered in his ear. "But we're so happy, aren't we?"

"Hmmm," Coleman said. He opened the paper.

A tentacle emerged from his ear and caressed her cheek. She giggled. He shuddered. Coleman tried not to think about the slithering sensation as he sipped his coffee.

• • •

Coleman drank four martinis and then thought about making dinner for Sandra. When the tentacle emerged from his left nostril, weaving back and forth, trying to open the refrigerator door, he grasped it with both hands.

He tugged. It resisted. He pulled and pulled and it stretched out long and thin. It hurt like nothing he had ever felt before as an amorphous sack squeezed out through his nose and plopped onto the kitchen table. It reformed into a translucent blob, pathetic and quivering. Coleman retched. He didn't feel drunk anymore.

He reached for the phone.

Julie picked up on the third ring.

"It's me," he said.

"What's wrong?" she said.

"I'm an empty old man," he said. "I'm going to die."

"You're not old," she said. "What are you talking about?"

"I love you."

She was silent a moment. "Why don't you come over?"

He grabbed his acrylic heart from the mantel and hauled his caved-in body to the car. He managed it somehow, using his own hands and feet on the wheel and pedals, surprised that he still knew how, that he had the strength.

He tried to imagine what would Sandra do when she got home and found the creature quivering on the kitchen table. Maybe she would let it go free. Maybe she would lay down her head and mourn its death. He decided he didn't care.

Julie met him outside her apartment, squinting through the rain at him.

The rain dripped down his nose, under his collar.

"Look at me," Coleman said. "There's nothing left but a hollow body. I don't want to live anymore."

She put a hand on his arm. "What about your bookstore?" she said.

"It's an unrealistic dream," he said.

"Is that what Sandra told you?"

He lowered his head.

"I don't think it is unrealistic," she said.

He felt the edges of his inside wound tighten just a little, start to pull together. Maybe it would fill in. Maybe the creature had not taken all of him. He stood up a little straighter.

"You broke up with Giles," he said.

"He was a jerk."

"I could have told you that."

The rain pattered lightly on the leaves of the jasmine bush near the walk.

"I've missed the rain," he said.

"I've missed the old Coleman," she said. "That crazy guy who bought dusty old books and piled them all over his apartment."

"Did I really do that?" he said.

He felt tears on his cheeks. He thought about saving and saving until he could afford the first few months rent on a store, about finding those books he had treasured so much as a child. Maybe Julie would want to help him with the bookstore. It suddenly didn't seem so unrealistic anymore.

She took the acrylic heart from under his arm. "I wish you could put it back in," she said.

He smiled at Julie, at the rain, at the city. "It will grow back," he said. And he knew it was true.

White Charles

SARAH MONETTE

The crate arrived at the Parrington on a Wednesday, but it was Friday before anyone mentioned it to me. Anything addressed from Miss Griselda Parrington, the younger of Samuel Mather Parrington's two daughters, was automatically routed to Dr. Starkweather's office, regardless of whose name she had written on it. I was, in truth, intensely grateful for this policy, for Miss Parrington most often addressed her parcels to me. She felt that we were "kindred spirits"; she considered me the only employee of the museum with the sensitivity and intelligence to appreciate her finds. Considering that she had inherited all of her father's magpie-like attraction to the outré and none of his discernment, her opinion was less flattering than one might think. I endured some teasing on the subject, though not nearly as much as I might have; in general, the curators' attitude was one of "there but for the grace of God." They were even, I think, rather grateful, if not *to me* precisely, then at least for my existence.

Miss Parrington's packages were inevitably accompanied by letters, sometimes quite lengthy, explaining what she persisted in referring to as the provenance, although it was no such thing. "I found this in a lovely antique shop in Belgravia that Mimi showed me," conveyed no useful information at all, since nine times out of ten she neglected to provide any further clues to Mimi's identity, and on the tenth time, when we managed to determine that "Mimi" was Sarah Brandon-Forbes, wife of the eminent diplomat, a polite letter would elicit the response that Lady Brandon-Forbes had never been in any antique shop in Belgravia in her life. The bulk of Miss Parrington's letters described, lavishly, what she *believed* the provenance to be, flights of fancy more suited to a romantic novelist than to even an amateur historian. But the letters had to be read and answered; Dr. Starkweather had been emphatic on the subject: they were addressed to me, therefore it was my responsibility to answer them.

It was perhaps the part of my job I hated most.

That Friday, when I found the letter in my pigeonhole, I recognized Miss Parrington's handwriting and flinched from it. My first instinct was to lose the letter by any means necessary, but no matter how tempting, it was not a viable solution. Dr. Starkweather saw through me as if I were a pane of glass; he would not be fooled by such an obvious lie. There was, therefore, neither sense nor benefit in putting off the task, unpleasant though it was. I opened the envelope then and there, and read the letter on the way back to my office.

It was a superbly representative specimen, running to three pages, close-written front and back, and containing absolutely no useful information of any kind. She had been at an estate sale—and of course she neglected to mention whose estate—she had recognized the name Carolus Albinus as someone in whom her father had been interested, and thus she had bid on and purchased a job lot of fire-damaged books, along with a picture she was quite sure would prove when cleaned to be an original Vermeer. She had not so much as opened the crate in which the books were packed, knowing—she said coyly—that I would prefer to make all the discoveries myself. But I would see that she was right about the Vermeer.

I propped my throbbing head on my hand and wrote back, thanking her for thinking of the museum and disclaiming all knowledge of seventeenth-century Dutch painters. I posted the letter, dry-swallowed an aspirin, and returned to the round of my usual duties. I gladly forgot about Miss Parrington's crate.

I should have known better.

On the next Tuesday, I was standing in Dr. Starkweather's office, helplessly watching him and Mr. Browne tear strips off each other over a *casus belli* they had both already forgotten, when we were startled by a shriek from the direction of the mail room. Dr. Starkweather raced to investigate, Mr. Browne and myself close behind, and we found Mr. Ferrick, one of the junior-most of the junior curators, sitting on the floor beside an open crate, his spectacles askew and one hand pressed to his chest.

"What on *Earth?*" said Dr. Starkweather.

Mr. Ferrick yelped and shot to his feet in a welter of apologetic half-sentences.

"Are you all right?" said Mr. Browne. "What happened?"

"I don't know," said Mr. Ferrick. "I was opening the crate and something—it flew into my face—I thought—" He glanced at Dr. Starkweather's fulminating expression and sensibly did not explain what he had thought.

A closer look at the crate caused my heart to sink, in rather the same way that reading the *Oedipus Tyrannos* did. "Is that, er, the crate from Miss Parrington?"

"Yes," said Mr. Ferrick, puzzled.

"Oh good God," said Dr. Starkweather in tones of utmost loathing, probably prompted equally by Miss Parrington and me.

"She said she, er . . . that is, she didn't open the crate. So it probably—"

"A bit of straw," Dr. Starkweather said, seizing a piece from the floor and brandishing it at us. "You've heard of the boy who cried wolf, Mr. Ferrick?"

"Yes, Dr. Starkweather," Mr. Ferrick said, blushing.

"Good God," Dr. Starkweather said again, more generally, and stormed out, Mr. Browne at his heels already girding himself to re-enter the fray.

I saw an opportunity to let Dr. Starkweather forget about me, and stayed where I was. Mr. Ferrick edged over to the crate as if he expected something else to leap out at him; it was with visible reluctance that he reached inside.

"What did you think it was?" I said.

"Beg pardon?"

"The, er, whatever it was that flew into your face. What did you think it was?"

"Oh. I've been spending too much time in Entomology," he said with a grimace. I waited while he lifted out a book so blackened with smoke that it was impossible to say what color the binding had originally been. "It looked like a spider," he said finally, tightly. "An enormous white spider. But Dr. Starkweather was right. It was just straw."

"Make out an inventory," I said, "and, er, bring it to me when you're done." And I left him to his straw.

Mr. Ferrick's inventory included several works by Carolus Albinus, one by the alchemist Johann de Winter, three by the pseudonymous and frequently untruthful Rose Mundy, and a leather-bound commonplace book evidently compiled by the owner of the library—a deduction which would have been more satisfying if he had signed his name to it anywhere. One of the Carolus Albinus books was rare enough to be valuable even in its damaged condition: the 1588 Prague edition of the *De Spiritu et Morte* with the Vermeulen woodcuts said to have driven the printer mad. The rest of them were merely good practice for the junior archivists. I heard from Mr. Lucent, who was friends with Mr. Browne's second in command Mr. Etheredge, that the "Vermeer" was no such thing and was sadly unsurprised. The crate and straw were both reused—I believe in packing a set of canopic jars to be shipped to San Francisco—and that was that. Another of Miss Parrington's well-meaning disasters dealt with.

Except that the night watchmen, a pair of stalwarts named Fiske and Hobden, began to complain of rats.

"Rats?" said Dr. Starkweather. "What nonsense!"

The rest of us could not afford to be so cavalier, and even Dr. Starkweather had to rethink his position when Miss Chatteris came to him on behalf of the docents and announced that the first time one of them saw so much as a whisker of a rat, they were all quitting.

"But there have never been rats!" protested Mr. Tilley, the oldest of the curators. "Never!"

Hobden and Fiske, stolid and walrus-mustached and as identical as twins, said they could not speak to that, but Mr. Tilley was welcome to tell them what else the scuttling noises might be.

Mr. Lucent rather wistfully suggested getting a museum cat and was promptly shouted down.

Dr. Starkweather grudgingly authorized the purchase of rat-traps, which were baited and set and caught no rats.

Mr. Browne was denied permission to purchase a quantity of arsenic sufficient—said Miss Coburn, who did the calculations—to poison the entire staff.

Frantic and paranoid inventory-taking revealed no damage that could be ascribed to rats, although Decorative Arts suffered a species of palace coup over an infestation of moths in one of their storerooms and our Orientalist, Mr. Denton, pitched a public and monumental temper tantrum over what he claimed was water damage to a suit of bamboo armor. Mr. Browne took advantage of the opportunity to start a campaign to have the main building re-roofed. Dr. Starkweather chose, with some justification, to take this as fomenting insurrection, and the rats were forgotten entirely in the resultant carnage.

Except by Hobden and Fiske—and by me, although that was my own fault for staying in the museum after dark. I was writing an article which required the consultation of (it seemed in my more despondent moods) no less than half the contents of my office. Thus working on it at home was futile, and working on it during the day was proving impossible, as the inventories were bringing to light unidentifiables overlooked in the *last* inventory, and everyone was bringing them to me. The puzzles and mysteries were welcome, but I had promised this article to the editor of *American Antiquities* nearly six months ago, and I was beginning to despair of finishing it. Being insomniac by nature, I found the practice of working at night more congenial than otherwise, and the Parrington was blessedly quiet. Fiske and Hobden's rounds were metronomically regular, and they did not disturb me.

And then there was the scuttling.

It was a ghastly noise, dry and rasping and somehow slithery, and it was weirdly omnidirectional, so that while I was sure it was not in the office with me, I could never tell where in fact it was. It was horribly intermittent, too, the sound of something scrabbling, and stopping, and then scrabbling again. As if it were searching for the best vantage point from which to observe me, and the night I had that thought, I went out to the front entrance and asked the watchman if they had had any luck at ridding the museum of rats.

He gave me a long, steady look and then said, "No, sir. Have some tea."

I accepted the mug he offered; the tea was hot and sweet and very strong. He watched, and when I had met whatever his criteria were, he said, "Me and Hob, we reckon maybe it ain't rats."

This was Fiske, then; I was relieved not to have to ask. "No?"

"No, sir. Y'see, Hob has a dog what is a champion ratter. Very well known, is Mingus. And me and Hob brought Mingus in, sir, quiet-like, feeling that what His Nibs don't know, he won't lose sleep over . . . "

"Quite," I said, perceiving that Fiske would not continue until he had been reassured on that point.

"Thank you, sir. So Hob brought Mingus in, and the dog, sir, did not rat."

"He didn't?"

"No, sir. We took him all over the museum, and not a peep out of him. And before you ask, sir, that dratted scratching noise seemed like it was following us about. Mingus heard it, sure enough, but he wouldn't go after it. Just whined and kind of cringed when Hob tried him. So we figured, Hob and myself, that it ain't rats."

"What do, er, you and Mr. Hobden think it is?"

Mr. Fiske looked at me solemnly and said, "As to that, sir, we ain't got the least idea."

Two nights later, I saw it, entirely by accident—and not "accident" meaning happenstance or coincidence, but "accident" quite literally: I fell on the stairs from the mail room to the west storage rooms. The stairs were of the sort that consist only of treads—no risers—and when I opened my eyes from my involuntary flinch, I was staring down into the triangular space beneath the stairs and watching something scuttling out of sight. I saw it for less than a second, but I saw that it was white, and it was not a rat. And I all too easily recognized the sound.

For a moment, I was petrified, my body as heavy and cold and unresponsive as marble, and then I scrambled frantically up the stairs, banging my already bruised knees, smacking my raw palms as I fumbled with the door. It was more luck than anything else that I got the door open, and I locked it behind me with shaking fingers, then slumped against it, panting painfully for breath. And then I heard that dry, rasping, scuttling sound from somewhere ahead of me in the storage room, and with the dreadful epiphantic clarity of a lightning bolt, I knew and whispered aloud because it was too terrible a thing to have pent and unvoiced in my skull, "It's in the walls." Even that was not the truth of my horror, for in fact that was no more than a banality. What made my chest seem too small for the panicked beating of my heart was not that it was *in* the walls, but that it was *using* the walls, as a subway train uses its tunnels.

Subway trains, unlike rats, have drivers.

And then I was running, my mind full of a dry, rustling panic. Later, I would reason with myself, would point out that it had not harmed anyone, or even any*thing*, that there was not the slightest shred of proof that its intentions were malicious, or indeed that it had any intentions at all. But nothing I came up with, no reasoned argument, no rational observation, could withstand the instinctive visceral loathing I had felt for that white scuttling shape. I remembered that Hobden's dog, a champion ratter, would not go after this thing. I remembered Mr. Ferrick, shaken and embarrassed, describing the "enormous white spider" that had flung itself in his face. And I wondered that night, pacing from room to sleepless room of my apartment, just what else Miss Parrington had bought in that job lot of worthless books.

Was it a sign of insanity that I assumed from the moment I saw it that it was not natural? I do not know. I do know that discovering it to be a gigantic albino tarantula would have been an overpowering relief, and by the very magnitude of that imagined relief, I knew it was no such thing.

The next morning, I prevailed on Mr. Lucent to ask a favor of one of his friends in Entomology, and the two of them met me in the mail room. I brought a flash-light. Mr. Lucent's friend was Mr. Vanderhoef, a shy young man who wore thick horn-rimmed spectacles and was an expert on African termites. Everyone in the museum, of course, knew about Mr. Ferrick's spider, and I explained that I thought I had seen it the night before. Mr. Vanderhoef looked dubious, but not reluctant, and contorted himself quite cheerfully into the awkward space beneath the stairs. I passed him the flash-light.

"A big piece of plaster is missing," he reported after a moment. "That must be how—oh! There is . . . something has been nesting here."

"Nesting?" Mr. Lucent said unhappily. "You mean it *is* rats?"

"No," said Mr. Vanderhoef, rather absently. "There aren't droppings, and it doesn't look . . . In truth, I'm not sure what it *does* look like."

"What do you mean?" I said. Mr. Lucent and I were now both peering between the treads of the stairs, but all we could see was Mr. Vanderhoef's shock of blond hair.

"There are no droppings, no caches of food, no eggs—nor viviparous offspring for that matter . . . "

"It couldn't be a, er, trap?"

"How do you mean?"

"Well, er, like a . . . like a spider's web."

"Ah. No."

"So, what is it using to nest in?" Mr. Lucent asked before I could find a way to get Mr. Vanderhoef to expand. "It isn't as if we've got a lot of twigs and whatnot in the museum."

"No, no," said Mr. Vanderhoef. "Paper. Newspaper, mostly, although I think I see the remains of one of Dr. Starkweather's memoranda."

"Paper," I said.

"Mr. Booth?" said Mr. Lucent, apparently not liking the sound of my voice.

"You're quite sure it couldn't be a spider?"

"That isn't what I said. This is not a *web*. There are spiders that don't build webs, but arachnids are not my specialty, and I cannot say for certain—"

"Is there anyone in the museum who would know?"

"Dr. Phillips is our arachnid expert, but he's on an expedition in Brazil until Christmas."

"Thank you," I said, because it was important to remember to be courteous, "you've been very kind."

"Mr. Booth!"

I stopped at the top of the stairs. "Yes, Mr. Lucent?"

"Did you . . . what were you . . . where are you going?"

"Paper," I said. "Will you ask Major Galbraith to get the plaster repaired?"

Mr. Lucent sputtered; I made good my escape and went to do what I should have done weeks ago and examine the commonplace book from Mr. Ferrick's inventory.

Mr. Ferrick was not happy to see me, though I could not tell if it was a guilty conscience—an affliction which seemed to be frequently visited on the junior curators in my presence—or simply that I irritated him. In either case, he stared at me as blankly as if I had asked about the second book of Aristotle's *Poetics*.

"The commonplace book," I said. "From, er, Miss Parrington's crate."

I noted that he had not been at the Parrington long enough for her name to have its full effect; we all winced reflexively, even Dr. Starkweather, but Mr. Ferrick merely frowned and said, "Is that the crate with the damaged books?"

"And the enormous white spider," I said before I could stop myself.

He gave me a look of mingled shock and reproach and said, "Oh! *That* commonplace book. I gave it to Mr. Lucent because it was holograph. Was that wrong?"

It was now obvious that he did not like me. I was glad he was a naturalist by training; once he had finished his probationary period, I was unlikely to have to deal with him again.

"No," I said. "That's fine." I was as pleased to leave as he was to have me go.

I spent the rest of the morning in a treasure hunt that was simultaneously ridiculous and nightmarish, pursuing the trail of the commonplace book from Mr. Ferrick to Mr. Lucent; from Mr. Lucent—who was miffed at me, he said, for rushing away in the middle of things and leaving him "holding the baby," although whether he meant by that the hole in the plaster, or Mr. Vanderhoef, or possibly Major Galbraith, I could not determine and did not like to ask—to Mr. Roxham; from Mr. Roxham, after a protracted and egregiously dusty search, to Miss Atterbury; from Miss Atterbury to Mr. Vine; and finally from Mr. Vine to Mr. Horton, who said, "Oh, I haven't gotten to it yet," and reached unerringly into the middle of one of the stacks of books waiting to be catalogued that surrounded his desk.

I retreated to my office with my prize and locked the door. The first few pages of the commonplace book told me that its owner was strongly antiquarian in his tastes, largely self-educated, and with an unhealthy penchant for the occult. Judging by the authors he quoted, he must have had quite the collection; the coup of the 1588 Albinus paled in comparison.

I flipped steadily through the pages, trying not to inhale too deeply, for the book reeked of smoke and secondarily of tobacco, and there was another scent, too faint for me to identify but sharply unpleasant. I was looking for quotes from Carolus Albinus or one of the other books that had been in the crate, and I found them starting about three-quarters of the way through. Albinus;

Mundy; a lengthy passage from de Winter on golems; a passage from an even more unpleasant author on the abomination called a Hand of Glory, although I had never seen these particular virtues ascribed to it before; and then the quotes began to be interspersed with dated entries such as one might find in a diary. These were written in a highly elliptical style, using an idiosyncratic set of abbreviations, and I could make neither heads nor tails of them, except for repeated references to "cllg"—"calling"?—someone or something called White Charles—the literal translation, of course, of Carolus Albinus, but the referent was decidedly not a book. And I did recognize the diagram drawn painstakingly on one verso page.

He had summoned something he called White Charles—presumably because he was using Carolus Albinus as his principal text, which ought to mean I could use my own knowledge of Carolus Albinus at least to make a guess at what he had been trying to do and what that white scuttling thing was.

So. He had summoned something, following—or improvising on—the rites of Carolus Albinus. Albinus had been a necromancer who dabbled in alchemy; White Charles was probably a revenant of some kind. The passage about the Hand of Glory suggested several further hypotheses; I was selfishly, squeamishly grateful that he had not discussed *that* matter in any greater detail. He had wanted power, no doubt, imagining it was something one could acquire like a new umbrella.

Whatever he had summoned, its actions indicated clearly that it had self-volition, unlike what very little I knew of golems. It had preserved itself from the fire, stowed away with the books—*its* books? I wondered. Did it know that those particular books were relevant to its existence, or was it mere coincidence? On reaching the museum, it had acted to preserve itself again, scavenged paper, made a nest. It had not, so far as I knew, harmed anyone, although it had greatly perturbed Fiske and Hobden—and Mingus—and had scared the lights and liver out of me. I certainly did not like the idea of a necromantic spider scuttling around the museum, but I could not immediately see any way of either catching or destroying it, and I quailed from the thought of explaining my theory to Dr. Starkweather—or even Mr. Lucent.

I would watch, I told myself. Probably before long, the thing would die or de-animate or whatever the correct term was, and it would not be necessary to take any action at all.

But over the next week, it became apparent that if I had decided to watch White Charles, White Charles had also decided to watch me. Any time I was in the museum after dark, the scuttling dogged my footsteps, and I could sit in my office and track the thing's loathsome progress from wall to ceiling and back to wall. The plaster under the mail room stairs had been patched, but that clearly hadn't caused White Charles more than a momentary inconvenience.

It unnerved me, but it still was not doing any harm, and surely it would disintegrate soon. Surely I would not have to . . . to hunt it down, or any of the other melodramatic imaginings that plagued me when I tried to sleep. I wanted desperately to avoid seeing it again, and most especially to avoid seeing it more clearly. This way, at least I could *pretend* I believed it was some sort of albino spider.

I was very carefully not thinking about Hands of Glory.

It was a Wednesday night when I finally finished my article for *American Antiquities.* I tidied the manuscript into an envelope and started for the mail room to leave it in the box for Miss Rivers the typist, but as I turned into the hallway leading to the mail room, I stopped so abruptly I nearly stumbled over my own feet. There was someone standing in the middle of the hall, a strange slouched figure who was certainly neither Hobden nor Fiske.

I had thought I was the only person left in the building save the watchmen. "Wh . . . who's there?" I said, my voice wobbling and squeaking embarrassingly, and groped toward the light switch.

"Noli facere."

It was not a human voice; it crackled and shirred like paper. And it spoke in Latin. I think I knew then, although I did not want to.

"Who are you? How did you get in here?"

"*In a box,*" it said, in Latin. It understood English, even if it would not, or could not, speak it. "*Full of smoke and straw and lies.*" It took a step toward me, rustling and crackling. I took a step back.

"What are you?" I said, although I did not expect an answer. I only wanted to distract it while I gathered myself to run for the front entrance and Fiske and Hobden.

But even as I began to turn, shifting my weight, it said, "*I am the ghost of a Hand of Glory.*" This time I did fall, sprawling my full ungainly length on the marble; before I could pick myself up, before I could even roll over, it was on top of me, paper scratching and scuffling, pinning me flat, holding my wrists in the small of my back. It should not have been able to hold me—even at the time I knew that, but I could not move, could not free myself.

"*He called me* White Charles" it said, the English words gratingly incongruous, and though it spoke in my ear, there was no breath, only the rustling and sighing of paper. "*But he did not know me to name me truly. You do.*"

"No, I don't!" I said vehemently.

"*You lie,*" it said, and I shuddered and cringed into the floor, because it should not have known that, no matter how closely it had observed me.

And what served it for eyes? Had it fashioned those out of paper, too?

"What do you want?" I asked.

It pressed even closer. I had often wondered morbidly what it would be like to be buried under one of the teetering stacks of paper that rose in my office like the topless towers of Ilium; now I knew that I did not want to know. It said, in the soft susurration of paper, "*I want freedom.*"

I tried to scream, but there was paper blocking my mouth. I heaved desperately against the—truly, almost negligible—weight on my back, bucking like a wild horse in a dime novel. I could not dislodge it; it seemed to have molded itself to me and merely waited until I was lying still again.

"*It must be you,*" it said. "*No one else knows what I am.*"

No one else was a threat to it, it meant, but dear God, neither was I! I had no idea how to banish it or to bind it—I did not even know how that foolish antiquarian had managed to summon it. Carolus Albinus alone could never have given him the idea of making a golem from a Hand of Glory, and I could not begin to imagine what mishmash of experiment and tradition and insanity he must ultimately have used.

The paper crinkled as the thing settled lower. I strained away from the paper covering my mouth and now also my nose, and realized that I did know one thing. The antiquarian had tried to fight his creature by burning his books; he had failed, but he had hurt it. It had taken White Charles several weeks in the museum to reach the point where it could be a danger to anyone. Moreover, it had stayed with the books when that was surely the most inconvenient and dangerous course of action. And although it said he had not known it, perhaps there was nevertheless a reason he had called it White Charles.

It was the ghost of a Hand of Glory, it said, yet it clothed itself first in paper.

Perhaps it was merely panic and lack of oxygen that made me so certain I was correct, but I twisted my head, freeing my mouth, and said, "White Charles," as loudly and clearly as I could. I felt the thing flinch.

"That *is* your name," I said. "Your name and your nature, and you cannot escape it."

Its hold on me loosened; I lunged free, crawled a few awkward paces, then got my feet under me and ran. I did not look back. The single sheets of paper that flew around me and slid under my feet were evidence enough. I had hurt it; worse than that, I had guessed its secret. It would not confront me directly again if it could help it.

I was not foolish enough to believe that that meant I was safe.

In the front entrance, behind the long curving counter that separated the coat check from the rotunda with its Foucault's Pendulum ceaselessly swinging, Mr. Fiske and Mr. Hobden came to their feet in alarm as I burst through the doors.

"I need your help," I said between heaving, panting breaths.

"All right, sir," said one, after exchanging an unfathomable look with the other. "What is it you need?"

"The furnace is going, isn't it?"

A stupid question, but they took it in good part. "Yes, sir," one of them said, taking a step forward. "First of October, just like clockwork. Takes a powerful amount of heating, the museum does."

"And you have the, er, the keys? To the boiler room?"

"I do."

"Then please, if you'd, er . . . That is, there's something I need to burn."

"All right," he said equitably, as if he had received stranger requests. Given how long the two of them had worked for the museum, I supposed it was possible that he had.

"What is it you're wanting to burn, Mr. Booth?" said the other, and I was appalled by my own inability to remember which of them was Fiske and which was Hobden.

"Ah," I said. "As to that, I, um . . . "

"Fiske, sir," he said, without any trace of surprise or resentment. I wondered in miserable distracted panic how many times he had faced that blank look from men who saw him every day.

"Fiske, yes. I, er, I'm going to need your help. I need to get into Dr. Starkweather's office."

"Oh," said Fiske. "Oh dear."

Most of the books from Miss Parrington's crate were readily accessible to me. The commonplace book was still in my office; the others were languishing in the communal office of the junior archivists. But the valuable one, Carolus Albinus' *De Spiritu et Morte,* Prague 1588, was immured in Dr. Starkweather's office against the alleged depredations of Mr. Browne and the Department of Restoration and Repairs.

Mr. Fiske had the key to Dr. Starkweather's office, of course, but he balked at letting me in to appropriate something I had already confessed I intended to burn. His position was entirely reasonable and understandable, and it made me so frustrated that I wanted to sit down and howl at the ceiling. Finally, in desperation, I said, "This will get rid of the, er, the rats that aren't rats."

Fiske's eyebrows rose. But he said, "Well, nothing else has, true enough. All right. But when he asks, I don't know anything about it."

"Absolutely. I'll tell him I picked the lock."

"*Can* you?"

"No, but I doubt Dr. Starkweather will, er, ask for a demonstration."

"Fair enough," Fiske said, and he escorted me—and my increasingly unwieldy stack of books—to Dr. Starkweather's office. It took me only a moment to find the *De Spiritu et Morte,* for unlike my own, Dr. Starkweather's office was immaculately tidy and oppressively well-organized. Fiske watched from the doorway, and he locked the door again when I came out.

"That it?" he said.

"Yes. This is all of them." I thought it likely that the only book it was necessary to destroy was the *De Spiritu et Morte,* but I was not prepared to gamble.

Hobden was waiting in the doorway of the boiler room, and he was not alone. For a moment, in bad light and panic, I thought the other person was

White Charles, but then he shifted a little, and I realized it was Achitophel Bates, the colored man who maintained the boilers and other machinery of the museum's infrastructure. I had thought—assumed—hoped—that he had already gone home.

"Good evening, Mr. Booth," he said. He was Southern by birth, and spoke with a slow unhurriable dignity even to Dr. Starkweather.

"Er . . . good evening. I . . . that is . . . " I looked at Hobden, who merely shook his head.

"Mr. Hobden says you're wanting to burn some books." Achitophel Bates was a tall, thin man, as tall as I, and when he looked into my eyes, he did not have to crane to do so. "Seems like a funny thing for an archivist like yourself to want, Mr. Booth."

I was unaccustomed to have anyone identify my profession correctly, much less a colored mechanic, and my surprise must have shown, for he said, "Not all colored men are ignoramuses, Mr. Booth. Some of us can even read."

"I . . . I didn't mean . . . " But I could not take back words I had not said, words I would never have said aloud.

Achitophel Bates waved the matter aside with one long hand. "But tell me, why are you burning books at this time of night?"

I did think of lying, but it was hopeless. Even if I had had any gift for deception, I had no story I could tell. I had nothing but the truth, and so that was what I told Achitophel Bates and the listening Hobden and Fiske. Achitophel Bates' eyebrows climbed higher and higher as I spoke, and when I had finished—or, at least, had run out of words—there was a long silence. In it I could see Achitophel Bates trying to decide if this was some sort of elaborate and cruel hoax. Certainly, it was a more plausible explanation than my lame and faltering truth.

"You remember the trouble we had with Mingus," said Hobden or Fiske.

"I do," said Achitophel Bates, and he looked thoughtfully from me to the watchmen and back again. "You think this is part of that same trouble, Hob?"

"Mr. Booth thinks so," said the watchman, and therefore he was Hobden and surely I could remember that if I tried. "And he's a learned man."

Achitophel Bates snorted. "*Learned* men. Haven't you been working here long enough to know about *learned* men, Hob?"

"Mr. Booth ain't like Dr. Starkweather," said Fiske mildly. "Or like that crazy man—what was his name?—who came down here and tried to get you to sabotage the boilers."

"Mr. Clarence Clyde Blessington," Achitophel Bates said, rolling the name out with a certain degree of relish.

"Oh dear," I said involuntarily. "Mr. Blessington is, er . . . "

"A committed Marxist and a card-carrying member of the Communist Party," Achitophel Bates finished. "Yes, I know. He told me. He showed me the card, even, when he was trying to persuade me that he knew what being oppressed by the bourgeoisie was like better than I did. Tell you the truth, I prefer Mr. Vanderhoef. He won't admit I exist, but at least he doesn't try to *improve* me." His sigh was a mixture of exasperation and contempt. "So just because he's a learned man, Fiske, doesn't mean a goddamn thing."

"I . . . I wouldn't . . . " But what was it, exactly, that I would not do? I settled on, "I wouldn't tell a lie like that," even though that was not, exactly, the point at issue.

"I admit," said Achitophel Bates, "that I would expect a liar to have a better story—and to tell it better, too. And I *do* remember the trouble you had with your dog, Hob, and that's not behavior I've ever seen out of a ratter. So, all right. Let's say it's true. Let's say there's some sort of monster wandering around the museum. I still don't see why you need to burn those books."

"I told you," I said despairingly. Had he not understood? "It's the only way I can think of to destroy it."

"And destroying it has to be the answer?"

"It tried to kill me!"

"Well, what choice did it have?" Achitophel Bates said reasonably, and I stared at him, abruptly and utterly bereft of words. "It doesn't want to be your slave."

"I don't want—"

"I know. And I believe you. For one thing, I figure if that's what you wanted, you could manage it for yourself, you being a learned man and all." And I winced at the derision in his voice. "But how is White Charles supposed to know that?"

And when I floundered, he pressed his point: "You'll forgive me if I have some sympathy for a slave who wants to be free."

He was not old enough to have been a slave—but of course, I realized, flushing hot with my own failure to think the matter through, his parents would have been.

"I . . . I don't want to enslave anyone. But I also don't want to be killed so that White Charles can be free of the slavery I'm not trying to . . . that is . . . " I became hopelessly muddled in my own syntax and fell silent.

"That's a reasonable position," Achitophel Bates said, so gravely that I suspected he was mocking me. "So what you need isn't to burn it. You need to talk to it."

"You, er, you are assuming that it is an entity with whom one can have a reasoned conversation."

"*You* said it had self-volition. And that it spoke to you. So what other conclusion should I draw?"

"And if you're wrong?" I said and hated how near to sullen I sounded.

"Then I'll throw the damn books in the furnace myself. But I'm not wrong. The only question is, how do you convince it to talk to you?"

"*It is not necessary,*" said a new voice, and even if it had not spoken in Latin, I would have known it to be White Charles, for it was a *new* voice in the most fundamental sense of the word, harsh and dull and not in the slightest human. It had spoken from inside the boiler room; Achitophel Bates turned and pushed the door all the way open and I saw why.

White Charles had abandoned its first body and built itself a second one out of newspaper and scrap lumber and an assortment of Achitophel Bates' tools. Where I had gathered only impressions of that first body, I saw this one all too clearly, slumped and strange, as if it could not quite remember what a human body felt like. Its hands were enormous, with screwdrivers and socket wrenches for fingers, its head no more than a suggestion, a lump between the hulking shoulders.

I thought, distantly and quite calmly, that if it did intend evil, we were all doomed.

But, "Audivi," it said. *I heard.* "*You do not wish to command me?*"

"No," I said. And then I realized that by speaking in English, the language in which White Charles had been given the name it hated, I was belying myself. I groped after my Latin; I read it fluently, but had not had to attempt composition since I graduated from Brockstone School. "*I do not,*" I said finally, haltingly—although at least in these circumstances I had an excuse for my habitual hesitations and stammers. "*I want no one to be hurt.*" Clumsy, but my meaning should be clear.

There was a silence long enough that I began to believe that self-assessment had been rankest hubris, but then White Charles said, "*I do not want to hurt.*"

I thought, suddenly and painfully, of the creature in Mary Shelley's novel, which had not done evil until it was taught that evil was all it could expect, and which had yet been so horrible of aspect and origin that it was never offered anything else. Certainly, White Charles was horrible—*the ghost of a Hand of Glory*—but that horribleness was not the fault of the intelligence which animated its scavenged bodies. Like Frankenstein's creature, it had not asked for the parody of life it had been given, and although, whatever my sins, I was not Victor Frankenstein, I had an obligation not to perpetuate evil for its own sake.

"*What do you want?*" I asked it, as I had asked it before, but this time I asked in awkward Latin, and this time White Charles stood and answered me, if not face to face—for indeed it did not exactly have a face—openly. "*I want freedom.*" It made a strange gesture with the massive armatures of its hands and said, "*I want freedom from this.*" *Iste.* This itself, and very emphatically.

"*The body?*" I said, guessing both at its meaning and at the right word.

"*It is not correct,*" said White Charles.

"*I don't understand.*"

"*That a ghost of a Hand of Glory should exist. It is not correct. It is not right. I do not want to be this thing.*"

"What is it saying?" Achitophel Bates said in an undertone.

"It says it wants to be free of being what it is," I said, which was a syntactic nightmare but—I thought—substantially accurate.

"It wants you to kill it? That's awfully convenient."

The irony and skepticism in his voice made me flinch, but I swallowed hard and said, "It understands English. If I were lying, it would know." And I looked, rather desperately, to White Charles.

"Verax," it said. And then slowly, and as if it were actually painful to it, "Truthful."

"But how can you want that?" Achitophel Bates demanded, almost angrily. "How can you want to die?"

"*I was not meant to live,*" White Charles said in Latin, and I translated. "*I am not a living thing enslaved, but a dead thing . . .*" Another of its strange gestures, which I thought perhaps meant it could not find a word to express its meaning. "*A dead thing called into life to be a slave. It is not the same.*"

"Frankenstein's creature was a new life created out of death," I said, half to myself, "but that's a poet's conceit."

"Sum mors vetus," said White Charles. *I am old death.* "*I am death that was never alive.*"

"The ghost of a Hand of Glory," I said. "Not even the ghost of the man whose hand was cut off."

"*You understand,*" said White Charles.

"The ghost of a book," I said, and only then realized that I was still carrying the entire unwieldy stack of books from Miss Parrington's crate.

"So that means we're burning the books after all?" Fiske said doubtfully.

"No," I said, purely on instinct, and was echoed by White Charles' clamorous voice. There was silence for a moment, as Fiske and Hobden carefully did not ask the next obvious question, and Achitophel Bates stood with his arms folded, waiting to see what I would do.

"*He brought you out of the book,*" I said, thinking of that paper body, of the name the creature bore and hated. Then I remembered something else and fell into English because I could not think of the Latin words quickly enough. "No. He called you out of the book. Called you and bound you and feared you so greatly that no binding could ever be enough."

"*He bound me to murder at his command,*" said White Charles, "*and he was not wrong to fear what I would do if the binding failed.*"

I did not, I decided, want to know anything more about the antiquarian or his death. I found my Latin again and said, "*If you were called out of the book, you must go back into the book.*"

White Charles said again, "*You understand,*" and although its voice was not expressive, I thought the emotion in it was relief.

Achitophel Bates was still angry, although I could not tell whether his anger was directed at me or at White Charles or at something else entirely. But he came with us to the rotunda, as did Fiske and Hobden, and watched disapprovingly as I opened the antiquarian's books and used them to lay out a rough circle, with the Carolus Albinus in the center. White Charles also watched, its low-slung head turning minutely to follow my progress.

My circle was somewhat cramped because of the Foucault's pendulum, but this was the largest open space in the museum that did not also contain a host of valuable objects. It would have to do.

Abruptly, Achitophel Bates blocked my path. "Do you know what you're doing?"

"More or less," I said. "Education is, er, not without value."

"I never said it was. But my experience has been that the *value* is in the man, not in what he knows."

I was assailed by examples confirming his contention. Learned men—learned persons, I corrected myself, thinking of my colleague Miss Coburn—were just as prone to be selfish, short-sighted, and stupid as anyone else. Or even more so, as the evidence of White Charles itself suggested. It took a learned man to make such a terrible and complicated mistake.

" . . . I do know what I'm doing. And I, er . . . that is, it's the right thing to do."

"*I want freedom,*" White Charles said thunderously from the other side of the circle, and Achitophel Bates raised his hands in a gesture of surrender.

"That word it keeps using. *Libertas.* Is that liberty?"

"Yes."

"All right," said Achitophel Bates. "I guess from where he's standing, liberty and death are the same thing. Not like Patrick Henry."

"It, er, *is* dead. The state it's in . . . there isn't a word for it, but it isn't alive. 'Awake' is closer. Maybe."

Achitophel Bates was frowning, but it seemed more concentration than anger. "Well, I can't argue a creature has free will and then argue it can't choose for itself. As long as you're sure what you're doing is going to do what it wants."

"As sure as I can be," I said.

He looked at me searchingly, but seemed to accept that I was telling the truth. "All right," he said and stepped aside.

I picked up the de Winter and closed it to create a door in the circle and said in Latin, "*Step inside.*"

White Charles did not hesitate. Its groaning, grinding body shambled past me to stand over the book in the center of the circle. I stepped into the circle myself, then opened the de Winter again and put it back in its place. I knelt in front of White Charles and opened the Albinus at random. It fell open, as books will, to a page that had been often consulted, adorned in this instance with a Vermeulen woodcut of a grave-robber—not inappropriate in a ghoulish Sortes Vergilianae fashion. I reminded myself not to wonder how the antiquarian had come by his materials.

I looked up at White Charles. It was still horrific in aspect, a crude approximation of the human form built by something that did not wish to be human, but I was no longer frightened of it. Achitophel Bates was right. When given the chance, it did not choose evil.

The longest part of my preprations had been working out the Latin; while awkwardness did not matter, imprecision might matter a great deal, and the consequences of using the wrong word could be rather worse than fatal. My words were inelegant, but I knew their meaning was correct.

"*You were called from this book,*" I said in simple, careful Latin, "*and now I call you back to it. Relinquish this unnatural existence. Rest.*" And, although even now I cringed from touching the creature, I reached out and guided one of its screwdriver-fingers to touch the page.

Around the circle, one by one, the books snapped shut.

The edifice that was White Charles was perfectly still for a moment; I saw—or thought I saw—something depart from it, and it went from being a constructed body to being simply an amalgamation of metal and wood. It swayed and sagged, and at the same time I realized what was going to happen, the entire thing came down on my head.

I regained consciousness on the sofa in the Curators' Lounge with the doubled bulldog visages of Hobden and Fiske staring down at me.

"You all right there, Mr. Booth?" said one. And I still could not tell one from the other.

"I, er . . . did it work?"

"As best any of us can tell," said the other.

Everything hurt. My right wrist was made of broken glass. My head was pounding; I felt that if I could observe it from the outside, I would see my temples pulsing like the gills of a fish. "Oh God, the books!"

I started to get up, but sagged and failed halfway.

"D'you reckon you ought to have a doctor, Mr. Booth? You've got a lump on your forehead like a goose-egg, and you're not a good color."

"I'm never a good color," I said. "But we can't leave the books in the rotunda—not to mention the, er, the tools and whatnot. It must be nearly dawn."

"Just past it," said one of them. "But don't worry. We took care of that part. Although Bates said he'd have a word with you later about his tools."

"I put the books back where you found them," said the other, who therefore had to be Fiske. "Including the fancy one in His Nibs' office. I may have got some of the others wrong."

"It doesn't matter," I said. I could not bear it any longer; I reached out with my left hand, caught the material of his sleeve. "Are you Fiske?"

"Yessir," he said, though he and Hobden exchanged alarmed glances.

I squinted to focus, first on his face, then on Hobden's. They were not identical lead soldiers, after all; they were men. And when finally, reluctantly, I met their eyes, first one and then the other, both frowning and worried, at last I saw. Fiske's eyes were brown. Hobden's eyes were blue. And around those eyes, dark and pale, their faces resolved. Nothing changed, for indeed there was nothing in them that needed changing, but I saw them.

But I looked away quickly, before they could see me in return.

On the Lot and In the Air
LISA L HANNETT

The crow's talons gouged new gashes into Jupiter's enamel as the orrery re-volved a clockwork orbit beneath him. Gaslights incandesced from the base of the carnival booth, projecting the solar system's rotations onto the canvas dome above the crow's head. Light strobed into his eyes each time Jupiter completed a rotation, which did nothing to improve the crow's temper. He lifted an articulated wing to shade his eyes; when he dropped it a moment later, he saw a gawking crowd congregating on the midway, its collective attention captivated by the golden gear held steady in his beak.

The midway's makeshift stalls had sprouted like rank weeds, hell-bent on doing damage before they were uprooted. As evening slid into pungent night, the carnival had colonized the city's neglected streets, transforming them with its garish gaslights and flea-bitten draperies. Tents had whorishly spread themselves along all surfaces, like the cheap skin show dames who plumped and corseted their wares in the fair's liminal spaces.

Now the thoroughfare teemed with noxious odors, secreted by a horde of notorious bodies, all crammed into collapsible houses of ill-repute. The buildings supporting the carnival's crooked pavilions dripped constantly, as if a giant pig was spitted in the sky, its juices left to fall like fatty rain onto the scene below. By morning, discarded candy wrappers and flocks of shredded ticket stubs would papier-mâché every tent, signpost, and tree, leaving archaeological layers of rubbish to congeal in the city's slime.

This whole place reeks, thought the crow.

"Forget cheap arcades with rubber-limbed benders! Forget dime museums, string-shows and flea powders! What y'all need is to let off some STEAM! Step right up and have a FREE shot at this Foul Fowl! Sock him in the block and win a plethora of prizes!"

The crow snorted as the sprocketed showman jangled out from behind a threadbare curtain. His stovepipe hat belched steam as he clanked over to the bally platform, which was girded in dusty organza. The showman's pliable tin shanks were clad in darted velor leggings; aluminum tails grafted onto his torso lent his outfit a certain panache, as far as tarnished suits go. Small beads of humidity or grease drip-dropped down his pockmarked cheeks and neck, watermarking the collar of his ruffled shirt with grey splashes. Leaning on a bamboo walking stick atop the dais, he surveyed his flock for a heartbeat. On the second beat, he raised a gloved hand to his breast and bowed like a courtly gentleman.

"Robin Marx, at your service," he said to rapt listeners, "on behalf of the Outdoor Amusement Business Association. That's right, folks—you've heard the rumors, and I'm here to prove 'em true—Robin Marx always gives the first shot for free! Win on that shot and the prize is yours! It's no sin to be a winner, my friends; so come and collect an easy dinner."

Revellers were drawn to Marx's stall faster than you could say shine on spit. He had greased more than a few palms to score such a choice locale; his bird-show was the first thing people'd see when they came in, set up as he was on the right-hand side of the midway, only two paces away from the carnival's main entrance. The showman smiled, and blessed the corruptible lot man as he surveyed his coffer-filling patch of turf.

It was proving to be the prime location for shooting marks.

Ladies and gents disembarked from a motley collection of dirigibles—steam-powered and boiler-driven, with leather balloons or finest silk, depending on the owner's station—directly outside Sideshow Alley's hastily erected plyboard fences. Two guineas were extracted from each heavy purse by way of an entrance fee; once inside, the gullible masses would sure as sugar leave a goodly portion of their remaining shillings to Robin Marx, proprietor and entrepreneur *extraordinaire*.

Pockets jingling, Marx wove through the crowd as if he were the Lord Mayor hisself; winking at the ugly girls and pinching the cute ones' bottoms; shaking hands with the gents and slapping sharpies on the back as he progressed. In the midst of his campaigning, Marx made his way over to the crow's slowly orbiting perch.

Night clung to the bird's mangy figure; his wings hung sodden tissue-like by his sides. The crow felt like a feathered showcase for their racket, a curio cabinet with an aching beak and flea-bitten wings. A cabinet that would do anything for a day off. He sighed, making sure not to knock the gear out of his beak as he did, and listened to the sideshow dames singing to their Johnnies:

" *—one fire burns out another's burning,*
One pain is lessen'd by another's anguish;
Turn giddy, and be holp by backward turning;
One desperate grief cures with another's languish . . . "

"Why don't you ever sing like that, bird?" Marx bent over and turned the ornate key jutting out of the orrery's bulbous base, and forced the slow-ing planets to rev into dazzling motion once more. The crow flapped his discontent. He growled down at the showman's oxidized head, much to the crowd's insipid delight. A mechanical band organ began to caterwaul across the thoroughfare, drowning out the crow's curses.

"Ah," said Marx, pausing before giving the key a final firm twist, 'the only sound more haunting than the calliope is the music of money changing hands, my friend.' And with a pseudo-sincere wink to his partner, he turned on his heel and directed his attention to the burgeoning audience.

Robin Marx hoisted his walking stick, jabbed it skyward to reinforce his ballyhoo. 'The winner of the day will get the key to the midway, straight from my two hands!' He flashed a large bank roll—a carny roll, thought the crow, or I'll be buggered—and made sure to expose the cash reward for only the briefest second before squirreling it away in his waistcoat pocket.

"Get the bird to release his bootlegged prize! Five pence a shot," the showman cried.

The crow made sure to tilt his head as Marx worked the bally; the golden gear winked in the gaslight, catching more than one poor sap's eye. As his roost lifted him skyward, he scanned the faces milling in the throng below him. Tried to guess which unfortunate sucker would reveal hisself—for it always was a bloke—to be Marx's front-worker.

Could be him, the crow thought, as a stocky gentleman in a bowler hat disembarked from a locomotive rickshaw and stepped onto the midway. But he changed his bet as the skin show dames peeled away from the shadows, snagging the bowler hat and its owner with their lurid insinuations. ["*Me they shall feel, while I am able to stand: and 'tis known I am a pretty piece of flesh,*" sang the dames down the way.] He'll be there for hours, the crow realized, or until his pockets (and other things) are sucked dry.

Jupiter convulsed on its brass frame, lurching further upward. The crow over-compensated for this movement and pitched forward at a precarious angle. His tomfoolery earned a round of raucous laughter from the carnival anemones swaying on the polluted floor beneath him. As he regained his balance, he saw a frogman wobble his way out of the ale den four stalls down, ribbetting up his dinner and the keg of piss-weak beer he'd consumed on a dare. Next door, a seedy-looking weasel in patched plus-fours emerged from the sky-grifter's tent. He slid across the frogman's spew, leaving a trail of putrid footsteps as he zigzagged his way up the noisy thoroughfare toward Robin Marx's stall.

The weasel's shifty eyes didn't blink twice to see the team of spontaneously combusting phoenixes bouncing on rickety trampolines in the center of the midway. His listless mouth didn't so much as twitch toward a smile, even when a row of constructs whirled a metallic dervish for his pleasure and coin. No, the weasel had the expression of a man on a mission. He had a job that wanted doing, just as sure as Old Cranker's sausages weren't stuffed with *bona fide* cud-chewer.

That's him all right, the crow thought. That's the shill.

He watched the weasel's stilted progress, humming a fiddley snippet one of the lads from Labrador had played while the caravan steam-rolled its way across barren plains the previous night. The crow tried to ignore the ornamental gear whose jagged spokes were doing their utmost to bash his beak into a less functional shape. Agonising moments passed; the crow's eyes began to water; his ears felt downright clogged with the midway's hubbub. Finally, the weasel stepped up and placed his grimy paws on the footprints Marx had painted on the cobblestones, no more than spitting distance away from the crow's orrery.

"Al-a-ga-zam, capper. Give the crowd a wave, and tell us your name," said Marx in a voice as slick as the carnival's boulevards.

"Trouper," said the weasel.

"Well, Trouper, as I've just been telling these here folk, this bird's a scoundrel of the nineteenth degree. That's right: this rotten crow is flaunting stolen merchandise in his good-for-nothing beak. He pinched that gear right out of my pappy's precious time-keeper"—he withdrew an unremarkable watch from his breast pocket and dangled it mid-air, just as he'd seen hypnotists do— "and now it's ticked its last tock. Irreplaceable, that's what this piece is. You've got to help me, Trouper! Help me get it back from that vicious crow so I can get my pappy's ticker started again!"

The crow pretended to bow his head in shame at hearing Marx's accusations. He swept his wings up before him in a gesture of mock supplication—his least favorite part of the act—and in so doing deftly swapped the golden gear for a confectioner's imitation while Marx explained the rules of the game.

"The first shot's always free, folks. Trouper, give it your best go. If you're a real lucky son-of-a-gun, you'll be the one to empty my purse after one sweet shot." As if of its own volition, Marx's hand stroked his waistcoat pocket while he spoke; and with each tender caress, the counterfeit bankroll bulged for all to see.

The crow gripped Jupiter more tightly as the weasel drew a jacked-up slingshot out of his leather satchel. Trouper braced hisself. He cranked the miniature catapult until its arm was fully cocked and in assault position. He took aim, his furry finger extending toward the trigger on the slingshot's wooden handle, and fired. Across the midway, a group of girls squealed as their teetering seats topped the Ferris wheel's luminous peak; the crowd at Marx's stall gasped as the slingshot snapped into action with an ear-splitting crack of released carbon dioxide.

The crow mimed he'd been hit. He creaked his sooty wings around in comical circles, then swallowed the confectioner's gear with a tinny gulp. The orrery shuddered to a halt. From beneath cracked eyelids, he watched his performance drain dollar signs away from the sea of greedy faces beneath him. He chuckled as he righted hisself on his now-stalled perch.

"Take that, you old shit," he squawked at Marx, ruffling his oil-slick plumage. "Try and get your precious gear now."

"You see, folks? You see what pain he gives me? Please—someone—*anyone*—step right up! Help me shut that miserable trap of his for good!" Right on cue, the bird started wheezing, hacking and choking, reeling the crowd in with faux suffering. He covered his beak with a wing—as all polite crows should do when they cough—and replaced the dissolved candy gear with its golden counterpart. Beams of golden light twinkled out of the crow's mouth as the clean gear was reinstated, wedged between the upper and lower sections of his beak.

The crowd fell quiet at Marx's feet. A chorus of accordions droned down the midway; coal-burners roared with delight as they powered bumper cars next door; whistles sporadically announced winners all across the carnival's crooked landscape; [" —yet I cannot choose but laugh, To think it should leave crying—" wafted out of the skin-tents]; but the group that had pressed in close to witness the crow's imminent demise was shocked into distrustful silence by the weasel's apparent failure, and the crow's derring-do.

Venus chose that moment to add insult to the audience's injury. The rose-colored globe, two prongs away from the crow's own Jupiter, flared on the orrery with a sudden brightness that blinded the already mute crowd, throwing the midway into unflattering relief. Yet when the yellow-blue afterimages faded from the spectators' eyes, their hands sprang together with gleeful applause. Tiny wind-up fireflies had escaped their Venusian cage: on Marx's command, they buzzed into formation, their minute bodies spelling out 'Golden Guinea' in a bewitching message of fortune.

"Never fear, my friends. What did I tell you? Everyone's a winner at Robin Marx's." The showman beamed with feigned magnanimity from his position on the stall's counter. He released the hidden lever that had unleashed the automatic fireflies, and blew contented smoke rings from his hat as he coddled the ersatz pocket watch. "Yes, the crow's still a crook, but good Trouper here shook him up a good one, didn't he?" Catcalls and wolf whistles punctuated general expressions of good humor in response.

"And as the Lady Venus wills, the Gentleman shall receive," Marx said. A newly-struck gold coin instantly appeared in Marx's hand, and disappeared just as quickly in Trouper's. The weasel snatched the throwaway as if it were the first and last coin he'd ever see, then forced a retreat through the jostling herd now vying to knock the crow senseless.

Mark after mark placed feet on painted footprints, squared their shoulders and threw—but none seemed blessed with Trouper's luck. Children began throwing tantrums instead of projectiles. One sniveling whelp kicked up such a stink that Marx gave both boy and mother a few ducats to go and see the Marx Brothers' Rocket-Powered Penny Farthings. This one tactical freebie was all it took; a deluge of 5p's avalanched across the countertop, and into Marx's purse.

More stones were launched the crow's way amid showers of minor coins; the first of these missed, but the latter staunchly met their target. "Sorry, matie," Marx said to one sour-breathed contestant, whose chest heaved against his sweat-soaked shirt after another pebble hurtled wide of its mark. "Your robust bear-huggers are just too strong for this game! You threw that one so quick, I reckon an African cheeter couldn't have caught it."

"C'mon, Marx. Give me a rehash. I'll slip you a free strudel next time you come past my bakery," said the blubbery man through his long mustachios. Marx walked behind the counter, tilted his bulk forward on the orrery's concealed pedals, and said, "Tell you what I'll do for you, matie: if you win on the next go, I'll give you back every penny you've gambled. Guaranteed. Peg this wretched bird with all your impressive might and you'll have more dough than you could ever knead at that bakery of yours."

Marx's tongue kept flappin' until he got his way; such smooth words never did the marks any good. Bitter smoke billowed from the street vendors' burners, following the losers home. Nightwatchmen changed shifts, grunting salutations and beating billies against enhanced meat-hooks, as adrenaline levels bloated the carnival's nihilistic avenues. ["*To see now, how a jest shall come about!*" laughed the dancing girls, "*I warrant, an I should live a thousand years, I never should forget it —*"] The disgruntled baker turned away from Marx's stall, stuffing his remaining two guineas into a ragged pocket. He nearly tripped over the fox wheeling its way up to the target.

Dressed in a chrome yellow top hat and matching damask suit, the fox was a dapper fellow, every inch a gentleman. The spiked wheels of his wicker invalid's chair sought purchase on the midway's greasy cobblestones; they skidded nauseatingly, and moved forward at an inchworm's pace. No matter if it took until morning for his master to reach his goal, the fox's kettledrum construct would not interfere. Only when he was contentedly puffing away on a mahogany pipe, his wheeled chair jauntily parked on the scuffed painted footprints, did the housebot approach. He draped a Burberry rug across his master's immobile copper knees, tucking it gently between the chair's arms and the fox's atrophied hindquarters, then stood off to his left-hand side.

The fox's eyes never wavered from their prize as he asked the bot to analyze the odds of his winning this game.

A slender ticker tape chugged out of a slit beneath the construct's speaker box. He tore it against his serrated teeth, and passed the results over to his master. "Immeasurably in your favor. As usual, Sir."

"Hey there, cowboy." Marx rearranged his features until they imitated a passably charming grin. He released a burst of steam from his top hat as he spoke.

The crow eyeballed the fox from his lofty perch. Those who balanced on wheels instead of legs were such simple targets. Weaker than children, and less confident. "Come have a go," he said, flicking the gear to the corner of his beak and projecting his voice for all to hear. "In fact, what's say we give him TWO goes for free, on accounta his poorly condition? Don't that sound fair, Robin?" he asked, seeking and receiving the showman's nod.

The fox tapped his pipe on the chair's padded arm, watched its sticky contents combine with the sludge lazily seeping around his wheels. ["*— let them*

measure us by what they will, We'll measure them a measure, and be gone . . ."]
He flicked a shred of tobacco off his lap, and gently cleared his throat.

"Indeed, I will take two shots, as you've so kindly offered, Mr. Black," said the fox.

It took a second for the crow to realize the fox was addressing *him*. Not 'bird', not 'jackdaw', not 'scoundrel', no. He was Mr. Black.

The fox feigned interest in the kaleidoscopic projections whirling around Marx's tent while the crow fluffed and preened his feathers.

Then he opened fire.

"Shot the first: a question. How did such a magnificent creature—genuine *Corvus corone*, pure flesh and bone, not a single enhancement—how did such a miraculous being come to be shackled and used as a cyborg's lackey?"

The crow spluttered, and nearly swallowed the gear in earnest.

"Shot the second," the fox continued, undaunted. "An offer. Work for me."

The crow cocked his head, and waited for the punch line.

"Let me set the terms," said the fox, "for I am sure you will find them suitably appealing."

"First," he said, "I will prohibit you from participating in any specimen of show—even though it would be an absolute delight to hear your dulcet tones raised in song, Mr. Black, old chap."

"But, no. No singing today. Instead, I would like to employ your golden sense. What does Mr. Marx pay you? Some flattering mirrors in front of which you might preen? Perhaps some chymical bird-feed?"

The crow kept silent.

[*"True, I talk of dreams,*
Which are the children of an idle brain,
Begot of nothing but vain fantasy . . ."]

"I will offer you a gentleman's fare, Mr. Black," the fox continued, quietly. "I am not interested in paying carny's fees for such a one as you are. Sneer all you like at the term, Mr. Marx; you cannot deny that you have treated this dark angel as nothing more than a lowly *carny*."

"I need a partner, Mr. Black, for a somewhat more lucrative . . . oh, let's call it a venture, shall we? Your guile, your cleverness, your wit: these are exactly the assets I need for this undertaking. You are far too intelligent for this braggart's show! In fact, the show's very success hinges on your intellect. Don't think I didn't see you exchange the false gear with the real, earlier—"

— the crowd stirred, grumbled as they fondled their weightless pockets —

— Marx fumed, "That's enough out of you, cowboy—"

" —indeed without your finesse, there would *be* no Robin Marx! And how does he repay you? By tying you to a moldy planet and shoving a gear down your gullet?"

[*"Ay, while you live, draw your neck out of the collar . . ."*]

"What horror will he perform next? Are you a crow, Mr. Black? Or are you a soiled dove, blackened much as this city has been of late, by too many trips up Marx's sooty arse?"

The paralytic's got a point, thought the crow.

He spat the gear out, propelling it with fury, loosening his tongue to ingratiate hisself to his new employer. The crowd dispersed like exhaled smoke. [Ladies, dames, raised their voices, "*To move is to stir; and to be valiant is to stand; therefore, if thou art mov'd, thou runn'st away . . .*"]

The tiny gear negotiated a haphazard path across the cobblestones, before spinning to a halt at the housebot's burnished feet. Before Marx could shift his frame off the counter, the bot had dropped a silk handkerchief onto the gear, collected it, and polished it properly. Then he lifted his master's damask coattails, exposing the clockworks inset in his narrow russet back.

Half of the works were still, while the other portion whirred out their quotidian functions. The bot gently laid the gear into the fox's lower back, and used his index finger to screw it into place.

"What do you want me to do, boss?" asked the crow, his eagerness to escape the ramshackle orrery hanging like a painful chandelier from his brief question.

"Why, you've already done it, old chap," said the newly mobile fox as his lower legs sprang to life. "You really have done it!"

["*O, Wilt thou leave me so unsatisfied?*"]

Yipping like a newborn pup, the fox switched his tail into overdrive. He sprang out of his redundant chair, blew the crow a grateful kiss as he sped past, fleeing the scene before he could get slicked.

["*What satisfaction canst thou have to-night?*" chimed the sideshow dames as the Johnnies were ejected from their parlors. The women's laughter was harsh and raw.]

A Woman's Best Friend
ROBERT REED

The gangly man was running up the street, his long legs pushing through the fresh unplowed snow. He was a stranger; or at least that was her initial impression. In ways that Mary couldn't quite define, he acted both lost and at home. His face and manner were confused, yet he nonetheless seemed to navigate as if he recognized some portion of his surroundings. From a distance, his features seemed pleasantly anonymous, his face revealing little of itself except for a bony, perpetually boyish composition. Then a streetlamp caught him squarely, and he looked so earnest and desperate, and so sweetly silly, that she found herself laughing, however impolite that was.

Hearing the laughter, the man turned toward her, and when their eyes joined, he flinched and gasped.

She thought of the tiny pistol riding inside her coat pocket: A fine piece of machinery marketed under the name, "A Woman's Best Friend."

The stranger called to her.

"Mary," he said with a miserable, aching voice.

Did she know this man? Perhaps, but there was a simpler explanation. People of every persuasion passed by her desk every day, and her name was no secret. He might have seen her face on several occasions, and he certainly wasn't the kind of fellow that she would have noticed in passing. Unless of course he was doing some nasty business in the back of the room—behaviors that simply weren't allowed inside a public library.

As a precaution, Mary slipped her hand around the pistol's grip.

"Who are you?" she asked.

"Don't you know me?" he sputtered.

Not at all, no. Not his voice, not his face. She shook her head and rephrased her question. "What do I call you?"

"George."

Which happened to be just about her least favorite name. With a reprimanding tone, she pointed out, "It's wicked-cold out here, George. Don't you think you should hurry home?"

"I lost my home," he offered.

His coat was peculiarly tailored, but it appeared both warm and in good repair. And despite his disheveled appearance, he was too healthy and smooth-tongued to be a common drunk. "What you need to do, George . . . right now, turn around and go back to Main Street. There's two fine relief houses down there that will take you in, without questions, and they'll take care of you—"

"Don't you know what night this is?" he interrupted.

She had to think for a moment. "Tuesday," she answered.

"The date," he insisted. "What's the date?"

"December 24th—"

"It's Christmas Eve," he interrupted.

Mary sighed, and then she nodded. Pulling her empty hand out of the gun pocket, she smiled at the mysterious visitor, asking, "By any chance, George . . . is there an angel in this story of yours?"

A gust of wind could have blown the man off his feet. "You know about the angel?" he blubbered.

"Not from personal experience. But I think I know what he is, and I can make a guess or two about what he's been up to."

"Up to?"

She said, "George," with a loud, dismissive tone. "I'm sorry to have to tell you this. But there's no such thing as a genuine angel."

"Except I saw him."

"You saw someone. Where was he?"

"On the bridge outside town," he offered. "He fell into the river, and I jumped in after him and dragged him to shore."

The man was sopping wet, she noted. "But now what were you doing out on the bridge, George?"

He hesitated. "Nothing," he replied with an ashamed, insistent tone.

"The angel jumped in, and you saved him?"

"Yes."

That sounded absurd. "What did your angel look like, George?"

"Like an old man."

"Then how do you know he was an angel?"

"He said he was."

"And after you rescued him . . . what happened? Wait, no. Let me guess. Did your angel make noise about earning an aura or his halo—?"

"His wings."

"Really? And you believed that story?"

George gulped.

"And what did this wingless man promise you, George."

"To show me . . . "

"What?"

"How the world would be if I'd never been born."

She couldn't help but laugh again. Really, this man seemed so sweet and so terribly lost. She was curious, even intrigued. Not that the stranger was her type, of course. But then again, this was a remarkable situation, and maybe if she gave him a chance . . .

"All right, George. I'm going to help you."

He seemed cautiously thrilled to hear it.

"Come home with me," she instructed him. And then she turned back toward the old limestone building that occupied most of a city block.

"To the library?" he sputtered.

"My apartment's inside," she mentioned.

"You live inside the library?"

"Because I'm the head librarian. That's one of the benefits of my job: The city supplies me with a small home. But it's warm and comfortable, with enough room for three cats and one man-sized bed."

Her companion stood motionless, knee-deep in snow.

"What's wrong now, George?"

"I don't," he muttered.

"You don't what?"

"Go into the homes of young women," he muttered.

"I'm very sorry to disappoint, but I'm not that young." For just an instant, she considered sending him to a facility better equipped for this kind of emergency. And in countless realms, she surely did just that. But on this world, at this particular instant, she said, "You need to understand something, George. You are dead. You have just killed yourself. By jumping off a bridge, apparently. And now that that's over with, darling, it's high time you lived a little."

Reverence has its patterns, its genius and predictable clichés. Many realms throw their passions into houses of worship—splendid, soothing buildings where the wide-eyed faithful can kneel together, bowing deeply while repeating prayers that were ancient when their ignorant bodies were just so many quadrillion atoms strewn across their gullible world. But if a world was blessed with true knowledge, and if there were no churches or mosques, temples or synagogues, the resident craftsmen and crafty benefactors often threw their hands and fortunes into places of learning. And that was why a small town public library wore the same flourishes and ornate marvels common to the greatest cathedrals.

George hesitated on the polished marble stairs, gazing up at the detailed mosaic above the darkened front door.

"What is this place?" he whispered.

She said, "My library," for the last time.

George was tall enough to touch the bottom rows of cultured, brightly colored diamond tiles, first with gloves on and then bare fingers.

"Who are these people? They look like old Greeks."

"And Persians. And Indians. And Chinese too." She offered names that almost certainly meant nothing to him. But she had always enjoyed playing the role of expert, and when the twenty great men and women had been identified, she added, "These are the Founders."

"Founders of what?"

"Of the Rational Order," she replied. "The Order is responsible for twenty-three hundred years of peace and growth."

George blinked, saying nothing.

She removed her right glove and touched the crystal door. It recognized her flesh, but only after determining that her companion was unarmed did the door slowly, majestically swing open for both of them.

"I can answer most questions," she promised.

Like an obedient puppy, George followed after her.

Sensing her return, the library awakened. Light filled the ground floor. Slick white obelisks and gray columns stood among the colorful, rather chaotic furnishings. Chairs that would conform to any rump waited to serve. Clean, disinfected readers were stacked neatly on each black desk. Even two hours after closing, the smell of the day's patrons hung in the air—a musky, honest odor composed of perfumes and liquor, high intentions and small dreams.

"This is a library?"

"It is," she assured.

"But where's the books?"

Her desk stood beside the main aisle—a wide clean and overly fancy piece of cultivated teak and gold trimmings. Her full name was prominently displayed. She picked up the reader that she had been using at day's end, and George examined the nameplate before remarking, "You never married?"

She nearly laughed. But "No" was a truthful enough answer, and that was all she offered for now.

Again he returned to the missing books.

"But our collection is here," she promised, compiling a list of titles from a tiny portion of the holdings. "You see, George . . . in this world, we have better ways to store books than writing on expensive old parchment."

"Parchment?"

"Or wood pulp. Or plastic. Or flexible glass sheets."

His eyes jumped about the screen. He would probably be able to read the words, at least taken singly. But the subject and cumulative oddness had to leave him miserably confused.

"This town isn't a large community," she mentioned. "But I like to think that we have a modest, thorough collection." Mary smiled for a moment, relishing her chance to boast. "Anyone is free to walk through our door and print copy of any title in our catalog. But I'll warn you: If we made paper books of every volume, and even if each book was small enough to place in those long hands of yours, George . . . well, this library isn't big enough to hold our entire collection. To do that, we'd have to push these walls out a little farther than the orbit of Neptune."

The news left the poor man numb. A few labored breaths gave him just enough strength to fix his gaze once again on the reader, and with a dry, sorry little voice, he asked, "Is this Heaven?"

"As much as any place is," she replied.

George was sharp. Confused, but perceptive. He seemed to understand some of the implications in her explanation. With a careful voice, he read aloud, "Endless Avenues. A thorough study of the universe as a single quantum phenomena.'"

"Your home earth," she began. "It happens to be one of many."

"How many?"

"Think of endless worlds. On and on and on. Imagine numbers reaching out past the stars and back again. Creation without ends, and for that matter, without any true beginning either."

Poor George stared across the enormous room, voicing the single word, "No."

"Every microscopic event in this world splits the universe in endless ways, George. The process is essential and it is inevitable, it happens easily and effortlessly, and nothing about existence is as lovely or perfect as this endless reinvention of reality."

The reader made a sharp pop when he dropped it on the floor. "How do you know this?" he asked.

"Centuries of careful, unsentimental scientific exploration," she replied.

He sighed, his long frame leaning into her desk.

"My earth is rather more advanced than yours," she continued. "We have come to understand our universe and how to manipulate it. Everyone benefits, but the richest of us have the power to pass to our neighboring worlds and then back again."

Once more, he said, "No."

She touched him for the first time—a fond, reassuring pat delivered high on his back, the coat still wet from the river. "It takes special machinery and quite a lot of energy to travel through the multiverse," she admitted. "Tying the natural laws into a useful knot . . . it's the kind of hobby that only certain kinds of people gravitate towards."

Poor George wanted to lie down. But he had enough poise, or at least the pride, to straighten his back before saying, "My angel."

"Yes?"

"He was just a man?"

She laughed quietly, briefly. Then with a sharp voice, she warned, "My world embraces quite a few amazing ideas, George. But there's no such notion as 'just a man'. Or 'just a woman', for that matter. Each of us is a magnificent example of what the infinite cosmos offers."

This particular man sighed and stared at his companion. Then with his own sharpness, he confessed, "You look just like my wife."

"Which is one reason why your angel chose this world, I suspect."

"And your voice is exactly the same. Except nothing that you're telling me makes any sense."

About that, she offered no comment.

Instead she gave him another hard pat. "There's a private elevator in the back," she told her new friend. "And first thing, we need to get you out of those cold clothes."

Once his coat and shoes were removed, she set them inside the conditioning chamber to be cleaned and dried. But George insisted wearing every other article on his body, including the soaked trousers and the black socks that squished when he walked.

She stomped the snow off her tall boots and removed her coat. Then before hanging up the coat up, she slipped the little pistol from its pocket and tucked it into the silk satchel riding on her hip.

He didn't seem to notice. For the moment, George's attention was fixed on the single-room apartment. "I expected a little place," he muttered.

"Isn't this?"

"No, this is enormous." Her ordinary furnishings seemed to impress the man, hands stroking the dyed leather and cultured wood. Artwork hung on the walls and in the open air—examples of genius pulled from a multitude of vibrant, living earths—and he gave the nearest sculptures a quick study. Then he drifted over to the antique dresser, lifting one after another of the framed portraits of her family and dearest friends.

She followed, saying nothing.

"Who are these two?" he asked.

"My parents."

George said, "What?"

"I take it those aren't your wife's parents."

"No."

She quoted the ancient phrase, "'The same ingredients pulled from different shelves.'"

George turned to look at her, and he gave a start. His eyes dipped. He was suddenly like a young boy caught doing something wicked. It took a few moments to collect his wits.

"My DNA is probably not identical to your wife's," she assured. "Not base-pair for base-pair, at least."

He wanted to look at her, but a peculiar shyness was weighing down on him.

She said, "George," with a reprimanding tone.

He didn't react.

"You know this body," she pointed out. "If you are telling the truth, that is. On this other world, you married to somebody like me. Correct?"

That helped. The eyes lifted, and his courage. With more than a hint of disapproval, he said, "When I found you . . . "

"Yes?"

"Where were you going?"

"To a pleasant little nightclub, as it happens."

His hand and her smiling parents pointed at her now. "Dressed like that?"

"Yes."

"You don't have . . . "

"What, George?"

"Underwear," he managed. "Where is your underwear?"

Every world had its prudes. But why had that anonymous 'angel' send her one of the extras?

George quietly asked, "What were you going to do . . . at this club . . . ?"

"Drink a little," she admitted. "And dance until I collapsed."

George dropped his gaze again.

"You were married to this body," she reminded him. "I can't believe you didn't know it quite well by now."

He nodded. But then it seemed important to mention, "We have children."

"Good."

"Your figure . . . my wife's . . . well, you're quite a bit thinner than she is now . . . "

"Than she was," Mary said.

His eyes jumped up.

"In your old world, you are a drowned corpse," she said. "You must have had your reasons, George. And you can tell me all about them, if you want. But I don't care why you decided to throw yourself off that bridge. Your reasons really don't matter to me."

"My family . . . " he began.

"They'll get by, and they won't."

He shook his head sorrowfully.

"Every response on their part is inevitable, George. And neither of us can imagine all of the ramifications."

"I abandoned them," he whispered.

"And on countless other earths, you didn't. You didn't make the blunders that put you up on that bridge, or you pushed through your little troubles. You married a different woman. You married ten other women. Or you fell deeply in love with a handsome boy named Felix, and the two of you moved to Mars and were married on the summit of the First Sister's volcano, and you and your soul mate quickly adopted a hundred Martian babies—little golden aliens who called both of you Pappy and built a palace for you out of frozen piss and their own worshipful blood."

George very much wanted to collapse. But the nearest seat was the round and spacious bed.

He wouldn't let himself approach it.

But she did. She sat on the edge and let her dress ride high, proving if he dared look that she was indeed wearing underwear after all.

"This club you were going to . . . ?"

"Yes, George?"

"What else happened there? If you don't mind my asking."

Jealousy sounded the same on every earth. But she did her best to deflect his emotions, laughing for a moment or two before quietly asking, "Did your Mary ever enjoy sex?"

Despite himself, George smiled.

"Well, I guess that's something she and I have in common."

"And you have me in common too," he mentioned.

"Now we do, yes."

Then this out-of-place man surprised her. He stared at her bare knees and the breasts behind the sheer fabric. But the voice was in control, lucid and calm, when he inquired, "What about that tiny gun? The one you took out of your coat and put in your purse?"

"You saw that?"

"Yes."

She laughed, thrilled by the unexpected.

Pulling open the satchel, she showed the weapon to her guest. "Every earth has its sterling qualities, and each has its bad features too. My home can seem a little harsh at times. Maybe you noticed the rough souls along Main Street. Crime and public drunkenness are the reasons why quite a few good citizens carry weapons wherever they go."

"That's terrible," he muttered.

"I've never fired this gun at any person, by the way."

"But would you?"

"Absolutely."

"To kill?" he blubbered.

"On other earths, that's what I am doing now. Shooting bad men and the worst women. And I'm glad to do it."

"How can you think that?"

"Easily, George." She passed the gun between her hands. "Remember when I told you that our richest citizens can travel from earth to earth? To a lesser degree, that freedom belongs to everyone, everywhere. It was the same on your home world too, although you didn't understand it at the time."

"I don't understand it now," he admitted.

"You are here, George. You are here because an angelic individual took the effort to duplicate you—cell for cell, experience for experience. Then your wingless benefactor set you down on a world where he believed that you would survive, or even thrive." With her finger off the trigger, she tapped the pistol against her own temple. "Death is a matter of degree, George. This gun can't go off, unless the twin safeties fail. But I guarantee you that right now, somebody exactly like me is shooting herself in the head. Her brains are raining all over you. Yet she doesn't entirely die."

"No?"

"Of course not." She lowered the gun, nodding wistfully. "We have too many drinkers on this world, and with that comes a fairly high suicide rate. Which is only reasonable. Since we understand that anybody can escape this world at any time, just like you fled your home—leap off the bridge, hope for paradise, but remaining open-minded enough to accept a little less."

George finally settled on edge of the bed, close enough to touch her but his hands primly folded on his long lap. "What are you telling me?" he asked. "That people kill themselves just to change worlds?"

"Is there a better reason than that?"

He thought hard about the possibilities. "This angel that saved me. He isn't the only one, I take it."

"They come from endless earths, some far more powerful than ours. There's no way to count all of them."

"And do they always save the dead?"

"Oh, they hardly ever do that," she admitted. "It is a genuine one-in-a-trillion-trillion-trillion occurrence. But if an infinite number of Georges jump off the bridge, then even that one-in-almost-never incident is inevitable. In fact, that tiny unlikely fraction is itself an infinite number."

He shook his head numbly.

She leaned back on her elbows. "Most of these benefactors . . . your angel, for instance . . . throw those that they've saved onto earths that feel comfortable with refugees like you. My world, for instance."

"This happens often?"

"Not exactly often. But I know of half a dozen incidents this year, and that's just in our district."

George looked down at his cold wet socks.

"Unlike God," she promised, "quantum magic is at work everywhere."

"Do you understand all the science, Mary?"

She sat up again. "I'm a librarian, not a high-physics priestess."

That pleased him. She watched his smile, and then at last she noticed that her guest was beginning to shiver.

"You're cold, George."

"I guess I am."

"Take off those awful socks."

He did as instructed. Then laughing amiably, he admitted, "There. Now you sound exactly like my wife."

They were both laughing when something large suddenly moved beneath the big bed.

George felt the vibration, and alarmed, he stared at Mary.

"My cats," she offered. "They're usually shy around strangers."

"But that felt . . . " He lifted his bare feet. "Big."

"Kitties," she sang. "Sweeties."

Three long bodies crawled into the open, stretching while eying the newcomer from a safe distance.

"What kinds of cats are those?" George whispered.

"Rex is the miniature cougar," she explained. "Hex is the snow leopard. And Missie is half pygmy tiger, half griffon."

With awe in his voice, George said, "Shit."

"I take that to mean you didn't have cats like this on your earth?"

"Not close to this," he agreed.

She sat back again, sinking into the mattress.

And again, this man surprised her. "You mentioned Mars."

"I guess I did. Why?"

"On my earth, we thought that there could be some kind of simple life on that world."

"You didn't know for certain?"

He shook his head. "But a few minutes ago, you mentioned something about Martians. Are they real, or did you just make them up?"

"They're real somewhere, George."

He frowned.

Then she laughed, explaining, "Yes, my Mars is home to some very ancient life forms. Tiny golden aliens that drink nothing but peroxides. And my Venus is covered with airborne jungles and an ocean that doesn't boil because of the enormous air pressure. And Sisyphus is covered with beautiful forests of living ice—"

"What world's that?"

"Between Mars and Jupiter," she mentioned.

George blinked, took a big breath and burst out laughing.

That was when Mary told her blouse to fall open.

He stared at her, and the laughter stopped. But he was still smiling, looking shamelessly happy, begging her, "But first, Mary . . . would you please put your gun? Someplace safe. After everything I've been through, I don't want even the tiniest chance of something going wrong now."

The Dying World
LAVIE TIDHAR

1. Bonsai

It's a beautiful world, easily worth killing for, but what would be the point? The world, encased in vacuum and glass, is blue-white, a miniature Earth, with a marble-sized sun rotating around it. It has a tiny atmosphere, tiny, lovingly-sculpted seas, three continents, numerous tiny islands, tectonic plate activity, miniature volcanoes, and some seriously large creatures for a world so small. It's a hot, humid place, this world. The glass orb that contains it protects it perfectly. Touching the surface of the orb, the old man magnifies a part of the tiny planet, watching, completely engrossed, as a sea creature the shape of a disc wraps itself around a creature shaped like a ball with many circular mouths full of sharp teeth. The ensuing fight attracts other creatures, and for a moment this particular point under this particular sea is swarming with life.

The man is so engrossed in his creation that he fails to hear the doors of the old church opening behind him. Outside it is dusk, and an enormous red sun is visible on the horizon, setting slowly. The man had always loved this place, with its ancient mausoleum and church spires shaped like ice-cream cones and its wide open square. It has an aura of faded grandeur, of stories having been worn deep into the stones by the passing of countless humans.

When he does hear the light footsteps approach it is already too late. Something cold touches the back of his head; he has only enough time to think he would like to be reborn as a butterfly before the assassin squeezes the trigger and the old man's head explodes all over the glass orb, covering an entire world in a violent red haze.

2. Black Rain

The assassin checks Mother Russia for the next forty-eight hours. Of the thirty of so humans living in the place one is still unaccounted for, which worries the assassin. He composes a message in Japanese, utilizing haiku for its brevity and sincerity of form. It is a quantum haiku, with meanings ranging from *Apologies For Disturbing One's Shape* to *Notification Had Been Sent in Advance*. He sends it to the church on Red Square in the biological form of a moth, the poem encoded into rapid wing movements. The moth fails to return. The assassin knows he can expect a counter-assassination at any moment, which he is quite looking forward to. He is using the ancient codes, Moscow Rules, to guide his behavior. Meanwhile he waits. The Entity on Everest, having requested he carry out this assignment, has not sent further instructions. By protocol, the assassin would not deliver the world directly. There will be a portal—a drop point.

And so . . . he should wait but, being as he is, he does not like to. It is why he is Assassin, rather than Maker, say, which certainly requires a fastidious kind of patience, or Explorer, which basically means—to the assassin's way of thinking—a way of further moving away from humanity, not to mention ice-sleeping in space for countless generations. The assassin is a humanist first and foremost, something he shared with his target, but he wonders now, a little uneasily, whether the target might be changing his mind about such things, which are a matter of philosophy, you could say, more than anything.

And so he decides, despite Moscow Rules, despite protocol, to act, to *do*— which is the human in him, still, the restless ape who doesn't like to wait. He steps out of the giant black cube of a building that he had been inhabiting on Dzerzhinsky Square—which turns out to save his life. As he turns to look at the building he sees clouds gathering over the roof; they form in mid-air and concentrate into discs that hover lower and lower. Where they finally touch the surface the entire building slowly grows transparent, the black leached out of it into the clouds, then slowly the entire edifice crumbles gently to the ground, the dust swirling lazily in the air. The black clouds above slowly dissipate into water, or perhaps it is ink. Where their rain falls it stains the pavement. The assassin opens an umbrella and walks away, meanwhile lodging a complaint with the Greater Moscow Entity regarding the destruction of a Monument of Historical Significance, not to mention the forbidden use of clouds, banned under a treaty too long ago for anyone to remember it. Inside, though, the assassin is pleased. So the old man wants to play after all.

3. Butterfly

The man does not return as a butterfly, of course. He returns as a cloud of butterflies, which is quite liberating after wearing human form for so long. A part of him watches the assassin walking through the inky rain, his feet leaving sootmarks on the pavement. The assassin is following Moscow Rules, one of which is Always Blend In. He is shifting—becomes a part of old brickwork, becomes shadow in the awning of a store, becomes glass, becomes reflection—a tedious mode of travel, the old man feels, but it does make it harder to follow him. The old man is spread all over the city now, a cloud of bright butterflies that beat their wings lazily in the dying light of the red sun. A part of him acknowledges the Greater Moscow Entity's complaint, sends back a Russian shrug, and watches as the old KGB building is reconstructed, the dust reassembling itself from the middle, up to the roof and down to the ancient foundations. He wants his world back, but it isn't there, and he wonders with some irritation where the assassin had hidden it. For a moment he scribbles a message in the sky, rearranging molecules to reflect light in a certain way, so that anyone glancing up can see the words: *Worlds Are To Be Given, Not Taken Away.*

The man sighs, millions of butterflies beating their wings as one. No one cares much for his worlds. He feels he should be flattered, and wonders what collector had sent the assassin after him. He did in fact receive Notification of Intent but had forgotten to follow it up, being too absorbed in a new ring-world that seemed quite promising. He decides to wait. It is the assassin's turn, after all, and he is curious to see what he would do.

4. Reflections

The assassin reconfigures himself into human form and for a moment watches his reflection in the air. His reflection stares back and nods in acknowledgment. It's a good form, he thinks. He shapes a few more reflections out of air and dust and sends them across the city. He knows the man is watching him, but he doesn't care. Where he is going the old man won't be able to follow.

He rings the bell.

The building used to be a hotel, a long time before. Its current occupant has had it restored some time in the past before moving in. He is a collector, and each former room is now a museum of sorts. He is another collector—the world is full of collectors—but a useful one, which makes him almost unique.

"Come in."

The door opens. He steps in and the door closes behind him, trapping a butterfly in the process. The butterfly emits a screech of what might be amusement before turning to dust.

"Second floor."

He climbs the steps. At the top of the landing on the second floor is a small chamber. The unseen voice says, "Get inside."

"Is this really necessary?" the assassin says.

"You know where the door is," the voice says, unhelpfully, and the assassin shrugs and steps through.

The ancient meme-washer starts to life, flooding the chamber with steam. It is like a sauna filled with tiny crawlers, who comb through the assassin's mind, searching for any meme he may have unwittingly picked up on his way and eradicating them. He feels a song go out of his head, a jingle for a soap that hasn't been sold in millennia, a religion, perhaps two, a theory of everything, a new concept of beauty and a recurring image of possibly alien origin, he can no longer remember.

"You're clean."

The doors open, and he steps through into the corridor, where the collector waits.

5. The Collector

The collector is a fat man with a toupee and a pipe and three very blue eyes. He smokes high-density encoded tobacco, which gives him a glazed look as he assimilates the data with each puff on his pipe. "Life forms on Carthage III," he says. "Fascinating." Puff. "The poetry of sentient asteroids." Puff. "Tasty. Ah, the Great Attractor, her life and cosmological significance for nearby galaxies. Did I ever tell you I met her once?"

The Great Attractor is two-hundred and fifty thousand light years away and the size of several galactic clusters. Apart from gravitationally affecting galaxies around her, she is also nosy, possibly senile, and generally believed to be, if not exactly God, then at least a high-level deity of some sort, in the same family as galactic center black holes and trans-dimensional sentient manifolds. "You did," the assassin says.

"Ah."

"I need a weapon."

"Indeed."

"Or at least the idea of a weapon."

The collector beams. "Then you've come to the right place!" he says jovially, and puts one podgy hand on the assassin's shoulder. "This place is full of good ideas."

6. Ideas

For the next several hours, or possibly it is several days, the assassin rifles through the collector's museum. There are memes preserved on anything from ink and paper to thought-globules, some in actual form, some in such exotic formats that he doubts even the collector can read them. He is looking for a weapons meme, which is the collector's specialty.

"I heard you made the old man peeved," the collector says some time into the guided tour. "Never understood it myself, that obsession with worlds. As if there aren't enough out there already."

"Contract," the assassin says shortly.

"Hmm," the collector says.

"Hmm?"

"If I were to venture a guess, I'd say one of the Entities put you up to it?"

"You know contracts are confidential."

"Of course, of course. Nevertheless . . . "

The assassin ignores him as he goes through concepts, blue-prints, essays, pictures, alternate-universe snapshots, snatches of alien music and all the rest of it.

"Pesky things, Entities," the collector says, undaunted. This time it's the assassin's turn to say, "Hmm."

"Hmm?" the collector says. "Do you know, I often wondered if one could take out an Entity."

"Don't let them hear you say that," the assassin says. The collector nods. "Grouchy, aren't they."

The assassin shrugs. He doesn't care much either way. Entities are like black holes or the common cold—they're just there. It is possible some were once human—or a conglomeration of millions of joined human lives—just as it is possible they are a machine amalgamation, or a hybrid of both, or some alien intelligence or even something out of a parallel universe that slipped in when no one was looking. At any given moment there are five or six of them on the planet, usually one or two on the moon, a few transient ones in the gas giants and several in the sun, either rebuilding it or hurrying its demise, no one is quite certain. The Everest Entity, his client, has been there forever, never comes down from a certain height, and has a fascination for human-made stuff like bonsai worlds or antique machine guns. Like this collector, the Entity is indiscriminate in its passions and, so the assassin thinks, has no taste besides.

"I'll leave you to it," the collector says, knocking the pipe against a wall. "Things to do, people to see."

"Actually," the assassin says, "I'm done."

"Oh? What did you find?"

"An old idea."

"Always the best ones," the collector says, then he sighs. "Very well. And my fee?"

The assassin finds the sealed packed, opens it, communicates it across. "An ant culture Eliminator from the Sigma-IV Universe," he says. "Black matter condenser, string-dimension automatic tuning, used between the hundred and fifth and the two thousand one hundred and second Grey Galaxy Wars."

The collector claps his hands gleefully. "A genuine ant weapon?" he says. "Where did you get this?"

But the assassin is already gone.

7. Dead Letter Box

There is a post box on Red Square though there hasn't been a postal service for millennia. It is kept for both historical and aesthetic reasons. It is also a portal, and the assassin's destination. Half-way there the Everest Entity contacts the assassin. Do *you have the item?* it says.

"I do."

You have shared the ant device? It has cost some effort to obtain.

"I'm sorry if you were inconvenienced."

You are exhibiting sarcasm.

"You think?"

There is a roaring in his head, like a million black flies trapped in a tiny space, all trying to escape at once. *Bring the world to the drop point."*

"I think the old man will be following," the assassin says.

Then do your job. Again.

Then it is gone, and he is alone, flying across the red sky, his reflections joining him so that they appear to be an arrow of birds, flying in formation.

He lands at the square. He knows the old man will be waiting. By the rules of the game, the only way to resolve a contract is for the two sides to face each other in the end. He waits.

A giant, silvery moon rises slowly in the sky. It looks like an alien spaceship, so heavy it might drop down at any moment. The assassin scans the area but sees no opposition. He begins to walk towards the mail box, his reflections following.

A thousand black butterflies rise before him, blocking the way. He spreads his fingers in front of him like a magician and fire spits out. The butterflies melt. Where they fall they ooze, and a wall rises, green and yellow like pus.

The assassin forms his hands into fists and punches the wall, but where he does the wall bends back and becomes butterflies again, and they latch onto his hands and snare them. The assassin curses.

There is the sound of light footsteps behind him.

He tries to turn, and can't.

"Give me back the world."

The voice speaks old Russian. It is rusty, almost a whisper. "You didn't," the assassin says.

The dead voice laughs behind him. "It seemed appropriate," it says. "After all, you cannot kill a dead man twice."

"You'd be surprised," the assassin says, and his hands become ice, a chill grows out of his body, and the butterflies holding him freeze and fall to the ground, breaking into thousands of tiny shards, the sound like a symphony. He turns.

"Give it back to me," Lenin says.

8. Wings

The doors of Lenin's mausoleum stand open. The mummy faces the assassin, a small smile playing at the corners of its lips. "The Greater Moscow Entity will complain," the assassin says, though privately he appreciates the sentiment.

"It is a true Russian," the old man says. "It always complains."

"We seem to be at an impasse," the assassin says.

"Not at all," the old man says. "Since you will never reach the drop box. I have sent it back to your client with a little gift of my own devising, alas."

"Oh?"

"From time to time I find the need for dead worlds," the Lenin Mummy says. "I sent the Entity a private composition, an anti-matter world which, sadly, had a malfunctioning casing. I'm afraid by now the world—this world, I mean—is short a mountain."

"I see," the assassin says, impressed despite himself. "Did it work?"

They both turn momentarily to the Kremlin, converting its walls into a giant display.

"I . . . see," the assassin says again.

"Unfortunate," the old man says.

"It will come back," the assassin says.

"No doubt. But that won't help you."

"Nevertheless," the assassin says. "A contract is a contract."

"Give me back the world."

"What do you need with miniature worlds, anyway?" the assassin says.

"They make more sense than the other kind," the old man says. The Lenin mummy takes a step closer, and another, its hands reaching out. The old man says, "Put it in the mummy's hands."

The assassin sighs. The orb materializes in his hands, the miniature world frozen inside it. "I'm sorry," he says.

"Oh? No harm done," the old man says.

The assassin coughs. He puts the orb in the outreached hands but, as soon as it leaves his hands, the scene inside it changes. There is the sound of a thousand butterflies buzzing and the old man says, "What have you d—"

"They did it to themselves," the assassin says. "I admit I helped accelerate the process a little, but . . . "

Inside the orb, dots of light flash across the world. The lights grow in strength and intensity, consume first one continent, then another, spread out across the oceans, their brightness blinding, the flash of the explosions ebbing out of the orb like bleeding light. A moment later, the tiny red explodes.

"Thermonuclear devices," the assassin says. "A shame—I became quite fond of them towards the end."

There is a moment of absolute silence. The assassin tenses, waiting for the old man's final strike.

It never comes.

The old Lenin body shakes, and it takes the assassin a moment to understand the mummy is crying. When it raises its head at last, its eyes are full of tears.

"It's beautiful," the old man says; and for a moment it seems to the assassin as if the voice is the sound of a thousand thousand butterflies, all fluttering their wings at once.

Advection

GENEVIEVE VALENTINE

The first day of fifth year a boy came in with the new eyeshields, a glossy expanse of black with no iris or pupil, and looking at him was like looking into an eclipse.

All the other girls said it made them uncomfortable; they teased him to take them out, to put on some normal sunglasses like everyone else. They said they'd never forgive him for hiding eyes in such a handsome face.

"Fortuni, it's a little much," said someone.

That was how I learned his name.

We were all Level Two intelligence, but before the first week was over the news was out that some had managed to find the money for a sixth year. Janik Duranti, who spent the history lectures drawing stick figures screwing on his computer screen, was getting a sixth year. I'd be cleaning his office someday. Answering his phones. Updating the registration on his blue ID cuff.

Carol Clarke opened the top button on her shirt as soon as the shades went down; obvious, but it was worth it to be married to a guy who had a sixth year.

The first time Fortuni opened his mouth was two weeks after start-of-year in geohistory, when Mr. Xi was talking about the five oceans.

"After the emergency desalinization," Mr. Xi said, "we held the first HydroSummit to determine the best use of resources."

"I think it's awful about the dolphins that died," said Kay, whose water ration was unlimited because her father was a diplomat, and that was how I first noticed her.

Mr. Xi opened the rain cycle diagram on our screens; the blue advection loop from a hundred years ago had been overlaid by a three-point process from the Atmo water collectors to the thirsty ground, and the green web of the surface sweat system that preserved the little underground things that managed to survive.

My grandfather sent my mom a postcard from Niagara Cliffs when there was still a river at the bottom (*RAIN! All my love, Dad*), and as Mr. Xi talked about desalinization I traced the advection circle, thought about the sky filling with wet clouds, about water sliding over everything.

I looked up, and Fortuni was watching me, his lashes casting shadows over his flat black eyes.

"I'm going to engineer some rain," he told me, and after a moment I laughed. That was how I met him.

It was nearly the end of year when I walked past the upper-class apartments and saw the plant in the garbage.

My heart leapt into my throat, and I checked to see if a cop was recording me, because nobody just left a clipping on the street. But besides the tram down the street full of commuters, there was nobody.

I knelt and stared at the glossy tops, the browned underside where it was drying out, the pale hairs on the stem. Even from this distance the smell was overwhelming, wet and clean, and without caring if the cops were watching I scooped it up and dropped it into the back of my hood where it would be safest from the sun.

The tram home was endless; I felt the stem pressing against my neck and shivered.

Half a day's water ration went into a glass bowl, and I looked up what plant it was (jade) and how much water it would need (hardly any. It was a survivor).

I sat up all night watching the pattern of leaves on the walls. I expected it to die; I cried like I'd already lost it, ended up dehydrated from tears and lack of water.

When Fortuni walked with me after school the next day I didn't ask why. I was making up my mind to show him the plant. My heart raced. He could turn me in. I didn't really know him. It was too dangerous. I couldn't.

"Come with me," I said, and he got in the tram without asking why.

Even before I opened the door I hadn't wondered why he walked me home, and when he smiled at the plant and said, "Beautiful," I knew.

He wasn't a Level Two. Everybody else was a fool.

He lifted his hand to the glass, closed his eyes over the black shields. He smiled like he knew he looked silly, or like the plant told him a joke.

"The water is cool," he said.

"I keep it under my bed at night."

He opened one eye, grinned at me. "Hiding it from your parents or trying for condensation?"

After a moment he took his hand off the glass and went home without another word.

The next day he messaged: *How is it? Dream about it?*

Stronger, I messaged back, didn't tell him what I dreamed.

At school we didn't talk about it—we didn't talk at all, because I had to work to pass exams, and he had to work to avoid tripping over girls who couldn't get enough of his bone-white skin and his blue cuff.

Kay ignored him. She sat one row in front of him in classes, and when he asked her a question she turned just enough to give him her profile, answered him curtly, turned back.

"This winter I'm going to my uncle's farm," she told Carol. "He's scheduled an Atmo so we can get rain."

"Oh, wow," breathed Carol.

My pen snapped, and I had to wait until end of class to get another one.

Mr. Xi talked about the Reclaimers and the class got into a screaming match about whether they were terrorists or guerillas. They yelled about the cave communities who harbored the sleeper cells; about whether wild rain was even a good idea anymore.

"It's a waste of water," said Janik, and I wanted to kick him.

When I looked over at Fortuni, he was gazing unblinking ahead of him, his eyes fixed on the knot of hair at the nape of Kay's neck, on her pale hand writing.

I didn't hear the rest of the class.

Fortuni messaged: *What do you think of Kay?*

I don't.

Try.

The plant was outgrowing the bowl, and I adjusted the stem, didn't get around to answering him.

The next day in geohistory Mr. Xi talked about Free Water, about the cave-towns authorized to collect condensation without reporting. The class got into it again about Reclaimers seeking asylum there.

I looked at the cliffs and thought how they were underwater once, about vegetation breathing into the sky, about water so big you couldn't see the end of it, about the wet slide of rain across skin.

"It's weird when you miss rain you've never felt," Fortuni said, like I'd spoken, and my fingers went cold.

"I know," I said.

He looked back at Kay, who had turned a little towards him as if by accident, resting a white hand on her throat.

When I got home he'd messaged me. *Clip it.*

I didn't think about Fortuni when the side-by-side clippings grew so fast; all I knew was my dreams filled with the creaky, quiet sound of growing.

Summer. The last day of fifth year Fortuni wasn't there. I didn't really think about it (he was Level Zero) except that Kay looked nervous, and it worried me that if something was wrong with Fortuni, Kay knew more than I did.

I stopped her as she was walking back to her seat with her certificate, said, "Have you seen—"

She pulled away from me like she was poisoned.

Carol laughed, and I hoped she had to marry Janick Duranti.

On the tram on the way home someone came up behind me, said in my ear, "Figured out rain yet?"

It was Fortuni's voice, and I was so relieved that I must have really been worried before.

I turned, but he was wearing a black UV hood and I couldn't see his face. It had a white bird outline on the side, and as I tried to find his profile behind the hood the silhouette took flight, wings beating.

My hood was from the bargain market, standard SPF 150 striped brown and purple, and I'd never wanted to be rich so much in my life.

"You weren't in class," I said. "Tapped for Level Zero?"

He looked at me like he couldn't help it, and for the first time I thought that maybe I'd managed to surprise him. "You think I'm special?"

I didn't answer that, and he grinned, shrugged. "Yeah, I wish. Just got held up with something."

For the rest of the tram ride he looked out the window, and I watched the bird flying on the taut black fabric between two of the ribs; when he put his hood back, the bird would disappear into the folds. It seemed really sad. I don't know why.

At my stop, I got off without asking him to follow me, and he took one step and changed his mind, gave me a half-wave as the tram pulled away from the stop and back onto the street.

At home I slid it out from under my bed so it could breathe for an hour. It was big enough to be illegal; I was a criminal.

I messaged him. *You should see it.*

The words sat on my screen, and he didn't answer.

Autumn. One of the big government offices was hiring, and I got my credentials and made coffee and shuttled lunches and watched sixth-years plan trajectories and irrigation patterns and wildlife preservation.

I made sure my plant had enough water.

Winter. The dreams about Niagara Cliffs and the water cycle never stopped, and I applied for a sixth year without telling anyone.

Spring. I went into one of the banks in my nice suit and folded back the expensive UV hood I borrowed from a nice sixth-year at the office, and arranged to go into a decade of debt for a year of Meteohydronics and a chance at a seat on an Atmo. My parents were surprised.

Summer. It was too big for the bowl, and I had to leave clippings on the sill with the shade cracked, five minutes at a time until the sun shriveled them and they were dry enough to burn.

A message came back from Fortuni.

Want to go to a concert?

It had been a year.

As I waited outside the back entrance of Roseland I couldn't think of anything but Fortuni's UV hood, black with a white bird silhouette that flew in place as you watched. I pressed against the grimy brick to avoid the swells of tourists sweating in their "NYC" rental hoods, and my breath fluttered in my chest as I looked for Fortuni in a sea of strangers. My hands were clammy.

When I saw him, bouncing along next to that little white bird was Kay's pale blue hood with her coat of arms on each side—two greyhounds and a pile of helmets and swords. Kay must have just finished her sixth year, because as the crowd parted for her (crowds always did) I could see she carried nothing except a smug expression.

I sucked in a sigh, and felt dust coating the inside of my mouth.

"Sarah, hi!" Kay stepped under the marquee and pushed back the hood, shook out her long blonde hair. She'd gotten a grey wash in between exams—the latest thing to make you look paler.

I made fists in my pockets.

When Fortuni pushed his hood back, the white bird spread its wings into the folds. "Did we keep you waiting?" he asked.

"Of course not," said Kay. "She doesn't have to worry about studying anymore." She grinned. "You must be so relieved that's all over."

"We should go inside," said Fortuni, and opened the back door. For a moment Kay looked disgusted by the shabby welcome, but she went. It was Fortuni, after all.

Music was already throbbing as we approached the bar, and Kay gave Fortuni a look of delight. Her hood was too big for her; folded down against her back it made her look like a crested lizard.

She brought him a glass. He passed it to me, and she had to go back for another one and look like it didn't bother her.

"This band is totally derivative," she told Fortuni, who had hung back with me.

He shrugged. "It's the opening act. I didn't pay much attention to the bill."

It was just like Fortuni to go to a concert without even knowing what band it was, and so I didn't think much of it. He just liked to stand in the crowd, eyes closed, feeling the breath of two hundred people.

I've never felt lonelier than when I was standing next to Fortuni in a crowd.

"Well, I figured you had better taste than that. I hear Hammond is amazing." Kay swung back and forth between baiting and appeasing Fortuni so quickly I thought she'd get whiplash.

"If you can hear anything around that stupid hood," I said under my breath.

Fortuni smiled into his glass, and his laugh, if he laughed, was drowned out by screams and applause.

Kay flirted with the bartender through two more free drinks, glancing backs at Fortuni to make sure it was all right.

"You've applied for a sixth year," he said.

He knew it the way he knew everything, and I didn't bother to answer him. I'd requested a year in Meteohydronics.

The study of rain.

"So," I said, "are you and Kay dating?"

He smiled, still not looking at me. "Nah. We just talk."

I thought about green leaves spilling over the edge of the bowl. "What about?"

"She has ambition," he said. "It's not something you run across often."

The ambition was her as the pretty shadow of some boy, and I saw that ambition all the time.

"I don't really feel like a concert." I pressed my drink into his hand. "I need to study. See you."

"No," he said, stepped forward. "Please, stay. Please."

He had his hand on my arm, the first time he'd ever touched me. I looked up and could see past the eyeshields into green, frightened eyes. He'd never asked me for anything, not one thing that whole silent year.

"Okay," I said.

He smiled as if he'd never doubted, and I wondered if I'd just imagined that I could see through him.

Kay materialized at his side, smiling, but her hand was wrapped around her glass so hard that the skin under her nails was red.

"Sorry," she said. "Am I interrupting? Hammond was announced, but if you want to be alone . . . "

Fortuni dropped his hand. My arm was cold where he'd touched it.

The band was loud, and when Fortuni leaned over and spoke he had to repeat himself, louder, before I heard him.

"Come with me," he said.

My heart constricted. "What?"

"You and Kay," he said. "Come with me."

"Where are you going?"

He half-smiled. "To engineer some rain."

I thought, Reclaimers, but didn't dare say it.

I thought about his fingers on the glass bowl as he listened to the plant growing, thought maybe he didn't even need the Reclaimers to make rain.

My lungs pounded against my ribs. "Me?"

"I want you with me for the first wild rain."

I don't know why he could still surprise me, but he could; he was a wondrous thing, and back then I was easy to surprise.

"And Kay?" I asked, because I was afraid, and it sounded like a spurned child asking.

He said, "Come with me."

I had signed up for a sixth year. I wanted to work with the Atmos.

I had a plant that would die without me.

In Fortuni's black eyes the reflection of the crowd was like wet clouds gathering, like the dream of rain.

The music washed over us, and I was half-dreaming about walking beside Fortuni, walking into some other unknown life that was full of water, and without Kay's white bracelet lighting up a warning we wouldn't have known the police were coming.

Kay moved first (she must have been used to getting out of something right before the cops got in), and shoved us towards the stairs, shouting something that was drowned out by the drums and the bass. As much as I distrusted her I ran, and beside me Fortuni ran, too.

When we took the turn on the landing I caught a glimpse of her in the crowd, swaying to the music like she didn't know us at all.

At the top of the stairs I saw the EXIT sign and ducked into the utility hall pulling Fortuni behind me; he crouched and slid along the wall, and I followed his lead.

"They're not after your plant," he said, which was the first time I thought they might have been.

"What were you doing all year?" I imagined him in a cave, drinking condensation, blowing up reservoirs, blowing up Atmos with people like me in them. My voice shook.

He turned and grinned. "Engineering some rain," he said, and as we heard footsteps echoing in the stairwell he held out a hand, said, "Come with me."

We couldn't make it to the fire exit before the cops got there, and he was holding out his hand, and I didn't understand what he was saying, what he was.

I hesitated, shook my head.

He turned and ducked into the door on his right; I saw a cluster of rooms before the door swung shut behind him.

As I moved to follow, the cops swarmed me.

They weren't all cops, some of them were kids drinking over-ration who got spooked and bolted, but it felt like a sea of uniforms and I covered my head to protect myself from the kicks, and I let myself be yanked up and handcuffed, listened for Fortuni to make his big escape.

He didn't. They stormed the dressing room (I bit my lips until they bled), someone shouted, the bang of a gunshot.

They had to drag me out by the cuffs because I was trying to run into the room, to see what had happened, to see them carry out his body.

I heard, " —nothing left!" just before the door swung shut and they yanked me down the stairs.

I thought of the little white bird, of the folds in his hood, how something could be so neatly tucked away. I stumbled. My eyes burned.

Kay was outside, talking to the cop with the most brass on. As I walked past them, Kay laughed.

"Her? Oh please. No way she's over ration. Can't afford anything."

And Kay stared at me like I knew something she didn't know.

I knew he had gone into the dressing room, and there was one shot—but maybe he was out by then, maybe he ran, he looked like a sprinter—and he would have run with me, taken me with him, but there was the shot, but even when his hood was folded back, and even when you couldn't see it the little white bird was flying away and away and away.

He would have taken me with him.

Kay looked sick and turned away, and I wondered if he had leaned in over the music and asked her to come with him, too.

They still play music there, not that anybody can get tickets unless they're willing to sit under the stage, and when my big brother did that for Goblin Dust he almost failed his service physical six weeks later because he couldn't hear.

The top of the balcony stairs is dark and quiet—everyone goes for the view over the railing, no one even sees the hall behind the utility door. Baby-blue walls, like Kay's hood, and two dressing rooms—one an inch deep in grime, makeup mirrors with all but two lights burned out, a pinball table rusted stiff.

The second door opens to a honeycomb of little rooms, cloth tacked to the walls, carpet crunching underfoot.

If there was ever an escape it's not there now, and I ram the walls until my shoulder wrenches in the socket, tear down the fabric and check for hidden doors, and I fall to my knees and drag my fingers along the floor looking for a crack that will open the way.

You have to apply at the Embassy to see anyone privately, even if you can recognize Ambassador Arnaun's crest in a sea of hoods, even if his daughter called the cops off you.

It's a paper form, and if it's not the Ambassador you want to see, then you write the person's name in a little box underneath, and in the box below that you fill out the reason for your visit.

I write, *Accepted into sixth year. Advice?*

A guard directs me to the proper line, and I stand between Visas and Water Permits, and some woman stamps my paper and tells me to look for a response in my email.

It takes six weeks, and then the image of my form is sent back so I can see that under ENTERED it has been stamped DECLINED.

I end up looking up the social calendar for her kind of people, and a week later I find her outside a club, smoking, bare-armed in the cold to show off the big white smoking permit on her wrist.

When she sees me she licks her lips, turns her profile to me like she used to do with Fortuni.

"Declined," she says when I'm close enough, "have they not gotten to long words in sixth year yet?"

I say, "Do you know where he is?" which I mean to say, and "I miss him," which I don't.

She says, "Well, I don't know, do I?" which I expect, and bursts into tears, which I don't.

I go home and look up her life until then, little mentions on the society sites and on the galleries of the most fashionable people, and I feel like I'm checking up on someone I used to babysit.

I get another message from the Embassy, which I expect, and accept the invitation, which I don't.

At night I pull the bowl out from under my bed and press my hands to the glass, feel with my palms for the voices of living things. When I sit back, the beads are already condensing, two handprints full of water.

"I'm going to engineer some rain," he told me, and I dream of him standing on the dry seabed, closing his eyes over black shields, spreading his arms, opening the sky.

Clarkesworld
Census

We would like to thank the following Citizens of Clarkesworld for their continued support:

Overlords

Renan Adams, Thomas Ball, Michael Blackmore, Nathalie Boisard-Beudin, Shawn Boyd, Jennifer Brozek, Karen Burnham, Barbara Capoferri, Morgan Cheryl, Gio Clairval, Dolohov, ebooks-worldwide, Sairuh Emilius, Joshua Faulkenberry, Thomas Fleck, Eric Francis, L A George, Bryan Green, Andrew Hatchell, Berthiaume Heidi, Bill Hughes, Gary Hunter, Theodore J. Stanulis, Jericho, jfly, jkapoetry, Lucas Jung, James Kinateder, Daniel LaPonsie, Susan Lewis, Paul Marston, Matthew the Greying, Achilleas Michailides, Adrian Mihaila, Adrien Mitchell, MrMovieZombie, Mike Perricone, Rick Ramsey, Jo Rhett, Joseph Sconfitto, Tara Smith, Elaine Williams, James Williams

Royalty

Paul Abbamondi, Albert Alfiler, Kathryn Baker, Nathan Blumenfeld, Marty Bonus, David Borcherding, Robert Callahan, Lady Cate, Carolyn Cooper, Mr D F Ryan, David Demers, Brian Dolton, Hilary Goldstein, Andy Herrman, Colin Hitch, Christopher Irwin, G.J. Kressley, Jeffrey L Lewis, Jamie Lackey, Jonathan Laden, Katherine Lee, H. Lincoln Parish, David M Oswin, Sean Markey, Arun Mascarenhas, Michelle Broadribb MEG, Nayad Monroe, James Moore, Anne Murphy, Charles Norton, Vincent O'Connor, Vincent P Loeffler III, Marie Parsons, Lars Pedersen, Matt Phelps, Rational Path, RL, John Scalzi, Stu Segal, Maurice Shaw, Carrie Smith, Paul Smith, Richard Sorden, Chugwangle Sparklepants, Kevin Standlee, Josh Thomson, TK, Terhi Tormanen, Jeppe V Holm, Sean Wallace, Jasen Ward, Weyla & Gos, Graeme Williams, Jeff Xilon, Zola

Bürgermeisters

7ony, Mary A. Turzillo, Rob Abram, Carl Anderson, Andy90, Robert Avie, Erika Bailey, Brian Baker, Michael Banker, Jennifer Bartolowits, Lenni Benson, Bill Bibo Jr, Edward Blake, Samuel Blinn, Johanna Bobrow, Tim Brenner, Ken Brown, BruceC, Adam Bursey, Jeremy Butler, Robyn Butler, Roland Byrd, Carleton45, James Carlino, Benjamin Cartwright, Evan Cassity, Randall Chertkow, Michael Chorman, Mary Clare, Matthew Claxton, Theodore Conti, Brian Cooksey, Brenda Cooper, Lorraine Cooper, James Davies, Tessa Day, Brian Deacon, Bartley Deason, John Devenny, Fran Ditzel-Friel, Gary Dockter, Nicholas Doran, Christopher Doty, Nicholas Dowbiggin, Joanna Evans, FlatFootedRat, Lynn Flewelling, Adrienne Foster, Matthew Fredrickson, Alina Fridberg, Patricia G Scott, Pierre Gauthier, Gerhen, Mark Gerrits, Lorelei Goelz, Inga Gorslar, Tony Graham, Jaq Greenspon, Eric Gregory, Laura Hake, Skeptyk/JeanneE Hand-Boniakowski, Jordan Hanie, Carl Hazen, Sheridan Hodges, Ronald Hordijk, Justin Howe, Bobby Hoyt, David Hudson, Huginn Huginn and Muninn, Chris Hurst, Kevin Ikenberry, Joseph Ilardi, Pamela J. Davis, Justin James, Patty Jansen, Toni Jerrman, Audra Johnson, Erin Johnson, Russell Johnson, Kai Juedemann, David Kelleher, Joshua Kidd, Alistair Kimble, Erin Kissane, Michelle Knowlton, JR Krebs, Andrew Lanker, James Frederick Leach, Krista Leahy, Alan Lehotsky, Walter Leroy Perkins, Philip Levin, Kevin Liebkemann, Susan Loyal, Kristi Lozano, Keith M Frampton, N M Wells Foundry Creative Media, Brit Mandelo, Matthew Marovich, Samuel Marzioli, Jason Maurer, Peter McClean, Michael McCormack, Tony McFee, Mark McGarry, Craig McMurtry, J Meijer, Geoffrey Meissner, Barry Melius, David Michalak, Robert Milson, Eric Mohring, Rebekah Murphy, John Murray, Barrett Nichols, Peter Northup, Justin Palk, Norman Papernick, Richard Parks, Katherine Pendill, David Personette, E. PLS, PBC Productions Inc., Jonathan Pruett, QLM Aria X-Perienced, Mike R D Ashley, D Randall Kerr, Paul Rice, James Rickard, Karsten Rink, Erik Rolstad, Joseph Romel, Leena Romppainen, Stefan Scheib, Alan Scheiner, Kenneth Schneyer, Bluezoo Seven, Cosma Shalizi, siznax, Allen Snyder, David Sobyra, Jason Strawsburg, Keffington Studios, Jerome Stueart, Robert Stutts, Maurice Termeer, Tero, Chuck Tindle, Raymond Tobaygo, Tradeblanket.com, Heather Tumey, Ann VanderMeer, Andrew Vega, Emil Volcheck, Andrew Volpe, Wendy Wagner, Jennifer Walter, Tom Waters, Tehani Wessely, Shannon White, Dan Wick, John Wienstroer, Seth Williams, Dawn Wolfe, Sarah Wright

Citizens

Pete Aldin, Elye Alexander, Richard Alison, Joshua Allen, Alllie, Imron Alston, Clifford Anderson, Kim Anderson, Randall Andrews, Author Anonymous, Therese Arkenberg, Ash, Bill B., Benjamin Baker, Jenny Barber, Johanne

Barron, Jeff Bass, Aaron Begg, LaNeta Bergst, Julie Berg-Thompson, Clark
Berry, Amy Billingham, Tracey Bjorksten, Mike Blevins, Adam Blomquist,
Kevin Bokelman, Michael Bonsall, Michael Braun Hamilton, Jennifer Bris-
sett, Thomas Bull, Karl Bunker, Jefferson Burson, Graeme Byfield, c9lewis,
Darrell Cain, C.G. Cameron, Yazburg Carlberg, Michael Carr, Nance Cedar,
Timothy Charlton, Peter Charron, David Chasson, Catherine Cheek, Paige
Chicklo, Elizabeth Coleman, Johne Cook, Claire Cooney, Martin Cooper,
Lisa Costello, Charles Cox, Michael Cox, Tina Crone, Sarah Dalton, Ang
Danieldeskbrain - Watercress Munster, Gillian Daniels, Chua Dave, Morgan
Davey, Chase Davies, Craig Davis, Maria-Isabel Deira, Daniel DeLano, Paul
DesCombaz, Aidan Doyle, Susan Duncan, Jesse Eisenhower, Brad Elliott,
Warren Ellis, Lyle Enright, Yvonne Ewing, . Feather, Fabio Fernandes, Josiah
Ferrin, Ethan Fode, Dense Fog, William Fred, Michael Frighetto, Sarah Frost,
Paul Gainford, Robert Garbacz, Eleanor Gausden, Leslie Gelwicks, Susan
Gibbs, Holly Glaser, Sangay Glass, Grendel, Damien Grintalis, Nikki Guerlain,
Geoffrey Guthrie, Richard Guttormson, Lee Hallison, Lee Hallison, Janus
Hansen, Roy Hardin, Jonathan Harnum, Jubal Harshaw, Darren Hawbrook,
Helixa 12, Jamie Henderson, Samantha Henderson, Dave Hendrickson, Dan
Hiestand, John Higham, Renata Hill, Björn Hillreiner, Tim Hills, Andrea
Horbinski, Clarence Horne III, Richard Horton, Fiona Howland-Rose, Jeremy
Hull, Dwight Illk, John Imhoff, Iridum Sound Envoy, Isbell, Stephen Jacob,
Radford Janssens, Michael Jarcho, Jimbo, Steve Johnson, Gabriel Kaknes,
Philip Kaldon, KarlTheGood, Sara Kathryn, Cagatay Kavukcuoglu, Lorna
Keach, Jason Keeton, Robert Keller, Mary Kellerman, Kelson, Kate Kligman,
Seymour Knowles-Barley, Matthew Koch, Lutz Krebs, Derek Kunsken, T.
L. Sherwood, Paul Lamarre, Gina Langridge, Darren Ledgerwood, Brittany
Lehman, Terra Lemay, Pontus Liljeblad, Susan Llewellyn, Thomas Loyal,
James Lyle, Allison M. Dickson, Dan Manning, Eric Marsh, Jacque Marshall,
Dominique Martel, Daniel Mathews, David Mayes, Derek McAleer, Mike
McBride, Roz McCarthy, T.C. McCarthy, Jeffrey McDonald, Holly McEntee,
Brent Mendelsohn, Seth Merlo, Stephen Middleton, John Midgley, Matthew
Miller, Terry Miller, Alan Mimms, mjpearce, Aidan Moher, Marian Moore,
Patricia Murphy, Jack Myers Photography, Glenn Nevill, Stella Nickerson,
David Oakley, Scott Oesterling, Christopher Ogilvie, Lydia Ondrusek, Ruth
O'Neill, Erik Ordway, Nancy Owens, Stuart P Hair, Thomas Pace, Amparo
Palma Reig, Thomas Parrish, Andrea Pawley, Nikki Philley, Beth Plutchak,
David Potter, Ed Prior, David Raco, Mahesh Raj Mohan, Adam Rakunas, Ralan,
Steve Ramey, Robert Redick, George Reilly, Joshua Reynolds, Julia Reynolds,
Zach Ricks, Carl Rigney, Hank Roberts, Tansy Roberts, Kenneth Robkin, Roy
and Norma Kloster, RPietila, Sarah Rudek, Woodworking Running Dog,
Oliver Rupp, Caitlin Russell, Abigail Rustad, Lior Saar, S2 Sally, Tim Sally,
Jason Sanford, Steven Saus, MJ Scafati, Jan Shawyer, Espana Sheriff, Udayan
Shevade, Josh Shiben, Aileen Simpson, Karen Snyder, Morgan Songi, Dr SP

Conboy-Hil, Terry Squire Stone, Kenneth Takigawa, Jesse Tauriainen, Paul Tindle II, Julia Varga, Adam Vaughan, Extranet Vendors Association, William Vennell, Vettac, Diane Walton, Robert Wamble, Lim Wee Teck, Neil Weston, Peter Wetherall, Adam White, Jeff Williamson, Neil Williamson, Kristyn Willson, Devon Wong, Chalmer Wren, Catherine York, Doug Young, Rena Zayit, Stephanie Zvan

Interested in immigrating to Clarkesworld?
Visit **clarkesworldmagazine.com** for more details.

About the Authors

N. K. Jemisin is an author of speculative fiction short stories and novels who lives and writes in Brooklyn, NY. In addition to writing, she is a counseling psychologist (specializing in career counseling), a sometime hiker and biker, and a political/feminist/anti-racist blogger.

Her short fiction has been published in pro markets such as *Clarkesworld, Postscripts, Strange Horizons,* and *Baen's Universe;* podcast markets and print anthologies. Several of her short stories have received Honorable Mentions in various Year's Bests; one of her stories has been nominated for a Hugo and a Nebula.

The Inheritance Trilogy: *The Hundred Thousand Kingdoms, The Broken Kingdoms* and *The Kingdom of Gods,* are out now from Orbit Books.

Ken Scholes is the author of the internationally acclaimed Psalms of Isaak series, published in the US by Tor. His short fiction has appeared in various magazines and anthologies for the last decade and is now collected in two volumes, *Long Walks, Last Flights and Other Strange Journeys and Diving Mimes, Weeping Czars and Other Unusual Suspects,* both published by Fairwood Press.

Scholes is a native of the Pacific Northwest and makes his home in Saint Helens, Oregon, with his wife and twin daughters. He invites readers to learn more about him and his work at www.kenscholes.com.

Nick Mamatas is the author of several novels, including *Sensation* and *Bullettime,* and of over eighty short stories. His work has appeared in *New Haven Review, Asimov's Science Fiction, Long Island Noir, Steampunk: Revolutions* and many other magazines and anthologies. As editor of the Haikasoru imprint of Japanese science fiction in translation, Nick was nominated for the 2010 Hugo award. As an anthologist, Nick co-edited the award-winning *Haunted Legends* with Ellen Datlow and *The Future is Japanese* with Masumi Washington.

Desirina Boskovich is a graduate of the Clarion class of 2007. As a freelance writer, she specializes in weird, fantastic and unlikely things—both true and imaginary. Her fiction has appeared in *Clarkesworld Magazine, Realms of Fantasy, Fantasy Magazine, Last Drink Bird Head* and *The Way of the Wizard,* and is forthcoming in *Nightmare Magazine.* Her nonfiction has appeared in *Lightspeed Magazine, Weird Fiction Review* and *The Steampunk Bible.* Find her online at desirinaboskovich.com.

Geoffrey W. Cole's short fiction has appeared in such publications as *Clarkesworld, Orson Scott Card's Intergalactic Medicine Show, Apex, On Spec,* and is forthcoming in *AE* - The Canadian Science Fiction Review and Michael Moorcock's *New Worlds.* When Geoff lives in Vancouver, BC, he manages the region's drinking water system and teaches science fiction writing. When he lives in Rome, Italy, he and his beautiful wife drink coffee, eat pizza, drink wine, and he writes as much as he can. Geoff is a member of SF Canada and SFWA. Visit Geoff at geoffreywcole.com.

Catherynne M. Valente is the *New York Times* bestselling author of over a dozen works of fiction and poetry, including *Palimpsest,* the Orphan's Tales series, *Deathless,* and the crowdfunded phenomenon *The Girl Who Circumnavigated Fairyland in a Ship of Own Making.* She is the winner of the Andre Norton Award, the Tiptree Award, the Mythopoeic Award, the Rhysling Award, and the Million Writers Award. She has been nominated for the Hugo, Locus, and Spectrum Awards, the Pushcart Prize, and was a finalist for the World Fantasy Award in 2007 and 2009. She lives on an island off the coast of Maine with her partner, two dogs, and enormous cat.

Berrien C. Henderson lives with his family in southeast Georgia. He was born in a small town and currently lives in a farming community. For fifteen years he has taught high school English. Ever-elusive free time he spends with family and late in the evening or late at night, writing speculative fiction and poetry.

John A. McDermott has been a bad bartender, a worse house painter, a fairly good copywriter, and a better actor. Now he teaches creative writing and American literature at Stephen F. Austin State University in Nacogdoches, Texas. A proud native of Madison, Wisconsin, he's not much of a Texan, but his students understand. His stories have appeared in a variety of journals, including *Alaska Quarterly Review, Cimarron Review, Meridian, Southeast Review,* and *Zahir.*

Mike Resnick is, according to *Locus,* the all-time leading award winner, living or dead, for short fiction. He had won 5 Hugos (from a record 36 nominations), a Nebula, and other major awards in the USA, France, Japan, Croatia, Spain and Poland, and has been short-listed in England, Italy, and Australia. He is the author of 71 novels, over 250 stories, and 3 screenplays, and the editor of more than 40 anthologies. His work has been translated into 25 languages. He was Guest of Honor at the 2012 World Science Fiction Convention.

Lezli Robyn is an Aussie Lass who loves writing sf, fantasy, horror, humor and even dabbles in steampunk every now and then. Since her first sale to *Clarkesworld,* she's made over twenty-five story sales to professional markets around the world, including *Asimov's* and *Analog,* and her first short story collection will be published by Ticonderoga Press in late 2012. Lezli was also a finalist for the 2009 Aurealis Award (Aussie) for Best SF Story, the 2010 Ignotus Award (Spanish) for Best Foreign Short Story, and a 2010 Campbell Award Nominee for best new writer. In 2011, she won the Best Foreign Translation Ictineus Award (Catalan) for "Soulmates", a novelette written with Mike Resnick, and first published in *Asimov's.*

Nnedi Okorafor is a novelist of Nigerian descent known for weaving African culture into creative evocative settings and memorable characters. In a profile of Nnedi's work titled "Weapons of Mass Creation", The New York Times called Nnedi's imagination "stunning". Her novels include *Zahrah the Windseeker* (winner of the Wole Soyinka Prize for African Literature), *The Shadow Speaker* (winner of the CBS Parallax Award), *Long Juju Man* (winner of the Macmillan Writer's Prize for Africa) and *Who Fears Death* (winner of the 2011 World Fantasy Award for best novel), is a dark, gritty magical realist narrative that evenly combines African literature and fantasy/science fiction into a powerful story of genocide and of the woman who reshapes her world. Nnedi holds a PhD in English and currently is a professor of creative writing at Chicago State University. Visit Nnedi at nnedi.com.

Jim C. Hines' latest book is *Libriomancer,* a modern-day fantasy about a magic-wielding librarian, a hamadryad, a secret society founded by Johannes Gutenberg, a flaming spider, and an enchanted convertible. He's also the author of the Princess series of fairy tale retellings as well as the humorous Goblin Quest trilogy. His short fiction has appeared in more than 40 magazines and anthologies. In his free time, he practices Sanchin-Ryu karate, fights a losing battle against housework entropy, and attempts ridiculous cover poses on the internet. Online, he can be found at jimchines.com.

Simon DeDeo is a scientist, writer and currently a postdoctoral fellow at the University of Chicago. His essays and criticism on poetics, epistemology and anarchism have appeared in *The Continental Review, absent,* and on his blog *rhubarb is susan,* and are forthcoming in *Mantis* and *The Chicago Review.* "batch 39" was completed during a stay at the Santa Fe Institute.

Jay Lake lives in Portland, Oregon, where he works on numerous writing and editing projects. His 2012/2013 books are *Kalimpura* from Tor Books, and *Love in the Time of Metal and Flesh* from Prime Books. His short fiction appears regularly in literary and genre markets worldwide. Jay is a past winner of the John W. Campbell Award for Best New Writer, and a multiple nominee for the Hugo and World Fantasy Awards. Jay can be reached through his blog at jlake.com.

Shannon Page was born on Halloween night and spent her early years on a commune in northern California's backwoods. A childhood without television gave her a great love of books and the worlds she found in them. She wrote her first book, an illustrated adventure starring her cat, at the age of seven. Sadly, that story is currently out of print, but her work has appeared in *Clarkesworld, Interzone, Fantasy, Black Static, Tor.com,* and a mighty number of anthologies, including *Love and Rockets* from DAW, Subterranean's *Tales of Dark Fantasy 2,* Flying Pen Press's *Space Tramps: Full Throttle Space Tales #5,* and the Australian Shadows Award-winning *Grants Pass.* Her debut novel, *Eel River,* will be published by Morrigan Books in 2013. Shannon is a longtime yoga practitioner, has no tattoos, and lives in Portland, Oregon, with lots of orchids and even more books. Visit her at www.shannonpage.net.

Karen Heuler's stories have appeared in *Clarkesworld, Weird Tales, Daily Science Fiction* and over 60 literary and speculative magazines and anthologies. Her most recent novel, *The Made-up Man,* is about a woman who sells her soul to the devil to be a man for the rest of her life. ChiZine Publications will publish her short story collection, *The Inner City,* in early 2013. She lives in New York with her dog, Philip K. Dick, and her cats, Jane Austen and Charlotte Bronte.

Don Webb has won both the Fiction Collective and Death Equinox Awards, been nominated for both the Rhysling and International Horror Critics Awards. He dwells in Austin, Texas with his wife the video artist Guiniviere Webb. He has several dozen short stories in anthologies, and as a Texan, a secret recipe for chili. He is a staple at Armadillocons in Austin, and despite having three mystery novels, loves the short story form the best.

Tobias S. Buckell is a Caribbean-born New York Times Bestselling novelist and short story author. His work has been translated into 16 different languages. He has published some 50 short stories in various magazines and anthologies, and has been nominated for the Hugo, Nebula, Prometheus, and Campbell awards. You can find him online at TobiasBuckell.com.

Ekaterina Sedia resides in the Pinelands of New Jersey. Her critically acclaimed novels, *The Secret History of Moscow* and *The Alchemy of Stone* and *The House of Discarded Dreams* were published by Prime Books. Her short stories have sold to *Analog, Baen's Universe, Dark Wisdom* and *Clarkesworld,* as well as *Japanese Dreams* and *Magic in the Mirrorstone* anthologies.

Alex Dally MacFarlane (alexdallymacfarlane.com) lives in London, where the foxes cross paths with her at night. Her fiction has appeared in *Clarkesworld Magazine, Strange Horizons, Beneath Ceaseless Skies* and *The Mammoth Book of Steampunk,* and her poetry in *The Moment of Change, Goblin Fruit, Stone Telling* and *Here, We Cross.* A handbound limited edition of her story "Two Coins" was published by Papaveria Press in 2010. The Devonshire Arms is a real pub in Kensington, London; for two years it was her local, and she always suspected it of keeping secrets.

Rachel Sobel is a biology student at the University of Washington in Seattle, and a graduate of the Alpha Writer's Workshop. She lives in a house full of people who consider her a dangerous lunatic, and generally manages to prove them right. Someday in the far future, she is going to be a scientist if she manages to survive her own education.

Corie Ralston has been a fan and writer of science fiction since the fifth grade, when she wrote her first story about a giant, time-travelling humanoid potato. She is glad to say that her writing has improved considerably since then, and she is very proud to be a contributor to *Clarkesworld.* She has been published in several other venues, including a writing contest sponsored by a synchrotron (light-reading.org/LightReading/MainCompetition.html), which might seem a little obscure until you know that she also works at a synchrotron. That particular story starred a giant, space-faring humanoid slug, so maybe she hasn't changed so much through the years after all. You can find out more about her at sff.net/people/cyralston/.

Sarah Monette grew up in Oak Ridge, Tennessee, one of the three secret cities of the Manhattan Project, and now lives in a 105-year-old house in the Upper Midwest with a great many books, two cats, one grand piano, and one husband. Her Ph.D. diploma (English Literature, 2004) hangs in the kitchen. She has published more than forty short stories and has two short story collections out: *The Bone Key* and *Somewhere Beneath Those Waves.* She has written two novels (*A Companion to Wolves* and *The Tempering of Men*) and three short stories with Elizabeth Bear, and hopes to write more. Her first four novels (*Melusine, The Virtu, The Mirador, Corambis*) were published by Ace.

Lisa L Hannett hails from Ottawa, Canada but now lives in Adelaide, South Australia—city of churches, bizarre murders and pie floaters. Her short stories have been published in *Clarkesworld Magazine, Fantasy Magazine, Weird Tales, ChiZine, Shimmer, Steampunk II: Steampunk Reloaded, The Year's Best Australian Fantasy and Horror (2010 & 2011),* and *Imaginarium 2012: Best Canadian Speculative Fiction,* among other places. She has won three Aurealis Awards, including Best Collection 2011 for her first book, *Bluegrass*

Symphony(Ticonderoga Publications). *Midnight and Moonshine,* co-authored with Angela Slatter, will be published in 2012. Lisa has a PhD in medieval Icelandic literature, and is a graduate of Clarion South. You can find her online at lisahannett.com and on Twitter @LisaLHannett.

Robert Reed has had eleven novels published, starting with *The Leeshore* in 1987 and most recently with *The Well of Stars* in 2004. Since winning the first annual *L. Ron Hubbard Writers of the Future* contest in 1986 (under the pen name Robert Touzalin) and being a finalist for the John W. Campbell Award for best new writer in 1987, he has had over 200 shorter works published in a variety of magazines and anthologies. Eleven of those stories were published in his critically-acclaimed first collection, *The Dragons of Springplace,* in 1999. Twelve more stories appear in his second collection, *The Cuckoo's Boys* [2005]. In addition to his success in the U.S., Reed has also been published in the U.K., Russia, Japan, Spain and in France, where a second (French-language) collection of nine of his shorter works, *Chrysalide,* was released in 2002. Bob has had stories appear in at least one of the annual "Year's Best" anthologies in every year since 1992. Bob has received nominations for both the Nebula Award (nominated and voted upon by genre authors) and the Hugo Award (nominated and voted upon by fans), as well as numerous other literary awards (see Awards). He won his first Hugo Award for the 2006 novella "*A Billion Eves*". He is currently working on a Great Ship trilogy for Prime Books, and of course, more short pieces.

Lavie Tidhar has been nominated for a BSFA, British Fantasy, Campbell, Sidewise, World Fantasy and Sturgeon Awards. He is the author of *Osama,* and of the Bookman Histories trilogy, as well as numerous short stories and several novellas.

Genevieve Valentine's first novel, *Mechanique: A Tale of the Circus Tresaulti,* won the 2012 IAFA Crawford Award and was a Nebula nominee. Her short fiction has appeared in *Clarkesworld, Strange Horizons, Journal of Mythic Arts, Fantasy Magazine, Lightspeed,* and others, and the anthologies *Federations, After, The Living Dead 2, Running with the Pack, Teeth,* and more.

Her nonfiction and reviews have appeared at NPR.org, *Strange Horizons, Weird Tales, Tor.com,* and *Fantasy Magazine,* and she is a co-author of *Geek Wisdom*(Quirk Books).

Her appetite for bad movies is insatiable, a tragedy she tracks on her blog, genevievevalentine.com.

About Clarkesworld

Clarkesworld Magazine (clarkesworldmagazine.com) is a monthly science fiction and fantasy magazine first published in October 2006. Via the heroic efforts of our talented and engaged staff, each issue contains interviews, thought-provoking articles and at least three pieces of original fiction. Our fiction is also available in ebook editions/subscriptions, audio podcasts, chapbooks and in our annual print anthologies.

Clarkesworld has been nominated for Hugo Award for Best Semiprozine three times and has won the award twice. Our fiction has been nominated for or won the Hugo, Nebula, World Fantasy, Sturgeon, Locus, BSFA, Shirley Jackson, WSFA Small Press and Stoker Awards.

For information on how to subscribe to *Clarkesworld Magazine* on your mobile device or ereader, please visit: clarkesworldmagazine.com/subscribe/

ABOUT THE EDITORS

Neil Clarke (neil-clarke.com) is the publisher and editor-in-chief of *Clarkesworld Magazine,* owner of Wyrm Publishing and a 2012 Hugo Award Nominee for Best Editor Short Form. He currently lives next to a wildlife refuge in NJ with his wife and two boys.

Sean Wallace is a founding editor at *Clarkesworld Magazine,* owner of Prime Books and winner of the World Fantasy Award. He currently lives in Maryland with his wife and two daughters.

Printed in Great Britain
by Amazon